"LIBBY IS CURED OF THE ALZHEIMER'S."

"Cured completely?" Jodie asked.

"One hundred percent," Roy said.

The hair on the back of her neck stood on end. "Do you know what the medicine is?" Jodie asked.

"The Cure?" Roy said. "Dr. Stirling explained it all to us. It has something to do with the whole process of moving messages around in the brain. Alzheimer's patients have a problem with that, apparently. Something about tangles and plaques. The Cure takes care of all that and makes the brain work right. I'm really not very good with the science of it all. I just know what I've seen with my own two eyes, what it's done for Libby. Whatever it does, it works. No doubt about that."

"You are aware that the medicine isn't FDA approved, aren't you?" Jodie said.

"Yup."

"That doesn't bother you?"

Roy glanced at his wife. "I don't care what the FDA says about it. Libby's better. That's all that matters."

THE CURE

By Kip Langello

The Clinic
The Cure

THE CURE

KIP LANGELLO

POCKET BOOKS

New York London Toronto Sydney Tokyo Singapore

This book is a work of fiction. Names, characters, places and incidents are products of the author's imagination or are used fictitiously. Any resemblance to actual events or locales or persons, living or dead, is entirely coincidental.

An *Original* Publication of POCKET BOOKS

POCKET BOOKS, a division of Simon & Schuster Inc.
1230 Avenue of the Americas, New York, NY 10020

ISBN: 0-671-54085-8

First Pocket Books printing July 1999

10 9 8 7 6 5 4 3 2 1

POCKET and colophon are registered trademarks of Simon & Schuster Inc.

Front cover illustration by Shasti O'Leary Soudant

Printed in the U.S.A.

For Dina

⚡ PROLOGUE

The pounding at the door awakened him.

Augustus Lohr had been dreaming that he was in the tropics, a sweltering, wretched jungle much like the one outside his shack tonight. As he rolled off the bony cot, his neck was clammy with sweat. He was breathing heavily from the violent images that had thrashed through his brain, unguarded while he slept. In the darkness, he felt a strange sense of uneasiness.

Something was wrong.

The drumming of heavy rain on the wooden roof throbbed like a headache. A mosquito buzzed around his ear. He ignored it, concentrating instead on why someone would come here at this hour, in the middle of a downpour.

His gaze dropped to the muddy boots at the foot of the cot. Protruding from one of them was a .45-automatic. He slid the pistol out and with his thumb disengaged the safety.

"*Quien es?*" he said.

Through the closed door, the voice said, "Is Raul."

Lohr let out a disgusted sigh. "Come back in the morning."

"Señor Lohr. Is important. There is much trouble."

"Much trouble . . ." Lohr coughed out the words sarcastically. As he walked to the door, dressed only in skivvies, he thought, *Much trouble to these beaners means their burro has the shits.*

He unbolted the door and stepped back as rain and a gaunt teenager in green fatigues washed in. Raul was soaked. From the knees down he was covered in mud. He had difficulty catching his breath. Obviously he had run all the way up here from the village.

"They are coming, señor!" he said, gasping.

"Who's coming?"

Raul took several short, shallow breaths, then said, "From the village."

"Who, damn it!"

In a hushed voice, somewhere between reverence and horror, Raul said, *"Coronel Mendez."*

Lohr grabbed Raul's shirt and yanked him close. "How do you know he's coming?"

"I see them on the road. I see them myself."

Lohr shoved him away and rushed back to his cot where he pulled on his fatigues and boots.

Colonel Mendez was the commander of the militia in this area. A visit from him now, in the middle of the night, could mean only one thing.

Their time was up.

Mendez never traveled alone. Lohr had never seen him with less than three dozen soldiers. How many troops would he bring here tonight? Surely too many to try to fend off.

"Why the hell are they coming here?" Lohr demanded, sticking the pistol under his belt.

Raul's nervous eyes darted around the shack like

mosquitoes afraid of being squashed. "For the doctor," he whispered. "They know, señor. Somehow they know."

"Goddamn!"

Lohr grabbed Raul by the shirt again and the two of them rushed outside into the rain.

Thick jungle rose out of the blackness surrounding Lohr's shack. The concealment provided by the heavy brush usually made him feel secure, but tonight all it did was make it impossible for him to see what lay waiting out there.

He hesitated for a moment, anticipating the sound of a gunshot ringing out. Instead he heard only the hiss of rain against the palm fronds and Raul's nervous breathing behind him.

A single roar of thunder echoed through the night, unnerving Raul.

"Señor—"

"Cállate!" Lohr said, telling Raul to shut up, then he tugged Raul down the muddy path.

Leaves the size of elephants' ears swatted at him as he ran. Vines grabbed at his legs, slowing his progress as though nature had conspired with Mendez against him. The wet night smelled of worms and mud. The air was always thin at this elevation; now, with the humidity, it seemed inadequate to fill his lungs.

The path snaked past a partially excavated altar left by Mayans hundreds of years ago. The two American graduate students who had begun to exhume it from its jungle grave last summer had been sacrificed by rebel troops who accused them of being spies.

For the uninitiated, this part of Central America could

be a very dangerous place. To Lohr, that was its only redeeming quality.

At the end of the path the clinic building poked up through the jungle palms. The crude structure built of boards salvaged from wrecked fishing boats and from several schools leveled by government bulldozers looked like it would collapse in a strong wind. The sheet metal roof was badly rusted. A moat of mud surrounded the clinic.

As Lohr ran toward the light glowing in the window, Raul following like a nervous puppy, he glanced down the side of the building to make sure his Jeep was there. They'd need it to escape into the mountains.

Lohr knew he had to get the doctor out of here. And more importantly, get himself out of here. If Raul was right about Mendez having discovered what the doctor was doing, they all were in deep shit. The brutal dream from which Lohr had awakened a few minutes earlier would be nothing compared to the real nightmare they would face if they were here when Mendez arrived.

As the doctor leaned close to the cage, his glasses slid down his nose. Clammy perspiration coated every inch of his skin. The lab's generator wasn't adequate to power an air conditioner, in addition to all the necessary equipment, so working in here was always miserable.

The doctor had no choice but to stay. His research needed to be conducted in this region—for now, anyway. Until he identified and cloned the specific protein that was responsible for the change. Once he achieved—

No, he was getting ahead of himself. First he had to

finish purifying it and make certain it was effective. Then he could concentrate on cloning the bioactive protein. That was the important step. That was going to win him a Lasker prize for sure. Possibly even a Nobel.

A Nobel, he thought, peering at his reflection in one of the dirty windows. Yes, it would be *that* momentous. He'd have to give it a different name, though. $BDNF_2$ lacked charisma. It was too dry. He'd need something exciting, dynamic. Maybe even something that would incorporate his own name . . .

But that was still months away. Many months. And he still had much hard work ahead of him. It would go more quickly if he had help, someone to grind through the boring biochemistry. But where down here would he find a technician who not only knew his way around a lab but could be trusted with the knowledge of what they were doing? He couldn't. That's why he was on his own.

He peered into the cage now, trying to tune out the annoying patter of rain on the metal roof and the stench of the rodents and their droppings. He raised his right hand and, monitoring the mouse's reaction closely, snapped his fingers once. Inside the cage, mouse #11 instantly turned away from its feed and peered at him. The doctor moved his hand slowly and watched the rodent's eyes follow it.

He smiled, then scribbled a brief entry in his lab notebook, recording the improvement in hearing and sight.

The tiny black rodent scampered from the left side of the cage to the right side, sniffed at the fecal matter in the corner, then scampered back to the left where it nibbled some more at the feed. The doctor was amazed by the mouse's vigor—or rather, not so much amazed as he was impressed. This was what he had hoped to see; he was just surprised at how well it worked.

Fifteen other cages were crammed onto three shelves in this corner of the lab, fifteen other C57bl mice. But #11 was the one with which he was concerned right now. He was eager to do the histology on its brain and further confirm his findings.

He opened the cage door, slid his hand into the opening and carefully grasped the mouse. It wriggled quite a bit in his fist, and made an attempt to nip at his thumb, but the doctor managed to remove it without getting bitten.

The doctor brought #11 to the lab bench. Holding it by the tail now, he set it down on the table, then picked up a pencil and placed it across the back of #11's neck, pinning it to the flat surface of the bench. With one swift pull on the tail, he heard the mouse's neck snap. It now lay perfectly still on the table, dead. He preferred cervical dislocation because it was quick and generally considered a merciful death for the mouse, but more importantly it would not affect the results of the histology.

He squeezed his hands into latex gloves and set the rodent into the dissection pan to catch whatever blood spilled out. His glasses slid down his nose again so he adjusted them, picked up his stainless steel scissors and began to snip through the rodent's neck.

When Augustus Lohr reached the clinic door, he found it unlocked. "Goddamn him," he said, kicking it open and rushing in. No wonder Mendez had found out. Lohr had told the doctor repeatedly to take precautions. But the doctor hadn't listened. His brain was buried too deeply in his books and test tubes and microscopic minutia. And his damn rats. If he had paid more attention to the real world around him, they'd both be a whole hell of a lot better off.

Now the result of his carelessness was on its way up from the village to squash him like a roach.

Lohr and Raul rushed through the empty waiting room, the wood benches smelling of the unbathed bodies that huddled here each morning. They left a trail of brown water on the plank flooring as they scrambled to find the doctor.

"What do we do, señor?" Raul asked, his voice breaking with fear.

"We get the hell out of here."

"Is much good I come to tell you, *si?*"

"Yeah, *si*, much good."

Lohr hurried down the hallway past the two examination rooms, past the primitively equipped operating room. He found the door at the end of the hall unlocked. He shoved it open and rushed in. The doctor was bent over a table, glaring down at the mutilated rodent on the lab table. The formaldehyde stench of the lab always reminded Lohr of death.

The doctor peered up, a surprised look magnified by his glasses. "What is it?" he asked, pushing up his glasses, which had slid to the tip of his nose.

"We have to go," Lohr said.

"Go?"

"Yes, go!" Lohr shouted. "Grab what you need. You've got about five seconds."

"What are you talking about?"

"Mendez. He's coming to get you. Do you understand that? He knows what you're doing!"

The doctor turned white. *"Oh my God . . ."*

"That's right. So we either get the hell out of here right now or we're dead meat."

"But . . . my work . . ." the doctor said, gesturing with his blood-stained gloves toward the lab, cluttered with overpriced equipment that had been a pain in the ass for Lohr to procure. "I can't just leave it."

"You're going to have to."

"But I'm so close to isolating the bioactive protein. I'm almost there. Do you know what that means? Do you understand the importance of this?"

"Do you understand what'll happen if Mendez finds you here? You'll be isolating that protein from six feet under. Is that clear enough for you?"

"Señor," Raul said, jittery, eager to go. *"Coronel Mendez está* much near."

"Take what you need and let's go," Lohr told the doctor. "Move it!"

The doctor spread his hands. "But I need everything. All the biochemical analysis I've done is documented in these papers, these notebooks, on the computer. No, no, I can't just leave. I've worked too hard to get this far."

He began collecting papers in his bloody hands and setting them on one of the lab tables, moving a couple cages of mice, reading labels on a stack of computer disks, deciding what to take.

Lohr turned to Raul. "There are two containers of gas in the back of my Jeep. Go get them. *Rapido!*"

The doctor turned when he heard this. "Why are you having him bring gasoline?" he asked Lohr.

"If you're as close to this big breakthrough as you claim you are, I don't want someone else coming in here and getting the jump on us. This is ours, and I'm going to make damn sure no one else steals it."

"What do you mean?"

"I mean whatever you don't take is going up in flames."

"You can't just destroy all my years of work."

"We have no choice. Take the important stuff and the rest gets torched."

"But I told you, *all* of it is important."

"You're wasting time just standing there. Grab what you need."

Raul returned with the gasoline. Lohr grabbed one canister and started pouring gas on the wooden floor and on the lab tables.

"*No!*" the doctor yelled. He rushed over to stop him. "No, I won't let you!"

He grabbed Lohr's arm, but Lohr easily shrugged him off and resumed pouring gasoline. The doctor lunged at him again, tearing at his shirt. This time Lohr shoved him over a lab stool. The doctor stumbled backward and landed hard on the floor.

"I told you to take what you need," Lohr said. "Either do it or get the hell outside." He turned to Raul, who was standing by the door, just watching. "Don't stand there like an ass," he said. "Dump that gas in here. Let's go."

"Si," Raul said, hurriedly pouring the gas around the lab.

The doctor, realizing he couldn't stop them, frantically raced around grabbing as much as he could and clutching it all to his chest.

Lohr poured the last of his gasoline into the drawers of the file cabinets and onto the black mice scampering in their cages, then tossed his canister on the floor. Raul emptied his container into the incubator filled with cultures.

"That's it," Lohr told the doctor. "Get out."

"I don't have it all yet."

"You have all you're going to take."

Lohr grabbed the back of the doctor's shirt and pulled him away from the desk where was scooping up papers.

"No, wait!" the doctor said. He tried to grab more paperwork and computer disks, but he took too much. Now he couldn't hold onto what he had already collected and as Lohr jerked him back, disks clattered to the floor, papers fluttered away.

"We're going. *Now,*" Lohr said.

"I need more time."

"We don't have more time."

"But I don't have everything! *Please*—"

"We're going."

As Lohr dragged the doctor across the lab, he pulled a book of matches from the pocket of his soaked pants and tossed it to Raul, who was standing by the door.

"Torch the place, then meet us in the Jeep," Lohr said, walking past Raul, pulling the doctor behind him.

"Si."

The doctor, struggling to break free, screamed, "No! You can't do this!"

Lohr just pulled him up the hall toward the waiting room. "You're going to thank me later," he said.

"You'll destroy everything!"

"That's the point."

"*Stop!*"

"Will you for Christ's sake shut up!"

"Let me go!"

Lohr shoved the doctor into the waiting room, toward the exit. The doctor stumbled over a bench and skidded across the floor, dropping all his papers and disks and notebooks.

Lohr blew out a breath of exasperation. "Grab your shit and wait for me in the Jeep."

He left the doctor and headed back down the hall toward Raul, who was standing in the doorway to the lab, peeling off a match. The matches were damp. Raul struck the first one several times but it wouldn't light, so he threw it aside and peeled off another.

Lohr glided toward him so swiftly and quietly that Raul didn't even notice him coming. In one smooth movement, Lohr pulled the pistol from his belt, placed the muzzle an inch from the back of Raul's head and without even a second's hesitation, fired.

Raul crumbled forward onto the lab floor.

The doctor was still on the floor in the waiting room, picking up the papers and disks he had dropped. Frightened by the sound, he jumped up and rushed toward the hall. When he saw Raul on the floor, a puddle of blood under his face, he gasped. "What . . . what did you do?"

"He knows too much."

"Oh God, no! You didn't have to do that. He wouldn't have turned us in."

"No? Who the hell do you think told Mendez?" Lohr said.

"But Raul came to warn us."

"You'll never understand these people, will you? Get in the Jeep. We need to haul ass out of here, *now.*"

Lohr took a Zippo lighter from one pocket and a bandanna from another, lit the bandanna, then threw it into a pool of gasoline. Instantly the lab burst into flames.

Lohr grabbed the doctor and dragged him out of the clinic and into the Jeep's passenger seat. Then he ran around to the other side and sped up the muddy path that wound into the mountains. As they left the compound behind, they could see the glow of headlights through the trees, Mendez's men approaching.

The doctor stared back at the burning building, looking like he had just lost a child. "I was so close," he said. "So close . . ."

Lohr leaned out the window and spat, tasting smoke and soot as he did so. "Close to dying," he told the doctor.

"No, not dying," the doctor said, leaning back in his seat and rubbing his eyes.

1

"They should have been here by now," Jodie Simms said.

Mike Bono looked at his watch. "Should have been here twenty minutes ago," he said. "How long do we wait?"

"I don't think we can wait any longer."

"Good. Sitting out here like this, in this neighborhood, at night . . ." Mike shook his head. "Not the best way to reach retirement age."

He reached for the key and was about to start the engine when Jodie stopped him.

"We're not leaving," she said.

"You just said we can't wait any longer."

"I know." It was ten till eight. If they were to have any chance of shooting and editing the package in time for the eleven o'clock newscast, they'd have to go in now.

"We can't wait any longer, meaning we're going inside now," she said.

"*Going in?* Without the cops being here?" Mike forced a laugh and reached for the key again. "That's a good one."

"I'm serious."

"You're out of your mind."

Jodie opened her door. The dome light inside the van glowed, exposing the two of them to anyone who might be watching. This made Mike even more nervous. His eyes darted from the abandoned house to an empty car across the street to the darkened alley behind them and back to Jodie.

"Say April fools', Jodie. Please say April fools'."

"It's January." She stepped outside. "Grab your camera."

"We can come back tomorrow, when the cops are here."

"We're here now. Let's just shoot it."

"I don't like the idea of us going in without police escorts."

"Neither do I," she said, and headed up the sidewalk toward the abandoned house.

"Jodie, wait!" Mike tried to whisper and shout at the same time. She hushed him and continued walking.

Realizing that he didn't have any choice, Mike grabbed the video equipment from the back of the van, locked the doors and hurried up the sidewalk after her.

Jodie was only five-feet-three, one hundred and five pounds. A few months shy of her fortieth birthday, she was still as thin and sinewy as she had been in college. She no longer had time for regular workouts, but her metabolism and the long hours of hustling between locations and the television station kept her in shape. Maintaining her energy level, however, was another story. With all that had happened over the last six months, she couldn't remember a single moment when she hadn't felt completely drained, physically and emotionally.

But tonight, adrenaline fueled her body as she hurried toward the abandoned house at the corner.

Debris was piled an inch thick on the front stairs. Jodie stepped over an empty bottle of Wild Irish Rose and a puddle of what looked like vomit and cigarette butts. The wooden planks beneath her shoes creaked and sagged.

"These steps aren't safe, Jodie," Mike said, testing the bottom step with his foot.

"They held me. Come on."

"Maybe they held you, but some of us are full-sized adults."

Mike reluctantly went up the stairs behind her, all two hundred and ten pounds of him. He placed each step as gingerly as someone tiptoeing into a bedroom to check on his child.

"We need footage inside," Jodie said. "We'll just go in, shoot a quick standup, get some shots of some of the rooms and we're done."

"What if someone's in there?"

"I didn't see anyone go inside in the last twenty minutes. Did you?"

"That doesn't make me feel any better about this."

"Let's just go in and do it."

"Do I have any say in this?"

Jodie tugged open the door and stepped inside.

"I guess not," Mike muttered.

The door opened into a hallway. Several doorways led off the hall in both directions. At the rear was a partially dismantled stairway. Mike shouldered his camera and turned on the spotlight, illuminating the narrow hall.

As he followed Jodie in, he whispered, "I hope you're wearing that silly angel pin you always have on."

"I am," Jodie said, touching the gold pin on her blouse. "And it's not silly."

"Turn it up to full strength, will you? We're going to need it."

Plaster, fallen from the ceiling and walls, coated the floor. On top of the plaster flakes were several malt liquor cans, a Burger King wrapper, many small piles of burnt ash. Mike panned the camera, the light illuminating a wad of human feces in front of one of the doorways.

"Let's not go in that room," he whispered.

Jodie pointed to a different doorway. Mike directed his camera toward it, lighting the room beyond. It looked like it had been a one-room apartment a long time ago. Now the walls were crumbling. Plywood covered the windows. Shards of broken glass protruded through the trash on the floor, warning them to be careful where they stepped.

The air was thick and difficult to breathe. It smelled of urine and pot. Jodie went in first. Mike followed, photographing all around him as he went. Jodie didn't see anyone so she turned back to Mike and said, "This is a good place to shoot the standup."

"Good. Let's shoot it and go."

"I want to make sure we have enough footage of the place in general."

"Don't worry, I've got plenty of coverage."

"I don't want to be short when we're editing it."

"If you want to be alive to edit it, let's just shoot the standup and go."

He unclipped the hand-held microphone from his camera and gave it to Jodie. The cable was knotted, and when Jodie raised the mike, the cord stretched tightly between them. Mike was so nervous about being in here that he didn't care about the cord being in the shot, but Jodie took a few moments to untangle it and position it out of frame.

"Come on, let's just shoot it," Mike said, glancing around anxiously.

"Give me a second." Jodie went over in her mind what she wanted to say, then she took a few steps back and asked Mike if her hair looked okay.

"It's fine. Can we just shoot this now?"

"Go ahead. Start tape. Three . . . two . . . one . . ." She started to walk slowly toward the camera as she said, "Police maintain that abandoned houses like this one are a haven for crack addicts and—"

"Goddamn light off!" a voice barked from deep in the room.

Jodie wheeled around. Mike jerked the camera toward the voice, the light illuminating a man, barely out of his teens, scrunched into what had once been the kitchenette. The door to the oven was lowered in front of him and on it were three white rocks and a crack pipe.

"Goddamn light out of my eyes!" he barked, throwing his hand up in front of his face.

Mike quickly directed the light away.

"Jodie," he whispered, his voice a nervous hiss. "Let's get out of here. Come on."

"Yeah, get out of here," the man said.

Jodie took a few steps toward the man.

"*Jodie!*" Mike whispered, worried. "What are you doing?"

She waved him to be quiet and moved closer. "I'm Jodie Simms," she said to the man. "Channel Ten News."

The man's hand quickly came up. In it was a dull gray utility knife with a rusted blade sticking out.

"Hell you come in here for?" he said.

Jodie stopped moving toward him but she didn't back off. Mike, however, quickly back-pedaled several steps.

"Jodie, come on, let's go!"

She ignored him and stared at the man on the floor. "I'd like to talk to you if you don't mind," she said.

" 'Bout what?"

"What you're doing here?"

"Sleeping, till y'all turned on that damn light."

"Is that crack cocaine?" Jodie asked, pointing to the rocks on the oven door.

The man saw her staring at his dope so he quickly brushed the crack and the pipe into his palm and stashed them in his shirt.

"I'd like to interview you for the news," Jodie said. She gestured toward the camera which was still pointed in the other direction. "Do you mind?"

"On TV?" he asked.

"Yes, that's right. Channel Ten. Would you talk to us on camera about this place and about the people who come here? We won't show your face if you don't want us to. But we would like to hear what you have to say."

The man stared at her a moment then turned and stared at Mike. Finally he said defiantly, "Ain't afraid of my face on TV."

"Good. The light's pretty bright but don't let it bother

you." She gestured for Mike to start taping again. He reluctantly turned the camera and the light on the man.

"You know the city is planning to tear down a lot of these empty buildings," Jodie said into her microphone then pointed it at the man.

He squinted into the light, stared for a moment at the camera, then turned back to Jodie. "Hell for?" he asked her.

"They claim it's a haven for crack users and they want to eliminate it from Jacksonville."

"It ain't gonna 'liminate shit. All it gonna do is put us out in the streets. We be doing it out there. Everybody gonna see us, all the tourists and business folk. City wants that? Hell . . ." he said and laughed a throaty smoker's laugh.

They stayed for fifteen minutes, interviewing the man and getting additional footage of the house. When they were done and starting to leave, a mouse scampered down the hall, almost crossing over Jodie's shoes. She shrieked and bolted outside. Mike, not knowing what happened, ran after her. He caught up to her at the van. When she finally told him what had startled her, he laughed.

"You don't have any problem going up to a crack addict with a knife," he said, "but a little mouse walks by and you run like a rabbit."

"Just shut up and drive. We have to edit this footage if we're going to make the eleven o'clock news."

When they returned to the station, Sheila Ward, the *Nightside* assignment editor, hurried over. "I'm glad

you're back, Jodie," she said. "The police called a few
minutes ago."

"A little late, I'd say," Mike Bono said. "Did you ask
them why they didn't show up tonight?"

Sheila didn't answer him. She stared at Jodie, the
troubled look on her face telling Jodie that something
was wrong.

"What is it, Sheila?"

"It's about your father."

≋ 2

As Jodie turned into the parking lot of Publix on Third
Street and saw the Jacksonville Beach police car parked
in the fire lane in front of the supermarket, the sour taste
of dread seeped into her stomach. They had not told her
much over the phone, just that her father was missing,
and now as she parked her Miata behind the police car, a
flood of fears washed through her.

A stiff wind blew from the ocean a few blocks away,
straining the palm trees that dotted the parking lot. The
night had the feeling of an impending storm. Jodie got
out into the damp wind, her hair blowing across her eyes,
and scanned the lines of cars. The market was busy
tonight. How could he just disappear amid all these
people? That question echoed through her head as she
rushed through the automatic doors and into the store.

The din of noise was disorienting. Voices coming
from everywhere, the discordant bleeping of the elec-
tronic scanners, metal grocery carts clanging as a boy

wheeled a long stack into place right next to her. She hurried toward the bank of cashiers, fighting the tide of customers pushing carts toward the door. Teenage girls rang up groceries as men in their sixties wearing tangerine-colored vests stuffed the items into bags, asking customers half their age, "Plastic or paper, sir?" "Plastic or paper, ma'am?"

Jodie squeezed past a woman struggling with three children and two full carts of groceries, and spotted the policeman at the customer service counter. Mrs. Kelly was with him, pacing in tiny, quick steps but covering no more than a couple feet of floor.

Normally as solid and sturdy as an elementary school principal, Mrs. Kelly looked a wreck. Her hair was mussed, her skin pallid, and when she pointed down the dairy aisle, explaining something to the police officer who was questioning her, her hand trembled so much that Jodie noticed it halfway across the store.

Jodie ran over. "What happened?"

"Jodie, dear God," Mrs. Kelly said, her Boston accent turning the last word into *Gaud*. "I'm so sorry. I don't know how it could have happened."

"You're Miss Simms?" the policeman asked, his calm, base voice a sharp contrast to Mrs. Kelly's squeal.

"Can you please tell me what happened?" Jodie said.

"From what I understand, your father—"

Mrs. Kelly cut in. "I was watching him the whole time. I was . . . he was . . . the next minute . . ." She struggled to catch her breath, hyperventilating from anxiety. "Then . . ." she said, sounding like a child afraid to tell her mother something bad. "Then he was just . . . gone."

That word—*gone*—brought a chill of terror to Jodie.

"We have a patrol car driving around the area right now, Miss Simms," the policeman said in a steady, reassuring tone. "I'm going to start looking myself. Would you like to come with me?" he asked.

"We can cover more ground if I go in my own car," Jodie said.

The policeman agreed.

Jodie turned to Mrs. Kelly. "What's Dad wearing?"

"Um . . . um . . ." She was still shaking. "Shorts, a blue windbreaker, that Jaguars cap you got for him."

"Okay. You stay here in case he comes back."

"Do you think he's all right?"

Jodie, seeing how frightened she was, squeezed her trembling hand and said, "We'll find him. Don't worry."

But Jodie was worried. As she ran back outside to her Miata and followed the police car across the parking lot to Third Street, she couldn't help but dwell on the darkness and on how busy the streets around here were. Carl could easily wander into a traffic lane. In his dark blue jacket, he wouldn't be easily seen.

The image of her father lying dead in the street frightened her. She had promised her mother that she would take care of him. She owed her father at least that much. Now, as she waited for a break in the traffic, she said a silent prayer that her father would be all right.

The policeman turned right, so Jodie went left and headed up Third Street toward Beach Boulevard. She kept turning her head from side to side, scrutinizing the dark sidewalks. The glare of oncoming headlights made it difficult for her to see. So did the tiny windows of her

Miata. She considered putting down the top but that meant pulling over and delaying the search for her father. Besides, the night was too cold and the wind too strong. She would just have to make sure she looked carefully.

She turned into the parking lot of another shopping center, rolled down her window and called out to her father as she drove between the rows of cars. People peered at her, some recognizing her from TV and waving, some just staring oddly. A couple of teenagers answered her when she called, "Dad!"

"What do you want?" one of them said. The other boy giggled and added, "I'm screwing your mother over here. Come back in ten minutes."

Jodie ignored them and continued searching. She asked an elderly couple waiting at the bus stop in front of Marshals if they had seen him and she described what he was wearing. She explained that his words might not have made sense if he had spoken to them.

"No, we haven't seen anyone like that," the man said. "But we'll keep our eyes open."

"Is he all right?" the woman asked.

Jodie couldn't answer.

She left the parking lot and continued down Third Street to Beach Boulevard. The traffic here was heavy. Jodie knew that the headlights, the traffic signals, the rushing cars, all the noise and confusion would frighten Carl; he probably would not try to cross here. So she turned the corner and drove past rows of apartment buildings, peering down the dark alleys and between the parked cars.

She stopped and asked a young couple on bicycles if

they had seen Carl. They hadn't. With each passing minute she became more worried. She could not stop thinking that something terrible had happened to him.

She wondered if the police had found him. Maybe he had returned to Publix on his own. Was he with Mrs. Kelly right now? Deciding to go back and check, she pulled into the parking lot of Beachside Deli to turn around. The small market was closed at this hour. As she began to turn, her headlights swept across the side of the building, illuminating for an instant the man seated on the pavement beside the dumpster, his knees bent up close to his chest, his arms wrapped tightly around himself.

She could not see his face but she could clearly see the windbreaker and cap he was wearing and she realized instantly that it was Carl.

She hit the brakes, left the engine running, and rushed over to him. Carl was sitting in a puddle of black water, his back to the wall of the deli. His face was tucked behind his knees and he was sobbing. His shorts were soaking wet.

"Dad, my God!" Jodie said as she knelt down beside him. "What happened?"

His head snapped up, a sudden, startled reaction, like a helpless animal turning toward a threatening sound in the woods. His eyes went wide with terror. He looked lost—not just lost in the sense of being on an unfamiliar street, but lost as though he were in an alien world, a world he could not fathom. Like someone who had suddenly awakened in the middle of an ocean, with no land in sight and no notion of how he had gotten there or how he could save himself.

Seeing him like this, Jodie wanted to cry.

In his panic, Carl tried to push himself back farther against the wall, afraid of Jodie, not recognizing her. His jaw quivered as he shuddered in the cold wind.

"It's okay, Dad," she said, trying to sound reassuring. The stink from the dumpster made it difficult for her to breathe. Even the stiff wind from the ocean wasn't enough to clear the air.

"It's all right," she said again. "It's only me. It's Jodie. Your daughter."

Carl, still shivering, peered up at her, struggling to understand what she was saying, struggling to recognize her face.

His face was soiled a ghostly shade of gray, dirt streaked by the flow of tears. Six decades of life had left his skin slashed with wrinkles, furrows that tonight looked deeper than Jodie had ever seen them before. His thick mane of ashen hair was caked with grease and dirt.

"It's me, Dad," she said, trying to sound friendly and familiar and maternal. "It's Jodie."

She reached down slowly to him, careful not to frighten him even more.

"It's okay, Dad," she whispered. "It's okay. It's me. It's only me."

Carl hesitated, watching her suspiciously. His eyes had a pathetic look of confusion and terror, one she had seen many times over the last five months since he had come to live with her. And she noticed an odor now, one other than the foul stench from the dumpster, an odor of excrement and urine. Her stare moved to the puddle beneath Carl and she understood now what it was.

"It's okay, Dad. Don't worry about that. That's no big deal."

The fear in his eyes turned to desperation. Slowly, his arm trembling, he reached up to her. She grasped his hand. It felt cold, fragile. She came a little closer. Suddenly he lurched forward, falling against her and wrapping his arms around her like a frightened child clinging to his mother.

"It's going to be okay, Dad," she whispered. She stroked his hair tenderly and tried to quiet him. "Everything's going to be all right."

"I couldn't find the bathroom, Helen," he said, sobbing, calling her by her mother's name.

"That's okay," Jodie said. "Don't worry about that."

"I tried to find it. I got lost. I got lost."

She held him tightly, protectively. "You're safe now," she said. "I'm here. Everything's going to be okay."

"I want to go home, Helen. I just want to go home."

"I'm going to take you home. I'm going to take care of you. Everything's going to be all right. I promise you. Everything's going to be just fine."

⇒ 3

Jodie awakened with a start.

The room was dark. The oldies station on her alarm clock was playing "You've Got a Friend," letting her know that it was seven A.M. and time to get up. She laid her head back down on the pillow and listened to the rest of the song, James Taylor's voice washing over her like warm bath water.

Last night she had been up for hours trying to reassure her father that he was safe and that everything was all right. The incident had left her exhausted. The few hours of sleep she had managed to get were not nearly enough to restore her energy. Another ten more minutes in bed would do her a world of good, she decided, so when James Taylor finished singing to her and the Cool 96.9 jingle came on, she rolled over to hit the sleep switch. That's when she noticed the time on the digital display: 7:39.

The radio hadn't turned on a moment ago as she had assumed. Rather, it had been on for thirty-nine minutes. She had been so tired it hadn't wakened her.

She couldn't spare ten more minutes of sleep now. Her day had not even begun and already she was half an hour behind.

Still groggy, not sure what had eventually roused her from sleep, she sat up and turned off the radio. Three paperback romance novels sat in a stack on the bedside table next to the lamp, none of them yet begun. They were thin enough to finish in a single night, but she didn't have the time or the ambition to read. Another book, Pat Conroy's latest novel, was on the ledge of the bathtub. She had managed to read a few chapters while soaking late one night after Carl had gone to bed, but the opportunity to finish it, or even to indulge in another long bath, evaded her.

Except for the hours she was at work, her father took

up nearly every minute of her time. Her schedule consisted of going to work, taking care of Carl, trying to sleep—and little else.

But the lack of time wasn't the only thing keeping her from enjoying things like a good book or a video. Concentration was another. She found it difficult to focus on the problems of fictional characters when worries about her father breaking something or hurting himself were always in her thoughts.

A noise. That's what had wakened her, she realized now as she shook the sleep from her head and things slowly began to register. But what noise? She hesitated for a moment, sitting at the edge of the bed, listening.

She hoped to hear silence. Silence meant Carl was still asleep, and as long as he was asleep, she didn't have to worry about—

Then she heard it. The faint clink of glassware coming from the kitchen. Her father was already up.

"Oh no," she said quietly, exasperated. She buried her face in her hands for a moment and prayed for strength. She wondered with a sickening sense of dread what the noise had been that had wakened her. Nothing in life had prepared her for the daily struggle she faced caring for her father, a struggle that seemed only to get worse as time went on.

Afraid of what she would find, Jodie threw on her robe and hurried out of the bedroom. In the mornings it was important that she got up before Carl. Since Mrs. Kelly didn't arrive until eight-thirty, Jodie was the only one here to look after her father. If she slept longer than he did, she risked him getting into trouble. She hoped she wasn't too late this morning.

With Carl here, she always needed to be on guard, she always had to expect the unexpected from him. Normal social rules of conduct did not apply to Carl anymore. As though an entire lifetime of learning right from wrong had vanished, he no longer knew what was okay for him to do. He was a child in a man's body. Left unsupervised, he was a disaster waiting to happen.

"Dad," she called out as she crossed the living room. Sunlight shone through the sliding glass doors, falling on her white furniture and illuminating all the stains that had accumulated over the past five months, since Carl moved in. Coffee. Ice cream. Dirt from her small backyard. The light brown ring that marked the beginning of his incontinence.

She hadn't thought about being practical when she decorated the place with white furniture three years ago. Why should she have? She had been living alone then. She had never considered that her father would come to live with her. And she had never, ever, imagined he would be in the condition he was in now.

If she were to furnish it today, she would do it completely in dark vinyl, something she could sponge off, something that wouldn't show the inevitable stains. And she would not own anything fragile. She used to keep her collection of angel figurines on the coffee table and on the bookshelf, but Carl had accidentally smashed three of them the very first day here. She had to remove the rest of them, bringing a few to her desk at work and hiding the others in drawers in her bedroom.

Everything else fragile she had placed out of reach. Even her first drama award, which she had won in high school for her role as Ado Annie in *Oklahoma*, was off the wall and stored away in the closet. She had removed all the Lenox from the china cabinet. It had taken her ten years to collect the settings piece by piece but it took Carl only one venture into the cabinet to chip two dishes and smash a saucer. They were packed in boxes under her bed now.

Even after Carl-proofing most of the house, some fragile items remained in the kitchen, cups and plates that she needed to keep out for everyday use. She feared Carl had gotten into them.

As she walked past the glass-top dining room table, now badly scratched, toward the kitchen, she said, "What are you doing, Dad?"

He answered just as she stepped through the doorway. "I'm making breakfast, Helen."

She stopped when she saw. For a moment she closed her eyes, asking for strength. When she opened them again, he was smiling. In one hand was a fish-shaped potholder, in the other a spray can of WD-40 lubricant. On the counter in front of him and on the floor around his feet were splattered eggs and spilled milk.

"Scrambled eggs," he said.

Mornings, before a full day of helplessness and hope-lessness took their toll, it was a little easier for her to remain calm when things like this happened. She always tried to remind herself that he was not responsible for his behavior. His actions weren't intentional. He was a prisoner of his failing brain and he couldn't help himself. She felt more pity for him than anger.

"Looks like you've got a little mess there," she said.

"Yeah, a little mess," he said, like an innocent child. "But I'm taking care of it."

He sprayed the counter with the WD-40 and tried to wipe up the eggs with the potholder.

"Why don't you let me take care of that," Jodie said. She came over and gently took away the WD-40. "This isn't really the best thing for cleaning."

"No?"

She put it in the cabinet under the sink and took the potholder from him. "Why don't you go get dressed and I'll have breakfast ready for you in a little while."

"You were sleeping late so I thought I'd help."

"Thanks, Dad. I appreciate that."

"I like to help," he said.

"I'm up now. I'll finish it."

"I can help you."

"That's okay. I can handle it."

He shrugged. "Okay." He started to leave but then stopped and said, "Oh. Good morning, Helen."

"I'm Jodie, Dad. Your daughter. Mom passed away."

He just stared at her, his head cocked, his eyes showing that he didn't understand what she was saying.

"Never mind," she said. "I'll call you when breakfast is ready."

Satisfied, he nodded and walked away.

When Mrs. Kelly arrived forty-five minutes later, Jodie still wasn't dressed and ready for work. "If you get a chance today," Jodie said, "will you wash the kitchen floor? It's kind of sticky in there."

"A little accident?" Mrs. Kelly asked.

"Dad tried to make breakfast."

"Poor thing. I'll take care of it."

Mrs. Kelly apologized again about last night. Jodie told her to forget about it, things like that happen. Carl was all right and that's all that mattered.

Jodie got to the TV station forty minutes late. As she walked toward the rear entrance of the building, she noticed that most of the Channel 10 News vans were already gone. Most of the other reporters were out putting together packages for today's newscasts.

Marvin Acker, the news director, was standing near the assignment desk when she walked into the news room. He was tall and slim and dressed as well as the anchormen, though he never appeared on camera himself. Appearance was important to him, not only his own appearance but the appearance of his reporters.

"Image matters in TV," he had said more than once. "This isn't the newspaper."

Reliability was a close second to image.

He watched Jodie as she came in, nodding a silent "good morning" and gesturing toward the chalk board with today's assignments on it. She had to cover an arraignment at the courthouse. She realized that she had probably already missed the defendant being brought in.

"Mike's down there getting some footage," Marvin said. "Do you think you could join him?"

"I'm on my way." She rushed to her cubicle, checked

her messages, then rushed back out and drove herself to the courthouse a mile away.

Though Marvin hadn't said anything about her being late, Jodie could tell from the way he looked at her and from the tone of his voice that he did not like it. Initially, when Carl first moved in, Marvin had been understanding. But lately he had hinted that Jodie could not continue coming in late. A couple weeks ago he took her aside and told her that while he sympathized with her, he had a newscast to produce and he couldn't do it effectively if his reporters were chronically late. And he needed his reporters' thoughts to be on their assignments, not on problems at home.

"It shows when a reporter doesn't give the story her all," he told her. His look when he said it made it crystal clear what he meant. Her performance was suffering because of Carl. But she didn't need Marvin to tell her that. She knew it already. She just didn't know what to do about it.

No doubt her father was a heavy burden on her schedule, as well as on her emotions and her finances, but she had no choice. Some friends had gently suggested she consider putting him in a nursing home. But every time she thought of that, she remembered her mother asking her if she would be able to take care of him.

Every single day, the week before she died, Helen had asked Jodie that question. "Will you be able to look after your father?" And each time Helen had asked, Jodie had answered "Yes, of course," relieving her mother's concerns. Jodie had wanted her mother to die in peace. And she had genuinely believed that she could take care of her

father. She had seen her mother do it for three years—by
herself, a sixty-year-old woman, dying from a brain
tumor. If Mom could do it, Jodie had reasoned, surely I
can.

Yes, she would take care of Carl for as long as she
possibly could, she told herself. But how much longer
would that be? Carl was getting worse. He needed more
attention. Her money wouldn't last indefinitely. She
would do what she could. She just hoped that it would be
enough.

It was only a week later when Sara Cassidy offered
Jodie a solution.

≡ 4

Jodie met Sara Cassidy for lunch at The Landing, an
upscale mall in downtown Jacksonville, overlooking the
St. John's River. Jodie bought a turkey salad but she
didn't have much of an appetite. She just picked at the
lettuce and sipped her Diet Coke.

Sara wolfed down a basket of chicken nuggets and
french fries, between glances at her watch. She had an
appointment with the public relations director of Blue
Cross and Blue Shield for a story she was writing about
supplemental Medicare insurance. She was supposed to
meet him in fifteen minutes so she had to eat, and talk,
fast.

But she had insisted that Jodie meet her today. When
she had called last night, she had said that she had

something important to tell her. Now, Jodie listened in disbelief at what her friend was saying.

"I'm convinced it works," Sara said.

"Sara, that's not possible," Jodie said. "There's no cure for Alzheimer's disease. I even took Dad to the Mayo Clinic here in Jacksonville. They have some of the best doctors in Florida, and they said they couldn't do anything for him. There are only two approved medications for Alzheimer's. Cognex and Aricept."

"I'm the *Sentinel*'s medical editor, remember?" Sara said. "So I know all that."

"Dad tried both medications. Cognex only made him sick and Aricept didn't do any good."

"Will you just listen to me. The doctor I'm talking about has helped this woman."

"What woman?"

"Her name is Libby Harden. I met her, I talked to her, I talked to her doctor in Daytona. I'm telling you, Jodie, she's better now. She had Alzheimer's, and now she's practically cured."

Jodie and Sara had met almost twenty years ago at Florida State University in Tallahassee. Jodie had been acting in the drama department's production of *Othello*. Sara had been assigned to review the play for the campus newspaper, *The Florida Flambeau*. After the performance, Sara came backstage and interviewed Jodie. Tray Parks, the actor who had played Othello, left without talking to her, so in Sara's review Desdemona came across as the play's main character. Sara wrote that Jodie's interpretation of the role was "well above the pedestrian performance of Parks's banal Othello." They had been friends ever since.

Physically, Sara was Jodie's opposite, tall, large-boned, overweight, awkward in her movement. Her voice was whiny, her manner sometimes overbearing. The written word was her strength. That and her keen intellect. Jodie knew no one smarter than Sara.

Jodie, on the other hand, was a performer, good with people and comfortable in most social situations. She moved with the ease of a dancer and could speak off the top of her head without resorting to the clumsy *um*'s and *you know*'s that many people use. Her grades had been good but not great. She considered herself smart in a different sense from Sara.

Their different talents and personalities explained why, after graduation, Sara went into print journalism while Jodie chose broadcast news as her career.

Jodie knew Sara as a pragmatic, skeptical reporter who was not easily misled. She was the type of person who wouldn't accept that the earth was round without corroboration from at least two sources. That was why Jodie found it so puzzling today that Sara would come to her with this tale of a "miracle cure."

"I just finished writing a three-part series on this woman," Sara said. "It starts running Sunday. I'll send you a copy." She leaned close and lowered her voice. "And I talked to a publisher in New York. They're interested in having me expand the series into a book. A cure this good, it's got bestseller written all over it." She winked and said, "Next time we have lunch, I could be working for *The New York Times*."

"I'm glad this is going to be such a good thing for you," Jodie said, realizing that was probably all it was, a career opportunity for Sara.

"And it's a good thing for *you* too," Sara said. "This clinic can help your father. You should go there."

Jodie, still not very interested, asked, "Where is it? In Orlando?"

"No, a little farther away than that."

"Miami?"

Sara looked down at her chicken nuggets, avoiding Jodie's eyes as she said, "It's in Cancun."

"Cancun? As in Mexico?" Jodie shook her head, losing all hope now. "In other words, it's a scam."

"It's not a scam."

"A miracle drug in Mexico, Sara? Haven't we seen this before? What was that cancer cure they had down there several years ago? Laetrile, wasn't it?"

"This is different. I told you, I met one of the patients myself, Libby Harden. Her doctor here in Florida confirms the she definitely had Alzheimer's, and now she's definitely better. And I called the neurologist who runs the clinic in Cancun and I talked to him myself. I also did some checking into his background. His name is Dr. Russell Stirling. He's not Mexican—he's an American. He's from South Carolina." She leaned forward and whispered with a giggle, "He's got the cutest Southern accent."

Jodie rolled her eyes. "You're basing your evaluation on how cute his accent is?"

"All right, forget the accent," Sara said. "He's got one hell of an impressive resume, let me tell you. He went to

medical school at Duke, did his residency at Columbia-
Presbyterian. That's in New York."

"I know where it is."

"After that he went into research. He was a big shot
neurologist at the National Institutes of Health in
Maryland. I talked to a few people who worked with him
there and they said he was a genius. He's won all kinds of
awards for the research he did there. He's been published
so many times it would take a month to read all his
papers—and by the way, I read a lot of them. He's really
well known in the field of neurology. He's not some
schmuck, Jodie."

"Then what's he doing in Mexico?"

"He left NIH to join the World Health Organization's
Hale Project."

"What's that? And what does the World Health
Organization have to do with Alzheimer's disease?"

"The Hale Project was a program designed to bring
advanced medical care to underdeveloped regions in
Latin America. It wasn't an Alzheimer's program. I'm
just telling you how he ended up in Mexico. He wanted
to help the less fortunate," Sara said.

"Oh come on."

"I swear. Anyway, after he was done with that, he
stayed down there and continued doing research on his
own. That's how he developed this cure for Alzheimer's.
From everything I've seen, this is on the level."

"How come I never heard of it before? When Dad first
got sick, I read everything I could get my hands on, and
I've never read a word about a cure in Mexico. And how

come the doctors at Mayo Clinic haven't heard of it? If this guy's so well known and this drug that he's developed is as good as you say, the doctors up here would know about it and would be using it."

"It's a new drug, Jodie. *Brand* new. It's not widely used yet. In fact, the clinic in Mexico where Dr. Stirling is, that's the only place you can get it right now."

"Why isn't this doctor of yours up in Manhattan where he can pull down a million dollars a year or more? If it's what you say it is, it has to be worth a heck of a lot more here than in Mexico. You're not going to tell me it's because he's such a great humanitarian and he's not interested in the money."

"First of all, from what I gather, he's doing pretty well down there in Mexico. He doesn't need anyone to hold any telethons for him. He has more patients than he can handle. And the therapy isn't cheap. He's making money, don't worry about that."

"That still doesn't explain why he's in Mexico."

Sara hesitated for a moment, fidgeting with her french fries, obviously reluctant to answer. Finally she pushed her fries away, took a deep breath and said, "The reason he's in Mexico is because the drug that he uses to help Alzheimer's patients doesn't have FDA approval yet and without that he can't prescribe it up here."

"Oh, is that all? It's hardly worth mentioning. Come on, Sara, you're a better reporter than that."

"Jodie, it works."

"If it works, why doesn't it have FDA approval? Didn't that question occur to you?"

"Of course it did. And I am a good reporter."

"I know you are, and that's why I can't believe you'd fall for this."

"I haven't fallen for anything. I've been checking into this for a long time, following Libby Harden's progress, talking to every expert I can, and grilling the hell out of Dr. Stirling and every Mexican health agency I could call. You should see the long distance phone bills I've racked up. I've done my homework, believe me. The reason the drug isn't approved yet here in the U.S.—and I know it will be, eventually—but the reason it doesn't have FDA approval right now is because it's still in the preclinical trial phase."

"Preclinical trial phase? That sounds like the medical equivalent of 'the check's in the mail.'"

"Jodie, it's no great secret that it takes forever and a day to get a new drug approved by the FDA. Dr. Stirling doesn't want to wait that long. And I don't blame him. People need it now. In Mexico he can prescribe it now. The health agencies down there that regulate this type of thing move much more quickly than the massive FDA bureaucracy in Washington does. Their medical experts reviewed this drug and looked at the trials Dr. Stirling did and they were impressed. They approved it. They concluded that it works and it's safe. It's only a matter of time before the FDA approves it, too. Something that works this well, they're going to have to. When that happens, I'll bet Stirling relocates up here, but for now he has to stay down there in order for people, who want the drug now, to be able to get it now."

Sara reached across the table and took hold of Jodie's

hand. "If it was my father," she said, "I wouldn't want to wait for the FDA bureaucrats to get off their butts and give this drug their stamp of approval. I'd want my father to have it now. Before it's too late."

If it worked, of course Jodie would want the same thing, but that was a big *if*. And there were other factors involved, too. It wasn't as simple as Sara made it out to be, Jodie realized.

"Let's just say this drug is everything you claim it is," Jodie said. "Even if it is, if the drug isn't FDA approved, how can I bring it back here? Even if I thought Dad should try it, how could he?"

Sara grinned. "You can chalk one up for the little guy," she said. "There's a loophole in the law that allows people like your father to bring experimental drugs into the country. It was put in because of AIDS patients."

"Now you're going to tell me that this drug is supposed to be a cure for AIDS, too?"

"No. But the loophole was put there in response to AIDS patients wanting to try whatever was out there without having to wait for the FDA to approve it. Since FDA approval takes so long, longer than most AIDS patients have to live, the government put in this loophole that makes it possible for anyone—not just AIDS patients, but anyone—to bring in a ninety-day supply of any drug, as long as they have a doctor's prescription. I guess they figured that's long enough to know if it'll work or not.

"Anyway, Libby Harden and her husband and her local doctor and the Mexican medical authorities all believe it works. And I do, too. I wouldn't be telling you this if I didn't. You should consider trying it, Jodie," Sara said. "If I were in your place, I definitely would."

It all sounded too good to be true, which was why Jodie wasn't sure about it. Experience had taught her that if something sounded too good to be true, it usually was too good to be true. But Sara sounded so sure . . .

"I don't know . . ." Jodie said, staring down at her turkey salad, torn between wanting to be hopeful and needing to be realistic.

Sara squeezed Jodie's hand again. "Talk to the Hardens," she said. "That way you can see for yourself. Let them tell you firsthand what they think about it. Daytona Beach is less than a two-hour drive from here. What have you got to lose? If you're not impressed, you've blown an afternoon. No big deal. But I promise you, you'll be impressed. If it turns out this can help your dad, don't you think it's worth the short drive down there?"

5

Sara called the Hardens and arranged for Jodie to visit them on Saturday morning. Mrs. Kelly said she could come over and stay with Carl until Jodie got back.

Even though it was chilly today, the sun was out, so Jodie put the top down on her Miata. The cool wind rushing across her face helped clear her head. As she drove down I-95, she wondered if there really was anything to this Alzheimer's cure Sara had told her about. She found it hard to believe something like that could exist and the doctors at Mayo Clinic not know about it. But with Carl's condition becoming progressively worse, Jodie was beginning to feel desperate. She had to do something.

The thing about Alzheimer's disease that she found so difficult to grasp was that no physical defect showed up on any tests. Her father had had an MRI when he was first diagnosed three years ago. The neurologist had showed Jodie and her mother the image of her father's brain. It had *looked* normal. No unusual physical aberrations. And yet the symptoms were so obvious.

A year later, when Jodie's mother had undergone an MRI herself, Jodie had seen the tumor so clearly. It had been right there on the MRI, a large white area on the gray brain scan. And yet her symptoms had remained invisible for months afterward, in fact not showing up until near the very end.

The images of those two MRI's remained in Jodie's memory after all this time, as vivid today as they had been the day she had seen them. Neither illness—her father's Alzheimer's, her mother's cancer—made any sense to her.

She remembered that the doctors hadn't been able to do anything for her mother, and all Jodie could do was watch her deteriorate. The feeling of helplessness had been the most difficult part. That's why now, if she could help her father, even if only slightly, she wanted to try.

She felt an uneasy mixture of excitement and anxiety as she exited the interstate and followed Sara's directions to the Hardens' house.

The Hardens lived in a small split ranch on the

Halifax River. The front yard had two large Royal Palms.
Flower beds thrived in neat rings around the palm trees
and in two long rows beside the front walk. Jodie pulled
into the driveway and parked behind a Cutlass that was
showing signs of Florida rust. She took a deep breath,
prayed that this wouldn't be a wasted trip, and got out to
meet the woman cured of Alzheimer's.

When Roy Harden answered the door, Jodie com-
mented on how nice the yard looked. He took her
around and showed her every bit of his work, including
the tomato plants and cucumbers on the south side of the
house, and the bed of roses in the back, facing the river.
He had been an auto worker in Michigan, he told her.
Now retired, he passed his days gardening.

The tour ended at the back patio. And, as if on cue,
the sliding glass door opened, and Libby Harden stepped
through.

"Hello," she said. "You must be Jodie Simms."

Libby was wearing a faded housedress, and carrying a
tray with a pitcher of iced tea and three glasses.

Jodie smiled and said hello. She watched Libby carry
the tray over to a table, and all she could think about was
her father trying to do that. If he tried to do that, the
three of them would have had tea and ice cubes on their
laps by now.

And this woman had Alzheimer's?

They chatted for a while about Jodie's drive from
Jacksonville and Roy asked her about her job, which he
found fascinating. They considered her a celebrity, even
though they didn't get Jacksonville channels here and
had never seen her on TV.

Jodie paid close attention to Libby to see how well she followed the conversation.

Libby noticed the angel pin Jodie was wearing and leaned close to examine it. "Isn't that just the loveliest thing," she said.

"Thank you. My mother gave me this one on my birthday two years ago."

"You have other ones?"

"I have a bunch of them. I collect angels."

"Really? See what I have there?" She pointed to a ceramic statue of an angel amid the rosebushes. Jodie hadn't noticed it until now.

"That's beautiful. Do you collect angels too?"

"I should, shouldn't I?"

Roy broke in. "No you shouldn't. We have enough junk in the house already."

"It's not junk," Libby said. She turned to Jodie. "Do you believe in angels? I do."

"I'd like to think they exist, yes. Sometimes I think I see proof of it, certain things that happen, certain feelings you get sometimes, as though there's some presence with you."

Roy sneered and said, "It's all a bunch of hogwash."

"Oh no," Libby said, very serious.

"I found a marvelous little book about angels," Jodie said. "*Where Angels Walk.* Have you read it?"

"No."

"I'll send it to you if you like."

"Thank you. That would be nice."

They talked about angels for a few minutes, then the conversation turned to the reason Sara Cassidy had interviewed them, the reason Jodie had driven here today.

"The Cure," Roy said. "That's what we call it. That's not what the clinic people call it, they have another name for it, but all the patients we talked to call it The Cure. The real name is one of those long ten-dollar medical terms that doctors dream up. I can never remember it. Even the abbreviation, it's something like NEPFE—or something like that—alpha. I remembered it ends with alpha. But we just call it The Cure."

"And you're convinced that it helped your wife?" Jodie said. She looked at Libby and said, "You feel it helped you, Mrs. Harden?"

"Oh yes."

Roy said, "Are you kidding? She's like a new woman. No, no," he said, correcting himself. "Not a *new* woman. She's back to being like she was before she got the Alzheimer's. That's what it's like. Like I got my *old* Libby back again."

"*Old?*" Libby said.

They all laughed. Roy apologized. Libby turned to Jodie, smiled and said with total sincerity, "It really does work."

Jodie didn't know what Libby had been like before she took the drug, but she was completely normal now. She wondered if Libby's condition had been less advanced than Carl's, or if Libby was just having an unusually good day today. Jodie knew that the dementia associated with Alzheimer's was not constant; on some days her dad was more lucid than on others.

"Is today pretty much normal?" Jodie asked, first looking at Libby then turning to Roy. His was the judgment she trusted more.

"What do you mean?" he asked.

"Does she have good days and bad days?"

"We all have good days and bad days."

"I mean . . . concerning her Alzheimer's," Jodie said. She glanced over at Libby. She felt uncomfortable talking like this with Libby sitting right beside her, but she had to know the answer. "On some days is she less . . . clear than other days?"

"Miss Simms," Roy said. "Libby is cured of the Alzheimer's. Every day is the same."

"Cured completely?"

"One hundred percent."

The hair on the back of her neck stood on end. Hope flowed into her heart. She wanted desperately to believe what this man was telling her.

"How long have you been on the medication, Libby?" Jodie asked.

"About four months now." Libby looked to her husband for confirmation. Roy nodded and said, "But we saw improvement right away. By the second week or so. I guess she was fully cured after a month. Wouldn't you say so, Libby?"

"Yes, I think so. A month."

Jodie warned herself to remain cautious, not to get swept up in the excitement, in the hope, but the proof was right in front of her. Libby seemed to be doing well. Jodie was certain that the Hardens weren't trying to deceive her. They genuinely believed. And Sara believed. Jodie knew Sara would have found out if these people weren't on the up and up.

Could it possibly be true? Could this drug really be a cure?

"Can you tell me a little about the clinic you went to?" Jodie asked Roy.

"What do you want to know? It's in Mexico. Cancun. They call that the Yucatan."

"It's real close," Libby said.

"Yeah," Roy said. "It's less than three hours by plane from Orlando. We have to go from Orlando because American doesn't fly out of Daytona anymore."

"I like Daytona airport better," Libby said. "It's smaller. It's nicer."

"But they don't fly from Daytona, Libby," Roy said.

"I know. I'm just saying it's a nicer airport."

"She doesn't care about that. She wants to know about the clinic."

Roy turned to Jodie again.

"You're thinking about trying it for your father, is that it?" he asked.

"I'm not sure."

"Did they tell you that it's not cheap?"

"How much does it cost?"

"Not including the plane tickets and the hotels, it costs about six grand. And Medicare doesn't pay a dime of that."

"Six thousand dollars, huh? That is expensive."

"But worth it," Roy said.

"Well, if it works . . ."

"Oh it works."

"I think I can afford six thousand dollars. Even if I have to take out a loan and spread the payments out over a couple years, that's only two-fifty a month."

"No, you don't understand. It's not six grand *altogether*," Roy said. "It's six grand . . . *each month*."

Jodie wasn't sure she heard him correctly. "Six thousand dollars *a month?*"

Roy nodded. "Yup. One month's worth of The Cure costs six thousand bucks."

"That *is* a lot of money." Jodie turned to Libby. "How long did you have to take it?"

"What do you mean?"

"How many months did you have to take the medication?"

Libby glanced at Roy.

"The Cure only works as long as Libby continues taking it," he said. "If she stops, she goes right back to the way she was before. It's six thousand a month . . . forever."

Jodie did the calculations quickly in her head.

"That's over seventy thousand dollars a year," she said.

"I told you it's not cheap. We had to sell our old house up north. We were going to sell it anyway. When the money from that runs out, we're going to get a reverse mortgage on this house. That's when the bank pays us every month instead of us paying them. Eventually they own the house, but they don't get to take it until we die. It'll be a good deal for us. And it should be enough to pay for The Cure. It really does work. It helped Libby. It might just work for your father, too."

Jodie swallowed hard. It might help her father—

might—but seventy thousand dollars a year? For the rest of his life?

Where in the world could she get that kind of money? *But if it worked* . . .

Was any amount of money too much to pay if it would make Carl better, if it would return the father she thought she had lost forever?

"Do you know what the medicine is?" Jodie asked.

"The Cure?" Roy said. "Dr. Stirling explained it all to us. I don't remember most of it. It has something to do with the whole process of moving messages around in the brain. Alzheimer's patients have a problem with that, apparently. Something about tangles and plaques. The Cure takes care of all that and makes the brain work right. I'm really not very good with the science of it all. I just know what I've seen with my own two eyes, what it's done for Libby. Whatever it does, it works. No doubt about that."

"You are aware that the medicine isn't FDA approved, aren't you?" Jodie said.

"Yup."

"That doesn't bother you?"

Roy glanced at his wife. "I don't care what the FDA says about it. Libby's better. That's all that matters."

⇒ 6

They walked slowly. Carl had to—his gait was not steady, not strong. He held Jodie's wrist with weak, bony fingers. He needed her arm for support. At times like this, he seemed much more like her child than her father.

She gazed at his profile beside her, his face set in an absent stare, and she wondered where the man who had raised her had gone.

It had taken her months after her mother told her about his diagnosis of Alzheimer's for her to accept the reality of the disease. The man she had always known as her protector and adviser, the stalwart backbone of the family, had come to depend on her for the simplest of things. No longer could he fry an egg or make coffee, go golfing or even take a walk around the block. And no longer could he help her with difficult decisions she faced. The man who comforted her in bad times and celebrated with her in good times had abandoned her. What remained was the outer shell of that person, a constant reminder of what he no longer was.

But could he be that person again? That was the question that occupied her thoughts now.

The Atlantic Ocean was gold with the morning sunlight. It was a chilly day, too chilly for the beach, but Carl so much enjoyed collecting shells that Jodie could not deny him this one distraction.

They had come here straight from church so they were both overdressed. Carl had taken off his shoes and rolled up his slacks to just below his knees. Jodie had left her shoes on the floor of the car. She was wearing a skirt so she didn't have to worry about the sand.

As they walked along, Carl's plastic Publix bag bulged with broken shells and pieces of coral. He let go of her arm now, doddered over to a shell fragment a few feet away and stooped to pick it up.

"Helen, look at this one!" he said, examining it closely.

All Jodie saw was a sandy orange shard the size of a quarter. It wasn't even a whole shell. He always walked right past the whole shells. Instead he stopped for pieces like this. She could not understand why. But Carl seemed to find something else in these broken shells, something valuable.

He reached into the Publix bag and took out his can of WD-40. Jodie had learned early on not to try to take it away. The can had a real calming effect on him.

He sprayed the shell, turned it over and sprayed the other side. Then he held it up so the sunlight would catch the flat surface, and he examined it. Satisfied, he smiled at Jodie, looking proud of himself, then stuffed the shell and the WD-40 into the bag, took Jodie's wrist again and continued up the beach.

As a wave washed up, Jodie scampered farther up the sand, dodging it. But Carl let the water flow over his bare feet, unfazed by its coldness.

"Dad, I've been thinking," she said.

His eyes swept the sand in front of them, searching for shells. She wasn't sure he was listening so she reached over and touched his shoulder. He turned toward her now.

"Hmm?"

"I've been thinking," she said again. "How would you like to go away for a few days?"

His face turned white, his eyes wide and afraid. "What do you mean?" he said.

"You and me, together," she said. "Take a little vacation."

"Together?"

"Of course together. We'll go away for a few days. To a place where it's warm."

He shook his head.

"You don't want to go?"

He shook his head again.

"Why not, Dad?"

"No," he said. "I don't want to go away. You want to get rid of me?"

"No. We'll go together. Like a vacation."

"A vacation?"

"Yeah. We'll stay in a hotel. In Mexico. It's warm and sunny there. I don't think you and Mom ever went to Mexico."

He didn't understand.

"It's warm there," she said and left it at that. "Anyway, they have a real good doctor down there. I thought we could see him, let him examine you, maybe he can help you."

"Dr. Harrigon?"

"You mean Dr. *Harrington*. No, he's your doctor here. This is a different doctor. He's a specialist. I think he might be able to help you."

Carl spotted a shell and hurried over to it. Jodie waited while he evaluated it, sprayed it and stuffed it into the bag with the others. When he came back to her and grasped her wrist, she asked him again.

"What do you think?" she said. "A quick trip to Mexico would be nice, wouldn't it? Just for a few days."

"What?"

"Mexico. To see that doctor."

"Dr. Harrigon?"

He had forgotten already.

"A different doctor, Dad. I think we should go down there and see him."

"I don't want to go anywhere."

"It'll be a nice change of scenery for you."

"No!" he said, shaking his head firmly. "I want to stay here."

He stooped for another shell, studied it, ruled it unacceptable and tossed it aside.

"They've got a beach down there," Jodie said.

"Where?"

"Mexico. They have a really good beach. Better than this beach probably."

Carl turned, his face wrinkled in thought. For the first time since she brought this subject up he looked interested. She didn't see that frightened stare in his eyes now.

"A real nice beach," she said.

"With shells?" he asked.

"All kinds, I'll bet. Better than the ones here."

He looked at his Publix bag then gazed out over the beach. Finally he turned back to her, and she saw him shiver slightly.

"It's cold," he said.

"It sure is."

"That other beach is warm?"

"Yeah. Warmer than here. You want to go?"

"Is it close?"

"It's in Mexico." He didn't understand the answer so she said, "We have to take a plane."

He thought for a moment then said, "I took a plane during the war."

"You've been on lots of planes, Dad."

"I have?"

"Yup. You and Mom. You've flown lots of times. You won't have any problem on the plane."

He thought again, then said, "Okay. Let's take a plane to the beach." He thought that sounded funny and started laughing.

⟩7

Sara Cassidy gave Jodie the telephone number for Dr. Stirling's office in Cancun, Mexico. When Jodie called on Monday, a woman who sounded like she was an American told her Dr. Stirling could see Carl immediately.

"Would this Saturday be convenient?" she asked Jodie.

"The doctor does the examinations on the weekends?"

"Weekends seem to work out best for most of our patients. They usually come on Saturday and leave Sunday. That way the family member who accompanies them doesn't have to miss work. Would that work out okay for you? I can schedule your father for this Saturday morning, eleven o'clock."

"I'll have to see what time the flights get there."

"American and Mexicana both have flights that get in before ten. That shouldn't be a problem."

"Okay. Eleven o'clock next Saturday it is."

She told Jodie to bring Carl's medical records and

reminded her that most U.S. insurance polices would not cover Dr. Stirling's fees, so payment was expected at the time of the visit.

"Can you recommend a hotel?" Jodie asked.

"We have an arrangement with the Salida Del Sol. It's a very nice place in the hotel zone. We're in downtown Cancun, which is about a fifteen minute ride by taxi from the hotel zone, but I wouldn't recommend staying downtown. The hotel zone is much nicer."

"Is the Salida Del Sol near the beach? My father likes the beach."

"It's right on the beach. It's a small hotel but it's well kept. It's newly renovated and the owner gives our patients a very good weekend rate."

She gave Jodie the phone number. Before calling them, Jodie tried a few of the major hotel chains to get rates. January was the high season in Cancun so most of the basic rooms cost between a $200 and $250 per night. When she called the Salida Del Sol and told them she was a patient of Dr. Stirling's, they quoted her the special rate of $100 for a room in the main building, with beach-front cabañas at $125.

Jodie booked a cabaña, thinking Carl would like that better than a regular room. Next she called American Airlines and made reservations for the flight from Jacksonville on Saturday morning. Lastly she called Dr. Harrington's office and arranged to pick up a copy of her father's medical records.

Everything was set.

Jodie told herself not to raise her hopes too high, in case it did not work. Even though her visit with the

Hardens had been encouraging, she wanted to maintain a healthy amount of skepticism. She did not want to set herself up for a big letdown later.

On Saturday morning, they took the seven A.M. flight out of Jacksonville. The crowds at Miami International when they changed planes made Carl nervous and every time a voice bellowed over the PA system, he tried to answer it, thinking the voice was talking to him. Once they boarded the plane to Cancun, he spilled his coffee and yelled at the flight attendant but Jodie was able to calm him, and they went through the rest of the flight without any further outbursts.

When the plane landed in Cancun, the sun was shining, it was eighty-five degrees, people were dressed in shorts and colorful shirts, there was laughter, smiles, no one was rushing. It was difficult to feel anything but relaxed.

The terminal did not have the gloss and overwhelming size of most major airports in the U.S. It felt transitory, as though the government had slapped it all together to accommodate the tourists and could just as easily dismantle it when the *gringos* stopped coming. Jodie also noticed an open-air sense about the place, a simple, comfortable, almost primitive milieu. And she liked it. She found herself walking through the place, feeling strangely lighter, breathing in slow, calm sighs.

Carl held Jodie's arm as they walked through the tiny terminal, past the group of Mexican men calling out the names of hotels and tour companies. She noticed these men, and most of the other workers in the airport, did not have the olive skin and fine features of Spaniards, of Europeans. With the exception of only a few, these Mexicans were clearly of Mayan lineage, with high-arched noses, long foreheads, dark brown complexion. They looked more like American Indians than the Latinos Jodie was accustomed to seeing back home.

As she and Carl made their way through the terminal, she wondered if Mexico had a class system, if the lighter-skinned Spaniards were treated differently from the darker Indians.

The feel of Carl's weak grip on her arm drew her thoughts back to her father. The way he was clinging to her right now, she felt a deep sense of responsibility for his health. He depended on her completely. He put his fate in her hands. She hoped she was doing the right thing by bringing him here. She hoped this doctor really could help him.

Outside, billboards in Spanish peeked through the palm trees circling the airport, advertising Portatel cellular phones and Café Kobà, a gourmet coffee grown in Mexico. On the concrete walls of the terminal building itself someone had painted a row of pink and yellow birds. The road in front of the terminal was more like a circular driveway than a street. Two lanes going the same way with only a handful of cars.

Taxicab drivers waited on the sidewalk, all of them dressed in white, smoking and speaking in a strange mixture of Spanish and something that sounded like American Indian. From the group, a Mayan man with a noticeable limp hobbled over and snatched the suitcases from Jodie and Carl.

"Hotel zone?" he asked as he scooted over to his cab at the curb, a tiny white Nissan Tsuru that looked like an old shrunken Sentra. He stuffed the bags into the trunk and slammed the lid.

"The hotel?" he asked.

"The Salida Del Sol," Jodie said.

"Ah! Is a very nice hotel. Very nice."

He held open the door for them. The back seat was so small that Jodie and Carl's knees were up against the seat back. The driver turned the air conditioner up high and drove off.

The two-lane road between the airport and Cancun was straight and flat, modern-looking except for the asphalt itself. The mixture felt stonier than roads back home, making for a rough, noisy ride. The cabby was going slowly for a road this straight, Jodie thought. She checked her watch, concerned that they would be late for the appointment with Dr. Stirling.

Other white and green taxis chugged along at the same speed. A rental car carrying two fair-skinned teenagers zipped past them all. The cabby watched the car speed away and shook his head.

"The roads are not good for to go that fast," he said.

On both sides of the asphalt was scrub brush as far as Jodie could see, with a web of power lines overhead. No houses. No hotels. No souvenir shops. No sign of habitation at all. It didn't fit her image of Cancun, the vacation mecca.

"Nobody lives here, Helen," Carl said, staring out the window at the emptiness.

"It looks that way, doesn't it."

"Not here," the driver said. "Everything is more far, in Cancun."

"Can Can?" Carl said.

Jodie giggled. "No, Dad, it's Cancun. That's the name of the city where we're going."

Carl looked at his wrist. He couldn't tell time anymore but he still liked wearing the watch. "We won't be late, will we?" he said.

"For the doctor's appointment?" Jodie asked.

"For the time!"

She had no idea what he meant so she just said, "We won't be late, Dad. We have plenty of time."

"Good." He sighed and sat back, more relaxed.

Cancun's hotel zone was a thin peninsula shaped like a "7" that jutted out from the mainland into the emerald waters of the Caribbean. A bridge at the top left corner of the "7" connected this strip of hotels and shopping centers to downtown Cancun. Another bridge at the bottom of the "7" took cars to and from the airport road.

The hotel zone had only one street through most of it, Kukulcan Boulevard. Massive hotels and time-share condominiums lined the east side, hugging the beach. The water was the clearest, brightest shade of emerald Jodie had ever seen. Gift shops and familiar restaurants like Denny's, Pizza Hut, Planet Hollywood, and the Hard Rock Cafe were strung along the west side, on the shores of the Nichupté Lagoon. Jodie and Carl rode past the Ritz Carlton, the Hilton, the Hyatt. Carl beamed when he saw the Caesar Park, a huge luxury hotel shaped like a Mayan pyramid.

For three miles, the entire shoreline of Cancun was

lined with these hotels, blocking out the view of the ocean. Scattered among the high-rises was the strange sight of half-finished construction, hotels begun and then abandoned.

A sidewalk snaked past the hotels, ducking in and out of the palm trees and patches of tropical flora. Teenage girls in bikinis flew along on Rollerblades, their ears plugged with Walkman earphones. Sharing the sidewalks were baby-boomers, jogging, sweating, panting. The men seemed unable to resist a prolonged gaze at the young, tanned bodies. Their wives were quick with elbows to their ribs, drawing their attention back to where it should be.

The Salida Del Sol was near the end of the hotel zone, close to downtown Cancun. It was nothing like the super luxury monuments at the south end of the strip. From the outside, it looked like a run-down Holiday Inn. The exterior needed a coat of paint. Two of the palm trees in the parking lot were dead. The concrete in front was dull gray and crumbling. Jodie wondered about the renovations that Dr. Stirling's nurse had mentioned.

Three Mayan men dressed in white sat on a bench outside the front entrance. Two rushed the cab and grabbed the suitcases, hustling them inside, giving Jodie the impression that their job was to keep the guests from turning around and finding other accommodations once they saw the building.

Carl looked leery as Jodie took him by the hand and led him inside. But once inside, they both felt relieved. The interior was much nicer than the exterior implied. Half the lobby was a tropical atrium. Palm trees and a small fountain made up the center section, with rattan chairs scattered throughout, providing a quiet place to sit and relax. From speakers hidden amid the palm fronds, mariachi music played quietly, giving the place a very relaxed, Mexican feel.

Carl sat by the fountain while Jodie went to the desk to check in. After the clerk finished all the paperwork and took an imprint of her VISA card, Jodie remembered to make sure the room had two beds.

"No, señorita," the young man said. "All of the cabañas have only the king bed."

"But the room is for my father and me. We need two beds."

"Only the rooms in the main building have the two beds. Not the cabañas."

Jodie wanted her father to be close to the beach. "Can we get a rollaway?" she asked.

"I don't think there is the place for two beds."

"Are you sure?"

The clerk signaled the porter to come over and spoke briefly to him in Spanish. The porter shook his head and looked sadly at Jodie.

"Las cabañas son muy chicas, señorita."

The clerk nodded. "Yes, the cabañas are much small," he told Jodie. "There isn't the place. The rooms here in the main building," he said, pointing to the ceiling, "they are very nice. They have the two beds for you."

"I wanted my father to be on the beach."

"I'm sorry. There is nothing I can do for that."

"Is there a problem?"

Jodie turned toward the voice. A man in his early

forties stood behind her, assessing her and the two Mexican hotel workers like an officer reviewing his troops. He had the air of someone accustomed to giving orders.

Jodie could tell he was an American. He had long blond hair, tied in a ponytail, and intense blue eyes. His chin was the kind of strong, square chin that male models coveted, only his had a faint scar across it. He was tall and straight and had a long, wiry physique. His skin had the deep tan of someone who spent much of his time in the sun.

"What's the problem, Tomas?" he asked the clerk.

"The cabañas only have the king bed and this lady needs two beds. I tell her she must use the rooms upstairs."

"A king size bed is going to be a problem for you?" the man asked Jodie.

"Yes." She assumed by the way the clerk addressed him that he was the manager. "The thing is," she said, "I'm with my father so we need two beds. A king size bed really won't work for us. But I wanted him to be near the beach. He, um . . . he's not well," she said quietly, glancing over at Carl sitting near the fountain.

The American looked over for a moment then turned to the porter and spoke rapid-fire Spanish. The porter said, "Si, señor," and hurried away.

"It'll just be a few minutes," he told Jodie.

"What'll be a few minutes?"

"I'm having them take out the king size bed and put in two twin beds."

"You can do that?"

He laughed. "It's my hotel. I can do whatever I want."

"I meant is it possible? They'll fit?"

"We'll make them fit. We do whatever it takes to make our guests happy."

"Thank you. I really appreciate it."

"No need to thank me. It's good to switch the beds once in a while. It's like rotating the tires on a car. The manufacturer recommends we do it every three thousand guests."

Jodie laughed. It was a corny joke, but he delivered it with an irresistible smile.

"I'm Neil Lancaster," he said, extending his hand.

"Jodie Simms."

He held her hand a moment longer than she expected, keeping his gaze on her until she finally looked away.

"Nice hotel you have here," she said, feeling nervous. "The front could use a little work, though."

"Haven't you heard? You can't judge a book by its cover."

"Did you just make that up?"

He took the remark as she intended it, light-heartedly. He had an effortless laugh and serene, affable bearing. That, along with his good looks, made for a charming package. Jodie was sure by the way he looked at her, the way he shook her hand, that he found her attractive and that caught her a little off guard. She hadn't anticipated meeting a man down here. Her thoughts had been limited to her father's appointment with Dr. Stirling.

"Will you be staying with us long?" Neil asked.

"We leave tomorrow."

"Just one night?"

"I hope you're not sorry now that you're having them change the beds in the room."

"Maybe a little," he said with a chuckle. "Why such a short stay? Are you here on business?"

"Sort of. We came down to see a doctor."

"Oh, I hope you're all right."

"My dad has the appointment, not me."

Neil glanced over at Carl again. "Is he going to be all right?" he asked Jodie, looking concerned.

"I guess that's what we're going to find out."

A moment of awkward silence followed, finally broken when Luis, the porter, rushed back into the lobby now, breathing heavily. *"Señorita, la cabaña está lista."*

"You're all set," Neil said. "They switched the beds for you."

"Thanks again."

"No thanks is necessary. I apologize for the delay."

"Don't be silly."

Jodie was about to go get Carl when Neil said, "Do you like seafood?"

The question threw her for a second, then she said, "Yes, sure."

He stepped a little closer. "I know the best seafood restaurant in all of Cancun. Perhaps you would do me the pleasure of joining me for dinner tonight?"

Jodie looked over at Carl who was staring across the lobby, looking lost and confused. "I really don't think I'll be able to," she told Neil. She couldn't leave her father alone at home in Jacksonville; she certainly couldn't leave him alone in a foreign country. "But thank you for asking," she said.

He nodded. "Enjoy your stay. And good luck with the doctor."

"Thanks."

Luis picked up the suitcases and headed outside. Jodie took Carl by the hand. As they walked out, Jodie glanced back once and saw that Neil was watching her. If only she were here alone, under different circumstances. But she reminded herself that they were taking this trip to help Carl. That had to remain her primary interest.

Luis took them through the pool area to the collection of cabañas set off from the hotel, scattered amid a collection of palm trees and tropical flora at the edge of the beach.

Stone paths wound past the huts, arranged so that each hut was secluded from all the others, but all had a view of the water. A cool breeze followed them along the path, gently scented with the aroma of flowers and sea life. Luis whistled *Via Con Dios*, accompanied by the faint lap of waves on the shore.

Carl nudged Jodie and whispered, "Helen, this is nice."

"It is, isn't it? It's incredible!"

"Who lives here?"

She giggled. "We do. For this weekend anyway."

Carl cocked his head to the side and stared at her, not understanding. She put her arm around him and said, "Never mind, Dad. Just enjoy it. We're on vacation."

Luis brought them to a thatched-roof cabaña tucked deep into the shade of several towering coconut palms. Through the trees, Jodie glimpsed the white beach and the brilliant water beyond. Chaise lounges were set up on the sand. Waiters in white uniforms carried colorful tropical drinks to the sunbathers.

Luis unlocked the door and turned on the air conditioner. The cabaña was furnished simply, with two beds, two wicker chairs by the window, a tall ceramic lamp on the bureau and a television. Luis showed them how the TV worked. It only got four channels—two local Mexican stations in Spanish, and CNN and ESPN in English. The bathroom was small but clean. Jodie noticed the faint scent of sewerage in the shower. That and the two bottles of purified water near the sink reminded her that they shouldn't drink or even brush their teeth with the water.

She thought it ironic that this place, with its magnificent beaches, year-round weather matched perhaps only by Hawaii, and some of the most luxurious hotels anywhere, could not provide a simple thing like clean drinking water.

She hadn't had a chance to change her money to *pesos* so she tipped Luis five U.S. dollars, grateful that he had switched the beds for them. She checked the time. It was ten-thirty already. Since Carl's appointment with Dr. Stirling was in half an hour, they could not unpack until later.

"We have to go, Dad," she told Carl, unpacking only the large envelope that contained his medical records.

"We just got here," he said.

"I know, but we have to go see the doctor. You have an appointment at eleven."

He stared at his watch then he looked up and said, "Dr. Harrigon?"

"No. This is a special doctor. He might be able to help you."

"I don't want to go to the doctor."

"Please, Dad. For me."

This was just what she needed, to come all the way to Mexico and then have him not want to keep the appointment.

"It won't take long," she said. "I promise."

He let out a long breath of exasperation. "All right, but this is the last time."

As they went out front to get a cab, Jodie said a prayer to herself, first asking that this would work, that the treatment would make her father better, then asking that if it did not work, at least it would not make her father worse.

≈ 8

The clinic was located in the center of Cancun. Even though this part of the city was still very touristy, Jodie was surprised at how congested and urban it was, how different it was from the resort atmosphere of the hotel zone.

The streets here were uneven cobblestone instead of asphalt. The traffic was stop-and-go. Their taxi zipped around one of the large concrete traffic circles rising out of the middle of every major intersection. This one had a large abstract sculpture in it, something like a giant conch shell twisting upward. Cars shot in from all directions, narrowly missing the fender of the taxi. Jodie noticed that no one was driving in lanes; everyone seemed to steer their cars wherever they could fit them.

The taxi drove down Tulum Avenue, a four-lane main street lined with gift shops and restaurants. This road had pedestrian crosswalks unlike any Jodie had ever seen before. They were twice as wide as crosswalks back home, but the major difference was that instead of being level with the road, these were elevated six inches above the pavement like speed bumps, forcing cars to come to an abrupt stop. These plateaus sliced across the street at irregular intervals, as though no regard had been given as to where to position them. They weren't at intersections. They weren't even where most of the people were crossing.

As the cab bounced up then settled back down to street level again, Jodie took in the surrounding architecture. Most of the buildings around here were two-story structures of concrete, painted in bright colors. They looked neither new nor old, and all of them were pretty much identical. Jodie had read that Cancun hadn't existed thirty years ago. Today, over a hundred thousand Mexicans lived here. The entire city sprang up around tourism. And it showed. In their haste to accommodate the needs of the large hotel chains, they had neglected to give the buildings the least bit of character.

She also noticed that downtown, as in the hotel zone, many buildings were half-finished. These weren't active construction sights yet to be completed, but old construction that had been abandoned. If the city did have distinguishing traits, they were its lack of character and the abundance of forsaken construction.

At the street level, stores sold tee shirts, onyx chess sets, straw sombreros and the ubiquitous linen blankets in bright Mexican colors. The sidewalk was a sea of tourists in shorts and sandals, with Mexicans handing out advertisements, others calling at the passers-by from storefronts, trying to entice them to buy.

The restaurants were not the American fast-food chains of the hotel zone, but medium-sized Mexican establishments, signs above saying CUISINE OF THE YUCATAN! Waiters stood at the doorways, menus in hand, trying to lure people in.

The cabby negotiated another traffic circle, then turned down a series of twisting roads, leaving Jodie confused about which direction they were heading. They left the tourist section of the city and entered what could have been any small American city if not for the Spanish signs everywhere. They passed a Sam's Club discount warehouse, a Blockbuster Video, a Chevrolet dealership.

One whole block of the city was an open air *mercado*, a collection of tiny booths selling food and crafts to the locals. The taxi stopped for a traffic light in front of the *mercado*. Looking out the window, Jodie saw one booth close to the corner with raw meat on a plywood table. Above it, hanging from ropes strung between two poles, were pale white chickens, plucked clean but with their heads and feet still intact. Flies buzzed everywhere.

As the cab drove on, Jodie smelled the unmistakable stench of fecal matter, as though there were an open sewer lid nearby.

Carl turned toward her, stared at her a moment, a quizzical look on his face. "Did you fart?" he asked.

Jodie couldn't help but laugh.

"No, Dad, I didn't."

He turned and looked out the window again. A moment later he turned back to her and said, "Did I?"

A few minutes later, the cab pulled to the curb in front of a line of storefronts that looked old and neglected. The sidewalk was uneven. Masonry sand was piled in one spot, forcing pedestrians to step down into the street to get by. Jodie wondered if this was the right place.

The sign over the one of the storefronts said RUSSELL STIRLING, M.D. Beneath it was NEUROLOGIST. Blinds hung behind the large display window, concealing the office inside. To the left was a shop that sold uniforms. Two mannequins stood in the window, one in a white waiter's uniform, the other in a white maid's uniform. Everyone who worked in a service industry, it seemed, from the cab drivers to the hotel bellmen to the men tending the flowers and shrubbery at the hotels, wore white.

On the right side of the doctor's office was an electronics store. A window air conditioner protruded through the wall, blocking part of the sidewalk. Water dripped down into a puddle that ran along the sidewalk, over the curb, and down the street.

Seeing how unprofessional this place looked, Jodie almost got back into the cab to leave, but she reasoned that they had come this far, they might as well keep the appointment, meet the doctor, see what he had to say. What harm could it do? She remembered that the Hardens had been convinced that the drug worked. She could not leave without at least talking to the doctor.

She took Carl by the hand and walked in. A blast of cool air hit them. The waiting room smelled of new carpeting and fresh paint. Soft music played over speakers in the ceiling. Scattered around were several tropical plants, green and healthy. The atmosphere instilled in her a sense of comfort.

"I'm tired," Carl said.

"As soon as we're done here we'll go back to the hotel and you can take a nap."

Carl sighed as he lowered himself into one of the chairs.

Jodie felt a sour sensation of guilt in her stomach.

"It won't take too long, Dad," she said, and put her arm around him. "We'll be back at the hotel in no time. You'll see."

Jodie walked over to the receptionist's window and tapped on the glass. A woman in her late forties came over and slid open the window. She had red hair and a brown tan. Her neck and arms were heavily freckled. She wore a white nurse's uniform.

"Miss Simms?" she said.

"Yes."

"Good morning. I'm Darlene Cummings. We spoke on the phone. I hope you had a good flight."

"Yes, fine. Thank you for asking."

"Did you have any trouble finding the office?"

"Not at all."

She handed Jodie a clipboard with several forms that needed to be filled out concerning Carl's medical history. Jodie gave her the envelope with the medical records from Jacksonville. While Jodie sat down and filled out the forms, she kept looking over at Carl, who was just staring across the waiting room. He didn't understand what they were doing here today, didn't comprehend the importance of this visit. But Jodie could not stop thinking how important this was—or would be if The Cure actually worked. Her father's future, her own future, depended on what happened here today.

When Darlene opened the door and said, "We're ready to begin now," Jodie actually trembled.

≡ 9

Carl looked puzzled as he followed Darlene down the hall and into the examination room. Jodie realized he had no idea why he was here. When Darlene weighed him, he stared at the scale with interest and wrinkled his face at the numbers.

"One-forty-six," Darlene said.

"Is that good?" Carl asked.

"You tell me."

"I don't know."

Jodie stepped over and put her hand on his shoulder. "That's good, Dad. You could stand to put on a few pounds, but that's good."

In fact he had lost nearly twenty pounds in the last two years. He stood five feet nine and at his present weight, he looked emaciated. But his doctors in Jacksonville had said that weight loss was common and Carl's weight loss wasn't yet severe enough to be a major concern. He told them they should keep an eye on it. Jodie didn't know where to draw the worry line, how much Carl could stand to lose, but she figured anything below 140 pounds warranted concern.

Carl didn't understand when Darlene asked him to sit on the examination table. She patted it a couple times, and he finally realized what he was supposed to do. With difficulty, he lifted himself up onto the table. He had lost a great deal of strength along with the weight.

Jodie sat on the chair in the corner and looked the room over while Darlene took Carl's vital signs. The place was large and bright and clean. Jodie was encouraged to see how well-equipped it was. The equipment looked new, state of the art, from the computer terminal on the desk in the corner, down to the digital wall-mounted gauge Darlene used to measure Carl's blood pressure. The counter beside the sink was stocked with antibacterial soap, boxes of latex gloves and separate receptacles for trash and hypodermic needles. It all looked as professional as the examination rooms at the Mayo Clinic, and that left Jodie with a good feeling about this.

Darlene quickly typed all of Carl's information into the computer, then excused herself. Only a moment later, the door opened and a doctor walked in.

Jodie was closer to the door than Carl, who was still seated on the examination table, so the doctor extended his hand to her and said, "Good morning. I'm Russell Stirling."

Jodie heard the Southern accent Sara had mentioned, but paid more attention to his handshake. His grip was weak, his palm damp. He seemed uncomfortable touching her.

"It's nice to meet you, Doctor," she said.

He gave a polite nod, hesitated for a moment as though more should be said, then turned to Carl, extending his hand again. "Mr. Simms?"

Carl nodded, looking at the doctor's hand for a moment. Finally he reached out and shook it.

"What time is it?" Carl asked.

Stirling checked his watch. "Eleven-thirteen."

Carl looked at Jodie. "We have to go soon or we'll be late."

"Late for what, Dad?"

Carl shook his head, annoyed, and looked away.

Jodie was about to explain to the doctor that Carl did this sometimes, that it didn't mean anything, but Stirling gave a knowing nod. He understood Carl's condition.

The doctor was in his mid-fifties, which was about what Jodie had expected. But she hadn't expected a man this tall. Stirling stood a few inches over six feet. He was very thin, almost *too* thin. His face had a gaunt look to it, the pallor of someone who spends most of his time indoors, working. His hair was full and dark, but combed haphazardly, the back almost entirely neglected, as though he did not have the time or the inclination to be concerned with his appearance. His white lab coat, as well as the dark wool pants and white dress shirt beneath, were baggy and in desperate need of pressing.

He wore large, wire-frame glasses, too large for his narrow face. And too heavy. They appeared to have slipped down his nose slightly. He nudged them back into place, a reflex that looked automatic, like he didn't even realize he was doing it. Now that the lenses were over his pupils, the strength of the glass made his eyes look unnaturally potent and focused.

What stood out most about him, however, was not these details of his clothes and hair and physical build, but rather his odd manner. As he sat in front of the computer, glaring at the screen, he looked unnaturally deep in thought, lost in pure concentration on what he was reading, and yet at the same time he appeared distracted.

He seemed more like an absent-minded college professor, a researcher most at ease in the sequestered environment of a laboratory, dealing with test tubes and specimen cultures, rather than a practicing physician accustomed to interacting with live patients.

As this filtered through her brain, she found her confidence wavering slightly.

He turned away from the computer now and walked over to Carl on the exam table.

"How are you feeling today, Mr. Simms?"

He spoke in a soft, almost shy, Southern accent, the kind of cadence and intonation Jodie associated with gentry from a much earlier age. She remembered Sara telling her how cute his accent was. Hearing him over the phone, perhaps a person might think "cute," but in person, seeing the man speak, "cute" was not the impression Jodie got. The word that came to mind for her was: *peculiar*.

Carl shrugged at Stirling's question and looked to Jodie for the answer.

"He's doing fairly well today," she said. "A little tired from the trip, but all in all, he's about normal."

Stirling checked Carl's blood pressure himself, even though Darlene had already done it, then he peered into Carl's ears with an otoscope, saying nothing as he did this, nodding to himself after each observation. He took out his stethoscope and without pausing to warm the diaphragm, pressed it to Carl's back and listened to his breathing. The whole time, he didn't say a word or look either Carl or Jodie in the eyes.

He returned to the desk and typed his findings into the computer, then turned so he was facing the empty space between Jodie's chair and Carl on the exam table, looking at neither of them.

"You should know," he said, speaking mainly to the floor, "that there is no infallible premortem test for diagnosing AD, Alzheimer's disease. The only way we can approach a diagnosis is by ruling out other aliments that can produce dementia similar to that seen in AD, such as stroke, Parkinson's disease, Huntington's disease, possibly cerebral tumors, head trauma. Altogether, there are more than five dozen disorders that can produce dementia. That's why I like to do a thorough examination with all my patients so we can be certain that what we're actually attempting to treat is in fact AD."

"Dad's had all kinds of tests back home," Jodie said. "CAT scans, PET scans, blood tests, psychological exams."

"Yes, I know. It's all in his record," Stirling said, pointing to the computer and making eye contact with Jodie for a brief instant. "Still, I prefer to run several tests myself so I can compare the results against the tests done earlier, see if there is any change."

Jodie didn't know what to say. She was glad that he was being thorough and cautious, but she doubted he would come up with a diagnosis different from the one the specialists at the Mayo Clinic had given. Carl definitely had Alzheimer's disease. She wondered if this doctor wanted to do the tests just to run up a large bill, but then she remembered how much the drug itself would cost and she realized he didn't need to pad the bill with tests.

"Whatever you think is necessary," she said.

What was necessary, it turned out, was an MRI, an EEG (both of which Carl had undergone at the Mayo Clinic), a urine specimen, and a final set of tests, which Darlene explained were designed to measure Carl's cognitive abilities. These Dr. Stirling conducted himself, in a small, windowless room.

Carl and Dr. Stirling sat at a simple table across from each other. Jodie stood in the corner behind Carl. Stirling positioned her there before he began, telling her that he didn't want Carl to be able to look to her for the answers.

First Stirling handed Carl a questionnaire to fill out. Carl stared at it a long moment, not knowing what to do with it.

"He can't read anymore," Jodie whispered.

Stirling glanced up at her and put his finger in front of

his mouth, hushing her. She realized that he must have known that Carl couldn't read and Carl's reaction to the paper was supposed to be the test itself.

Stirling took the paper back, pushed his glasses toward the bridge of his nose, made some notes on a white legal pad, then read from another questionnaire a series of terse, to-the-point queries.

"What is two plus two?"

Carl considered it a moment then said, "Two."

Without looking up at him, Stirling wrote something and asked several more math questions, all of which Carl got wrong.

Then he said, "I'm going to read you a story, after which I'll ask you questions pertaining to it." He glanced up. "Do you understand?"

Carl shrugged.

Stirling read a brief, trivial tale about a man who took his car to the mechanic to be fixed, then he questioned Carl on the details, such as the color of the car and what the mechanic said about the engine trouble. Some of the things he asked, Jodie could not remember being in the story. Did she just miss them? she wondered. Or were they trick questions?

Carl did poorly on the test, remembering only that the mechanic's name was Jack. Jodie herself had forgotten that part.

Next Stirling told Carl to close his eyes, then asked him to perform some simple tasks such as touching his right ear with his left index finger, folding his hands, pushing his tongue against the inside of his cheek.

With Carl still not looking, Stirling touched Carl's

right temple and asked him what side of his face he had touched.

Carl answered, "Eyes."

The psychological tests continued for almost an hour, Stirling testing Carl's memory, his language abilities and attention span, his capacity for abstract reasoning.

"Odd numbered streets run east to west, even numbered streets west to east. Lettered avenues run north and south; however unlike the numbered streets, they are not one-way. If you're at Third Street and J Avenue and you want to visit a store east of you on Fifth Street and K Avenue, what is the most direct route to get there?"

Carl had no idea how to answer. He just stared, saying nothing. Jodie needed a few moments to figure out the answer herself—J Avenue south to 4th Street, then 4th east to K, and finally K south to 5th. She realized Carl didn't stand a chance of getting it.

Next Stirling asked Carl to copy drawings of a circle, a square, a cross, and wavy lines. After that he took a puzzle from a box and scattered the pieces on the table for Carl to assemble. Carl did well on those two tests, and it seemed to perk him up a bit, but he was tired and he was becoming bored and frustrated with most of the tests. Finally he just stopped cooperating.

"We're done anyway," Stirling said, collecting his notes and testing materials. "If you two would wait in the waiting room, I'll review the data and then we can talk about a possible treatment plan."

They sat in the waiting room for twenty-five minutes before Darlene came out.

"The doctor is ready for you now."

10

As they followed Darlene down the corridor, Carl tugged on Jodie's hand and said, "We're going to go home now, right?"

"In a little while. We're just going to talk to the doctor first."

"We've been here all day."

"Not all day."

"We have to go soon or we'll be late."

"Late for what?"

Carl looked puzzled. He tried to find an answer but had none. He looked at his watch now and shook his head. Then he turned away and stared off blankly as they reached the door at the end of the hall.

Darlene tapped on it then opened it and ushered Jodie and Carl in. Jodie was surprised at how small and cluttered the office was. It didn't have any of the bright, modern qualities that the examination rooms had. It looked almost like an afterthought.

Dr. Stirling was sitting behind a desk covered with file folders and loose papers. On top of the file cabinets behind him, on a chair in the corner, on the floor under the desk, books and journals lay folded open as though partially read, then set aside. Every bit of wall space in the office was covered with a strange mixture of physiological diagrams and Mayan carvings.

"Come in," Stirling said, looking up from the computer. "I must apologize for my office," he said, looking past

Jodie and Carl at the clutter behind them. "My practice has grown considerably since we opened the clinic a year ago. We really do need a larger facility. I could use more room in which to disperse my clutter."

"A neat office is a sign of a sick mind," Jodie said.

Stirling laughed. "I should repeat that to Miss Cummings the next time she petitions me to spruce up the place."

"Do you have a lot of patients like my father?" Jodie asked.

"Oh yes. We treat more patients every month, patients with AD such as your father, as well as patients with different medical problems. We've had excellent success treating several types of neurological disorders."

Carl interrupted. "What are you two talking about?"

"The doctor was just telling me about the patients he's been able to help."

"Who cares about that?"

Stirling looked over, a little surprised.

"I'm sorry, Doctor," Jodie said.

"No need to apologize."

Carl scoffed at her, then turned to Dr. Stirling. "My wife doesn't know what she's talking about," he said.

"I'm your daughter, Dad," she said. "I'm Jodie."

"I know that." Carl turned to Stirling. "I know that."

Stirling nodded, adjusted his glasses, then turned his attention back to the computer monitor. Using the mouse, he scrolled through a few screens and said, "Well, I feel confident that I have a complete picture of your father's medical situation from the tests we did today and from the records you brought down with you. I don't think there's any question about the diagnosis."

He made no attempt to segue into this. He just came out and said it. Jodie noticed again that he did not seem comfortable dealing with people. He seemed much more at ease with the computer. In fact he spoke to it more than he did to her and Carl.

"Your father appears to be in the middle stages of Alzheimer's dementia," he said, glancing only momentarily at Jodie.

She nodded. This was no surprise to her. She already knew what Carl had. She was anxious to hear what Stirling could do to help him.

"Let me say I understand the position you're in, Miss Simms," Stirling said quietly. "I know it's not an easy one. And I feel for you." The words sounded forced, awkward, and yet at the same time they sounded genuine. When he stole a brief look at her, she saw empathy in his eyes.

"I've seen many patients come through here similar to your father and I do realize how difficult it is for both the patient and the caregiver."

"Thank you, Doctor," she said.

He nodded, glancing momentarily at Carl, who was staring at a Mayan carving on the wall, unable to follow what they were saying.

"Do you think you can help him?" Jodie asked.

Stirling watched Carl for a moment, then looked down at the papers on his desk and said, "I should tell you that there's no guarantee that the therapy we use will help him."

He lifted his gaze toward Carl for an instant then glanced at Jodie and finally looked down at his desk again.

"I can tell you that we've had many patients who have experienced remarkable results, but we've also had a few patients who haven't shown the improvement we anticipated." He peered up. "I want to make sure you understand that this type of therapy may not bring about the result for which you are hoping," he said.

Jodie nodded. Carl's doctors in Jacksonville had all but given up on him. They had admitted that they could do nothing. If there was a chance that Dr. Stirling could help him, even a small chance, that was much more than her father could get anywhere else.

"Let me explain a little about the therapy I'd recommend for your father," Stirling said. He put his forearms on the desk and folded his hands. He looked directly at her through his thick glasses, which was a little surprising. His oversized eyes were distracting.

"It would involve regular injections of a neuroplasticity enhancing factor."

"Is that what they call The Cure?" she asked. "I spoke with a patient of yours who lives in Florida," she explained. "Libby Harden. She and her husband told me a little about the clinic and the medication. They said everyone calls it The Cure."

"Yes, well, some patients do call it that," he said, looking embarrassed by it. "I feel it would be a bit . . . presumptuous of me to call it that. I usually refer to it as NPEF-alpha."

"For people to call it The Cure, it must work," Jodie said.

"As I said, we have had excellent results, yes. But I guess you know that, having spoken with the Hardens. You already know a great deal. That will save us time." He turned back to his computer and started clicking the mouse, scrolling through screens, apparently satisfied that no further explanation was needed.

"The Hardens really didn't tell me a lot," Jodie said. She wanted to hear what he had to say about it. She wanted to understand it better. "I was hoping you could explain how it works," she said.

"Certainly."

He thought over his answer for a moment, then folded his hands on the desk again and spoke directly to her.

"In simplified terms, proper functioning of the brain's communication system is dependent upon what are called neurotransmitters."

Talking impersonally about the science, he appeared much more comfortable than he did talking about Carl personally. He had no problem maintaining eye contact now.

"You see," he went on, "all brain function is a matter of communication, of messages moving between the brain's various parts. These messages move from neuron to neuron until they reach the part of the brain where they're supposed to be, and then they tell the body what to do. AD results from a disruption in the brain's communication system. In an AD patient, the neuro-transmitters that carry messages across the brain no longer function properly due in part to neuron loss associated with the disease. Do you know about tangles and plaques?"

"I've read some articles and books that mentioned them but I'm not sure I understand it completely."

"The distinguishing characteristic of AD, along with neuron loss," Stirling explained, "is the presence in the brain of what we call senile neuritic plaques and neurofibrillary tangles. Plaques are accumulations of an insoluble protein we call beta-amyloid. These accumulations are very hard, like rocks. They form in one of the brain's memory centers—the hippocampus—"

"Hippopotamus," Carl blurted, grinning first at Jodie then at Stirling. When neither of them replied, he shrugged and looked away again.

Stirling continued. "You need not remember the name, just that it is a memory center. Accumulations here are associated with memory deficits.

"Tangles," he said, "are made up primarily of another protein called tau. They result from the destruction of minute cytoskeletal elements in the brain, called microtubules. What happens is that these microtubules crystallize and fall apart. The resulting minute particles then form together into masses, again in the brain's memory centers, the hippocampus"—he glanced at Carl, expecting him to say something, but Carl wasn't even listening, so he continued—"along with the amygdala. But in addition, tangles form in the cerebral cortex, which is the site of most of the brain's higher functions—math, reasoning, logic and such.

"I know I'm giving you a great deal of information," he said, "but the thing to keep in mind is that it all boils down to the blocking of messages from one part of the brain to another. When this happens, what the brain does is lock in on a single message, blocking any other messages from being transmitted. In effect, the brain seizes up. This seizing up, if you will, can last for a short period—perhaps a second or two. For instance, when the patient is trying to do some common everyday task, like brushing his teeth, and can't remember how to do it at first. But then with a little help he is able to do it."

"Yes, I've seen that in my father."

"When that happens, the little nudge you give him sort of reroutes the message through the brain. The message finds an alternate, functional pathway, providing access to the information needed to perform that task.

"This seizing up can also last for longer periods, hours or days. When this happens, the little push you gave him to get him to brush his teeth doesn't work any longer. That's because an increasing number of the alternate routes have also become nonfunctional. Finally, when the disease reaches the advanced stages, what you have is a permanent seizing, a permanent interruption of the normal flow of neurological messages. There are no alternate routes left. At that point the brain, for all intents and purposes, ceases to function in any kind of effective manner, and well . . ."

He looked away from her now, turning his attention back to his computer and sliding the mouse around on the tiny pad. "We don't want our patients to get to that stage," he said. He glanced at Carl, then told Jodie, "Your father isn't anywhere near that stage yet."

"And The Cure can prevent him from reaching that stage?" she asked.

"NPEF-alpha is a neuroplasticity enhancer. As the name implies, it enhances the plasticity of neurons in the brain, improving brain function and ameliorating the symptoms of AD."

"I don't understand what you mean by plasticity?"

Stirling thought about it for a moment, then said, "In many lower animals, insects for example, brains are hard-wired, so to speak. In other words, there is only one correct wiring pattern for the brain's signals to follow. Think of neurons as the wiring and the brain's signals as electricity. The wiring is already in place from birth. The benefit of such a brain is that it's more or less prepro-grammed from inception—insects don't really have to learn anything. The downside is that they aren't really *capable* of learning anything. A disruption in the normal flow of neural signals is devastating because the wiring pattern is difficult to change. Mammals, on the other hand, are not hard-wired. They must learn many of their complex behaviors. Their wiring changes in direct re-sponse to their experiences."

Stirling looked directly at Jodie as he spoke, again at ease as long as he was discussing the science and not particular patients.

"This same plasticity, this rewiring process, is what allows the brain to reroute messages when there is neuron death—for instance from stroke. The brain can recover without exactly healing."

"I'm not sure I understand that distinction," Jodie said. "Recover without healing?"

"When we cut our finger," Stirling explained, "the lesion can be healed by proliferation of skin cells. Neighboring skin cells divide and make new skin, closing the wound. The brain, however, doesn't have that capacity. Dead brain cells cannot be replaced by new ones the way skin cells can. However, the brain does have a unique response all its own. Instead of making new cells, new neurons, the remaining neurons compensate for the lost function of the dead neurons by rearranging the wiring pattern, allowing the signals, the electricity, to travel through a new route, through different wires. This, again, is plasticity.

"Now, a young brain has the plasticity to develop new routes through which the neurotransmitters can travel. But as the brain ages," he said, "its capacity for this kind of rerouting greatly diminishes. This affects learning. The young learn more readily than the old because their brains are more plastic."

"I guess there's medical truth to the saying you can't teach old dogs new tricks," Jodie said.

"It is harder for an old dog to learn, yes," Stirling said, missing the humor completely. "This same diminished capacity for compensation, or loss of plasticity," he went on, "is also prevalent in certain neurological disorders, such as Parkinson's disease, but especially in AD, which is what we're concerned with in reference to Mr. Simms."

"Here I am," Carl said.

The interruption jolted Stirling from his thoughts. He glanced at Carl for a moment, looking a little lost, as though his neurotransmitters weren't functioning properly. Then he turned back to Jodie and gathered his thoughts.

"NPEF-alpha," he said, "dramatically increases the brain's plasticity, enabling the neuroglial tissue to carry out that rerouting process I mentioned, to develop new pathways through which the neurotransmitters can travel, thus compensating for the neuron loss and circumventing the blockage created by the tangles and plaques symptomatic of AD. This, in effect, restores the brain's communication system to the way it was before the onset of AD."

"And that's something other Alzheimer's medications can't do?" Jodie asked.

"The other AD drugs on the market right now are intended to prolong the amount of time normal neurotransmitters are present in the synapse and therefore enhance stimulation at remaining synapses. However, the enhancement a patient experiences from these drugs is minor at best. They certainly don't increase the brain's plasticity."

"My father tried those medicines before," Jodie said. "They didn't help him."

Stirling looked in Carl's file again. "I see here that he did try Cognex and Aricept. They work for some people, but not for others. And even for those patients who do benefit, at best we've seen only a slowdown in the decline of cognitive abilities, and that's only temporary. We've certainly never seen a reversal in the disease. None of those medications is a cure. NPEF-alpha, on the other hand, when it works at its best, can literally halt the neurological degeneration and enhance plasticity in the remaining neurons so they can generate new routes for information to flow. In the majority of patients, this will actually reverse the behavioral symptoms of AD."

"That would be wonderful if we could do that," Jodie said.

"Let me make it clear once again that I cannot guarantee that it will work for any one individual, but we have had remarkable success with many patients."

"Can you tell me what is it?" Jodie asked. "Chemically, pharmacologically, what exactly is NPEF-alpha?"

"It's what we call a nerve growth factor. What in some circles is referred to as 'chicken soup for the brain.' Nerve growth factors are proteins produced in different areas of the body for the purpose of development and maintenance of neurons. In the case of NPEF-alpha, we've discovered that it affects the plasticity of neurons in the brain."

"Where does it come from?"

"It's secreted by the cerebral cortex."

"No, I mean the injections you give the patients, the shots my father will be getting—where does that come from?"

"Oh, I see what you're asking," Stirling said. He turned to the computer and typed for a moment. Without looking at Jodie, he said, "We obtain the NPEF-alpha that we use from the cortex of a transgenic animal source. The growth factor is purified in our laboratory and then combined in a bacteriostatic solution. The patient then receives the NPEF-alpha through intramuscular injections."

"Wait a minute," Jodie said, ignoring what he said

about *bacteriostatic* and *intramuscular* and concentrating on the first part. "You get The Cure from animals?" she asked, shocked.

Stirling smiled, an affectation that looked uncomfortable on him.

"It must sound strange," he said.

"To be honest with you, it does sound kind of strange."

"As strange as it may sound, it's not as unusual as you might think. This sort of xenogenic therapy—utilizing chemistry arising from different species—is used in many ways for various types of disease. Many types of proteins are conserved between species—in other words, some animal proteins work the same way as human proteins. I assure you, it is quite safe and effective."

It still sounded strange to Jodie, but she saw that Stirling had no reservations at all about using an animal source. It must be okay, she thought.

"What animal do you get The Cure from?" she asked.

"They're from genetically modified porcine donors."

"Pigs?"

He chuckled stiffly. "Through many years of testing," he explained, "we've discovered that the cortical matter from pigs produces the best results when it comes to enhancing the plasticity of the brain."

"Ordinary pigs?"

"No, not ordinary at all. We use specially raised pigs into which we have introduced specific human genes. Consequently, these pigs produce human proteins. This is the only way we've found to produce a growth factor that will have the desired results in human recipients. So no, they're not ordinary at all. They're special, very special."

That was a little reassuring to Jodie.

"And you think this—" She glanced at her father, concerned about him hearing the rest of the question, concerned he might reject it just because it sounded strange. "You think this special pig tissue," she whispered, "might help my father?"

Stirling turned his attention back to data on the computer screen. "Judging from his tests results here," he said, "I think he'd make a viable candidate, yes. The earlier in the disease's development that we treat a patient, the better the results are, we've found." He glanced at Carl. "Your father is still early enough in the progression of this disease that we should be able to anticipate positive results."

Jodie hesitated for a moment, then said, "I have another question, Doctor."

"Yes, of course."

"Why are you the only doctor prescribing this therapy? I mean, if it's so good, why isn't everyone using it?"

He paused, thinking over his answer like a witness in a court of law.

"I believe eventually everyone will be using it," he said finally, and Jodie was relieved to see him make eye contact. "But right now we haven't had sufficient clinical studies to present it to the FDA for approval. The more patients we treat, the more data we'll amass, and the sooner we can make NPEF-alpha more widely available."

"Is there any possibility that my father can have an

adverse reaction to the therapy? When he took Cognex he had to stop because it made him very sick."

"That's not uncommon with Cognex. Many patients have the same problem. Cognex is not for everyone."

"Will he have problems like that with The Cure?"

"Let me assure you that the growth factor your father will be taking is very safe. We haven't encountered any patients experiencing any kind of immune response, so you won't have to worry about the body rejecting it. The only side effects we have encountered are minor nausea and a general feeling of lethargy. But this is only for the first day or two and not every patient experiences these symptoms. In any case, these symptoms disappear as the body adjusts to the new synapses. Some patients get headaches on the day they take the injections, but that's only with very few patients, and the headaches don't last more than an hour or so. None of our patients have had discomfort severe enough to cause them to discontinue the therapy. I understand your concern for your father's safety, and rightfully so, but I can assure you that we've encountered no adverse side effects from NPEF-alpha. Of course, there are no guarantees with any medication. Ultimately it has to be your decision."

"If we did go ahead and try this, what would be the next step?"

"The initial therapy is a one month trial period. You'll have to give your father the injections yourself. Miss Cummings will instruct you on how it's done and we'll provide you with everything you'll need for the first month's treatment. After one month, your father will return here for reevaluation, at which point we measure his cognitive abilities. If he is progressing, if NPEF-alpha is helping him, we'll give you the next supply, adjusting the dosage at that point if necessary. After two more months, your father will return again, and we'll test him again. From then on, he must come back every three months for testing and for additional NPEF-alpha.

"You should know that the therapy is very expensive and most insurance companies will not cover it."

Jodie nodded. "Yes, I knew that before we came down here."

"I wish we could charge less, but the process of retrieving and purifying the cortical tissue is very time-consuming and costly. You have to remember that NPEF-alpha cannot be synthesized. We have to purify the protein from source tissue. This makes the therapy very expensive. Hopefully, soon we'll come up with a way to use recombinant DNA to synthesize it so we can bring the price down, but right now I'm afraid it is a very costly therapy. There's no way around that."

"And Dad will have to take it indefinitely?"

"I'm afraid so. If he stops, the symptoms of AD will immediately return. Your father will have to take injections of NPEF-alpha for the rest of his life."

"Assuming we did try it," Jodie said, "how long would he have to take it before we'll know whether or not it's going to help him?"

"We should know that very early in the therapy. By the second or third week we should see results. Certainly by the time the initial four-week supply is exhausted and your father returns for his follow-up exam, we'll know if NPEF-alpha is helping him."

"Well," Jodie said, "I have to admit it sounds encouraging, but I'll need a little time to think about it, talk it over with my father."

"Yes, absolutely. This isn't something you should rush into. You're scheduled to leave tomorrow, right?" Stirling asked, checking the computer. It seemed that everything about them was in the computer already.

"Yes, in the afternoon," Jodie said.

"As long as you let us know in the morning, we can have everything ready before you leave."

≈ 11

Jodie and Carl had a late lunch at Denny's near the hotel, then they returned to their cabaña and changed into their bathing suits. In Jacksonville she had promised Carl he could collect shells once they got here. That was the only thing in months he actually remembered her saying.

Since she hadn't thought to bring along a Publix bag for him to carry his shells, she took the hotel's plastic laundry bag out of the bureau and gave him that.

"This isn't the same," Carl said.

"I know, but it's just as good. It'll hold the shells."

He examined it for a minute, let out a breath of disapproval, then took the can of WD-40 from his suitcase, stuffed it into the plastic bag and followed her down the path to the beach.

Jodie took off her sandals and went barefoot. The sand was warm and powdery under her toes. The sun felt good on her face. A slight breeze blew off the sea, tempering the heat just enough to make it comfortable.

She watched Carl lumber toward the water. Usually he wore a shirt and long pants or Bermuda shorts. Today, he had on only swimming trunks, no shirt, and Jodie saw that his skin was an unhealthy shade of white, his body gaunt and weak. Staring at him, she found herself comparing the way he looked to someone who had just emerged from a prisoner-of-war camp. He did not look at all healthy.

She joined him at the edge of the water and stepped in up to her ankles. Here in Mexico the surf was much warmer than back home in Florida. And the water was as clear as tap water. And calm today—not even the slightest of waves ruffled the surface.

"There's a couple shells there, Dad," she said, pointing.

He looked at them and shook his head. "No good."

"Really? You don't think they look kind of nice?"

"No good."

He turned and started walking up the beach. Jodie followed.

Many other hotel guests shared the beach with them this afternoon, most stretched out on chaise lounges, soaking in the sun, a few wading in the surf. A plywood booth with palm thatching for a roof was set up just above the tide line. Wave runners were beached at the edge of the surf, signs on them offering them for rent at: $35 U.S. PER HALF HOUR. A black man with a Canadian flag tattooed on his shoulder sat near them, reading a damp, tattered issue of *Sports Illustrated*.

Waiters carried colorful drinks out onto the sand, serving supine guests in chaise lounges. A volleyball game was in progress on the other side of the rental booth, a humorous mixture of chunky European men in scanty bikinis and slim Americans in baggy trunks. Someone nearby had a radio playing a blend of salsa and rock.

Even with all these people around, all the activity, Jodie still found this place peaceful and relaxing. Perhaps it was the gentle sun, the whisper of tiny waves, the clean breath of air that blew in from the Caribbean, or maybe just the lazy pace she had adopted since stepping out onto this beach. Whatever it was, it opened her mind to the many questions she needed to resolve.

Much had happened today, much for her to digest and evaluate. She needed to make a decision by tomorrow morning. It would not be an easy one.

She turned to her father, reasoning that since it involved him, she should consider his opinion. The difficult part was getting him to comprehend it all.

"Dad," she said. "How did you like that doctor we went to see today?"

"What doctor?"

"The one who examined you a little while ago. Dr. Stirling. Do you remember him?"

He shrugged.

"He seemed like a good doctor, didn't he?" Jodie said. "Not the most outgoing, personable guy, but he seemed to know what he was talking about. Don't you think?"

She noticed Carl wasn't listening. He was concentrating on the sand, looking for shells. Jodie stayed close to him, in case he needed to hold her arm. Getting him to understand all this was going to be a challenge.

With his thoughts on his search for shells, she fell silent and reflected on this morning's visit with Dr. Stirling. She had mixed feelings about the man. His manner was a little unsettling. He was not the friendliest doctor she had ever met. He did not have the kind of personality that inspired confidence, the way her father's doctor at the Mayo Clinic had. But Jodie got the definite impression that he did seem to know what he was doing. When he spoke about Carl's illness and about the treatment he offered at his clinic, he demonstrated a keen understanding and—not passion, exactly—perhaps the word she was looking for was . . . sincerity.

In spite of his caution, his reluctance to guarantee that the treatment would absolutely work, Jodie could tell that he *believed* in it. He may not have been comfortable dealing with patients the way Dr. Harrington was, but he was very much at ease with—and even committed to— the Alzheimer's cure itself.

In that respect, Jodie felt she could trust him—at least as much as she could trust any other doctor she had consulted. And Dr. Stirling was going to *try* to do something to make Carl better, which was much more than any other doctor was willing to do.

"Dad," she said, drawing his attention away from the sand for a moment. "That doctor we went to today, he has a medicine that he thinks will make you better."

"Better what?"

"Make you feel better. Help you to think a little better."

He gazed at her in thought, looking like he understood, then he said, "I don't like the shells here."

She told herself to be patient with him. "They have nice shells here," she said.

"No, I don't like them."

"Well, we're going to go home tomorrow, then you can get the good shells again."

"Good," he said with a satisfied nod. He turned away from her and went back to looking for "bad" shells.

"So anyway," Jodie said, still trying to get him to understand the real reason they had come here. "The doctor you saw this morning—"

"What doctor?"

"Dr. Stirling. He examined you this morning. Remember?"

"Wait a minute. Maybe . . ."

"You think maybe you remember?"

"Hmm?" He made an annoyed gesture toward her with his hand and turned his attention to a shell half buried in the sand. He labored over and stooped to examine it. Spiral and unbroken, the shell was the color of a ripe peach and had the texture of glass. After a brief inspection he tossed it aside. "Nah?" he said, making a distasteful expression with his mouth, as though he had just bit into a lemon.

"You didn't like that shell?" Jodie asked.

"No good."

"I thought it was a nice one."

He scoffed at her and continued up the beach.

Carl's attention was back on shells. Jodie realized he really wasn't capable of understanding all that was involved. He couldn't help her. This decision was hers and hers alone.

She needed to weigh the risks of taking The Cure against the possible benefits. The reality of Carl's illness was such that without a cure or a miracle he would become progressively worse. That was the cold, hard fact. No way around it. Dr. Harrington had estimated that Carl probably wouldn't live more than another three or four years—three or four years that would find him in much *much* worse condition than he was now.

Dr. Harrington had explained that before long, Carl would lose the ability to feed himself and take care of his toilet needs. Eventually, too, he would become too weak to stand, too weak even to sit up or hold his head erect. Not only that, but his mental acuity would quickly deteriorate as well. Jodie realized that as bad as Carl was today, he was as good as he would ever be. That was the harsh reality of his disease, leaving no hope, none whatsoever.

If The Cure might—just *might*—help him, didn't that outweigh the possible risks?

When she looked at it in that light, she was satisfied that the therapy was worth trying.

The only other consideration that made the decision difficult was the issue of cost. Seventy thousand dollars a year was an awful lot of money. And considering that Carl was only sixty-eight years old and could easily live for another ten years—assuming The Cure eliminated his Alzheimer's—the cost would be three quarters of a million dollars. The prospect of having to come up with that much money actually frightened her.

She didn't see any way she could possibly afford that. Her annual salary from the TV station was less than seventy thousand. Much less. Add the cost of four trips a year to Mexico—airfare, hotel, food—plus the medical exams, and the figure became dauntingly high. She simply did not have that kind of money. And neither did her father.

Even if she combined her salary with her father's pension, that would just barely cover it. But she still had to pay the mortgage and taxes on her house, her own medical bills, her car, her insurance, and food for both of them along with all her other bills. And Carl's bills. His house in St. Augustine and the one in Connecticut were two more drains on her finances.

No, she didn't have seventy thousand dollars to pay for his treatment, and that was a frightening realization when she considered that it might just cure him. The thought of Dr. Stirling's treatment working and Carl not trying it solely because she couldn't come up with enough money sickened her. She knew she wouldn't be able to live with herself if she let that happen.

Sure, it was a lot of money, but if it would make Carl better, if it would bring back the father she used to have, it was certainly worth it. To make her father better, to cure him, was worth any amount of money. She would have to find a way to pay it. Whatever it took, she had to do it.

She thought again about the house in Connecticut and the one in St. Augustine. The St. Augustine house was small and probably worth less than a hundred thousand dollars. But the house up north, the one she had grown up in, was surely worth much more, probably three times that. Three hundred thousand dollars was a lot of money, a lot of The Cure.

Until last summer, her parents used to drive up to Hartford every May and spend the summer in the old house, driving back to Florida the week after Labor Day. Selling it had never been a consideration since they lived there part of the year. But now that Jodie's mother was gone, the house remained empty year-round, nothing more than an additional expense—insurance, taxes, heat, repairs. More money she didn't have.

Jodie doubted Carl would ever be able to make the trip to Connecticut again, and even if he were able, even if The Cure did cure him, he probably wouldn't want to go back to the old house alone, without his wife. Too many memories up there. Perhaps she should sell the house.

Jodie realized she couldn't make that decision. Not now anyway. Maybe someday she would be forced to do it, but right now she put that out of her head and concentrated on The Cure's effectiveness. She realized that considering the yearly cost was premature. She should be thinking about whether or not it would work. To find out whether or not it worked would cost her one month's supply of injections, about six thousand dollars. She had that much money in the bank, and while it was still a considerable sum of money to spend, she knew she couldn't afford *not* to spend it on this drug, not if it meant curing her father.

They would try it, she told herself, watching Carl stoop down for a shell. They would try the drug and hope it was the miracle everyone claimed it was.

12

The next afternoon, when Jodie and Carl walked into Dr. Stirling's waiting room, an elderly couple was at the receptionist's window. The man was writing a check, the woman commenting on Darlene Cummings's blouse. The fact that Jodie couldn't tell which of the two was the patient strengthened her resolve that she was doing the right thing.

After the elderly couple left, Darlene brought Jodie and Carl back to one of the examination rooms. She helped Carl up onto the examination table and wheeled the doctor's stool over for Jodie to sit on.

"It'll be up to you to administer the injections for the first month or so," Darlene told Jodie.

"I expected that."

"After that, your father should be able to do it himself."

Jodie found it difficult to imagine Carl manipulating a hypodermic needle, but she would wait to see how he was a month from now.

"Your father will be receiving one injection of NPEF-alpha every four days," Darlene explained. "Since today is Sunday, and he's having his first shot today, you should give him the next shot on Thursday and the next shot the following Monday, then Friday, and so on."

From a small refrigerator under one of the counters, Darlene took out a plastic case a little larger than a VHS cassette tape.

"This is your NPEF-alpha home-use kit," she said.

She opened it, exposing eight individually wrapped hypodermic syringes, each already filled with one milliliter of clear liquid. Beside them in the case were several sterile cotton pads and a small bottle of antiseptic solution.

"You keep it refrigerated?" Jodie asked.

"Absolutely. And you should, too. That preserves the potency of NPEF-alpha. The shots are administered intramuscularly," Darlene said. "That means the needle goes into the muscle, not a vein. So you won't have to worry about tying off the arm and finding a vein. You make the injection directly into the upper arm or the thigh, much the way a diabetic would inject insulin. It's very easy. You'll see."

She showed Jodie how to prepare the syringe, then she swabbed a spot on Carl's arm with an antiseptic solution and told Jodie where to inject him. Jodie's hand trembled slightly as she brought the tip of the needle to her father's skin. Darlene put her hand on top of Jodie's hand and helped her jab the needle into Carl's arm. Carl winced as it went in.

"Helen, that hurt!" he said.

"I'm sorry, Dad."

Darlene put her arm around Carl and rubbed his back. "You'll be just fine, Mr. Simms." She looked at Jodie who was holding the needle in Carl's arm. "Now you depress the plunger slowly," she told Jodie. "Keep steady pressure on it until all of the solution is out."

Jodie did this.

Darlene instructed her to remove the needle, then she

pressed a small piece of cotton over the tiny mark on Carl's arm and taped it in place with a Band-Aid.

"There, that's it," she said. "Now that wasn't so bad, was it?"

Carl shrugged and stared at the bandage on his arm. As Jodie let out a long sigh of relief that it was over, Darlene squeezed Jodie's hand reassuringly and said, "You did real well. I'm sure you won't have any problems."

"I hope not. It's a lot harder than it looks."

"After you give him a couple shots, it'll be second nature to you."

There was a tap at the door, then Dr. Stirling walked in. "Hello," he said, nodding to the three of them, looking uncomfortable in the crowded room. He was carrying a clipboard with a single sheet of paper on it.

"Afternoon, Doctor," Jodie said.

"Miss Simms." Stirling turned to Darlene. "Would you bring Mr. Simms to the waiting room? Miss Simms will join you in a moment."

"Yes, Doctor."

Jodie feared immediately that something was wrong. Had Stirling found something in Carl's tests that would prevent the medicine from working? Could it be even worse than that?

She watched apprehensively as Darlene took Carl by the hand and led him toward the door. He started to get nervous when he noticed Jodie didn't follow, resisting Darlene's gentle coaxing, peering around the room anxiously. He glared at Jodie and said, "Come on. You, too."

"I'll be right there, Dad."

"Where am I going? What are you doing? *Helen.*"

"Dad, it's all right. I'm just going to talk to Dr. Stirling for a minute. I'll be there in just a second."

"It's all right, Mr. Simms," Darlene told Carl, patting him on the back. "We're just going to be right down the hall. Hey, how would you like a cup of coffee? Come on, let's you and me go have a cup of coffee."

"I don't want coffee."

"How about a Coke?"

"What about Helen?"

"Let's you and me see if we can find one for her, too. Okay? You can help me find a Coke for your daughter."

Carl reluctantly left with Darlene. As they walked down the hall, Jodie could hear Carl saying, "I can't leave Helen alone too long."

"We won't."

"She can't be alone."

"She's okay."

"She needs me."

"I'm sure she does . . ."

Stirling walked over to the door and closed it, silencing the voices in the hall. He turned back to Jodie and stared uneasily at the clipboard in his hands.

"Is there something wrong, Doctor?" Jodie asked.

"No, nothing's wrong."

"*Whew.*" Jodie let out a nervous chuckle. "When you asked them to leave, I thought there was a problem."

"No, it's nothing like that." He looked down at the clipboard and said, "I just needed to bring this to your attention before you left. It's not something I particularly like doing, but . . . well, it's . . . necessary."

"What is it?"

He handed Jodie the clipboard. The paper looked like a legal document with a blank line in the middle of the first paragraph for her to print her name and another line on the bottom for her signature and the date. The heading at the top of the page said: COVENANT OF NONDISCLOSURE.

"What's this?" Jodie asked.

From his flushed expression and the trouble he had standing still, Jodie could tell that Stirling was very embarrassed about this.

"What that is . . . I mean to say . . . I don't know how familiar you are with the pharmaceutical industry," Stirling said. "With some of the less than honorable practices of a few companies and their researchers . . ."

"I'm not sure I follow you, Doctor."

"I really hate to have to mention this." He came a little closer to her and lowered his voice, as though he were whispering inside a church. "Some of them are not above peculating the scientific breakthroughs of others and exploiting them for their own benefits."

Peculating? "You mean you're concerned someone might steal the formula for The Cure?" Jodie asked.

~~Until it is patented~~—which won't be possible until I finish developing the process for synthesizing NPEF-alpha—until then, usurpation of my research by one of the pharmaceutical companies is a very real possibility that I must try to protect against. I have invested a significant amount of time and money in this project,

and well . . . it's not something I like having to do
but . . . if there were another way . . ."

"I think I understand," Jodie said.

"Yes, well, that's why I have to ask all my patients to
sign this document," he said, pointing to the clipboard.
"It means you agree not to turn NPEF-alpha over to any
other pharmaceutical or medical entity. I'm not at all
suggesting that it is your intent to do that. Your father's
well-being, obviously, is your primary concern and relin-
quishing any of the NPEF-alpha would only jeopardize
his health. I know you realize that. It's just that the state
of research being as it is . . ."

"Helen!" Carl called from the hallway. *"Helen, where
are you?"*

Jodie sighed, exasperated. Carl could be so tiring at
times. She started to read the document but then her
father called again. She heard him struggling with
Darlene, who was trying to get him to go to the waiting
room.

"Duty calls," she said with a forced chuckle. She
quickly scribbled her name, signed and dated it, then
handed the clipboard to Stirling.

"Once again," Stirling said, "I apologize for having to
ask you to do this . . ."

"No need to apologize. I understand."

"Helen, I'm lost!"

"You'll have to excuse me, Doctor."

"Yes, of course."

Jodie hurried out of the room and found Carl rushing
up the hall toward the MRI room, Darlene chasing
behind. They managed to catch him and calm him down.

He told Jodie to be more careful and held on to her arm so tightly she thought he'd leave a bruise.

Back in the waiting room, Jodie wrote a check for $7,700—$1,700 for yesterday's examination and test, and $6,000 for the eight injections of The Cure.

"I hope this does some good," she said as she tore off the check and handed it to Darlene.

"Trust me, it will. I've seen dozens of patients since I started here and the improvements have been remarkable. You'll see."

"I hope you're right."

Jodie took Carl by the hand and was about to leave when the door flew open and a small Mayan woman the same age as Jodie rushed in. Her clothes were old and faded. She wore sandals on feet that were rough and thick like saddle leather, feet more accustomed to going shoeless. And she smelled as though she had worked outside in the sun all morning and had come right here without showering. She looked first at Jodie and Carl, and Jodie saw fierce hostility in her charcoal eyes.

"*Donde está el doctor?*" the woman barked.

Jodie remembered enough from her high school Spanish to understand that the woman was asking where Dr. Stirling was. And she was clearly irate about something.

"*Quiero ver al doctor!*"

Darlene quickly came out of the back. In relation to the small, dark Mayan woman, she looked like a giant albino. In that brief instant, Jodie realized that Darlene and Stirling, as well as Carl and Jodie herself, were outsiders in somebody else's country, somebody else's world.

"*Señora,*" Darlene said. "*Como—*"

The woman wouldn't let Darlene speak. "*No! Tengo que verlo! Donde rayos está ese doctor? Donde está Cassandros?*"

"*Señora, por favor—*"

The woman started screaming, "*Cassandros! Cassandros!*"

"*Señora—*"

The woman wouldn't listen. She kept screaming: "*Cassandros! Cassandros!*" Jodie realized she wasn't looking for Stirling; she wanted another doctor, someone named Cassandros. Jodie wondered if Stirling had any associates. The sign outside had only Stirling's name. Who, then, was Cassandros?

Then the Mayan woman said something in Spanish, loud and fast and ringing with fury. Jodie missed all of it except the last word. The woman said, "*Muerto!*" Jodie knew what that word meant. "*Dead!*"

Dr. Stirling hurried into the waiting room now, and the Mexican woman turned her anger toward him. She screamed and waved her hands furiously. He remained calm and talked softly to her in Spanish, never losing his cool. He spoke the language much more naturally than Darlene, with the rapid cadence of a Mexican.

Jodie, confused by all that was happening, was unable to understand any of what Stirling and the woman were saying, but she detected something unspoken and grievous in the woman's anger.

Somehow Stirling managed to mollify the woman enough that she went with Darlene into the back.

Stirling, noticing Jodie and Carl watching all this, came over, looking troubled and uncomfortable.

"I have to apologize . . ." he said, making a vague gesture toward where the woman had been standing a moment earlier. "Poor woman . . ." He glanced down the hall behind him, his face creased with sympathy. "She recently lost her son," he said quietly.

Jodie nodded, feeling bad for the woman. "Who is Dr. Cassandros?" she asked.

"Some of the physicians down here are not the best." He shook his head sadly and said, "A lot of people come to me when there's a problem. Unfortunately sometimes it's too late for me to help them." He glanced down the hall again, where Darlene had taken the Mayan woman. "I'm sorry, but I really have to go." He gestured toward the back office. "If you'll excuse me."

"Yes, of course."

He started to leave, then turned back, a concerned look on his face. He came over to Carl and put his hand on Carl's shoulder.

"Mr. Simms," he said. "You're going to do just fine."

Carl didn't understand what Stirling was saying, but the doctor looked at Jodie and gave a reassuring nod. This instance of closeness seemed awkward for him, but Jodie saw in Stirling's face genuine compassion for her father.

"Thank you," she said quietly.

Stirling nodded and hurried away.

Jodie put the hysterical woman out of her mind. The only thing that really mattered was whether The Cure would help her father. That was her only concern. And as the plane took off and they headed back to Florida, she realized that within a month she would have the answer.

⬥ 13

"Ever hear of shock absorbers?" Sam Rogoff grunted as the taxi bounced and lurched over the crude dirt road, sending jolts up his spine.

"*Que?*"

"Nothing. *Nada.* Let's just get there," Rogoff grumbled under his breath.

When the World Health Organization said they were sending him to Mexico, this was not the kind of trip he had envisioned. He'd been thinking of sandy beaches, salty margaritas, and beautiful señoritas. Not the taxi ride from hell.

Suddenly the driver steered his cab to the side of the road. Palm fronds scraped the fender, but he didn't seem to give a damn. He pulled as far to the right as he could, as if he were trying to make room on the road for another car to pass. And then he just stopped.

Sam Rogoff didn't see another car ahead of them. He turned his neck and saw only empty road and desolated scrub brush behind them. His first thought was that he was about to get mugged.

Oh great. First they lose my luggage. Now they're going to steal the few lousy pesos I'm carrying.

The driver shut off the engine and peered over his

shoulder at Rogoff. He smiled, a gold tooth catching the glint of the sun and he said, "No more road, señor." He pointed to a narrow path in the palmetto bushes, barely wide enough to walk down. "We must to go on feets."

"You're pulling my leg, right?"

"Señor? Pull the leg?"

"Forget it," Rogoff sighed, realizing there was no way out of it. They were going the rest of the way "on feets."

The car was too close to the bushes for Rogoff to open the door on the right side so he squirmed across the back seat to the left side and shoved open the door. To ride in a car like this, he thought, it would be a big plus if you didn't have legs. Or if you were Willie Shoemaker.

Sam Rogoff was only five-nine, an average height back home, but in this car his knees were pressing up against the seat back and his thinning hair brushed the top. Suddenly he felt sorry for all those overpaid Knicks players who tried to ride in normal cars.

With a moan, he climbed out of the cramped back seat and struggled to straighten his legs, stiff and sore from the ride. As soon as he stood up on the sand road, he felt the intense heat of the tropical sun beating down on his bald spot. There were no trees here to offer shade, just scrub palms that went up to his chest.

"Just what I need," he grumbled. "A walk through the woods in ninety degree weather."

The air was so heavy with humidity that Rogoff was sweating already, after only a moment out of the air conditioning of the cab. He didn't know which was worse, being squeezed in like kippered herring or standing out here in an open-pit Mexican barbecue.

He wasn't even close to being appropriately dressed for this place. Not in the least. The wool slacks and long sleeve dress shirt he had worn on the plane, the only clothes that had survived the Mexicana baggage handlers, belonged in an office building back home in civilization, not out here in the Yucatan version of the suburbs. At least he had the good sense to leave his tie in the cab. But then again, he thought, maybe he should take that along in case he decided to hang himself later.

His wing tips weren't going to survive the trek over the sand, he realized as he peered down at his shoes. He made a mental note to put in for some new clothing when he got back to New York. One way or another, either the airline or the World Health Organization was going to come up with some cash.

Another thing about his *gringo* clothes, he realized, was that they weren't going to help endear him to the locals. They certainly weren't going to speak openly around a *gringo* giant in wool and cufflinks. Now as he prepared to enter "the bush," he hoped the long flight, the uncomfortable drive in the minicab, and the even worse walk he was about to endure, did not end up a waste of time.

Rogoff's neck was already sticky with sweat. He unbuttoned the second and third buttons on his shirt to try to get some more air under the collar. Now he looked like Rico Suavé with his chest showing. A couple gold chains and he'd be in business. Gnats swarmed around his head, probably drawn by his cologne. One of the little bastards flew into his mouth and he practically choked on it. He flailed his arms in front of his face and tried to blow the bug out but it was down too deep. The little bastard was probably pigging out on airline food right now.

Another gnat landed on his lip, but he managed to spit it out before it joined its *amigo* inside his gut. He kept his hand in front of his face now as he spoke.

"How far do we have to go?"

The driver, Juan, who was barely as tall as the fender of the cab, came around the front, tugging on a Dodgers baseball cap he must have had under the seat. "No much far," he said.

Rogoff pointed to the hat. "You got a Mets cap for me?" He felt his scalp blistering already.

"No, Los Angeles Dodgers." Juan pointed to the name. "Dodgers."

"Yeah, I can see that. But do you have another one? One for me? Any damn team, it doesn't matter. Even the friggin Red Sox, if that's all you've got."

"Red Sox, no. I like the Dodgers only, señor."

Juan missed the meaning of Rogoff's question completely. Or was he pretending not to understand? Natives—uh, make that indigenous peoples—often came down with sudden language deficits when they didn't want to answer something. Rogoff hadn't yet learned to tell when they were faking and when they really didn't understand, and he hoped he wouldn't have to spend the amount of time in places like this necessary to learn to tell.

"Never mind," Rogoff said. "Let's just get going." Under his breath, he murmured, "And not for nothing, but the Dodgers suck."

Rogoff followed Juan down the path, palm fronds

swiping at his arms, snagging the sleeves of his shirt. He removed his cufflinks and stuffed them into his pocket, then rolled up his sleeves, exposing his forearms and his Movado watch to the attack of the palm branches.

The path wound through the brush for only a hundred feet or so, then opened into a clearing fed by several other paths and containing half a dozen traditional Mayan huts. Rectangular in shape, with rounded ends, the huts were constructed of thin, straight branches, stripped of bark and lashed together with homemade rope. Most of the roofs were brown thatching, but a few had rusted sheet metal on them. They gave the word "flimsy" new meaning.

Low stone walls circled each hut. Chickens ambled freely. A small pink pig was tied to a stone outside one hut.

They were twenty feet from that hut when Juan called out, "*Hola, Maria. Yo soy Juan, paal de Santiago. Hu'chabal in naats'kimbae.*"

Rogoff spoke a little Spanish, enough to get the gist of what Juan was saying, even though Juan was mixing in some Mayan words. He was identifying himself as some relation to Santiago and asking permission to come to the house.

"Why don't you wait till we get to the door?" Rogoff said.

"No, señor. It is the custom of the Maya to announce when you are visit." He turned back to the hut and shouted, "*Hola, Maria!*"

A tiny woman with wrinkled skin the color of cocoa opened the flimsy door of the hut and peered out. Maria

Ticas de Garcia, Rogoff assumed. The old woman's expression was not at all friendly when she noticed Rogoff standing behind Juan.

"*Hola, Maria?*" Juan said, smiling at her, nodding deferentially. "*Hu'chabal in naats'kimbae?*"

Maria considered the request for a moment, then nodded. "*He'le'.*"

Juan turned to Rogoff and whispered, "She said we go in."

"She doesn't look too friendly to me."

"The Maya are careful with *gringos*, foreigners."

"Is she going to talk to me?"

Juan shrugged.

"Wonderful," Rogoff murmured.

"Oh, señor," Juan said, remembering something. "When you talk, only say Maria. Maya don't like for the strangers to know the family name."

"Why?"

"All you need to talk to someone is the first name. They believe more information give you control over them. Say only Maria. Okay?"

"Whatever turns her grass green."

"*Que?*"

"Yeah, yeah, I'll just say Maria. Let's go inside," Rogoff said, prodding Juan to lead the way.

They walked past the chickens and the pig. Rogoff had to duck as he entered the shack behind Juan. Compared to the majority of the people down here he was practically Shaquille O'Neal.

The inside of the hut smelled of an unsettling mixture of unwashed bodies and chili peppers. He assumed this was what a Mexican soccer team's locker room smelled like. The entire home was the size of Rogoff's bathroom back in Manhattan. But even as small as this place was, it had so few furnishings that it looked empty.

To the left was a mesh hammock, hanging between two of the four posts that held up the roof. Someone lay asleep inside it, a featureless body that resembled a net full of fish more than a human form. Rogoff didn't have the least idea if it was a man or a woman.

The right side of the hut had a crudely made wooden table, two chunks of a tree stump for chairs, a couple shelves with religious mumbo jumbo on it. The cooking area was nothing more than three bowling-ball size stones on the concrete floor with a metal griddle laying over it. A pile of warm ash was still heaped beneath the stones.

Maria positioned herself behind the table, keeping it between herself and Rogoff. The stance she took reminded him of a linebacker waiting for the running back to come through the line. Or in this case, waiting for Rogoff to ask her questions.

He tried to make himself look sympathetic, friendly, feigning a smile even though he was clammy with sweat and struggling to breathe in the stagnant, foul air of this hut.

He glanced back at the form in the hammock, then spoke to Maria in a whisper, hoping she would be impressed if he came across as not wanting to wake whoever was asleep over there.

"Yo soy un doctor," he whispered.

But he realized from the hard look that came across

Maria's face that informing her that he was a doctor was probably a mistake. Maria obviously didn't like doctors. Or was it more than dislike? Was it distrust that he saw in her face?

His thoughts lingered on that face, on the shallow wrinkles. Her skin showed some signs of aging, but she wasn't nearly as wrinkled as he expected a 70-year old woman to be, a woman who spent her life working outdoors in the sun. Also, this old woman stood much too straight, walked much too smoothly, and the brief utterance she made was much too clear for someone who had suffered the kind of stroke Maria had suffered just ten weeks ago. If Rogoff hadn't seen the CT scans with his own two eyes earlier today, he never would have believed that someone Maria's age could rebound from a cerebral insult so completely. But the evidence was standing right in front of him. Maria Ticas de Garcia, who should have been paralyzed and probably even dead, had recovered fully.

"Como se siente, señora?" Rogoff said, hoping that asking the woman how she felt would break the ice, would make him appear friendly.

Maria answered reluctantly with a silent nod.

The recovery from the stroke certainly intrigued him, but that wasn't the reason he was here. He decided to get to the point and get out before he suffocated.

Since his Spanish was only remedial, to save time he told Juan to explain to Maria that he was from the World Health Organization and that he was *not* a medical doctor. Mayans, he remembered, and Mexicans in general, put more faith in *curanderos*, in herbalists, than in

M.D.s. If he intended to get her to open up, it was important that she not mistake him for an M.D.

"Tell her I'm here to investigate the death of Hector, her husband," Rogoff told Juan.

When Juan finished translating, Maria simply nodded again, saying nothing. She stared at Rogoff, her face still betraying distrust.

"I understand that Hector had appendicitis and that he had to have his appendix removed," Rogoff said, then gestured for Juan to translate.

Again Maria responded with a silent nod. Rogoff sighed. He needed to get this old lady talking, explaining what happened.

"Hector stayed in the hospital for three days?" Rogoff asked. *"Tres dias en la hospital Hector?"*

Maria nodded.

"And then what happened? Tell me as much as you can remember," Rogoff said. Lowering his voice, he said to Juan, "See if you can get her to talk, will you? It's like interviewing Helen Keller."

"Who?"

"Just get her to talk. There's a hundred pesos in it for you if you can get her to tell me what the hell happened here."

Juan understood that well enough. He smiled and winked. Apparently fifteen bucks had a lot of pull down here. Back home, you couldn't get a wino to tell you what brand he drank for fifteen bucks. Here you could probably buy a national election and still have some change left over for a burrito and a Corona.

Juan spoke with the old woman for a few moments

and finally Maria answered in Mayan-Spanish, speaking to Juan and not to Rogoff. Juan translated.

"When Hector come home, he was not right."

"Not right, how?"

"*Pol,*" Maria said and pointed to her head. She spoke a few more words in clipped Mayan, then Juan told Rogoff what the old woman had said.

"Hector was bad. He was cry for no reason. He was . . . *agitación,*" Juan said, struggling for the appropriate translation. "Not right," he said. "Then is the . . . *ataques.*"

"*Ataques?*" Rogoff didn't understand. "You mean attacks, like heart attacks?"

"No, no. Not the *corazón,* not sick of the heart. Of the *cabeza,* the head," Juan said. "*Ataque,*" he repeated. Unable to find the right word, he stuck out his tongue, extended his arms and started shaking. "*Convulsiónes,*" he said.

"You mean convulsions, seizures?"

"*Si.* He has the see-zhor. Many the see-zhor."

"Like epilepsy?"

Juan shrugged, then asked Maria. She spit out several words angrily, leering now at Rogoff as she said them.

"She say the *clinica* give Hector the *ataque.* He have no the *ataque* before he go to the *Clinica Centro.*"

"Hector had no history of epilepsy, of seizures?"

"No, no see-zhor before the *clinica.*"

"Never? None at all?"

"*Nunca,*" Maria said. She spoke a few more words and Juan translated.

"Hector go back to the *clinica,* to the doctor. He make

the picture of the head to see why the see-zhors. But he don't help Hector. The last see-zhor make Hector no can breathe. Maria call the *hmen*, the *curandero*, and he give Hector the *xiw*."

Gesundheit, Rogoff thought. He said, "What's *xiw*?"

"The *hierba medicinal*."

"Herbs?" Rogoff said in disbelief. "You're saying her old man Hector was having a seizure, he couldn't breathe, and this medicine-man-whatever-he-is forced herbs down Hector's throat?"

"The *curanderos* are very good, señor," Juan said. "They can treat many sickness better than the doctor."

"Yeah, sounds like it." Rogoff let it go—no sense arguing the point. "So, what happened next?" he asked.

"Next is too late." Juan lowered his voice and said, "Hector, he die . . ."

Maria spoke again, her voice a malignant hiss. "*Ts'ats'aak kinsik Hector*," she said.

Rogoff looked to Juan for the translation.

"She say the doctor kill Hector."

"Does he know the doctor's name?"

Juan asked Maria who answered with a single word.

"*Cassandros*."

≋ 14

Jodie watched her father closely Sunday night when they arrived back in Jacksonville, looking for any change in him at all, anything that would indicate that the injection of The Cure was working. When they watched *60*

Minutes, he talked back to Andy Rooney, as though the commentator were in the room with them. Carl had always liked watching that show, even though he usually had no idea what anyone was saying. The ticking clock before each segment was his favorite part. Tonight his reactions were the same as always: he understood nothing.

After the show was over, he went into the kitchen for some ginger ale and got angry at the refrigerator when he couldn't figure out how to open the door. He seemed just as confused and frustrated as he had been last week, before the injection.

The next morning, after she cleaned up the breakfast dishes, Jodie went into Carl's room and she found him standing in front of the bureau, spraying WD-40 on his face.

She rushed over and took the can away. "Dad, what are you doing?"

"I'm shaving."

"You don't use this. You use the electric shaver. It's in the bathroom."

He stared at her, not understanding. She took him to the bathroom and helped him wash off the WD-40, then showed him how to shave.

"I know how to do it!" he said angrily after she got him started.

"I know you do, Dad. You go ahead and shave. I'll be back in a little while."

She left him alone in the bathroom, but stayed in the hallway and watched him without him knowing it. When he started to rinse off the shaver in the sink, she hurried back in. He had no idea what he was doing was wrong.

The trip to Mexico was supposed to have changed all this, she thought. She was already beginning to lose hope. Even though Dr. Stirling had said it could take two or three weeks for the effects of The Cure to show, she wanted it to work immediately, wanted her father better *now*.

Because of the extra time she spent with Carl this morning she arrived at the TV station half an hour late. Most of the vans were gone. Mike Bono was sitting in the rear opening of his van, his feet hanging out, tightening something on his camera, waiting for her.

"Sorry," Jodie said. "Be ready in a sec."

She rushed inside to check the assignment board and see if she had any messages. Since Marvin didn't have anything he wanted her to do, she drove downtown to the police station. Reporters from the two other TV stations and from Jacksonville's newspaper, the *Florida Times Union*, were already there when she walked into the records office on the second floor. They were going through the stack of white incident sheets and yellow arrest reports from the weekend, looking for something worth following up.

"Late again, Simms," the *Times Union* reporter said.

"I didn't know you were keeping track."

"I always keep an eye on what the competition is doing."

"Well, at least you consider me competition."

"I don't really," he said. "I was just saying that to be nice."

"Being nice doesn't agree with you."

"That's what I tell my wife."

The four of them passed the reports around the table, with cops walking in and out of the room, talking freely around them as though the reporters were fellow officers. As Jodie flipped through the pages, she listened to the chatter. The woman from Channel 17 was pregnant and she gave them the daily update. The man from Channel 4 was moving to Charlotte next month to buy an AM radio station. The police sergeant who ran this office was upset at someone named Brody for smashing his car.

Jodie didn't mention her trip to Mexico.

No newsworthy arrests had been made over the weekend. Jodie scribbled some notes from two incident reports, one about a decapitated dog found in the alley behind the Maxwell House Coffee plant, another about a couple of nine-year-old girls suspended from school for smoking crack. Hoping there'd be a decent story in one of them, she went back to the station and talked them over with Marvin. He didn't like either possibility. Instead he assigned her to do a story on a woman who turned one hundred years old today.

"I do investigative reporting," she said. "Can't you get one of the feature reporters to do this?"

"I'm short-handed today. Beth is sick and Lenny is stuck in Palatka, the van broke down. I need you to do this for me."

"I feel like Willard Scott," she said, grumbling as she walked out of his office.

She and Mike Bono drove across town to the Riverview Manor Nursing Home. The sight of elderly men and women wandering the halls as though lost, others strapped in wheelchairs calling out to no one, talking to themselves, saddened Jodie. She knew she had a job to do and told herself to concentrate on that, get it done, and go.

They found Pauline Tuttle in the sun room, staring out the window at the river. She looked surprisingly good for one hundred. And she was sharp and funny when Jodie talked to her. The interview went well. Afterward, they staged a few shots with Mrs. Tuttle potting a plant in the day room, sitting by the river outside, smoking a cigarette on the patio. She still smoked half a pack a week and swore that tobacco was responsible for her longevity.

While Mike shot some footage of the birthday party they threw for Pauline at lunch, Jodie spoke with a few of the workers to get background information for the voice-over track she would record later at the station. When she was finished, she headed back toward the dining room to see if Mike was done.

One of the nurse's aides, a young black man, came up alongside her in the corridor and whispered:

"They killed a man last week."

Stunned, Jodie stopped and looked at the man.

"Yeah, my wife's a big fan of yours," he said, suddenly smiling and speaking loudly so the nurses at the end of the hall could hear him. He was smiling at her but he looked nervous. "She watches you on the news all the time," he said.

Jodie realized what he was doing. "Thanks," she said, glancing up the hallway at the nurses.

"You know who else likes to watch you? Mrs. Cotton-wood. Her room's right over there," he said, pointing to an open door. "I'll bet she'd love it if you'd stop in and say hi."

Jodie glanced at the nurses again. They smiled at her, nodding that it was okay, then turned back to their work.

"Yeah, sure," Jodie said.

"Come on, I'll take you."

The man led Jodie into a room where a woman was sitting on a chair in front of a TV, sleeping. The room had the sterile feel of a hospital, with just a few extras—a digital clock beside the bed, a hand-knitted afghan over the chair, a photograph of the woman's family hanging on the clothes-cabinet door. The rest was depressing institutional issue.

The nurse's aide turned the TV a little louder and gestured for Jodie to follow him to the window, far from the open door.

"I don't want them to hear," the man whispered.

"Won't it wake her?" Jodie asked, concerned about the old woman.

"A hurricane couldn't wake Mrs. Cottonwood."

"What do you mean they killed a man?" Jodie asked.

"Mr. Litkey in one-eighteen. He had a heart attack."

"You said they killed him."

"They did."

"How?" She thought he was going to say they gave him something to cause him to have a heart attack. She wondered if he was crazy or just trying to get himself on TV.

"It happened last Friday night," the man said. "Mr. Litkey was in bed. He started having a heart attack. See, his ticker wasn't good for a long time but he was still a cool old guy. Anyway, he had these chest pains and he started calling for help. But the nurses wouldn't go check on him. He kept calling them, saying that he was dying, but they still ignored him. They just let him die. The poor old guy, he really must have suffered in there. They didn't check on him until the next morning. By then he was already dead. On the death certificate the doctor put that he died in his sleep. Can you believe that?"

"Were you here when it happened?"

"No. I don't work nights."

"Then how do you know it happened the way you say it did?"

"One, I know Mr. Litkey. He gets the slightest pain and he's calling at the top of his lungs. He used to call out like that about three, four times a day, just about every day. The nurses never go check on him."

"The boy who cried wolf," Jodie said.

"Exactly."

"If you weren't here the night he died, how do you know he called for help, how do you know he said he was dying? He could have died in his sleep like they said."

"I know he called for help because Mrs. Winston told me he did."

"Who's Mrs. Winston?"

"She's got the room directly across the hall from his. She heard the whole thing. She told me he was calling so loud that she couldn't sleep. She said she even called the nurses herself. They came to see what she wanted and when she told them to check on Mr. Litkey, all they did was close his door so he wouldn't wake everybody else up."

"Are you sure about this?"

"I'm sure."

Jodie thought about it a minute. She glanced over at Mrs. Cottonwood asleep on the chair. *The Price Is Right* was on TV. The din of the audience calling out prices irritated Jodie. She turned back to the aide.

"Where is Mrs. Winston?" Jodie asked. "I want to talk to her."

"That's the thing. They won't let no one talk to her."

"What do you mean? They can't stop people from talking to her."

"Wanna bet? They put a sign on the door saying she has TB and that no one is allowed in and she ain't allowed out. And since she don't have family close by, no one to visit her, no one questions it, no one complains. Mrs. Winston don't know what's going on herself. She don't even know that Mr. Litkey died."

"I'll need to talk to her to verify what you're saying."

"They won't let you in to see her."

Jodie thought for a moment, then asked, "Is her room on the ground floor?"

"Yeah."

"Maybe there's another way . . ."

Jodie had the aide show her and Mike where Mrs. Winston's room was. As they walked down the hall past the room, Mike held the camera at his hip so no one would know he was photographing the door and shot some tape of the sign forbidding anyone from going in. They didn't stop; they just kept walking down the hall, as though they were finished here. They said good-bye to the nurses and went outside. First they started walking toward the van. When they were certain no one was watching them, they circled around the parking lot and scurried down the side of the building.

Jodie counted the windows. They stopped at the fourth one from the end, Mrs. Winston's room. She peered in. Mrs. Winston was sitting in a chair with her back to the window. Jodie couldn't tell if she was asleep or awake—or, for that matter, dead. The TV was on, *The Price Is Right* again. They were doing the showcase, a Winnebago, a fishing boat, a Cadillac Catera.

Jodie told Mike to keep the camera out of sight, thinking it might frighten the woman, then she tapped on the glass to try to get Mrs. Winston's attention. Mrs. Winston didn't hear so Jodie tapped harder. Finally the elderly woman looked over. She wasn't dead after all.

When she first saw the two of them standing outside the window, she looked surprised, nervous, but then Jodie waved and smiled. Mrs. Winston's expression turned to one of recognition. She pointed to the TV then pointed to Jodie. Jodie nodded and smiled again. Mrs. Winston, grinning now, waddled over to the window.

It took her a few minutes to figure out how to unlock the window but finally she managed to open it.

"You're that nice young girl on the television, aren't you?" she said to Jodie.

"Yes, ma'am."

Mrs. Winston looked at Mike. "I don't know you."

"He works with me," Jodie said, which satisfied the kind old woman. "If you don't mind," Jodie said, "could we talk a bit about Mr. Litkey? . . ."

Jodie had to climb inside to get the interview. Mike was too heavy to fit through the window so he shot it from outside. The whole time Jodie was talking to Mrs. Winston, asking about Mr. Litkey, she kept thinking of Carl ending up in a place like this. It was difficult for her when the old woman related the events of Mr. Litkey's final night.

Maybe they couldn't have helped him, Jodie reasoned. Maybe the heart attack would have killed him even if they had rushed in when they first heard him. But even if nothing could have been done for him, it still pained her to think that this lonely old man had spent his last hours screaming for help, with no one coming into the room to be with him. He had died alone in this place. And no one cared. She did not want her father to end up that way.

☞ 15

Jodie, Mike Bono and Marvin Acker stood in front of a monitor in the news room, several other reporters and producers gathered around, squeezed in between a desk and the row of editing bays. They were watching the five o'clock broadcast. Jodie's story about Mr. Litkey's death was on.

On the screen, Jodie stuck the microphone into the face of Ralph Pervis, the chubby, effeminate director of the nursing home. As soon as she brought up Mr. Litkey, the man's face reddened and his eyes darted around nervously. Mike had zoomed in so tight that the lens picked up the beads of sweat dripping down the man's fleshy cheek.

"Nice, Mike," Marvin said.

On the television, the nursing home director said, "I'm not going to discuss individual patients. This interview is over." He turned and marched toward his office.

Marvin murmured, "Follow him, follow him . . ."

Jodie had done just that, following him toward the office. The camera was unsteady as Mike hurried behind.

"Mr. Pervis, one more question," Jodie said. "Has this happened before, with other residents?"

Pervis wheeled around. "Has *what* happened before?" He spoke like a linguist, picking out each word individually. "Nothing happened," he said. "And that is all I have to say."

He started to leave but then he turned one last time and said, "This was supposed to have been an interview about a wonderful resident of this facility who turned a hundred years old today. It was not supposed to be an ambush about . . ."

Frustrated and irate, he couldn't finish the thought. He stormed into his office and slammed the door.

The video cut to more of the interview with Mrs. Winston in her room and the footage of the sign on her door. When the story was over, the other reporters congratulated Jodie and Mike. A commercial for Hooters came on and the news staff drifted away to finish up their work and go home. Jodie was alone with Marvin Acker now.

"Simms," he said, "I sent you to do a fluff piece on a perky old broad and you come back with hard news. Maybe I should give you that kind of assignment every day."

"You do and I'll kill you."

Marvin laughed. "Today almost makes up for all those late days," he said.

He patted her on the back, a gesture that seemed to her like a coach patting one of his players, and he told her to keep up the good work. Two other women reporters came over while Jodie was getting ready to leave.

"Good story tonight, Jodie."

"Thanks."

"We're going to Casper's for some drinks and maybe something to eat. We haven't seen you there in a while. Why don't you come by tonight, celebrate?"

Reporters from all three stations and from the newspaper congregated at Casper's after work. Jodie used to go there once or twice a week for a quick drink and to catch up on industry gossip. But that was before her father came to live with her. She couldn't afford to pay Mrs. Kelly to stay many evenings. Just paying her to be there weekdays along with the few evenings Jodie had to work was already more than she could afford.

"Thanks," Jodie said, "but I can't. I have to get home."

"Another time then?"

"Yeah, sure."

When she got home, Carl didn't recognize her for the first ten minutes. He insisted he was married to Mrs. Kelly and that he was supposed to leave with her. Finally he started calling Jodie by her mother's name again and settled in for the evening.

With an hour till dark, Jodie took him for a short walk to the beach, Publix bag in hand, WD-40 ready in case he found any "good" shells. Later they watched TV together. She left him for a minute while she went to the bathroom and when she returned he was spraying WD-40 all over the ferns in the living room, thinking he was watering them.

The next morning she overslept and found Carl in the kitchen, pouring water into the sugar bowl. She tried to stay calm.

"Dad, what are you doing?"

"I'm making coffee."

"Let me do that from now on, okay?"

"For God's sake, Helen, I can make coffee."

"I know you can, but you shouldn't have to. That's my job."

"Suit yourself," he said and went into his room to get dressed.

She was twenty minutes late for work again this morning. When she arrived at the police station to go through last night's reports, the other reporters congratulated her on yesterday's nursing home story, then they all hurried out to begin playing catch-up.

Jodie did a follow-up piece on Riverview Manor. The State's Attorney announced that he was ordering an investigation into the incident. Marvin Acker asked Jodie to do a series about nursing homes in general, a story that made her very uncomfortable.

Thursday morning she awoke early so she would have time to give Carl his second injection of The Cure. Without Darlene Cummings there to guide her, this shot was more nerve-wracking than the first one had been, less than a week ago in Mexico. She worried that she would do something wrong, that somehow she would hurt him, puncture something vital, break the tip of the needle off in his skin.

Her hand trembled as she brought the needle close to Carl's arm. She winced when she jabbed it in, as though she were the one feeling the prick.

"Ouch!" Carl said, glaring angrily at her. "That hurt, Helen!"

"Sorry, Dad."

"What are you doing?"

"The hard part's over," she told him.

She depressed the plunger and emptied the solution into his arm, then put a Band-Aid over the needle mark.

"All done," she said.

"I don't like that."

"I know. But it's going to make you better."

He shook his head. "I don't like it, Helen. I don't want to do that anymore. It hurts."

"I know, Dad. I'm sorry."

"No more," he said.

She didn't argue. She knew that he would forget all about it by the time he was due for his next injection.

When Friday evening came, she was relieved that the week was over. It had been five hectic days. Between work and her father, she barely had enough energy to do everything she needed to do. She was looking forward to the weekend and her two days off. But while she did not have to go to work, she still had to take care of Carl, eliminating any chance of getting rest.

The only change she noticed in her father after two injections was that he wasn't as tired as he used to be, which meant he slept less, which meant *she* slept less too. She could not leave him alone in the mornings, fearing what he might do in the kitchen or in the bathroom.

Carl kept her on her toes all weekend. By the time Monday morning rolled around, she was as tired as she'd been Friday night. Right before work, she gave him his third injection of The Cure. She was losing confidence in the medicine, having seen no change in him yet. She was beginning to fear it would not work. Maybe it was a scam, she thought. Maybe she had put her faith in a bogus elixir. The whole thing simply might be a way to bilk money out of desperate people. And she had fallen for it.

But she needed so much for it to work. She needed it even more than Carl did. She wanted her life back—a normal life. She wanted to be able to do things like other people, to go to bed without having to worry about her father breaking something or hurting himself while she slept, to go to work and be free to concentrate on her job. She wanted to be able to go to Casper's after work with the other reporters. She wanted to be able to date again.

She wasn't getting any younger. With her fortieth birthday frighteningly close, she was keenly aware of her biological clock ticking down. If she intended to start a family of her own, she needed to do it soon. But that was wishful thinking.

As long as she had to care for Carl, marriage and motherhood had to wait.

Almost as much as Carl did, she needed The Cure to be real.

⇌ 16

The next week was the usual chaos. Jodie and Mike covered stories all over the area, driving up to Fernandina Beach on Monday, down to St. Augustine on Tuesday, to Gainesville Wednesday to cover a sexual harassment charge brought against a University of Florida professor. She spent Thursday in downtown Jacksonville reporting on the arraignment of two high school football players who allegedly raped a female Naval officer on shore leave from Kings Bay, Georgia.

On Friday morning, after Jodie gave Carl his fourth shot, she and Mike drove all the way out to Lake City to do a story on a woman who had been beaten nearly to death by her ex-husband four months earlier and was now in court with their son, trying to convince the judge to terminate her ex-husband's visitation rights.

The judge ruled that the man could not go near the woman, but that the woman couldn't keep the man from seeing his son. Interviewing the woman afterward helped Jodie forget her own troubles for a while. The woman broke down and wept several times. Jodie signaled Mike to stop taping, then she held the woman in her arms and did her best to comfort her.

By the time they drove back to Jacksonville and finished editing and doing the voice-over track for the package, Jodie was exhausted and eager for the day to be over. She told herself that next week would bring better things. But as she drove east toward the beach, she thought about the problems she would face when she got home. No longer did she look forward to weekends.

Carl was waiting for her in the kitchen when she trudged in. It was past seven. As usual she was running late. Mrs. Kelly should have left half an hour ago.

"I'm sorry I'm late," Jodie said.

Mrs. Kelly waved off the apology and said, "Your father wants to show you something."

"What is it?"

"Let him show you."

Jodie walked into the kitchen. "Hi, Dad."

"Well, finally she comes home," he said.

"Sorry. Busy day. Mrs. Kelly said you wanted to show me something."

"Yup." On the table was an ossified starfish. He placed it carefully in his palm and held it out for her to see.

"Isn't that beautiful!" she said.

He usually only picked up broken fragments of shells. She was surprised that he would come back with something like that.

"Where did you get it?" she asked.

"I found it. Mrs. Kelly and I went for a walk on the beach this afternoon."

"That's beautiful, Dad." Jodie turned to Mrs. Kelly. "Thank you for taking him." That would save Jodie having to do it this evening. She was much too tired.

Carl tapped Jodie on the shoulder and said, "Know what I'm going to do with it?"

"No. What are you going to do with it?"

"I'm going to give it to you, Jodie."

"Oh, that's so nice, Dad. I really appreciate—"

She stopped mid-sentence as his words finally registered in her head.

"What did you say?" she asked.

"I said I'm giving it to you."

"You . . . you called me Jodie."

Carl tilted his head as he looked at her, confused by her words. He glanced over at Mrs. Kelly who was smiling widely. She looked like she would cry at any minute. He turned back to Jodie and said, "Of course I called you Jodie. That's your name, isn't it?"

Jodie couldn't control herself. Her lips stretched into a smile, then her smile grew into joyous laughter. "Yes," she said, unable to stop laughing. "That's my name. Jodie."

⇒ 17

Jodie saw the change clearly in Carl's eyes.

The vacant eyes that had stared at her every day for the past six months, those eyes that gave the impression no one was behind them, those frightened, confused, sad eyes were no longer there.

Now it was her father she saw in those eyes.

She stared across the kitchen table at him. Was "The Cure" really working?

"How do you feel, Dad?"

He shrugged. "I'm hungry."

Mrs. Kelly, who left a few minutes ago, had baked some chicken. Jodie took it out of the oven and removed the foil.

"Smells good," she said.

Carl moaned. "I don't like chicken."

"I thought you liked it."

"I hate it."

"Oh, well, we can have something else. What would you like for dinner tonight?"

"What do you mean?"

She came back over to the table. "What would you like to eat?"

"What do you mean, Jodie?" He was becoming irritated by the question.

Jodie reached across the table and touched his hand to calm him. "Never mind, Dad. I'll choose."

He nodded, looking at her as though he only partly understood.

"How about I order us a pizza?" she said. "We'll celebrate. You like pizza, don't you?"

"Of course I like pizza."

"Good. Me, too."

"We'll celebrate," he said.

"Yeah, we'll celebrate. We'll celebrate you getting better, Dad. How does that sound?"

He nodded and said, "I like pizza."

The next morning was Saturday. Jodie didn't have to go to work, but she was out of bed even before the sun came up. She hadn't slept much at all. Most of the night she had lain awake thinking about Carl: she was eager to see what his condition would be. She made coffee, waited impatiently until it grew light outside, then hurried into his room.

Asleep, he looked no different than he had looked yesterday or last week or last month. But that didn't mean anything, she reminded herself. Sleeping, he had always looked normal, healthy, looked like the father she remembered from her adolescence.

She stood by the bed and stared at him for fifteen minutes. Finally she could wait no longer. She leaned over and gently touched his shoulder.

"Dad," she said softly. "Dad, time to wake up."

He opened his eyes slowly, blinking for a moment in the morning light.

"Good morning, Dad," she said. She needed to hear him speak, needed to know if he could communicate like an adult. "How are you feeling?" she asked.

He yawned and looked around the room. Finally his gaze returned to her.

"Dad," she said again. "How are you feeling?"

He nodded. For a moment he didn't speak. But then finally he opened his mouth. "Good," he said. "I'm good. How about you, Jodie?"

She laughed from the joy. "Me, I never felt better," she said. "I feel so—"

It came so suddenly she wasn't prepared. A swell of emotion choked the words in her throat. She tried to hold in her feelings, but she couldn't contain them. They were too strong. Still smiling, she started to weep.

"Jodie?" Carl said, concerned.

She turned away, not wanting him to see her cry. She didn't want him to think she was sad. She wasn't. Just the opposite. She felt happier than she had felt in a very long time.

"Sweetheart, are you all right?" he asked.

"I'm okay, Dad. I'm good."

She wanted to say more but every time she opened her mouth the weeps of happiness came stronger. When Carl sat up and put his arm around her, the way he used to do thirty years ago, she broke down and sobbed openly, no longer even trying to hold back.

Her father had returned. The exuberance she felt because of this was too much for her to keep inside.

That afternoon the two of them took a long walk on the beach and had an actual conversation. They talked about Jodie's job. Carl asked her if she had a boyfriend. They discussed living in Florida; Carl liked the warm weather and the ocean here, but he said he missed the fall colors.

"Seasons," he said. "I like seasons."

"We have seasons here, Dad. We have the mosquito season, the hurricane season, the love-bug season."

He just stared at her, not understanding the joke. He wasn't completely better, she realized. But he definitely had improved.

Carl asked about Helen for the first time since her death. When Jodie told him about her mother's brain tumor and how she had died last August, he fell into her arms and wept.

First thing Monday morning, even before she left for work, Jodie called the Mayo Clinic and made an appointment with Dr. Harrington. She wanted her father evaluated before they returned to Mexico. She wanted to make sure this was real, that she wasn't imagining it. It was hard for her to believe it could be true, but Carl definitely seemed to be getting better—much better.

His appointment was for the following Monday, and in the week leading up to it, his improvement continued steadily. She gave him another shot of The Cure on Tuesday and saw even more change a few hours afterward. He grilled her about the last time her house had a termite inspection.

"Florida isn't like up north," he said. "You give termites a foothold and you might as well just sign over the deed."

"I'll call someone this week," Jodie said.

"I'll do it. Leave it to you and it'll never get done."

Each day after work Jodie rushed home, eager to see how he was, what new ability he had regained. She took him out for dinner Friday night, then he asked her if they could go to a movie, something he hadn't done in years.

Saturday morning she awoke to find him sitting in the living room, going through the newspaper. She stood in the doorway behind him, not letting him know she was watching. As he flipped through the pages, she could tell he was struggling to read the words. But he seemed to be able to make sense of some of them. He chuckled once.

Another time, while he was looking through the sports section, he blew out a breath of exasperation, shook his head and tossed the paper down.

He noticed her now. "I didn't know you were up," he said.

"Reading the paper?" she asked.

He shrugged. She gave him his shot of The Cure, then he said, "How about some coffee?"

"Sure, I'll make it right now."

He grinned. "Already made."

"You made it?"

She went into the kitchen expecting to see coffee on the floor or the can of WD-40 beside the coffee maker and an oily film on the coffee, but instead she saw a full pot of actual coffee. She sniffed it; it smelled good, the way coffee was supposed to smell. She poured two cups and took a sip of hers. It was stronger than she normally made it but it was still pretty good.

Carl came in and sat with her at the table. "Well?" he said after she drank some.

"It's good, Dad." She took another sip. "A little strong."

"That's how you should make it. Yours tastes like dishwater."

She just laughed.

Jodie arranged to have Monday morning off. She drove Carl down to the Mayo Clinic where nurses ushered him from floor to floor for two hours of physical and psychological tests similar to those he had undergone in Mexico. Jodie watched the mental agility tests closely. Excitement built inside her with each correct answer Carl gave the psychologist. He did much better than he had done in Cancun. His short term memory was still weak at times but all in all he did well.

After the tests were completed, they went in to see Dr. Harrington.

"I have to admit," Harrington said, speaking directly to Carl, rather than to Jodie, "you are doing remarkably well."

"Thank you," Carl said, grinning.

"He is, isn't he?" Jodie said.

"I don't understand it, but yes he is."

Harrington was in his late fifties, tall and slightly overweight. Jodie liked his easy-going, avuncular manner. He did not hide his thoughts or emotions at all. And after seeing him with Carl several times in the past, she had come to trust his medical judgment implicitly. The diplomas on his wall bore the names of such institutions as Notre Dame and Yale Medical School. There were plaques from the Cleveland Clinic and the Mayo Clinic in Rochester, Minnesota. He was probably the finest doctor Jodie had met, so she was very eager to hear his opinion of the change in Carl.

"We retested your mental agility," Harrington told Carl. "Gave you the same tests we did last year when your wife brought you in. I have the scores right here," he said, picking up a sheet of paper from Carl's chart. "The numbers are up in every area—mathematical aptitude, abstract reasoning, memory recall." He shook his head, showing genuine surprise, and said, "I've never seen anything like this." He gazed up at them, his cheeks red with excitement, threw up his hands and said, "I don't know how to explain it."

"I think I should tell you," Jodie said. "Dad's been taking something."

Harrington looked puzzled. "What do you mean? Taking what?"

"It's called NPEF-alpha. They also call it The Cure. Have you heard of it?"

"No I haven't. What is it? Where did you get it?"

"Mexico," Carl said, blurting it out.

Jodie turned, surprised that Carl even remembered they had been there.

"Mexico?" Dr. Harrington said.

"Yes," Jodie said. "There's a special clinic in Cancun that helps people with Alzheimer's disease." She told him briefly about Dr. Stirling and the injections she had been giving her father.

"At first there was no change," she said. "But then about a week ago . . ." She gestured toward Carl. "Well, you can see for yourself that he's better."

Harrington fixed his stare on Carl again, scratching his chin in bewilderment. "It would certainly appear that you are better," he said. He turned back to Jodie. "But these injections you mentioned, I've never heard of anything called NPEF-alpha. What else can you tell me about it?"

"The doctor called it a nerve growth factor," Jodie said. "He said it comes from genetically engineered pigs. It's supposed to do something to make the neurons in the brain work better—make them more *plastic*," she said, remembering the word Stirling used. "It's not available in this country yet, but Dr. Stirling said they're in the process of getting FDA approval."

"I have heard of nerve growth factors," Harrington said. "But not the one you mentioned. There is a lot of research being done in that area, new growth factors being identified all the time. On the whole, though, clinically speaking, it's still a very experimental area. I would be careful about taking something like that, especially if it's not FDA approved."

"But it seems to be working. Dad seems to be better. You said so yourself."

Harrington flipped through Carl's chart again. He appeared confounded by what he read, but he also looked impressed.

"There's no question that your scores have improved in every area," he said to Carl. He looked at Jodie. "I'd really like to see exactly what it is he's taking. Could you bring some in? I think it might be a good idea to have it analyzed, to find out exactly what it is. I don't think it's such a good idea to be taking something when you don't know what it is." He turned to Carl. "Okay, Mr. Simms?"

Carl shrugged and looked to Jodie for the answer.

Jodie remembered the Covenant of Nondisclosure she had signed when Stirling gave her the medicine, prohibiting her from turning over The Cure to any pharmaceutical or medical entity that might steal the drug and patent it first. She was sure the Mayo Clinic would not do that, but still she felt uneasy breaking the agreement she had signed.

"I only have enough to last this week," she told

Harrington. "I don't want Dad to miss a shot, he's been doing so well."

Harrington leaned forward, looking very serious now. "You need to be aware that many countries don't have the same strict standards of drug safety that we have," he said. "True, the injections your father is taking appear to be helping now, in the short term. But we want to make sure that in the long run they don't end up causing harm. Do you understand my concern?"

Jodie nodded. His tone made it quite clear how important he thought this was. And she realized he was right, it was important. She should make certain that it was safe for her father to continue taking The Cure. She did not want to see him hurt in any way.

She did not think Dr. Harrington would try to steal Stirling's medicine. But even if someone else here was not as honest as Harrington, someone in the lab or someone Dr. Harrington brought in to consult on this, Jodie would testify for Stirling, make sure everyone knew that she provided the sample of The Cure, that Stirling had it first. Besides, the doctor who tried to steal it would not have the genetically altered pigs that Stirling had, would not have the years of research data and clinical tests that Stirling had. Stirling had told Jodie he was close to synthesizing and patenting The Cure. Jodie justified to herself that since Stirling was that close and had such a large head start on everyone else, he would still get there first, even if someone tried to steal The Cure.

Rationalizing further, Jodie told herself that having the Mayo Clinic test The Cure might actually help speed the approval process. If it impressed the doctors here, that would surely impress the people at the FDA more than Stirling alone could. And furthermore, if someone thought it good enough to steal, that would be further evidence supporting its effectiveness and safety.

"I'll tell you what I can do," Jodie said. "We're supposed to go to Mexico next weekend to get more of The Cure. I can bring some in when we get back."

"I think that would be a good idea. With something like this, it's always better to be safe than sorry."

≈ 18

When they landed in Cancun, the sun was shining, smiling faces greeted them in the terminal, and Jodie felt good about being here. Not simply because they were returning to the doctor who had helped Carl, though that was part of the anticipation she felt—a large part. But in addition, this was to be something of a vacation, a chance for her and Carl to relax and spend some time together. For so long she had been his caregiver instead of his daughter. She was looking forward to being his little girl again.

They took a taxi to the Hotel Salida Del Sol. Last week, when she called to make the reservations, she had requested twin beds. She didn't want to go through the same problem as the first trip. Today, the front desk clerk, Tomas, recognized her and Carl. He smiled and said, "Two beds, señorita. We make it very nice for you."

"Thank you, Tomas."

As Jodie and Carl followed the porter down the path toward their cabaña, Carl said, "This time let's have a little fun, okay?"

"What do you mean, Dad?"

"I don't want to stay in the room all day. Let's do something."

Jodie laughed. It heartened her to see him so full of life. "We'll do whatever you want," she said.

Carl pointed to the colorful para-sails dotting the blue sky over the Caribbean. "Let's do that," he said.

Jodie laughed again and said, "We'll see."

When they walked into the cabaña, Jodie found a bouquet of flowers and a huge basket of tropical fruit on the table by the window.

"What's that doing here?" Carl said.

Jodie picked up the note attached to the bouquet.

Dear Miss Simms,
*   I hope this will brighten your room and make your stay in Cancun more enjoyable. If there is anything you need, please don't hesitate to call on me personally.*
                                        Best,
                                        Neil Lancaster

"Well? . . ." Carl said.

"It's from the owner of the hotel."

"Oh." Carl shrugged, not impressed, and began unpacking.

Jodie read the note a second time, her interest stirred. She remembered Neil Lancaster from the first trip here, remembered him arranging for the beds in the cabaña to be switched. And she recalled he had asked her to dinner, an invitation she had been unable to accept. She had assumed he had long since forgotten her, just another woman passing through his hotel, an assumption that obviously was wrong. She was surprised he even knew they were here this weekend. She certainly hadn't expected this.

While Carl continued unpacking, Jodie sat on the bed, her back to him, and picked up the phone. She was a little nervous making this call in front of her father but she went ahead and dialed anyway. Tomas at the front desk picked up and told her Señor Lancaster was not in this morning, would she like to leave a message?

"Just tell him thank you for the flowers and fruit and I hope I have a chance to see him before we leave tomorrow."

She hung up, worried that the message sounded adolescent and a little too obvious.

Once she and Carl were settled in, they took another taxi to Cancun Centro. Darlene Cummings smiled when she saw them. She went right up to Carl and said, "How are you feeling, Mr. Simms?"

"Couldn't be better."

She turned to Jodie, reached out and squeezed her hand. They exchanged a look. No words were necessary. Darlene seemed as happy about Carl's improvement as Jodie was.

"Are you ready to come back with me," Darlene asked Carl, "so I can take your blood pressure, weigh you, poke you with some needles, all that good stuff?"

Carl glanced at Jodie for the answer. She nodded and said, "I'll be right here waiting for you."

They came back ten minutes later, Darlene holding Carl's arm as through they were on a date, both of them laughing.

"What's so funny?" Jodie asked.

"Your father is a real character," Darlene said.

"Why? What did he do?"

"Well, I asked him if he was . . . you know, regular. He said—" She broke up, all giggles. "You tell her," she told Carl.

"Tell me, Dad. What did you say?"

He shrugged as though it were nothing and said, "I told her I move my bowels every morning at seven-thirty sharp, like clockwork."

Darlene giggled again.

Jodie didn't get it.

"Problem is," Carl said, "I don't get out of bed until eight."

They all laughed. Carl smiled, proud of himself. Jodie couldn't remember the last time he had told a joke. She still couldn't get over how much better he was, how much he had returned to the father she used to have.

They waited fifteen minutes, then Darlene took Carl back again for the rest of his tests. Jodie went along this time. Darlene brought them to the small room with the table in the middle and a chair on either side. A moment later, Dr. Stirling came in.

He didn't say much. He managed something resembling a smile and extended a weak hand first to Jodie, then to Carl. The way he avoided looking directly at either of them was a little disconcerting at first, but Jodie remembered it was Stirling's way. She realized she should not expect him to have a salesman's personality. That wasn't what he was. And he wasn't like Dr. Harrington, at ease with patients. Everything about him reinforced her original image of him as a scientist, a lone researcher constantly absorbed in internal reflection on his work.

Stirling sat across the table from Carl and put him through the same series of psychological tests he had undergone a month ago, the same type of tests he had taken at Mayo Clinic on Monday. Jodie watched from behind Carl, impressed by how much better he did today than just a week earlier in Jacksonville. After fifteen minutes, he became bored with the tests, and Jodie reasoned that his results probably suffered a bit from that, but even so, he impressed her by how sharp he was.

Next, they walked down the hall to an examination room so Stirling could give Carl a thorough physical. All this to determine how well the therapy was working. Jodie laughed to herself. None of these tests were necessary to prove that Carl was better. It was quite obvious. *Just talk to him, just look into his eyes, and you can tell that he's cured.*

After the physical, Stirling led them back into his office.

"I'm quite impressed by how well you have done over the last month," he told Carl.

Carl didn't know how to respond. He shrugged and said, "Thanks."

Stirling turned to his computer. He almost seemed to be speaking to it when he said, "The NPEF-alpha injections have certainly brought about a marked improvement since your last visit."

"I feel great!" Carl said.

"Do you remember how you felt a month ago?" Stirling asked, looking at him only briefly.

Carl shrugged. "Good, I guess." He glanced at Jodie, his face showing that he really didn't know what to say.

"How about a year ago?" Stirling asked.

"A year ago?" Carl thought about it a moment then chuckled and said, "Tell you the truth, Doc, I really don't remember back a year ago, but I guess I was feeling pretty good." He turned to Jodie. "Wasn't I?"

"Not exactly, Dad."

"I wasn't?"

"It's not unusual," Stirling said to Jodie, "for AD patients not to remember the state of their health prior to beginning NPEF-alpha therapy. It's similar to amnesia in many ways. For the last few years, your father," he said to Jodie, then turned to Carl and said, "you, Mr. Simms, lacked the neural capacity to form any kind of memory imprint, both short-term and long-term."

Carl stared at him, trying to understand, but Jodie saw from the look on his face that he really didn't comprehend all of what Stirling was saying.

"Your brain couldn't store what was occurring over that period the way it does for me or for your daughter," Stirling told Carl. "Or the way it does for you now. That's why you have no distinct memory of the last couple of years. And I'm afraid you won't be able to get it back with time, either. That period was never committed to memory."

Carl just gave a vague nod.

"It's sort of like taking pictures without film in the camera," Stirling said.

Carl chuckled, understanding that.

"Is that going to be a problem?" Jodie asked.

"No." He looked away now, directing his focus to the computer as he said, "I just wanted you to be aware of some of the limitations of your father's capacity to recall events from the past. He should be able to remember events prior to the onset of AD. Perhaps not everything right away, but gradually many of the memories from several years ago and earlier will begin to return."

Stirling looked over at Carl who was listening intently, nodding.

"You are doing exceptionally well," Stirling said. Then he turned back to the computer. "The scores on all the mental agility tests are up. There's a significant increase in physical strength. We'll know how the blood work looks tomorrow but I don't foresee there being any problem."

Carl winked at Jodie. He was beaming with pride.

"I'd like to continue with the same dosage of NPEF-alpha," Stirling said. "That seems to be working well. Have either of you noticed any adverse reactions?"

"No, none."

"Good. I'll have Miss Cummings prepare an eight-week supply of injections for you. It'll be ready tomorrow. After I look at the blood results, if there's anything to be concerned about, I'll give you a call, but as I said, I really don't anticipate anything."

He finished with the computer and turned to Carl. "Can you come back in two months?"

Carl shrugged, then looked to Jodie for an answer.

"Sure," she said.

Carl said, "Mexico's nice."

Stirling nodded and stood up, first shaking Carl's hand, then Jodie's.

"Thank you, Doctor," Jodie said. "I really appreciate all you've done."

Stirling's response was something between a nod and a smile, the uncomfortable look of someone who didn't quite know how to answer but didn't want anyone to realize it.

⇒ 19

When they returned to the hotel, Jodie thought Carl might be tired from the trip and would want to lie down for a nap, but he insisted on going to the beach instead. They stopped briefly in the lobby gift shop so she could buy half a dozen post cards. She needed something to do while Carl went treasure hunting for shells. He kept nagging her to hurry and pick out her cards, finally saying that he was going to leave without her. She paid in a rush and hurried out after him.

He looked almost comical strutting across the pool area, with his gaunt body, ribs showing, skin as pale as flour. He wore his dress shoes and black socks, along with baggy red lifeguard trunks a size too large for him. Jodie noticed him checking out women in bikinis as he walked by. Giggling, she ran over, took him by the arm and walked with him to the beach.

She, too, was pale, but not as pale as Carl. She had left her shoes in the cabaña and now enjoyed the warm sand under her bare feet. She picked out a chaise lounge shaded by a palm tree. Carl tugged off his shoes and socks and headed toward the water.

"You going shelling?" Jodie asked.

"Nope. Swimming."

"In the water?"

"It works better in the water. You coming?"

"No thanks. I'm just going to lie here, write my post cards and soak up some of this nice tropical shade."

He scoffed at her and walked away.

"Be careful, Dad," she called out.

He didn't even look back as he said, "Yes, dear."

She realized how patronizing she sounded, but she still worried about him. As he waded out into the water, she watched him attentively, still feeling motherly toward him, wanting to make sure nothing happened while he was swimming.

A waiter came over and convinced Jodie that she needed a margarita. She sipped the cool, salty drink as she wrote the post cards and kept an eye on her father in the water, feeling better than she had felt in a very long time.

"Jacksonville, eh?"

Jodie looked up, startled by the voice.

Standing alongside her chaise lounge was a man

wearing light blue Bermuda shorts, a white dress shirt with the collar open and the sleeves folded up a couple turns, leather sandals. He looked to be in his late forties, with a gut that strained at the buttons of his shirt. His skin was paler than hers, paler than Carl's, making the ink black hair covering his arms and legs look like a fur coat. It was unfortunate that he couldn't transplant that to his head because his hair was thinning so badly that his scalp was sunburned. He was carrying a bottle of *Dos Equis* beer and peering over Jodie's shoulder at the post card she was addressing.

"Home of the Jaguars," he said. "Not a bad outfit for an expansion team."

"Do you mind?" she said, moving the post card so he couldn't see. She made sure her expression let him know she did not welcome his company.

"You ever take in the games?" he asked. "Or is football not your thing?"

Jodie didn't answer.

"Me, I could watch any sport there is. Football, basketball, hockey, you name it."

He stepped over to the chaise lounge beside Jodie's and sat with an old man's moan. As he started picking the sand from under his toenails, he said, "I have a sister who lives in Gainesville. That's not far from Jacksonville."

Jodie tried to ignore him but he kept talking.

"She teaches at the University of Florida," he said. "Women's studies," he said with a snort of contempt. "Imagine graduating with a B.A. in that? Or maybe it's a B.S." He snickered at his own joke. "What kind of job

does Women's Studies prepare you for? Can you tell me
that?"

Jodie considered moving to another chaise lounge but
she worried that her father would look this way, not see
her, think she left, and panic.

"So, what do you do in Jacksonville?" the man asked.

"Look," Jodie said. "I'm sure you're a nice person, but
I'm here with my father, we just want to relax and spend
some time together. I'm really not interested."

"What aren't you interested in?"

"Anything." She tried to be tactful but clear. "I'm not
looking to make any new friends. Okay?"

"Oh, I see, you've got too many friends. Yeah, I could
see where that could be a real dilemma. I understand
they're holding a conference on just that very issue later
this year in Brussels. Big problem, too many friends.
Especially in Third World nations."

He waited for her to laugh, but she looked away, not
wanting to encourage him.

"I'm just asking what you do," he said. "What line of
work you're in. We call that small talk where I'm from."

"Really? I thought small talk was what your dates do
when they describe certain parts of your anatomy," she
said, hoping it would send him on his way once and for
all.

But instead he chuckled and said, "Touché. Good
comeback. But I admit, you're right, I do have small
feet." He wiggled his toes, snickered, proud of himself,
and said, "By the way, the name's Dr. Rogoff. You can
call me Sam."

Jodie just nodded.

"Now you're supposed to tell me your name," he said. Then he slapped his forehead and said, "Oh yeah, I forgot, you've got that too-many-friends problem."

She let out a loud breath, to show him that he was only annoying her, but he didn't seem to get the message.

"That's your father over there, huh?" Rogoff said, pointing to Carl, who was talking to two women in the surf. "I saw the two of you together a few minutes ago."

"Yes," Jodie answered, avoiding eye contact by looking down at her post cards.

"Looks like he's having a good time. I guess he doesn't have the too-many-friends problem like you, huh?"

Jodie sighed and gave in. "Jodie Simms, all right?" she said.

"Nice to meet you, Jodie Simms. You know, for someone from Florida, you don't have much of a tan. You're going to give the Sunshine State a bad name."

She decided his comment didn't deserve a response.

"So," he said. "First time in Cancun?"

"No."

"You've been here before?"

She peered at him with an annoyed look. "If it's not my first time," she said, "then obviously I must have been here before."

Her sarcasm didn't deter him. In fact, he seemed to take it as encouragement.

"Second time for me," he said. "I was here about a month ago. My luggage didn't make it but I was here." He chuckled at himself. "This time I've got clothes," he said, gesturing toward his goofy attire.

Jodie wanted to say, *You'd be better off if the airline had lost your bags this time too*, but she decided it would be best to say nothing.

"Not a bad place, if you ask me. Hot enough for you?" he asked. "When I left New York—that's where I'm from—when I left the city, it was snowing. Here it's eighty degrees."

"How about that."

"Yeah," he said, scanning the beach. "Not the best place in the world I've ever been, not even close, but it's not bad. They've got that whole thing about not drinking the water. Take it from me, don't drink anything that doesn't come out of a sealed bottle or you'll spend your time down here staring at the wall of the john. And the food's nothing to brag about either. Top it off, the only sports they have on TV is soccer, and who the hell can watch that? But it's still all right, I guess. Cheap enough. You like it?"

Jodie answered with a vague gesture that meant nothing. She tried again to concentrate on writing the post cards.

"So, what brings you down here?" he asked. When Jodie didn't answer, he said, "I'm here on business. You here on business?"

"No."

"You still haven't told me what you do in Jacksonville. What racket are you in?"

She put down the post cards and looked at him. "You're not going to leave me alone, are you?" she asked.

"Unlike you, I don't have a too-many-friends problem."

"I'm not surprised."

"*Touché* again."

"I'm a reporter for a television station," she said. "Okay? Satisfied?"

"No kidding? Sounds interesting."

She just nodded and turned her attention back to the post cards.

Rogoff asked himself, "So, what do you do, Sam? Since you ask, I'll tell you. I'm an epidemiologist for the World Health Organization. Really? Sounds interesting. Well, yes, it can be. I travel a great deal, meet all sorts of interesting people, not all of them as talkative as you, however."

Jodie glared at him. "Do you have conversations with yourself often?"

Rogoff just grinned and continued talking to himself. "What does an epidemiologist for the World Health Organization do, you ask?" he said.

Finally she gave in. "All right. What does an epidemiologist do?"

"Actually it all depends on the circumstances."

"Don't make me sorry I asked. Just give me the *Reader's Digest* condensed answer."

"We study outbreaks of disease—their cause, their distribution, how they spread and how to control and prevent them. What makes it interesting is that every investigation is different. For instance on this trip," Rogoff said, "I'm looking into a health problem down here that's recently come to the attention of the WHO. An unusual number of Mexicans—Mayan Indians, to be more specific—have been suffering epileptic-like symptoms, seizures and the whole nine yards, and in a few cases there have even been some deaths."

He paused for a moment for dramatic effect, just staring at her and nodding. Then he lowered his voice and said, "It's very mysterious, wouldn't you say?"

"I wouldn't know. Is it?"

"Oh, yes. Very. We wouldn't expect to see this many cases in a single area like this. And this is among a population, I discovered, that ordinarily have a very low incidence of degenerative brain disorders, like Parkinson's, Alzheimer's, that type of thing."

"Alzheimer's?" Jodie said, thinking about her father.

"Yup. Practically nonexistent. The whole spectrum of degenerative disorders doesn't affect these people. On top of that, they appear to have a remarkable ability to recover from trauma to the brain, like stroke. Conditions that you would expect would debilitate them, they quickly recover from. And that's why the sudden outbreak of epilepsy is so odd. There's no history of epilepsy. It's something that just appeared out of nowhere. Oh, yes, it's very mysterious."

"And you don't know what's causing it?"

"Well, it appears there's a problem, an abnormality, with the cortex of their brains, but how and why such an abnormality would suddenly show up in such numbers, we just don't know yet. Needless to say, we're concerned."

"Maybe it's environmental?" Jodie said.

"That's usually the first thing we look at."

"And is it?"

"To tell you the truth, I'm beginning to think that it might not be."

"Then what do you think is the cause?"

He glanced around, as though he was concerned someone might be listening, then he leaned a little closer to Jodie and in a whisper said, "It might just be . . . medical care."

"You mean the lack of doctors?"

"Let's just say that people don't realize that the problem in places like this isn't always so much the *lack* of medical care. Sometimes it's simply that the medical care they do have isn't always—how should I put it?— beneficial. Some of the doctors down here can do more harm than good, if you know what I mean."

"There are bad doctors everywhere."

Rogoff took a long gulp from his beer, picked some more at his toenails, then said, "There's one doctor in particular down here. He practices at a clinic that a lot of poor Mexicans go to, the only place they can afford. A lot of his patients aren't doing too well—to put it mildly." He leaned closer again and whispered, "Back home they'd yank this quack's license. Down here . . . well, you know how it is."

Rogoff was silent for a moment, just staring at Jodie in a way that made her uncomfortable. He looked at her as though the two of them shared some unspoken connection, as though they hadn't just met, as though they knew each other much better than they actually did. *Or as though* he *knew* her *better*.

"The doctor's name," he said, staring at her again, "is Cassandros."

The name—*Cassandros*—struck a familiar chord. It took her a moment to remember where she knew it from. She had heard it the last time she was here in Mexico. A Mayan woman had come into Dr. Stirling's office screaming that name. Dr. Stirling had explained that some of the doctors in Mexico were not very competent and often he had to try to repair the damage they had done. Jodie hadn't realized that this particular doctor— Dr. Cassandros—was so bad that word of what he was doing had reached the World Health Organization. He must be *really* incompetent, she thought.

Before Jodie could say anything, Rogoff snapped his fingers and pointed at her, acting like he had just remembered something. *Acting*, she realized. The whole thing seemed oddly unnatural to her.

"Hey, you know what?" he said. "I may be mistaken, but didn't I see you downtown today? Yes, that was you, wasn't it? You and your father? Weren't you at a doctor's office a few hours ago?"

Jodie was surprised that he knew where she had been. She stared at him, not sure what to say, and then it suddenly occurred to her that maybe he hadn't just *happened* upon her sitting here at the beach. Maybe he had followed her here.

But why?

This thought wiped all concern about the incompetent doctor named Cassandros out of her mind, leaving her feeling very uneasy being near this guy.

"Stirling, I think," Rogoff said. "Yeah, I'm pretty sure that was the doctor's name. Stirling. Wasn't that you and your father I saw there earlier?"

She didn't answer him. Instead she said, "Are you staying at this hotel?"

"Me? No, I, um . . . I just came in for a drink." He held up his *Dos Equis*. "It looked like a nice place from the outside so I thought I'd just stop in and have a drink, see how the place was, maybe stay here next time I'm down here."

"You were impressed by the *outside?*"

The outside was about as *un*impressive as a building could be, making it clear to Jodie that he was lying.

He must have realized his mistake because he chuckled and said, "The outside looking from the beach. I was walking up the beach. My hotel's just down the beach. Down there." He made a vague gesture toward the shoreline and chuckled nervously.

Jodie glanced at his sandals and feet. Some sand was tangled in the hair and between his toes, but not nearly enough for someone who had walked up from the beach. He had followed her here. But why?

Rogoff leaned forward in his chair now, staring intently at her. Suddenly he wasn't the comic figure he'd seemed a minute before. Sam Rogoff had something deadly serious to tell her.

Just then a voice behind Jodie said, "Miss Simms?"

Jodie turned and saw Neil Lancaster walking over. When Neil saw Rogoff, the look on his face changed. He seemed disappointed that Jodie was with another man.

"Oh, I thought you were with your father," he said to Jodie. "I can see you're busy at the moment . . ."

"No, no, I was just going to get a refill." She grabbed her half-full margarita glass and quickly stood up, joining

Neil. Whatever Rogoff wanted to tell her would have to wait.

"Was he bothering you?" Neil said, looking back over his shoulder at Rogoff, who was now scurrying off in the other direction.

"I think he was following me." She shivered. "He's kind of . . . creepy."

"That little gnat. Wait here. I'm going to go squish him like a—"

"No, don't," Jodie said, holding his arm to keep him from going after Rogoff. "He's leaving now anyway. He won't be back."

"He better not."

"He was just being a typical man."

Neil chuckled. "I don't know if I should take offense at that, being a man myself."

"Well, I get the impression that you're not *typical.*"

"I'll give you the benefit of the doubt that that wasn't an insult either."

She laughed. "Thanks. And thank you for the flowers you sent this morning. They're beautiful."

They reached the bar. Neil gestured to the Mexican bartender who immediately began preparing a margarita. Neil turned to Jodie.

"At the risk of being a typical man," he said, "I'd like to invite you to have dinner with me tonight."

"I'm flattered that you're asking," she said, "but I really shouldn't leave my dad alone."

"He looks like he's doing okay on his own right now," Neil said, gesturing toward Carl, who was sitting in shallow water, laughing and joking with the two women.

"My dad's turning into Casanova."

"How is he?" Neil asked.

"Actually, he's better. Much better."

"But not good enough for you to have dinner with me?"

"He's still not one hundred percent yet. I wouldn't feel right leaving him all alone, especially in a foreign country like this."

"So you're turning me down again? That's twice now. I don't think my ego can stand that."

"You're a big boy. I think you can take it."

He chuckled, then he thought for a moment and said, "What if there's a way you could have dinner with me and still keep an eye on your father?"

"What do you have in mind?"

⇌ 20

Carl had been so active today that by evening he was exhausted. He fell asleep a little before nine. Jodie left the bathroom light on in case he woke up, then she went outside to the pool area. Neil was already there.

"You look beautiful tonight," he said.

She hadn't packed anything fancy for this trip, never thinking she would have a date while in Mexico. But she managed to put together an outfit with a turquoise blouse she found in the hotel store and white leggings and white shoes she had brought along. Gold angel earrings and Poême perfume added the finishing touches.

He had on a light gray linen suit with a white shirt and Italian loafers. The ponytail was gone; instead his hair fell loose on his shoulders. He had a tiny earring in one ear, a gold cross, and he was wearing the faintest hint of a cologne Jodie found captivating.

"Your table is ready, señorita," he said, making a sweeping gesture toward the beach. He held out his arm for her to take and together they walked to the edge of the sand.

Set up under a coconut palm tree was a small table with a bleached white tablecloth. From the palm fronds above hung a string of yellow lights. A Mexican waiter stood at the table holding a bottle of white wine.

"I don't believe this," Jodie said, impressed by all Neil had done.

"You don't make it easy to take you to dinner," Neil said. "A man does what he has to do, even if it means bringing the dinner to you."

When she leaned against him for support while she took off her high heels, she felt the firm muscle under his sleeve. She took a deep breath of his cologne, spiced by the scent of the sea, and found herself imagining her fingers running through his hair.

Surprised at how much she felt like a schoolgirl, she walked with him across the sand to the table and started giggling.

"What's so funny?"

"Nothing."

"Do you usually laugh like that for no reason?" he said.

"Sometimes."

He held out her chair. Because of the sand, everything

was a little off balance, but Jodie didn't mind at all. The
atmosphere out here could compensate for almost anything. This was much nicer than she had expected.

The waiter filled their glasses, then left them alone.

"You picked a nice restaurant," Jodie said.

"And if you look through the trees," he said, pointing,
"you can see your cabaña from here, so you don't have to
worry about your father being alone."

"You have it all figured out, don't you?"

"I always do."

"I believe that."

Just then a trio of musicians appeared near the pool, as
though by magic. The pool light cast a flickering
turquoise glow. The men started playing softly, the
melody of their strings and voices drifting through the
night like a cool breeze from the sea.

Jodie tingled everywhere. She hadn't been on a date in
months, not since her father came to live with her. But
even with the dates before that, she didn't remember any
of them ever being this good. She didn't remember ever
feeling this enchanted.

Neil gazed across the table at her and smiled. He
raised his wineglass.

"To a beautiful evening that is long overdue," he said.

They touched glasses and sipped wine, staring at each
other for a moment in silence.

"This is really nice," Jodie said.

"If you like the ambience, wait until you taste the
food."

The waiter returned with steaming soft tortillas and
several dishes of salsas. A busboy came behind him,

turned over their water glasses and filled them from a bottle of purified water.

"Down here we call that *agua gringo,*" Neil said, pointing to the water.

Jodie giggled. "An appropriate name. What do you call tap water?"

"Obviously *agua Montezuma.*"

She giggled again, feeling giddy and charmed.

After the waiter left, she said, "You know what I don't understand? How come the local people can drink the water and we can't?"

"That's because their physiology is different from ours."

"Maybe their skin color is different, maybe the shape of their facial features, too. But inside we're all the same."

"Obviously not, otherwise they wouldn't be able to drink the water without getting sick. Races differ, beyond exterior characteristics." He stopped and suddenly looked embarrassed. "God, I sound like a neo-Nazi. That's not how I meant it, believe me. I'm just saying that some races—people from different parts of the world—" He was struggling for the right words.

"Take sickle cell anemia, for example," he said. "Black people are more prone to that than white people are. That's fact, that's not prejudice. And that's because of genetic, physiological differences. It would be foolish to assume that in the entire world, sickle cell anemia is the one and only physiological difference between the many races, wouldn't you agree?"

"Besides running a hotel, you're also an anthropologist, I see."

"In an amateur sense aren't we all?"

The two waiters returned now, carrying several large trays and a folding table. They left the food on the serving table and walked back up to the hotel. Neil got up to serve.

"There's enough food to feed an army," Jodie said.

"I thought you might want to try a little of everything."

"You've got a *lot* of everything."

"I'm counting on it being a long dinner."

As he served the individual selections, he explained what each was. *Caracol al ceviche* was conch marinated in lime juice, tomato and cilantro. Next he gave her some barbecued grouper that the Mayans called *tikinxic*, flavored with *achiote*, a seed the locals used to add color and subtle spiciness to the dish. They had *langosta al mojo de ajo* which was clawless Caribbean lobster fried in garlic butter. There were dishes of steamed shrimp, stuffed crab, and even a whole blackened red snapper called *hauchinango al carbon*.

It was a feast of seafood delights that Jodie had never tasted before. Neil continued filling her dish every few minutes, pouring more wine, signaling the waiters to bring more *aqua gringo*. They ate for hours and talked as easily as two people who had known each other for years.

When Jodie told him that she worked in television news, he said, "That must be an exciting and glamorous job."

"It *sounds* more exciting than it is. As for being glamorous, it's a far cry from that."

She told him about the evening she spent in the crack

house, stepping over garbage and feces to interview a stoned junkie with a knife. She also told him about the mouse that had practically scared her to death.

"Something that small scaring you," he said. "I find that hard to believe."

"Me too." She sipped some wine and explained. "When I was a little girl growing up in Connecticut, I accidentally locked myself in my grandmother's cellar. I was stuck down there for three hours. There were two mice down there and I was petrified. I thought I was never getting out and they were going to eat me." She laughed nervously. "I was little, what can I say? Anyway, ever since then I kind of freak out around mice."

He reached across the table and touched her hand. "That just means you're human," he said.

They talked some more, and she also told him about the nursing home story she had broken a few weeks ago. He was impressed.

"You do something that makes a difference in people's lives," he said. "That must be very gratifying."

"I don't do as much of that as I'd like."

"Even if it's just once, that's more than most people get the opportunity to do in their jobs."

"I guess so. But it's difficult to do the kind of in-depth reporting that would really make a difference. The time constraints working in television are so tight. And that's really not what TV news is all about, anyway. That's for the newspaper people. At least that's what my boss keeps saying."

"I have a feeling that even with those limitations, and

that boss, you manage to put together stories that mean something, that touch people."

Jodie laughed. "You determined that just from spending one evening with me, did you?"

He smiled, the cocky grin of a man quite sure of himself.

"Enough about me," Jodie said. "What about you? What are you doing down here in Mexico?"

"Hiding."

She couldn't tell from the casual way he said it if he was serious or joking.

"What are you hiding from?" she asked.

"I haven't figured that out yet. I guess I wanted a simpler life than what I had back home and I found it down here."

"Where's back home?"

"Seattle. I had a consulting business there. I did real well at it. I made a good living. A hell of a good living. I had all the toys I always wanted—I always *thought* I wanted. Big house, a Porsche, overpriced designer suits."

"Like the suit you're wearing now? I see some of the toys made the trip down here with you."

"Well, I had to keep a few things," he said with a chuckle.

"Were you married?" Jodie asked.

"A lifetime ago. I have three kids. Two boys and a girl. All grown now. Really terrific kids. I've been lucky in that regard. How about you?"

"I haven't been as lucky. No kids. I've never been married."

"How did you pull that off, a beautiful woman like yourself?"

"Easy. Career came first. And second. And third."

He nodded knowingly. "The dilemma of our age."

"Then, once my career was pretty well set," she said, "Dad got sick and, well . . ." She didn't bother finishing the thought. He understood.

"But we're supposed to be talking about you, not me," she said. "Tell me why you left Seattle, besides wanting to run this hotel and pursue your own special brand of anthropological research."

"I guess I got a little burned-out. I started hating my work, hating the things I had worked so hard to get. I hated my life, period. I felt old and tired and I would have given anything to have the last twenty years over again. Then I got an offer to do some consulting work in Guatemala. It sounded like the escape I needed so I jumped at it. From there I came here, fell in love with Mexico, and the rest, as they say, is history."

"What kind of consulting did you do?"

"Oh, foreign trade, that kind of thing. Boring stuff. But it was a change of scenery. It was exactly what I needed."

"How did you end up owning a hotel?"

He grinned and said, "I can't tell you all my secrets. Not right away. I have to leave something for our second date."

"You're taking a lot for granted, aren't you? What makes you think there'll be a second date?"

"You mean you won't see me again?"

"I'm going back to Florida tomorrow afternoon."

"But you're going to come to Cancun again, aren't you?"

"Probably."

"Well? . . ."

Jodie laughed. "I was right before. You do have it all figured out."

He just grinned.

The waiter cleared the table then brought dessert, *tamales* sweetened and flavored with cinnamon, candied fruits, chopped almonds and pine nuts. On top was a scoop of mango sherbet and a slice of fresh mango.

"So your father's doing better?" Neil asked.

"A lot better. The medication he's on has really made a difference."

"What was—or is—wrong with him, if it isn't too intrusive of me to ask?"

"He has Alzheimer's disease."

"Really? You can't tell it to look at him."

"No, not now, not at all. But before he started going to Dr. Stirling, you could definitely tell. But like I say, he's a lot better. The medication Dr. Stirling has been giving him seems to be working wonders."

"Good. I'm glad to hear that."

"Do you know Dr. Stirling?"

"Stirling?" Neil shook his head. "No, I don't believe I do."

"He's an American. I just thought that with you being an American and he being an American and your hotel giving discounts to his patients, I thought you two might know each other."

Neil chuckled. "There are a lot more Americans than you think living down here. Quite a few of us, actually. As far as the discount, we have arrangements with many different businesses and groups. I don't handle that part of the business myself."

"Oh, I see."

"You say he's a good doctor, though?"

"Well, if what he's done for my father is any indication, he's very good."

"You're fortunate then. There are a number of doctors down here that—how should I word it?—are less than competent. Mostly Mexicans, I'm sorry to say. And the people who suffer are mostly Mexicans, too."

Jodie thought again about the doctor whom Rogoff had mentioned this afternoon, the doctor whose name the Mexican woman in Stirling's office had screamed.

"Do you know a Dr. Cassandros?" she asked.

"Cassandros?" He thought a moment then said, "No, can't say that I do. Why? Your father isn't seeing another doctor down here, too, is he?"

"No, nothing like that." She told him about the woman at Dr. Stirling's office the first time she and Carl had come to Mexico. And she told him that the man who had been hitting on her this afternoon had been interested in Dr. Cassandros because of some kind of problem with some of his patients.

"I don't know the doctor," Neil said again, then he chuckled and added, "But I can see the reporter in you is always at work."

She smiled. "Occupational hazard."

The waiter brought two snifters and a bottle of *Sarao Pulido* mescal. Neil poured it and handed Jodie a glass.

"Mescal was once the drink of Mexico's elite," he said.

"I've never had it before."

"You're in for a treat."

Jodie took a whiff and asked, "Is it anything like tequila?"

"A very distant cousin. Unlike tequila, this is all made by hand, no huge distilleries churning out this stuff. Making mescal is an art form in Mexico. Go ahead and taste it," he said.

She took a sip. It had a delicate, smoky taste at first, but as it went down and only the residue remained on her tongue, she discovered an interesting hint of fruit and pepper in the flavor.

"What do you think?" Neil asked.

"I like it. This is good."

They stayed on the beach, sipping mescal and talking until after midnight. The time passed too quickly for Jodie. She didn't want the evening to end. Neil walked her back to the cabaña. At this hour all the other rooms were dark. Soft colored light illuminated the path. The only sounds were her and Neil's bodies brushing the palm fronds, and the quiet whisper of waves lapping the shore. The moist breath of the sea wiped over them, leaving Jodie feeling warm and awkward and oddly winded.

"I really had a wonderful time tonight," she said as they walked.

"The pleasure was all mine."

"I was surprised that you even remembered me from the last trip."

"How could I not remember you? You're not the kind of woman a man easily forgets."

She was glad there wasn't much light out here because she didn't want him to see her blushing. When they reached the cabaña they stood at the door in silence for a long moment. Jodie giggled in the awkwardness. Neil reached out and brushed her hair off her shoulders then gently ran his hand down her arm. Her whole body quivered with his touch. He gazed into her eyes for what seemed like an eternity, then he slowly drew her against him and surrounded her in his arms. When they kissed, her whole body tingled. She tasted the mescal on his breath. But mostly she felt his passion. It left her feeling safe and desired in a way she hadn't felt in years.

When their lips finally parted, she whispered, "I'm going to be thinking about you tonight." She wiped the lipstick off his mouth and said, "You'd better go . . ."

He squeezed her hand one last time, then turned and retreated down the stone path. Jodie watched him disappear into the night, feeling out of breath as though she had just been running.

This evening had been special for her, and she wanted to tell someone all about it, tell her father. But Carl was asleep when she walked into the cabaña, so she turned off the bathroom light and went to bed with all of her emotions burning inside.

She lay awake for almost an hour thinking about Neil and their date on the beach, thinking how much better her father was, thinking how good life had suddenly become. When she finally drifted off to sleep, she felt like a fairy princess, and dreamed pleasant dreams of what lay in store for her.

≈ 21

Jodie and Carl had breakfast at the hotel restaurant. Afterward they stopped in the lobby gift shop. Jodie bought an onyx angel to add to her collection of figurines at home. Carl bought a baseball cap that said CANCUN. He also pocketed the Mexican coins the clerk gave them as change. He liked the *pesos* even better than the hat.

When they got back to the cabaña, the phone was ringing. Jodie picked it up while Carl went to the bathroom to brush his teeth.

"Don't forget to use the *agua gringo*," she told him.

"The what?"

"The bottled water. Hello?" she said into the phone.

"Good morning."

She recognized Neil's voice instantly and a smile came to her face.

"Good morning to you," she said.

"I didn't get much sleep last night."

"There must be something in the air," she said, "because neither did I."

"I couldn't stop thinking about you."

Carl poked his head out of the bathroom, toothpaste foaming around his mouth. "Who's that on the phone?" he asked.

"Neil."

"The guy with the hair? But he just saw you last night."

"Why don't you go finish brushing your teeth, Dad."

Carl chuckled. "I'd say he's got the hots for you."

Jodie put her hand over the mouthpiece. "Dad, will you please! . . ."

He laughed and went back to brushing his teeth.

When Jodie was alone again, she said to Neil, "Thanks for last night."

"I should be the one thanking you."

"I had a really good time."

"Good enough that you'll let me take you and your father to Chichén Itzá today? You haven't been there yet, have you?"

"No. But we're leaving this afternoon. I don't think we have time."

"When's your flight?"

"Five o'clock."

"You've got plenty of time. Meet me in the lobby in half an hour?"

"Let me ask my dad."

Carl poked his head out of the bathroom again. "Ask me what?"

"How would you like to go to Chichén Itzá today?"

"Chicken pizza?"

She laughed. "Chichén Itzá. It's an ancient Mayan ruin. Neil wants to take us."

He shrugged. "Yeah, why not? Give me a chance to get to know this girly-haired guy who's after my little girl."

* * *

Chichén Itzá, located in the middle of the Yucatan peninsula, is a hundred and thirty miles southwest of Cancun. Neil rented a Ford Taurus for the three hour drive this morning. He usually drove an open-topped Jeep, but he told Jodie he didn't think she and Carl would be comfortable in it for such a long trip. She said she wouldn't have minded, but she thanked him for showing concern for her father.

They arrived at Chichén Itzá early in the afternoon. Admission was ridiculously low, Jodie thought, at three dollars per person. For another ten dollars, Neil hired a private tour guide outside the entrance, a man Carl's age named Arturo, with one arm amputated and distinctive Mayan features. He spoke English well and had the kind of face that, just by looking at it, you could tell he had lived an interesting life.

He and Carl chatted quietly as they walked through the visitors' center toward the entrance. Jodie and Neil walked behind them, holding hands. She felt very much at ease with Neil, as though they had been on many day trips together.

As they went through the turnstiles, he leaned close and whispered to her, "This place is going to blow your socks off."

A sign at the entrance warned them that some merchants might approach them and that they should not do business with these people because they were on the grounds illegally. From the way the sign was worded, Jodie expected to see a few people sneaking carvings and handiwork under their clothes, whispering to tourists to persuade them to buy. But what she found, only a few yards beyond the sign, were hundreds of vendors lining the path through the jungle, with tables and chairs set up, selling all sorts of blankets, onyx figurines, wood carvings, paintings, knives and *machetes* with intricate detail on the blades and handles.

Arturo ushered them past the vendors. "There will be time after to buy the souvenirs," he said. "If we stop now, they will never let you go, you will never see all of Chichén Itzá."

As they walked up the jungle path, Arturo began the tour by saying, "No one knows for certain how old Chichén Itzá is. The earliest date the scientists have found on the hieroglyphics is fourteen hundred years ago. But they believe this city is much more older. There is evidence that Maya have been in the Yucatan for ten thousand years. We are a very old civilization," he said, his chin high, his chest swelling with pride.

At the end of the path they came to a clearing. Stone ruins spread out to the left—temples, platforms, pillars—but the edifice that stood out the most was the massive terraced pyramid straight ahead.

"El Castillo," Arturo said, gazing up at it with veneration. He must have seen it thousands of times before, yet he still looked enthralled. "This was built to honor the Maya god Kukulcan," he explained.

Jodie had seen photographs of this pyramid in books, read a little about its history, but now, seeing the stone walls rising above the trees, the carvings of the plumed serpent on the stairways, the temple on top touching the blue sky, she was awestruck by its majesty and historic significance. This had been built centuries before Columbus discovered the New World. Some archeologists believed it had been here even before Jesus Christ. And here it still was, still standing, still commanding reverence.

"What is especial about El Castillo," Arturo said. "If you add the number of steps on all the four sides, and count the top platform as one step, there are 365 steps altogether. This number is familiar?" he asked.

"That's the number of days in a year," Carl said.

Arturo acknowledged the answer with a professorial nod. "It is not a coincidence," he said. "The ancient Maya used architecture in the way we now use the calendars. El Castillo is built to align with the sun and the moon. Where the shadow falls tells them when to plant and when to harvest."

He told them that twice a year a shadow was cast on the steps, resembling an undulating serpent. This shadow, believed to be Kukulcan, appeared to ascend in March and descend in September, a 202-minute phenomenon that prescribed when to plant and when to harvest. He also explained the Mayan mathematical system, which used a base of 18 instead of our base of 10, and how the 9 levels of the pyramid, divided by the stairways, correlated with the 18 months of their solar calendar.

"The Maya were much advanced, you know," he said.

Dozens of tourists scampered up the stone steps on two sides of the pyramid. Though the pyramid had stairways on all four sides, the ones on the east and south steps were impassable because of centuries of deterioration. On the east side, Mayan laborers hoisted buckets of mortar up by rope and toiled to rebuild their ancestors' stonework.

"You must go up," Arturo said. "From the top of El Castillo, you have the best view of all of Chichén Itzá."

Carl hurried to the steps first, excited about going up. Jodie worried he might not be able to climb all the way by himself. His mind was clearer than it had been in years, but he was still thin, still weak. To be safe, she walked on one side of him and silently signaled Neil to walk on Carl's other side. They held him by the arms and helped him climb. Arturo waited below.

Once they started up, Jodie found the stairs to be even more steep than they looked. They were nothing like the stairs in a home. The rise on each step was twice that of normal steps, making it more like stepping up onto a chair instead of climbing stairs. The pyramid had no handrails, nothing for Jodie to hold onto for support except the step directly in front of her. The tread where she placed her feet was slightly shallower than the soles of her shoes, leaving her heel hanging over the edge. The Mayans must have had small feet and strong legs, she decided.

And little fear. One glance back and she realized that if she fell, there was nothing below except stone and other tourists.

Twice on the way up Carl stopped to rest. Jodie was thankful because she was out of breath herself. When they finally reached the top platform, eighty feet up, she fell flat against the wall of the temple, keeping as far from the edge as possible. Gasping for air, she peered out at the ancient city before her.

Chichén Itzá was much larger than she thought. Not only were there ruins in this clearing, but trails snaked off through the jungle in all directions, leading to more stone buildings. She was surprised to see there was an entire city of Mayan ruins hidden in this jungle.

They stayed on top for fifteen minutes, just marveling at the sights below. When they finally came down, Arturo led them through the sprawling city to several other, smaller temples. One of them, the Temple of Jaguars, had a ball court in front of it where, Arturo explained, the ancient Mayans used to play a game similar to soccer.

"But the stakes of the game were more higher than futbol," he said. "The captain of the team that fails was decapitated and his blood used to fertilize the earth and appease the gods. Some history people say the head was kept and covered with rubber to be used for the ball the next time."

"That's gruesome," Jodie said.

"The Mayan version of the Roman gladiatorial games," Neil said.

"Different," Arturo said. "I tell you why. The Romans kill for amusement. The Maya don't kill for amusement. Maya kill only for the gods."

Arturo led them down a path crowded with souvenir vendors, to an astrological observatory and told them that the Mexicans called it *El Caracol,* the conch shell, because of its shape. It was the only round structure in the entire city.

"The archeologists believe this is not Maya, is built by the Toltecs from *Méjico,*" Arturo said.

"Isn't this Mexico?" Carl said.

Arturo answered with a coy smile. "Señor, this is no *Méjico*. This is the Yucatan."

Arturo led them down another path to more temples, the ancient market, the Mayan sweat house, and he related more of the city's history.

"Chichén Itzá has much different culture in the history," he explained. "Maya, Toltec, Espanish. Many Maya tribes from the Yucatan and the Toltecs from *Méjico* conquer Chichén Itzá. The last independent Maya tribe to be here is where the name Chichén Itzá is from. The tribe is call the Itzá. Did you know there is different Maya tribes? The Dzul, the Poot, the Haustec. No just one Maya—many Maya. The Itzá Maya come out of the west and take over this city from the Yucatec Maya. The scientists believe the Itzá were not Yucatec, not like the Maya Indian here before them. They were from another place, but we don't know where."

"From Mexico?" Carl said with a wink.

Arturo grinned. He and Carl were like elder statesmen. They seemed to like each other.

"The name Itzá," Arturo continued, "means 'Foreigners who speak our tongue broken.' The Itzá are a very mysterious people. Some Maya believe the Itzá had especial powers. They give to Cortes the most trouble of all the Maya tribes," he said with a sense of pride. "To last against Cortes as long as they do, they must be especial. The Conquistadoros attack and defeat them only three hundred years ago. There are still Itzá alive now," he told them as though revealing a great secret. "But not many."

"Are you one of them?" Carl asked.

With a rakish grin, Arturo said, "I think I have a little bit of Itzá in my blood."

Arturo took them down another path, north of the central clearing.

"The name Chichén Itzá," he said, "means 'Mouth of the Cenoté of Itzá.'" With reverence in his voice, he said, "I now take you to the Sacred Cenoté."

The path ended at what looked like a quarry, a giant pit a hundred feet across. A flat shelf stood at one end, an altar looking out over the descending wall of limestone, straight and smooth, impossible to climb. Sixty feet below was a placid surface of brackish water. Arturo explained how the ancient Itzá threw many valuables into the water to please the gods and how foreign scientists came later and dredged the cenoté, taking all the valuables back to museums in their own countries, stealing the antiquities of the Maya.

He told them how the Itzá, as part of their sacrificial ceremonies, often threw children into this sacred well.

"If they do not drown," he said, "then the god is pleased and the city will be cured of a bad illness."

"It sounds like they were big on human sacrifice," Jodie said.

Neil said, "It's only relatively recent in history that human sacrifice wasn't the predominant way of insuring health and well-being."

"Certainly not the health and well-being of the one being sacrificed," Jodie said.

"No, but the health and well-being of the community

as a whole. And most cultures, with the exception probably of ours in the U.S., believe that the good of the community outweighs the good of the individual."

"The flaw in that thinking is that human sacrifices were not only bad for the individual being sacrificed, but they didn't do the community any good either," Jodie said.

Neil laughed and said, "Your twentieth century beliefs make it impossible for you to objectively evaluate whether the sacrifices did any good."

Jodie thought he sounded like he was only half-joking.

"Common sense lets me evaluate it," she said. "Human sacrifice didn't do any good."

Arturo said, "Will you say the same about prayer? Does prayer do good?"

Jodie avoided answering by saying, "Isn't it supposed to be bad form to discuss religion?"

They all laughed and dropped the subject.

A covered refreshment stand was tucked into the trees beside the cenoté. Neil bought cold drinks for everyone, then they headed back toward the center of the city. Before they left, Jodie haggled with a few of the vendors, buying some Mexican blankets and hand-carved jade spice containers.

They got back to Cancun a little after four, picked up the luggage at the hotel, then Neil drove them to Dr. Stirling's office to get the supply of The Cure, and finally they headed to the airport.

Carl had to use the men's room in the terminal, giving Jodie and Neil a few moments alone before the flight. They stood near the metal detector, holding hands and gazing into each other's eyes, other passengers hurrying past them.

"When are you coming back?" Neil asked.

"My father has an appointment with Dr. Stirling in two months."

"You don't have to wait for your father's appointment to come to Cancun. People come all the time, you know, even people whose fathers don't have appointments."

"I'll try. But it's hard to leave him alone."

"He seems to be doing pretty well. Try to come see me," Neil said.

"Planes fly both ways," she told him. "You can come see me, too."

Carl came out of the men's room now. He walked over, looked at the two of them still holding hands and said, "Will you two hurry up and kiss. Get it over with so we can get on the plane. I don't want to be stuck down here."

Neil laughed. "Your dad has a point," he said to Jodie.

Jodie turned to Carl who was staring at them. "Dad, why don't go through," she said, pointing to the metal detector. "I'll be right behind you."

Carl let out a loud breath of exasperation. "All of a sudden she's bashful around me." He turned and went through the metal detector and headed up the terminal toward the gate.

Jodie turned back to Neil. "So, this is it . . ." she whispered.

"I'm going to miss you, Jodie Simms."

Carl, halfway to the gate now, turned back and shouted, "Come on, get it over with, will you?"

They both laughed. Finally Neil placed his hands on Jodie's face and held her as he moved in and kissed her lips. It was a long, passionate kiss that ended in a sad hug. Jodie broke away and hurried through the metal detector, glancing back and waving only once.

She had gone so long without this kind of romance, and now that she found it she hated to leave.

Two months, she told herself. They would be together again in two months.

≋ 22

Sam Rogoff pulled his car to the curb two blocks away, worried that if he parked closer, some joker he didn't want knowing he was here might spot his rental car and spill the beans. It would be like telling the other team when you were going to blitz. He wanted a clear shot at the quarterback and he didn't want the doctor doing the equivalent of throwing a screen pass. So parking this far away would keep them from getting wind of his game plan—he hoped.

Nine P.M. found this section of Cancun with few streetlights to break the darkness. This block had no sidewalk; the doorways of businesses opened right onto the street, a street that in some places was pavement, in others was dirt. A pothole the size of Delaware forced Rogoff to walk out into the middle of the road. Fortunately there were no cars driving past to squish him like a slow cat on the Bruckner Expressway. But the empty street made him realize now just how alone he was. No cars, no pedestrians, no bums or two-dollar hookers hanging around in front of the doorways. Just him. This area had a strange abandoned feeling that made him shiver in the muggy night.

Shaking those thoughts from his head, he glanced at the mesquite branch someone had stuck into the pothole. A strip of cloth hung from the end, warning off cars. If someone drove over that hole, it would take a hell of a lot more than Mr. Goodwrench to get him going again.

Beside the hole a pitcher's mound of sand was piled up, apparently to be used for fill. Rogoff got the impression the sand had been there quite a while. They were probably going to get to it *mañana*, which to the Mexicans could mean tomorrow or a year from tomorrow.

As he got closer to the clinic building, he saw a few shops still open. A grocery store that looked like it had been looted; all the shelves were barren. An ice cream parlor smelling of overripe bananas. A gym that would be laughed out of existence back home. One weight bench, one barbell and a heavy bag hanging in the corner.

From the open doorway of the gym, two dark Mayan faces watched him as he walked by, two short round men who looked neither friendly nor hostile, instead showing only an odd glare of curiosity.

Gringos didn't often come around this part of Cancun. But the lack of tourists in this area, of outsiders of any kind, and the predominance of Mexicans, more specifically of poor Mexican Indians, descendants of ancient

Mayan tribes, was exactly the reason Sam Rogoff was here tonight. The clinic he had come to investigate existed solely for these people.

So far his investigation had turned up some interesting facts about this place, facts that defied all logic. As he expanded his search these last few days, he had discovered evidence pointing to one thing, and one person, an explanation so surprising he hadn't believed it initially. It can't be, he had told himself. No one could get away with that. Why would anyone even want to? It defied not only logic, but reason.

Those answers would only come with a full-scale, all-out, no-holds-barred investigation. Rogoff's job at this point was to make sure such an investigation was launched. He needed to provide the WHO with enough evidence to justify a sweeping probe. He intended to get it tonight.

He grinned as he thought of himself as the hero, the Joe Montana of epidemiology. If only the WHO put out trading cards, he thought, little Mexican kids and American kids alike would fork over two Darryl Strawberrys and a Mark McGwire for one Sam Rogoff.

He approached the clinic building with an exaggerated sense of stealthiness, crouching behind a palm tree, peering through the fronds at the entrance at the end of the block. He felt like James Bond tonight. *Rogoff, Sam Rogoff.* Two yellowish lights illuminated the doorway. He saw a woman and three children leaving. Other than that, the area was deserted.

Disregarding the front entrance, he detoured through the staff parking lot beside the building. Unlike at hospitals back home, very few workers here owned cars. Most rode the bus to work, including many doctors. So the parking lot didn't need to be large; it was a strip of asphalt the size of a handball court squeezed between the clinic building and a vacant shop, resembling little more than a cluttered alleyway. Half a dozen cars were parked here tonight, including the Nissan he was hoping to find. He checked the license plate to make sure it was the same car. *Bingo!*

On the door at the side of the building was stenciled: NO ENTRADA. This entrance was for staff only. Rogoff tried the knob anyway and the door opened.

"Base hit," he said as he stepped inside and closed the door behind him. Through another doorway straight ahead was the main floor. The hallway was dimly lit, several of the bulbs burned out. He saw a nurse wheeling a cart of empty food trays and he ducked to the side so she wouldn't see him. She turned the corner and disappeared. He hesitated for a moment, then went in.

The air smelled of bleach and fecal matter. He had come here earlier this afternoon and saw enough to get a pretty good idea of the layout, of where he needed to go. A few of the nurses had been naive enough to talk to him. He even got one lab technician to spill his guts, though much of what the man had said Rogoff had been unable to comprehend because Rogoff's Spanish was a bit rusty and the man spoke too quickly.

On the wall ahead of Rogoff were signs directing him toward URGENCIA. RADIOLOGIA E IMAGEN. LABORITORIO. QUIRÚRGICO. The last one, *quirúrgico*, which he knew was Spanish for surgery, was where he wanted to go. That section of the clinic was where he hoped to find the proof he needed.

He followed the arrow down a hall and around the corner to a pair of doors marking the beginning of the surgical wing. He looked back to make sure he was still alone. He hadn't passed anyone since he came in and he hoped it would stay that way just a little longer.

He eased open the door enough so he could see into the surgical wing. All but one of the lights were off, and that light was a dim bulb at the very end, providing just enough illumination for him to see the wing was empty. He glanced back one last time to make sure no one saw him, then he slipped through the doorway.

His slow, careful footsteps echoed off the tile floor, sounding in his head like the ticking of a time bomb. He wasn't the type to feel reticent about sticking his nose where it didn't belong, but tonight a peculiar feeling of uneasiness swept over him. For a brief instant he wondered if he should be doing this.

He quickly dismissed that thought. Sure, he should be doing this. If his suspicions were right, horrendous things were being done down here and someone had to stop them. Rogoff's job was to do this. Any reservations should have been left at the airport when he cleared Customs.

He walked past a small nurse's station and two recovery rooms. Just past them, on the left, were double doors with NO ENTRADA stenciled on them. Two tiny glass portholes provided a view into the surgical ante-room and just enough light for Rogoff to see the scrub sinks and storage closets. At the back of the scrub room was another set of doors, propped open to reveal the clinic's one and only operating room, looking prehistoric compared to ORs back home.

That's where it happens, Rogoff realized. *That's where the doctor is killing people.*

But why?

He continued past the operating room to the door at the end of the hall, a solid wood door with JEFE DEL DEPARTAMENTO DE CIRUGIÁ stenciled on it. *Chief of Surgery.* Earlier today, a nurse had told him where to find this office. Now he hesitated and listened to see if anyone was in the room. Hearing nothing, he stepped back and peered up at the transom over the door. The glass was dark, no lights on behind it. No one was in there, he reasoned, so he stepped up to the door again and tried the knob. He wasn't surprised it was locked. He came prepared.

He had to admit to himself that he didn't have the strength to pull himself up to the transom, and even if he could get himself up there, he certainly wasn't lean enough to squeeze through such a narrow opening. But he wasn't a pull-up, squeeze-through type of guy. Growing up in Brooklyn, he had learned there were easier ways.

He reached into his pocket and took out the small zippered case. Back home it would be illegal for him just to have this in his possession. He wasn't sure about the law here, but he doubted they looked favorably on it, even though the locksmith who had sold it to him didn't seem the least bit concerned once Rogoff put three hundred pesos in the palm of his hand.

Rogoff looked back up the hallway to make sure no one was coming, then he unzipped the leather case, revealing the tools inside. For two hundred pesos more, the locksmith had given him a quick lesson, let him try it on a few locks in his shop. Rogoff had practiced at the hotel until he felt comfortable. Now he manipulated the tools with ease. He felt the tumblers move, heard the latch spring. He tried the knob again and the door opened. Well worth the five hundred pesos, he thought.

He looked down the corridor one more time, then darted into the room like a tailback shooting through a hole off tackle. He quickly closed the door behind him, and to be safe he locked himself in. He also decided it would be best to leave the lights off. If someone happened to come to this wing for anything, he didn't want them seeing light through the transom. The room would look dark, empty, and they would not suspect that he was in here.

He took the penlight from his pocket and shined it into the office. There were no windows. The only ventilation came from the transom over the door, left open a few inches. The air seemed dense, too dense to breathe. Rogoff felt his lungs constricting. He heard himself wheezing and felt that unfamiliar sense of uneasiness again.

The beam of his flashlight fell on the doctor's desk. Rogoff went over and was about to open the drawers when he noticed the doorway right beside him. He had almost missed it in the darkness. He tried the knob and found it unlocked.

He eased the door open and stepped through, shining

the tiny beam of his flashlight into the dark room. The
first thing he noticed was the chill in the air. This lab was
kept cold with air conditioning, probably the only room
in the building with such luxury. He felt an odd shiver
rattle his bones as he stepped deep into the lab.

The light swept over a long table in the middle of the
room, illuminating a fluorescent microscope, a micro-
fuge, an assortment of vials and test tubes. A counter
along the right wall was filled with more lab supplies. On
a separate bench near the back of the room was a
complete electrophoresis system, set up to analyze protein mixtures, with modules, buffer tanks, lids, cooling
cores and several unused gel sandwiches. Another bench
had a sophisticated sequence analyzer, a system used to
identify amino acids in proteins.

Why would this doctor have these items? Rogoff
wondered. They were used predominantly for biochemical research. Certainly not something a physician in
clinical practice would need to have.

Unless curing patients wasn't his objective.

Hanging on the wall to the left was a lightbox for
viewing x-rays, and just left of that a desk and a bank of
old wooden file cabinets. Farther along the wall on that
side of the room were shelves stacked with mice cages.
Rogoff moved a little closer, shined the light into a few
of the cages and noticed the tiny circles punched into the
ears of the mice, signifying they were being used for
experiments. The patterns of the punches acted as
number designations.

Rogoff peered at #6. The tiny mouse had a deep black
coat: a C57bl. He glanced at the other cages. All of them

were C57bls. Why would the doctor have an interest in this particular strain of inbred mouse?

Rogoff remembered using C57bls once, years ago, when he was in research, back in the days when he spent hour after hour in a boring lab at the University of Rochester. He had chosen C57bls because they had been the perfect model for the sensory degeneration study he had been doing.

The thing that stood out in his mind now as he stared at these black rodents is that they were used predominantly in molecular studies, not for clinical diagnosis. So why would this doctor have these mice in this kind of clinic? It made no sense at all.

"What the hell is this guy up to?" Rogoff wondered out loud.

Another question unanswered. Another facet of this investigation that didn't make a whole lot of sense. Another item he would report to the WHO when he got back to the States.

He turned away from the mice and continued scanning the lab. He noticed another doorway in the back of the room and wondered if it was a closet or if it led to another room or hallway, something he should check out. He made a mental note to explore back there later, but right now he turned his attention to the desk.

He sat in the uncomfortable wood chair behind it. The desk was nothing more than a sheet of wood with legs under it. It had no drawers. Some papers were scattered on top. The phone looked like it belonged in a museum. A plastic model of the brain was partially dismantled and scattered about. Rogoff began lifting up the brain parts and searching through the papers. Right away he found something.

"Exhibit number one," he whispered to himself in the darkness.

It was an invoice from the Chemicon Corporation in Temecula, California, near San Diego. Chemicon was a commercial supplier of antibody reagents. Scientific labs and research facilities ordered compounds from companies like Chemicon, but clinical practitioners should not be doing business with them, certainly not doctors with the kind of practice that this doctor at this particular clinic had.

This invoice indicated that the doctor had purchased one hundred micrograms of BDNF antibodies two weeks ago. Rogoff knew that pathologists used many different antibodies to do immuno-histochemistry stains; researchers used them for Western Blot analyses and ELISA assays. Both would have reason to use anti-BDNF. But a clinician would not. He might use antibodies for some diagnostic purposes, but not BDNF antibodies. So why did this doctor have anti-BDNF? Why antibodies directed against this particular growth factor?

Once already in this investigation Rogoff had come across that same growth factor, when he questioned a fast-talking Mexican lab tech earlier today. Now he wished like hell his Spanish was better. At least he should have thought to bring a translator along with him so he would have known what the guy had been saying. It might have helped clarify some of the things he was learning tonight.

He set the invoice aside and searched the desk for more evidence. Nothing. He focused his attention on the file cabinets.

He shined his light on the front panel of one of the drawers, illuminating the letters: G–J. He pulled on the drawer but it was locked, so he took out the leather case again and easily picked the lock. *Yes, best five hundred pesos I ever spent.*

He slid open the drawer and found it stuffed with file folders from which papers and x-ray films stuck out. These must be patients' records, he reasoned. He couldn't resist a fat grin, having found exactly what he was looking for.

He reached into his pocket for his notepad and the list of patients he had gathered, but the pad wasn't there. *"Damn it!"* he whispered, realizing that he left it on the car seat.

He couldn't go all the way out to the car, get the pad, then come back here. He wasn't O.J. Simpson—it would take too long and he might get caught. Since he was already here, he had to try to remember the names he had written just a few hours ago.

Hoping to trigger his memory, he began thumbing through the folders, looking at the names handwritten on each tab. Each of these represented a person's life, he realized. Some of them represented a person's death—a death falsely explained. How many deaths? he questioned. He knew of only nine, but he kept wondering if there were others he did not know about.

A hand-printed name glowed under the beam of his penlight, triggering his memory. ESCONDITA GARCIA

DE PELEZ. Yes, he had a Garcia on his list, though this wasn't the patient. He hurriedly thumbed through several more files, looking for his Garcia.

All the G's were in this drawer but they weren't arranged alphabetically. Everything was mixed in. Even the Hs and Is were sandwiched between names beginning with G. He found a Gonzalez, two Gongoras, an Ibenez and a Huaxtitlan before he came to the patient he was looking for. HECTOR ITZÁ GARCIA.

Rogoff pulled out the folder and opened it with nervous anticipation. Among the papers stuffed inside the folder was an x-ray film with gray bands that Rogoff recognized immediately as a Western Blot analysis. The molecular weight markers were written on the edges of the blot, as were notes about which samples were run in which lanes and which antibody was used to probe it. This one said the doctor used BDNF antibodies.

"So *that's* what he's doing with the anti-BNDF?" Rogoff said. But he still didn't know why the doctor ran a Western Blot on this patient.

A sheet of paper clipped to the blot had several typewritten notations on it. Beneath Hector Itzá Garcia's name it said POSITIVE FOR $BDNF_2$ PRECURSOR.

"Exhibit number two," Rogoff said. Another piece of evidence he could use to prove his case to his superiors.

Rogoff still didn't quite understand what it all meant, and he didn't understand the meaning of the notation typed beneath the $BDNF_2$ entry. It said: FAMILY AVAILABLE: IMM—son, sister, brother. EXT—grandson (1), cousins (11), nephews (6), nieces (4). Available for what? Rogoff wondered. After this entry the doctor had listed the names of all these relatives, many of whom had either Garcia or Itzá in their names. Two were also named Hector. The list was followed by: PROSPECT—9+. Rogoff couldn't imagine what that meant. But it was the next entry that grabbed his attention. Handwritten across the page was the notation:

Watch for this lineage.

This indicated to Rogoff that this doctor was interested in tracking something that was heritable. But what? And why? With his experience in epidemiology, his first thought was that it was a disease the doctor was tracking. But there was no mention of a disease in the notes. So what was it? Obviously it was connected to BDNF, but how? Not knowing the answers made Rogoff uneasy. Still, he knew enough to be convinced that something bad was happening here and he was determined to expose it.

He continued looking through the file until he found Hector Itzá Garcia's CAT scan, the one thing that would emphatically prove what Rogoff suspected the doctor was doing. According to Hector's wife, Hector had returned here after the seizures began, before they went to the Indian herbalist. The doctor had taken films of Hector's brain, probably to make it look like he was actually trying to help them. Was it more deception, or did he just want to see his handiwork? If it was more deception, this deception was going to help put the quack away for a very long time. If the CAT scan showed what Rogoff believed it would, all hell was *definitely* going to break loose down here.

He brought the film over to the lightbox, eager to see

once and for all if he was right. He had to hold down the switch on the viewer for a few seconds before the light finally flickered on. The bright glow stung his eyes as he held the CAT scan up to it, illuminating the eerie gray image.

He couldn't believe what he saw.

There it was, Exhibit #3, the proof he needed. He just stared at it for a long moment. Even though he had suspected this, he was still shocked to find out he was right. It was difficult to spot if the person looking at it didn't know where to look, didn't suspect it would be there in the first place. No larger than the opening of a McDonalds' straw, it barely showed up on the film as a light gray spot. But it was there. It definitely was there.

And it definitely should not be.

Why was the doctor doing this? Rogoff asked himself. He had a pretty good idea *what* the doctor was doing, but he could not imagine *why* he was doing it. Why was he killing these people? It made no sense at all.

Rogoff remembered another patient's name now, one whose last name was the same as Hector Garcia's middle name. Itzá. The same name as the ancient Mayan ruin, Chichén Itzá. He had read enough about the native Indians to know they often took Mayan tribes for their name, like Itzá, Ticas, Pooc, Dzul. Having the same name didn't mean people were necessarily related by blood, but rather linked by a common tribal history. It would be like Apaches having the word Apache in their name.

The name Hector Itzá Garcia reminded him of Elena Fuentes de Itzá. Elena was an elderly Mayan woman who lived near Hector, but they were not related, as far as Rogoff knew. She had no living family either. A friend of hers had told Rogoff her story, about the woman's visit to this clinic for TB and the seizures that followed, the seizures that finally took her life.

Rogoff kept out her and Hector Garcia's CAT scans, Western Blot films and the pages with the notations, tucked them under his arm, then stuffed the folders back into the cabinet. He tugged on another drawer and found it unlocked. The doctor might know medicine, but he had little sense of secrecy. *Thank God.*

The name Petán popped up at him. Manual Lamas Petán had been only ten years old when he died. His mother had given Rogoff much of the information that led him to this point. Rogoff stared at the boy's CAT scan, disgusted by what he saw.

The doctor had to be stopped. He had to be stopped immediately.

Rogoff decided he would fly back to New York tonight rather than go straight to the local authorities. The local people wouldn't know how to handle this. They wouldn't even understand it. No, instead he would have his superiors at the WHO contact Mexico's federal authorities. They'd need law enforcement and health officials involved in this. The WHO had the clout to convince the Mexican government to act swiftly, properly. Rogoff knew that since much of the evidence he would be turning over was obtained in a less-than-legal manner, this had to be handled with tact, but he was confident that the bigwigs at WHO would be able to deal with it. This wasn't the first time he had bent local laws. This wasn't the first time his superiors had to make things right.

As he remembered another patient's name—Carmela Zapata de la O—and took out her CAT scan, he heard a faint noise in the hallway. He froze, holding the woman's scan in his hand and peering out the lab door and into the dark office. He heard the sound again, a soft jingling of keys. The tumblers clicked and he suddenly realized someone was unlocking the door.

Rogoff quickly turned off his flashlight and jabbed the button on the x-ray viewer, throwing himself into darkness. He needed to find another way out of here, but with the lights off he couldn't see more than an inch in front of his face. He remembered seeing another door in the back of the room when he had come in a few minutes ago so he started moving in that direction, hoping it was an exit, not just a closet. But even a closet would provide a place to hide.

In the darkness he bumped into the table in the middle of the room and stumbled.

He dropped the CAT scans, blot films and notes.

They fluttered to the floor, spreading all around. He fell to his knees and felt along the cold tile, gathering up the paper and film. The door in the outer office opened and the light snapped on, throwing a wedge of illumination into the lab.

He froze again, not sure what to do. He saw the door in the back of the room now and sprinted toward it. Just as he tugged it open, the overhead lights flickered on.

He froze, caught in the light.

It was the doctor, and another man. The other man caught Rogoff's eye, and smiled. The look on his face reminded Rogoff of an animal eying prey.

Rogoff rushed through the doorway and down the stairs, barely able to keep from stumbling. The sound of footsteps coming after him echoed through his head. A cold spike of fear ran through his heart. In all the years he had been doing this, he had never faced death. Suddenly, tonight, survival was the only thought in his head.

⇶ 23

On Tuesday after work, Jodie swung by the Mayo Clinic to drop off the syringe of The Cure. She got there a few minutes before Dr. Harrington's office closed.

"Do you know how much of this you'll need?" she asked the nurse.

"I don't know. That depends on what tests Dr. Harrington ordered. That's something the lab will have to determine."

Jodie had spent the day agonizing over her decision to hand over the syringe to the clinic. The $750 syringe. "If there's any left over afterward," she said, "I'd like to have it back. This is pretty expensive medicine."

"I'll make a note of that."

Remembering the Covenant of Nondisclosure Stirling had her sign a month ago, and conscious of the doctor's concerns that someone might steal the drug, Jodie told the nurse that it was very important no one but Dr. Harrington and the individual lab technician doing the tests have access to medicine or the test results.

The nurse looked a little surprised. "The lab tech is the only one who will have access," she said. "We'll be delivering it downstairs in just a few minutes and when the results are in, they'll go straight to Dr. Harrington. I can assure you that nothing will happen, Ms. Simms."

Only Dr. Harrington knew how well The Cure worked. To the nurses and lab techs, the syringe would probably be just another substance to be analyzed. Jodie was satisfied that Stirling's research efforts would not be usurped here.

When Jodie got home, Carl was in the kitchen with Mrs. Kelly, helping her make dinner. He stood over the sink, peeling potatoes. Seeing him with the sharp peeler in his hands made Jodie a little nervous but she also saw how steady he was, how deftly he manipulated the blade.

"Well, look who's home," he said when he saw her. "How's my girl?"

"I'm good, Dad. I see Mrs. Kelly has you working."

He winked and said, "She's a slave driver, that woman."

"Idle hands do the devil's work," Mrs. Kelly said, punctuating it with a firm nod of her head.

Mrs. Kelly left shortly after Jodie got home. Dinner was already in the oven so all Jodie had to do was take the roast out and slice it. Carl helped her clean the kitchen afterward, then they sat together in the living room and

watched an old movie on AMC, Barbara Stanwyck and
Gary Cooper in *Meet John Doe*. Jodie got choked up at
the end. Carl seemed preoccupied with something else.

"Is everything okay, Dad?" she asked.

He said, "I've been thinking about something." He
was silent for a moment, looking for the right words.
Finally he took a deep breath and said, "About living
here."

"What do you mean?"

"I don't think I need to have you take care of me
anymore."

"I don't take care of you, Dad."

"Your mother and I bought a beautiful house in St.
Augustine," he said. Suddenly he looked concerned—
something just occurred to him. "We still have the
house, don't we?" he asked. "After your mother died, you
didn't sell it, did you?"

"No, I didn't sell it."

He looked relieved. "It's not rented or anything like
that, is it?"

"No. But Dad—"

"Let me finish."

"I know what you're going to say," she said.

"There's no reason why I can't move back down there.
I'm perfectly capable of taking care of myself. This house
is much too small for two grown people. You have your
own life and you don't need me around interfering."

"You're not interfering. I like having you stay with
me."

He smiled and said, "Maybe I don't like staying with
you."

"You're just saying that because you think you're a burden. You're not, Dad. I mean that."

He got up from his chair and came over to the couch where she was sitting. "Jodie," he said. "There's no reason why I shouldn't be living on my own. I'm a grown man. I miss being in my own house. I miss just doing things the way I want to do them. And yes, I don't want to be a burden on you. And I know I am so don't say I'm not. You're a wonderful daughter but you're not Mother Teresa. You should have a life of your own. You need to be able to do things without having to worry about coming home to take care of me."

"Do we have to have this conversation?"

"Yes, we do. You've been paying Mrs. Kelly to look after me for God knows how long. I'm sure that costs a lot of money. She's a nice woman, but you shouldn't have to spend all that money. Besides, it's just not necessary anymore. I don't need a baby-sitter."

"She's not a baby-sitter. She does a lot of work around here to help me out. She cleans and cooks and does the wash and a lot of other things. I don't know what I'd do if I didn't have her helping me, whether you're here or not."

"Then keep her if you need her, but don't keep her to look after me. I don't need it. I didn't want to have to tell you this," he said with a chuckle. "But I think she has the hots for me."

"Oh, Dad," she said and hit him on the arm.

Carl became serious again and said, "I really mean it, sweetheart. I want my old life back. I know it won't be the same without your mother, but I want to feel like I'm

useful again. I don't want to feel like a little baby. And
that's how I feel living here."

"I don't think of you that way, Dad."

"That's good. You shouldn't. Because I'm not. I'm a
man. I'm your father. And I have a home in St.
Augustine that I worked very hard to be able to afford.
Now I want to go back there. I want to go home, Jodie.
Please don't ask me not to. Please."

≈ 24

On Saturday, Jodie and Carl drove down to St. Augustine to get the house ready for Carl to move back in.
They took A-1-A instead of the Interstate, driving along
the beach, past the expensive homes in Ponte Vedre.
Jodie had the top down on her Miata, letting in the warm
March sunshine. Carl's hair flew about in the ocean
breeze but he didn't seem to mind at all. His face was
fixed in a satisfied grin. He stared out at the sand dunes
and blue Atlantic beyond, looking like a man just paroled
from prison.

The house Carl had lived in before Helen died, before
he came to stay with Jodie in Jacksonville Beach, was in
an age-restricted development off US-1 called Sunny
Palms. No one under fifty-five was allowed to live there.
That equated to no loud music, no kids playing in the
streets, no one driving through in the middle of the night
waking the neighbors. Grandchildren were permitted for
a week at a time, never longer, no exception, with four
weeks of visits total per year, per house. Also, no dogs

allowed, cats only because they didn't bark; lawns had to be maintained below ankle height; no clotheslines; no boats or motor homes could be parked in the yard. The resident association and the board of enforcement were stricter than most city councils and police departments.

Jodie couldn't imagine ever wanting to live in a place like this. But plenty of people, transplanted northerners mainly, did not share her feelings. When her parents had bought the property six years ago, only a handful of lots had homes on them. Now, identical white stucco cookie-cutter homes occupied nearly every acre of land.

The main road snaked past a thinning stand of pine trees and a murky swamp the association called a pond. Jodie remembered seeing an alligator sunning itself on the bank the first time she came here. How many of the approved cats had been served up as dinner since then?

She steered around an elderly couple driving a golf cart down the road. Many of the driveways had these golf carts. St. Augustine Shores Golf Club was a short distance away and it was one of the main draws for the seniors living here.

In Carl's driveway was the blue Ford Taurus Jodie's mother had bought the year before she died. It hadn't been driven in almost eight months and was covered with a patina of grime. Jodie parked her Miata behind it.

"You think it still runs?" Carl asked, staring at the car.

Jodie shrugged. "The battery's probably dead."

Carl continued staring at it for a moment, then finally got out and stepped cautiously between the cars, toward the side door of the house. Jodie went with him.

The steady sounds of traffic and ocean wind she

always heard at her house were missing here. No barking. No voices. Nothing at all. She found the silence a little unnerving. It felt too much like a cemetery.

She unlocked the side door and walked into the house ahead of her father. With the windows closed and the air conditioner off, the air inside was stuffy and hot. The place had a stale, abandoned odor, like a house vacated hurriedly, left to waste away. But beneath it, Jodie could still smell the faint scent of her mother's presence in the house—the powder she always sprinkled on herself in the morning, the perfume she would dabble behind her ears when she went out.

Carl followed her in, stepping gingerly on the welcome mat just inside the door. The carpet was an impractical shade of pearl. Years of Helen's admonitions about dirty shoes must have come back to Carl because he slowly began wiping his feet as his gaze gradually took in his surroundings.

The oversized sofa with its tropical pink and turquoise print. The collection of photographs on the bookshelf, pictures of Carl in his blue Postal Service uniform, of Helen wearing a flowered apron and holding up a chocolate cake with HAPPY RETIREMENT! on it. The white curtains Helen had made from a pattern she found in *Family Circle*. Jodie remembered driving all over Jacksonville with her, trying to find the perfect fabric.

Carl moved cautiously through the living room, like a visitor through a museum, and stepped into the kitchen, the sound of his shoes on the cobalt blue tile making an uneasy scratch in the silence of the house. He stared at the sliding glass doors that led to the patio out back. The curtains were open, revealing the PVC table where Jodie's parents used to sit each morning and sip coffee and talk. Many evenings they would watch the sunset from that same table, enjoying Helen's favorite, lady finger cookies and a glass of Harvey's Bristol Cream.

Carl turned his head now, studying the rest of the kitchen, as though reacquainting himself with a place out of his distant past. His gaze lingered on the note Helen had stuck to the refrigerator door eight months ago. Jodie stood behind him and read it silently. CALL CABLE TV MONDAY. NO CHANNEL 33. She wondered if her mother had lived long enough to make the call. Probably not, if it was still there. She had become sick on a Saturday and had died the following Friday night. The note, stuck to the refrigerator door by a watermelon-shaped magnet, was a painful reminder of her last week of life.

Carl turned away from the kitchen now and stepped back onto the living room carpet. His eyes drifted up the hall leading to the bedroom. On his face Jodie saw more than just sadness. She saw anguish.

"Dad," she whispered. "Maybe it would be better if . . ."

He silenced her with a look, then slowly walked up the hall toward the bedroom, like a man walking toward the altar in a church. Jodie chose not to follow him. She felt it would be an intrusion. He needed to be alone.

To keep herself from thinking too much, she busied herself by opening the windows to air out the place. There wasn't much breeze here so she turned on the ceiling fans and started the air conditioner. It hadn't been used in eight months and at first blew a foul, chemical odor through the ducts, but then cool air followed. She was relieved that it still worked; one less thing she had to have fixed.

Dust covered all the flat surfaces, reminding Jodie that the house needed a thorough cleaning before Carl moved in. Her mother had mentioned a woman named Andrea who used to come in once a week to clean. In the kitchen near the phone she found a list of numbers her mother had written long ago. Andrea's number was on it so she called while Carl was still in the bedroom and arranged to have the house cleaned on Tuesday. She'd leave the key in the mailbox for Andrea.

In the drawer by the phone she found her mother's checkbook and two credit cards. The balance in the bank account was $2,311. In the months since her mother had died, Jodie hadn't used any of the money. She didn't fully understand why, but she felt uncomfortable spending her parents' savings, even though she realized she would have been spending it on Carl, not on herself.

Now she was glad he had this money to use when he moved back in. She assumed she would still have to pay the bills for him—he hadn't been the type of person who could remember to write checks the first of every month even before his Alzheimer's. She left the checkbook on the counter for him to use at the grocery store or Wal-Mart. She would have to show him later how to write a check and use the VISA card.

All last week, she had observed him closely, watching him shave, watching him in the kitchen, watching him operate the television. And she had noticed he was much better doing these everyday tasks, better than he had been just two months earlier. She was still worried about him living alone, but she had come to accept that he could take care of himself.

Carl tottered back up the hall now. He lowered himself into the easy chair and stared past the television at the window. His cheeks were red, his eyes puffy. Jodie knew he had been crying. She came over and just held his hand for a few moments, neither of them speaking.

The silence was interrupted by a knock at the screen door. Jodie saw Jack Costello, Carl's neighbor across the street, standing outside.

"I saw the car in the driveway," Jack said through the screen. He noticed Carl on the chair. Speaking to Jodie, he whispered, "Is he . . . ?" and made a vague gesture pointing to his head.

"He's doing well," Jodie said. She turned to Carl. "Hey, Dad, look who's here." She motioned to Jack and said, "Come on in."

Jack opened the door slowly, as though uncertain what to do, what to say. Carl saw him and smiled.

"You son of a bitch," Carl said, which instantly put Jack at ease. "You're still ugly as hell."

"Look who's talking, old fart?"

Jack and Carl shook hands and sat and talked about the house, golf, arthritis—two old friends who had worked together in the same post office for twenty years. Jack and his wife had moved down here on the urging of Carl and Helen. The four of them used to play golf together three times a week. They were always having dinner at each other's house. And every summer, they shared the ride up north. Jack's wife had suffered a stroke and died only a few months before Helen.

When Carl told Jack that he was moving back in, Jack was thrilled.

"We can get the old poker game together again," Carl said.

"That might be a problem. Oscar had a heart attack in October and Benny moved back to New Jersey first of the year cuz Louise got homesick for the kids and the grandkids."

Carl scoffed at the thought of moving back there. He said, "We'll find two new pigeons."

"You're on."

Jack had to run, he was on his way to the barber shop. "They can cut all day, you're still going to be ugly," Carl told him.

Jodie and Carl stayed another hour, straightening out a few things, getting the house ready. During the week that followed, Jodie made the rest of the arrangements for Carl to return to the house permanently. She had the cable TV and the telephone service turned back on and arranged for Meals-On-Wheels to deliver dinner to Carl five days a week. She called a pest control company to spray around the house—black, hairy spiders and fat, winged palmetto bugs had taken advantage of the long vacancy and settled in around the windows and under the eaves.

On Friday, after work, Jodie helped Carl pack his clothes, then drove him down to St. Augustine again, this time knowing she would be returning to Jacksonville alone. Carl sighed when he walked in and set his bags down to stay. Jodie saw in his body language how much this meant to him.

They were there only ten minutes when someone knocked at the door.

"Hi, dear," an elderly woman said to Jodie when she opened the door. She had an ink-black dye job, her hair twisted into something resembling Princess Leia's buns in *Star Wars*. Her lipstick was much too heavy and was smeared on her teeth. "I'm Dot Luden," she said. "From down the street. I brought this for your father."

She held out a casserole dish filled with stroganoff.

"That's so nice of you," Jodie said.

When she tried to take the dish, Dot pulled it away and squeezed past her through the door. She brought it to the kitchen herself, then spent a few minutes with Carl to make sure he knew where it came from and which house she lived in. She showed him her house from the living room window.

"See, you can see it from here."

After she left, several other women stopped by with food. They had heard from Jack Costello that Carl was moving back in. Within an hour, the refrigerator was filled with Tupperware and foil-covered dishes. Jack came over after the last widow made her delivery. He inventoried the food and grinned.

"Carl, we're going to make out like bandits around here. I'll bet widows outnumber widowers five to one."

He couldn't stay and eat with them because he had a date with Mary Coughan. She was making her famous meat loaf tonight.

Jodie and Carl tasted a little of everything. Most of it

was good. She felt a little relieved, certain that her father was going to be eating well, probably better than she would.

"It's getting late," Carl said after they ate. "You should be leaving."

"It's not late." Jodie sat in the living room and picked up the *TV Guide*. "Maybe there's something good on," she said.

"It's Friday night. Shouldn't you be on a date or something?"

She laughed. "Sounds like you're trying to get rid of me."

"I am."

"I'll leave in a little while. I just thought we'd watch a little TV. There's a good movie on TNT."

Carl got Jodie's purse from the table and handed it to her, then he walked over to the door and opened it. "Good night, Jodie," he said.

"What's the rush, Dad?"

"Look, I'm going to have to get used to staying alone. And so are you. Now is a good time to start."

He walked over to the chair where she was sitting, took her by the wrist and practically pulled her to the door.

"I can take a hint," she said. "I'm going."

"Thank you."

"If you have any problem, you call me. I put my number on the speed dial on the kitchen phone. Number two. Number one is nine-one-one. If you need the police or an ambulance you push that one. You know how to work it, right?"

"You showed me twice already."

"I just want to make sure."

"You've made sure."

He kissed her on the cheek and gently pushed her out the door.

"Goodnight, sweetheart."

"Goodnight, Dad. I'll call you later."

"Don't call for two days."

"I'll call tonight when I get home."

"Don't call for two days," he said again.

"I'm not waiting two days."

"All right, don't call until tomorrow night."

"I'm calling later tonight."

"Tomorrow night."

"Tonight," she insisted.

"You call tonight and I'm not going to answer the phone."

"If you don't answer the phone then I'm driving right back down here."

"All right, call tomorrow morning, and that's my final offer."

When Jodie got home half an hour later, the phone was ringing and her first thought was that something had happened to Carl. But when she grabbed the phone in the living room and nervously said, "Yes, hello," she was surprised to hear Neil Lancaster's voice on the other end of the line.

"You sound terrible, Jodie," he said. "What's wrong?"

She blew out her anxiety in a long sigh, sank down onto the couch and explained it all to him. They caught up on what each of them had been doing since their time together in Mexico—time that had been so short, Jodie thought now, but time that had stirred feelings she hadn't allowed herself to feel for so long.

It touched her heart when Neil asked how Carl was feeling and how Jodie was holding up under all the stress in her life. He really seemed to care. It was so good to hear his voice, but it reminded her how much she missed him, how much she wished they were together now.

"When are you coming back down here?" Neil asked.

"My dad isn't supposed see Dr. Stirling for nearly three months."

"I like your dad, don't get me wrong, but he's not the one I want to see. I miss you, Jodie."

"I miss you too."

"Then come back."

"I can't get away right now," she said. "I still have to look after Dad and then there's work. Can you come up here? I'd really like to see you."

"I wish I could, but this is the busy season down here. I really can't leave."

Jodie sighed, disappointed. "I guess the phone will have to do for now," she said.

"The phone isn't nearly enough."

"At least we have each other's voice."

"I want all of you, Jodie," Neil said, and the passion in his words and in his tone made her shiver with emotion. She was surprised by how strongly he felt, but even more so by how strongly she suddenly realized she felt.

"Three months," he said with a long breath of resignation. "It's going to be a long spring."

"I'll be thinking about you."

"You're all I'll be thinking about."

They talked for another half hour. After she hung up, Jodie lay on the couch thinking about him as darkness enveloped her house. She wished she could get away so she could see him. Maybe she could manage it in a few weeks, if Carl continued improving the way he was. Work would prevent her from staying long, but she figured she could swing a weekend. And what a weekend it would be . . .

She called her father before she went to bed. He was doing just fine, he said, and told her to stop worrying about him. First thing the next morning, she called him again.

"I died in my sleep," he told her.

"You sound pretty good for a dead man."

"Are you ever going to stop worrying about me?"

"Nope. What are you going to do today? Do you want me to come down there?"

"I want you to go out, have a good time, and leave me alone."

She worried about him all day, even as she took advantage of the free time to do some shopping at Regency Square. In the evening, she filled the tub, added some mint salts she had bought at the mall, and finished the Pat Conroy novel begun months earlier. She called her father before she went to bed and listened to him tell her again to stop worrying about him.

She didn't drive down to St. Augustine to see him until Tuesday morning. She made the trip before work, so she could give him The Cure shot. On Saturday she drove down again to give him another shot. She planned to spend the day with him afterward, but he had other plans.

"I'm going golfing with Jack," he said. "Then we're going to the VFW. They're having a dinner-dance tonight. We're going stag."

"What am I supposed to do?" she said.

"Go home and have some fun."

Unaccustomed to having all this free time, Jodie didn't know what to do. She spent the afternoon at the beach, saw a movie with some girls from work that night, then lounged around all day Sunday, reading the newspaper and unpacking all her china and angel figurines, putting them back out where they belonged.

In the evening, she left the lights off, lit a candle, then sat by the flame, with a Roberta Flack CD on the stereo, and wrote Neil a long letter telling him about her week, about Carl, about how much she missed him. She scented the envelope with a mist of Poême, the same perfume she had worn the night of their date on the beach in Mexico. She hoped he would recognize it. She still remembered the smell of his cologne and the taste of his lips when he kissed her.

Early Wednesday morning, before work, she drove down to St. Augustine to give Carl his injection. He forced her to take some of the "widow food" back with her. Between Meals-On-Wheels and the widow brigade, he had enough food to feed a football team.

His skin had color for the first time in months. The afternoons on the golf course were doing him good. Jodie hated to admit it, but he had adjusted well to living alone. Now if only she could make the adjustment.

Friday night after work she took him out for a shrimp dinner. They ate at a small restaurant in Old St. Augustine, overlooking the San Marcos Fort. Afterward they walked along the cobblestone streets and talked about all that had happened over the last few days. She came back Saturday morning and found Carl leaning over the Taurus with the hood open and a collection of tools on the bumper. The driveway smelled of gasoline.

"What are you doing?" she asked.

"You got jumper cables in that little car of yours?" he said, gesturing with is head. He had a screwdriver in his hands and was adjusting something in the motor.

"Why do you want jumper cables?"

"Battery's dead."

"You want to start it?" she asked.

"Can't drive it unless I start it, right?"

"You can't drive, Dad."

"Of course I can drive. I was driving before you were born. I'm a good driver."

"But Dad, you haven't driven a car in more than three years."

"Then it's about time I started up again."

"But Dad—"

"It's like riding a bike. You never forget."

"I don't know about this . . ."

"I do. I need to drive to get to Publix, to Wal-Mart, to the golf course, anywhere I want to go. A man's gotta drive, Jodie."

She argued for a few minutes but he won. He said if she didn't have cables, he'd get them from Jack later. Jodie relented and helped him jump-start the Taurus. He wanted to drive off right away, but she insisted on putting him through a test-run first. She drove him to St. Joseph's High School. Since it was Sunday, school was closed and the parking lot was empty except for the line of yellow school buses parked in one corner. Jodie drove to the opposite side of the lot and put the car in Park.

"You remember how to stop the car, right?" she asked.

"Sure. I stomp real hard on the gas pedal."

"No. The brake, not the gas pedal. The brake is this one here," she said, stepping on it several times to show him.

"Are you sure?"

"Yes, Dad. The brake stops the car. The gas pedal makes it go faster."

"Then how do you make it turn?"

"The steering wheel. This," she said, showing him.

He shook his head and scratched his chin, looking bewildered. "That's not how I remember it. I thought the radio steers it, and the air conditioner makes it go faster."

"No. Listen to—"

He started chuckling, and she finally realized that he was teasing her. "I know how to drive," he said. "I'm the one who taught you. Remember?"

"I just wanted to make sure you didn't forget."

"I didn't forget."

They switched seats. Carl pulled away slowly and circled the parking lot three times, then he steered the car toward the street. Jodie was holding the arm rest on the door so tightly that her fingers went numb.

"Careful now, careful," she said.

He winked at her.

He pulled out into traffic and headed up the street. He drove slowly, overly so, which she appreciated, but it annoyed the drivers behind them. Carl didn't seem to care about them. His face glowed with excitement. He looked like a child riding his bike for the first time.

He drove all around St. Augustine, then headed back to Sunny Palms. Jodie heated some macaroni casserole she found in the refrigerator and they ate outside on the patio. Carl asked her if she had a date for tonight.

"Not tonight, no."

"You're never going to find a husband if you don't start dating."

"I really have to get you a calendar so you'll know what year it is. The eighteen hundreds are long gone, Dad. A woman doesn't *have* to get married."

"Don't you want to?"

"If I meet the right man."

"Well, you're not going to meet the right man unless you start dating on Saturday nights. You're certainly not going to meet any men hanging around me."

"I don't know about that. That's how I met Neil."

The name didn't mean anything to him.

"Neil Lancaster," Jodie said. "In Mexico. Remember, he took us to that Mayan ruin last time we were down there."

"Chicken pizza, yeah, I remember."

Jodie laughed. "It's Chichén Itzá, Dad."

"Neil, yeah, right, I remember him. The guy with the long hair. Lancaster is his name, huh? Any relation to the actor?"

"I don't think so."

Carl shrugged, a little disappointed. "He's too far away. You need someone here in Florida."

"They invented telephones and airplanes, Dad."

"Listen to your old man once in a while. Go out and get back in circulation—with someone in Florida."

"I can't believe we're having this conversation."

"Believe it."

"I'm leaving. I'll see you tomorrow morning, early."

"What for?"

"To give you your shot."

"I want you to show me how to do it myself," he said. "I can't have you driving down here twice a week for this."

"I don't mind."

"I mind. I'm a grown man. I can give myself a shot, for God's sake."

Jodie tried to convince him to let her continue doing it but he insisted she teach him. The next morning, when they sat at the kitchen table and he held the syringe in his right hand and brought it up to his left arm, Jodie was surprised how steady his grip was. He trembled less than she had the first time she gave him the injection.

He jabbed the needle into his arm, wincing only slightly. Then he depressed the plunger and pumped the The Cure solution into his arm. When he pulled the needle out, he said, "Is that all there is to it? I could have been doing this a long time ago."

"You're just determined to make me obsolete, aren't you?" Jodie said.

Carl smiled. "Absolutely."

He had eight more syringes of The Cure left in the kit Darlene had given them.

"I'm going to make reservations to go to Cancun in a month," Jodie said. "And don't tell me that you can go alone because I'm going with you."

"I *can* go alone," he said. "But I know you want to see that Lancaster guy again."

"I think I liked you better before, when you didn't know every little thing that was going on," she said.

Carl laughed, looking proud of himself.

As Jodie was getting ready to leave, he came over and said, "That medicine you've been getting for me . . . that has to be expensive, huh?"

"Don't worry about that, Dad."

"I'm not worried about it. I'm just asking. It is my medicine. I'd like to know what you've been paying for it."

"I can take care of it. That's not a problem."

"I'd still like to know how much it costs."

"Dad, will you let me worry about that?"

"Why won't you tell me?"

"You have enough to worry about. You don't need to concern yourself with that."

He chuckled. "I don't have anything else to worry about. You're the one with the job, the mortgage, the car payments. What do I have to worry about?"

She kissed him on the cheek and said, "Staying healthy. That's enough for anyone to worry about." She headed for the door. "I'll call you during the week," she said.

"Jodie, I want to know."

"Good-bye, Dad."

"Jodie," he said, his tone harsh, insisting.

She stopped at the door and turned toward him. "Come on, Dad, let's not get into this right now. We'll talk about it another time."

"Why won't you tell me? It's a lot of money, isn't it?"

"No, it's not a lot of money."

"Then tell me how much it is."

"All right. Do you want to know. It's hardly anything. It's only—"

"And tell me the truth," he said as though he had read her thoughts.

She didn't say what she was going to say, realizing that he would know she was lying. She walked back into the living room and sat at the edge of the couch. She took a deep breath.

"It costs seven hundred and fifty dollars for each shot," she said.

Carl tried not to show any reaction but Jodie saw the shock in his eyes. He nodded then said, "Okay. Thank you for telling me."

"I know it sounds like a lot of money, but—"

"It *is* a lot of money."

"But it's definitely worth it to me to have you the way you are now."

"How long do I have to take the medicine?" he asked.

"They're not really sure, because it's a new treatment."

"They must have told you something."

Peering at him across the living room, Jodie could not lie. She sighed and said quietly, "It'll be for a long time, Dad."

"Months? Years?"

Jodie nodded. "Years. A long time."

Carl was silent for a few moments, contemplating what Jodie had just told him. Finally he said, "I figured it was going to be expensive."

"It's worth the money, Dad, believe me."

"I've been doing a lot of thinking lately."

"Dad, really, you shouldn't worry about this. Let me worry about it. Okay?"

"I'm not worrying about it. I've just been considering our options. It would be foolish not to do that. First of all, you shouldn't have to pay for my medicine."

"Dad, please, I want to—"

"Please," he said, "let me finish. It's not right for you to pay. Even if you want to pay, even if you could afford it—and I don't see how you can afford it—"

"Let me worry about that, Dad."

"Even if you could afford it," he said, "and even if you wanted to pay for it, it's still not right. Your mother and I must have some money put away, right?"

"You have a couple thousand dollars, but—"

"Do I still have those stocks? The ones from a long time ago."

"Yes, but—"

"And I think your mother used to pay for a life insurance policy on me. That's not doing any good right now. I want to cash that in. And sell the stocks too."

"I don't want you to start cashing in everything you own. Besides, it won't come to much. It'll pay for a month or two and that's about it. Why don't we just leave all that alone for now."

"I was talking to Jack," he said.

"Jack Costello across the street?"

"Yes."

"About this?"

"More or less. About going up north for the summer."

"That's a long way off. Let's not talk about that right now."

"Jack said I could stay with him."

"Dad, why don't we wait and—"

"The point is, I don't need the house up there anymore," he said. "That has to be worth quite a bit, right?"

"I'm sure it is, but—"

"Do you think you'll ever move back to Connecticut?"

"What?" The question surprised her.

"If you think you will, I won't sell it. You should be allowed to have it if you want to move back. Your mother always said that."

"Dad, I don't want to talk about selling the house."

"Do you think you'll move back there?"

"No, but I don't want you to sell it. I can pay for—"

"How?"

"I'll worry about that. You just concentrate on getting better."

"I am better and I'm going to pay for the shots and that's all there is to it. I'm going to sell the house. I'm just sorry that there probably won't be anything left to give you when I die."

"Dad, please! I don't want you to leave me anything. God! I really don't like talking about this."

"It has to be talked about. I'm going to pay for my own

medicine from now on. And I'm going to write you a check for what you've already paid out."

"I don't want a check."

"I'm going to give it to you anyway."

"I'm not going to cash it."

"Listen to me. I want to pay for my own medicine. When I run out of money, then you can pay, but for right now there's no reason why I shouldn't pay for it."

"Dad—"

"Please don't argue with me about this," he said. "This is the way I want it to be. I don't want you to have to take care of me. I want to feel like a whole person again. Please don't take that away from me."

"Are you sure you want to do this?"

He came over and put his arms around her. "As sure as I've ever been about anything."

"Do what you think is best," she said.

"Thank you."

"It's good to have you back, Dad."

He chuckled. "What are you talking about? I haven't been away."

"Yes, you have." Jodie hugged him, kissed his cheek and whispered, "But now you're back and I'm not going to let you leave again."

25

On Wednesday morning, Jodie and Mike Bono went along with a special police task force working to stop gang violence on the north side of Jacksonville. Marvin Acker had said he wanted footage of the police interacting with "suspicious youths." The sergeant in charge of the task force, trying to accommodate them, stopped and questioned two black teenagers standing on a corner. When he discovered that one of the boys was carrying three crack cocaine rocks, it turned into an arrest.

Jodie felt a little uneasy that the boy was being arrested only because a TV station needed footage. She tempered her guilt somewhat by telling herself he was a drug dealer and the arrest was a good thing.

As the police cuffed the teenager and placed him into the back seat of a squad car, Mike followed it all closely with his camera.

"Got some great footage," he told Jodie.

The police agreed to let her interview the boy if he consented. He said, "Yeah, sure I'll be on TV," so they did the interview with him in the squad car. Jodie stuck the microphone through the window. Mike shot over her shoulder.

"How do you feel about the increased police presence in this area?" she asked him.

"Bullshit, man. Homies out cappin this dude, that dude, and five-ohs burnin my ass for nuthin? You know what I'm sayin? Bullshit, man. That's all it is. Bullshit."

"How do you think it will affect your business?"

"What bidness you talkin bout?"

"The drug business."

"Hell you talkin bout! Get that damn camera out my grill. I ain't talkin no more."

They shot a standup with Jodie at the corner, explaining the new police presence, then Mike rode back to the police station in one of the squad cars to get footage of the teenager being processed into jail. Jodie returned to Channel 10 to time-code the video and start writing the story.

The editing bay was a cramped room the size of a small closet, with a sliding glass door, an uncomfortable chair, and a narrow shelf for scribbling notes. Jodie sat in front of the TV monitor and the computer that electronically encoded the raw video tape and spent half an hour breaking the footage down into increments of 100ths of a second, selecting portions as she went along to use for the two-minute package that would air on tonight's news. She also made notes to help her later, when she would write the script for the voice-over track.

She was almost finished reviewing the last part of the video when the assignment editor tapped on the glass door, slid it open and poked her head in.

"Jodie, you have a phone call."

"I'm kind of busy. Do you know who it is?"

"He said his name is Dr. Harrington. Want me to take a message?"

"No, I better take it." Harrington would only be calling about Carl, she knew. "What line is it?" She picked up the extension in the editing bay and punched the button. "Hello, Dr. Harrington."

"Miss Simms, I have the results from the lab, the analysis we did on that medicine your father is taking."

"Oh, good. What did you find out?"

Harrington hesitated. "You did say that the medicine is a solution derived from porcine donors, didn't you? From pigs?"

"Yes, that's what the doctor in Mexico told us."

"Hmm. That's odd."

"What do you mean? What did you find?"

"That's a little difficult to say, exactly. Let me try to explain. The lab ran several different tests on the sample you gave us, and from those tests they were able to catalog some of the components in the shots your father is taking. The majority of the solution, more than ninety percent—" Jodie heard Harrington shuffling paper. "To be more precise," he said, "ninety-four point one percent of the solution is bacteriostatic water."

"I recall Dr. Stirling did mention that word bacteriostatic. What is that?"

"Bacteriostatic water is a common base for injections. There isn't anything unusual about that. But it certainly isn't the component that's having the effect on your father."

"What is helping him then?"

"Well, the lab identified traces of nonspecific endocrine tissue, an extremely small quantity of prostaglandins and several different types of polypeptides."

"Doctor, I don't know what any of that means."

"Yes, I'm throwing quite a few medical terms at you, aren't I? The important thing to know is that I don't think any of those things are what has been helping your father."

"Then what has? Something definitely has." She was becoming impatient for answers. "Do you know what's responsible for his improvement?" she asked.

"The lab found something else that might provide a

clue," he said. Then he added, "That is, if we knew what it was."

"What are you talking about?"

"Well, a small quantity of the solution, approximately eight tenths of one percent, appears to be a protein that resembles BDNF. It has a different molecular weight than BDNF. The lab couldn't determine if it was a mutated form of BDNF or some other protein that was antigenically similar. Whichever the case, I would guess that this protein may be what has been helping your father, since the rest of the solution is more or less innocuous. But that's just a guess. We can't be certain."

"I don't understand what all this means. Is this protein something that's harmful?"

"We don't know enough from the tests to determine if it's harmful for him to keep taking," he admitted. "If it is in fact BDNF, then it probably isn't harmful, but by the same token if it is BDNF, I'm not sure that's what's helping him. It might be. But we just don't know."

"So what you're saying is we're still right where we started from?" Jodie said.

"No, not exactly."

"You just said you don't know what it is that's making Dad better, you don't know if it's safe, you don't know anything new."

"There is one thing . . ." he said.

"What?"

"I can tell you that the shots your father is taking do not come from porcine tissue."

"Wait a minute. What do you mean?"

"They're not derived from pigs," Harrington said.

"You must be mistaken, doctor."

"That is the one thing we are sure about. The neuroglial cells the lab isolated were definitely not porcine."

"Then what were they?"

"The best we can determine from the sample you gave us," he said, "is that they are human."

Jodie was too stunned to speak. In her mind, she kept hearing that word, over and over. *Human. Human. Human.*

The editing bay seemed to shrink around her. The sounds of a dozen people working to put together today's newscast buzzed in her brain, adding to her confusion: phones ringing, voices speaking words she could not understand, the steady chatter of several television sets scattered throughout the room playing the last half hour of some afternoon talk show.

"I don't understand how that can be," she said to Harrington.

"Are you certain the doctor in Mexico told you that the shots your father is taking are derived from porcine tissue? Could he have said something else? Could you have misunderstood him?"

"No, that's what he told me. I'm sure of it. There has to be a mistake."

"There's no mistake on this end, I assure you."

Jodie wasn't sure what to believe. Her thoughts were racing at a hundred miles an hour, trying to make sense of this.

"What is that protein you said you found?" she asked.

"The one you said might be helping my father? BD-something?"

"BDNF. What I said was the protein we found appears to be antigenically similar to BDNF, but that it has a different molecular weight. It might be a mutated form of BDNF or it might be something altogether different. There was an antigenic response to BDNF antibodies, but it was not altogether conclusive. We just don't know exactly what it is, and we don't know if that's what is helping your father."

Groping for information, wanting desperately to understand, Jodie asked, "Well, what is BDNF?"

"It's called a nerve growth factor. It's a protein produced naturally in the brain, secreted by different areas, such as the hippocampus, the cerebellum, the cortex and so forth."

The more he told her, the more confused Jodie was becoming. But one thing stood out. His mention of the cortex. For some reason, that struck a familiar chord with her, though she couldn't remember why. Had Dr. Stirling mentioned anything about the cortex? Possibly, but she couldn't remember for sure. She definitely remembered hearing someone talk about it recently, and she was fairly certain it had some connection to Mexico.

"Miss Simms," Harrington said. "You really should find out exactly what it is your father is taking. I don't feel comfortable having him injecting himself with this, not until we fully understand exactly what it is and whether or not it is safe for him to be taking. I'm quite concerned."

"But it seems to be helping him," Jodie said, surrendering for a moment her need to understand what it was, concentrating on the irrefutable results. "You said so yourself, he was better."

"Yes, I know. That's what is so puzzling. I think it would be a good idea if I examined him again, maybe brought in a few other specialists. There's a doctor in Rochester who might be able to come down here. And I think it would be prudent to have the lab do further analyses on that solution your father is taking."

"I agree," Jodie said. "I'll talk to him tonight. I don't think this is something I should tell him over the phone. We'll come in next Monday if you can fit us in."

"I'll absolutely make sure we can fit you in."

≋ 26

Jodie found it difficult to concentrate on her work for the rest of the afternoon. And it showed in the way she wrote the gang story. She didn't like the way it turned out, knew it needed to be rewritten, but she gave it to Mike to edit anyway, then went into the sound booth and recorded the voice-over track. She didn't stay to see the package air on the five P.M. newscast. Instead she drove down to St. Augustine, to her father's house.

She found him sitting in the easy chair in the living room, a bottle of Budweiser on the table beside him. He had on Channel 10 and looked surprised to see Jodie here.

"I still can't get used to you being on TV and here at

the same time," he said, shaking his head. He took a sip of beer and said, "I just saw your thing about the gangs."

"It was pretty bad," she said.

"I thought it was good. How did you happen to be there when they arrested that kid?"

"It's called a made-for-TV arrest."

He didn't understand. She told him it wasn't important. He waved to the kitchen and told her to help herself to a beer. She sat on the sofa and for several seconds just stared at him, saying nothing. She didn't know what to tell him.

When a commercial came on, Carl muted the TV and looked at her.

"Still worried about your old man, eh?" he said. "I'm doing just fine. You don't have to worry about me anymore. And you don't have to keep driving all the way down here every other day."

"I don't come down that often."

"Sure seems like it," he said with a snicker and sip of beer.

She took a deep breath and finally came out with it.

"Dad," she said. "I'm concerned about the shots you're taking."

"You don't think I can give myself the shots? Hell, I showed you last Sunday I could do it."

"I know. That's not what I mean."

"Then what do you mean?"

She hesitated, searching for the right words. "The shots," she said, still struggling. "They might not be . . . not what we think they are."

"What are you talking about?"

"I don't . . . we can't be sure . . . if they're good for you or not."

He laughed. "Of course they're good for me. Doesn't take a genius to see that."

"I, um . . . I talked to Dr. Harrington this afternoon."

"Harrington? What does he have to do with anything?"

"I had him run some tests on one of the syringes of The Cure."

Carl's eyes spread open wide in shock. His face became sanguine. "You gave him a dose of my medicine?" he said, angry. "You know how much that stuff costs. Are you crazy?"

"I wanted to make sure it was safe."

"That's seven hundred and fifty bucks down the drain!" Carl said. "That's a hell of a lot of money. Not to mention what you paid for the tests. Jesus Christ, Jodie . . ."

"I wanted to make sure it was safe," she said again.

Carl coughed out a disdainful laugh. "And I suppose Harrington says it's not safe."

"He's not sure."

"Oh, *he's* not sure? Harrington's not sure?" Carl sat forward in his chair. "What the hell does Harrington know about this stuff anyway? We went to him before and he couldn't do a damn thing for me. Remember? Now I'm supposed to believe him about this? Like hell . . ."

"Dad, Dr. Harrington is a good doctor."

"He's a quack."

"He's not a quack. He's one of the best doctors in Jacksonville and I want you to go see him on Monday."

Carl pursed his lips and blew out a loud breath. He flopped back down in his chair and grabbed the beer. "In a pig's eye I'm going to go see him," he said. "Not on Monday or any other day."

"Dad, I want him to examine you again. And he needs another dose of The Cure so he can run more tests."

"Forget it."

"It's important that—"

"I said forget it."

"He's concerned that you—"

"I don't care if *he's* concerned. I don't need to be examined by Harrington. And I damn sure am not going to give him another dose of my medicine for his ridiculous tests."

"Dr. Harrington said the medicine he tested isn't what Dr. Stirling told us it is."

"I told you, Harrington doesn't know what he's talking about."

"Dad, he tested it. He has the results."

"Then the results are wrong."

"How can you say the results are wrong when you don't even know what they are?"

"I don't care what they are. I feel good and that's all that matters."

"Don't you want to know what it is you're taking?"

"Hell, I've been taking aspirin for sixty years and I still don't know what that is. The answer is no. Whatever the medicine is, it works. That's all I need to know. Besides, at seven-fifty a pop, there's no way in hell I'm going to fork over another dose to Harrington or anyone else." He sat forward again and glared at her. "And I'm still upset that you gave him one dose," he said. "Don't ever do that again."

"I'll pay for it myself," Jodie said.

"When did you hit the lottery?"

"It's worth the money to me to be certain that it's safe for you to be taking it."

"It's safe. The answer is no and it'll always be no. Now stop asking."

"Dr. Harrington's concerned about you."

"I don't need another mother."

"I'm concerned, too."

"Now I've got two extra mothers. I wish people would just leave me alone."

Carl picked up the remote control and turned the volume up so Jodie couldn't talk anymore. She walked over to the TV and slapped the power button, turning it off.

"Hey! What are you doing?"

"Dad, you're not being reasonable. Dr. Harrington just wants to make sure everything is okay."

"Everything *is* okay."

"Dr. Harrington said—"

Carl scoffed. "Harrington said this, Harrington said that. Harrington just wants to drive up a big bill so he can afford that house of his in Ponte Vedra."

"Come on, Dad, you know that's not it."

"I don't need Harrington's examinations. And I don't need my medicine tested. I don't want to talk about it anymore."

"Dad—"

"I said I don't want to talk about it anymore, and that's final."

"Will you do me one favor then?"

"I'm not going to see Harrington."

"This is something different. Will you wait before taking any more shots?"

"*What?*"

"Give me a chance to look into it. Just a few days."

"I'm supposed to take a shot tomorrow."

"Please, Dad. Hold off for a few days. Just until I can make sure that everything's all right."

"Everything is all right."

"Maybe they gave us the wrong medicine last time. That's possible. Maybe they gave us someone else's medicine. Or maybe it got contaminated. Things aren't the cleanest down there, you know that. You remember the water situation, right? Something like that could have happened very easily. If the medicine got contaminated or mixed up with something else by mistake, it could make you worse. You don't want to get worse, do you?"

Carl thought about what she was saying now. Jodie could see that he wasn't dismissing it as easily as he did before. She realized he was very much afraid of getting worse, of going back to the way he was before, more afraid of that than of the medicine harming him in some other way.

"Let me make sure it's the right medicine," she said. "Just give me a few days. I'm sure you can miss the shots for a few days without it making a difference."

He looked at her much the way he used to, before The Cure, looked at her with eyes confused and afraid. "Just a few days," he said. "You make sure that's all it is."

☰ 27

When Jodie got home, she phoned Sara Cassidy in Orlando and told her what Dr. Harrington had said.

"How can that be?" Sara said. "No, it has to be a mistake."

"He was certain about the test results," Jodie said.

"I once went to a doctor who was certain that I was pregnant, but you don't see any babies running around in my apartment, do you? Doctors make mistakes all the time."

"What if it wasn't a mistake? Did you have The Cure tested when you did your article on it?"

"Well, no, I didn't actually have it *tested*, not if by that you mean analyzed in the sense that you had it analyzed."

"Yes, that's exactly what I mean," Jodie said, snapping at Sara. "How else is there?"

"The more important way to is to go by the effectiveness of it. That's the real test. How is your father doing?" she asked.

"That's just it. He's doing unbelievably well."

"Well . . . ?" Sara said, almost as though that settled it. But for Jodie, "well" didn't settle it.

"Sara, I'm still concerned," she said in a frightened whisper.

"I understand, but—"

"Did Libby Harden in Daytona Beach ever say anything to you about The Cure not being what Dr. Stirling told her it was?"

"No. In fact I talked to her and her husband three weeks ago. For my book. Remember I told you a publisher was interested? I'm writing that now. Oh, by the way, I wanted to come up there and interview you and your dad for the book."

"I'm not interested in the book right now, Sara," Jodie said, snapping at her again.

"Jodie, listen to me. Libby Harden is doing just fine. It's like she never had Alzheimer's. And she hasn't had any problems. She's healthier than I am. She and her husband are really happy with the medicine. And so is their doctor. I'm sure your guy up there made a mistake."

"I'm worried, Sara. I don't know what to do."

"Look, I'll tell you what. Let me see what I can find out. Tomorrow I'll make some calls, ask around, maybe I can find out something that'll shed some light on all this."

"I appreciate it. I really do."

"Don't worry too much. Okay? Like I said, Libby Harden is fine and your father's doing well. I'm sure everything is all right. I'll call you tomorrow. Try to get some sleep."

"Not much of a chance of that."

"Take something then. It won't do you any good to stay up all night worrying."

But that's exactly what Jodie did. She was too troubled to sleep. She lay in bed for hours, thinking, worrying, trying to make sense of what she knew. She thought about calling Neil, talking to him about it. Even if he couldn't help, at least hearing his voice would fortify her. But she realized it was too late at night to call. He was probably already asleep.

Then, in the dark hours of early morning, she finally remembered where she had heard mention of the cortex of the brain.

It had been during the second trip to Mexico. She had been sitting on the beach watching Carl swim in the surf. Sam Rogoff, the epidemiologist from the World Health Organization, had come over to her chaise lounge and tried to hit on her. In an attempt to impress her, he had told her all about his work. One of the things he had mentioned was the inordinate number of people with epilepsy and how abnormalities in their cortices might be responsible.

A few hours ago, Harrington had told her that The Cure contained a protein similar to one secreted by the cortex. Was it possible that these two things were connected? *No, how can they be?* That didn't make any sense at all.

But as the hours wore on and she remained awake, rehashing this whole thing over and over in her mind, she could not stop wondering if a connection might actually exist.

The next morning, before she and Mike Bono left the TV station to cover a burglary investigation at Orange Park High School, she phoned the World Health Organization's office in New York. It took fifteen minutes for her to find the right department.

"I'd like to speak with Dr. Sam Rogoff," she told the woman who answered the phone.

The woman on the other end said nothing. Jodie wondered if she had been cut off.

"Hello?"

"Who is calling?" the woman asked.

"My name is Jodie Simms. Dr. Rogoff and I met in Mexico a few weeks ago."

"In Mexico?"

"Yes."

The woman was silent again.

"Hello?" Jodie said. "Are you there?"

"Yes, I'm here."

"Would you tell him it's very important that I speak with him."

The woman hesitated again then said, "One moment please." She put Jodie on hold.

Jodie remembered Rogoff had told her he was concerned with a specific clinic in Cancun. She hadn't thought much about it at the time, hadn't considered asking him the name of it, but now it suddenly seemed important, as did the doctor he had mentioned.

Cassandros. She remembered him telling her that name. She had dismissed it at the time, but now she questioned who this doctor was. *Cassandros.* The same name the Mayan woman had screamed in Dr. Stirling's office two months ago, when Jodie and Carl first went there. Jodie couldn't help but wonder if somehow Cassandros, the clinic Rogoff was investigating, and The Cure were all somehow connected.

A man came on the line now. "Hello, can I help you?" He spoke with a slight British accent. It wasn't Rogoff.

"I'm trying to reach Dr. Sam Rogoff," she said.

"My name is Arthur Maxwell. I'm the assistant director of the Latin American department. I understand you know Sam from Mexico."

"Yes. We met in Cancun a few weeks ago. I need to speak with him about something we discussed down there."

"I see. And you're with? . . ."

"I'm not *with* anyone. I'm just a friend," she said, stretching the truth a bit. "I have to talk to him about something—it's very important."

Mike Bono poked his head over the wall of her cubicle and whispered, "Got to get going."

She held up her hand to silence him, then gestured that she needed a minute. He pointed to his watch, shrugged impatiently and wandered away.

Jodie turned her attention back to the man on the phone, Arthur Maxwell.

"If Dr. Rogoff isn't there right now," Jodie said, "I'd like to leave a message to have him call me as soon as he gets in. As I said, this is very important."

Maxwell hesitated. "Um . . . Miss Simms," he said. "I'm sorry to be the one to tell you this, but Sam . . . passed on three weeks ago."

Jodie was shocked. "He's . . . dead?"

"I'm afraid so."

"What happened?"

"He suffered a heart attack while in Mexico. They found him in his hotel room. They think it happened while he was asleep. They say he probably didn't suffer. He was alone," he said, as though he assumed Jodie were Rogoff's lover and it would make her feel better to hear that he was not with another woman.

Jodie was silent for a long moment, so much going through her head she couldn't make sense of it all. Human brain tissue in The Cure. The question of who Dr. Cassandros was and how he was connected to Dr. Stirling. Dr. Harrington claiming that the solution didn't come from pigs—which meant Dr. Stirling had lied. The connection, if any, with the cortex. Rogoff, the man who might be able to help her to understand it all, was dead. He had died in Mexico. Only days after he and Jodie had spoken.

"Miss Simms," Maxwell said. "Are you going to be all right?"

"Yes."

"If there's anything I can do? . . ."

"No. Thank you for telling me." Then she had a thought. "Wait, maybe there is something," she said.

"Yes?"

"Sam told me he was investigating some medical problems down there and a certain doctor he had heard reports about. My father may have a connection. Is there some way I can find out what Sam learned about the place and the doctor he was checking up on?"

"I'm surprised he discussed that with you. All of our investigations are confidential until they've been completed and released publicly. The case that Sam was working on is no exception."

"Please. This is very *very* important."

"Even if I could give out information about it, I don't have any to give. Sam didn't file his report before his death so I don't know what he learned."

"You must have his notes."

"No."

"Wouldn't he have taken notes?"

"Probably. He had one of our computers with him, one of those small notebook computers. But it was blank."

"He didn't type any notes in it, none at all?"

"It was blank. The hard drive was empty. No notes, no programs, no Windows, nothing. It must have crashed or whatever they call it. Maybe it was erased when he went through the airport metal detector."

"Did he have any written notes?" Jodie asked.

"If he did, we don't have them either. I spoke with his sister. The Mexican authorities sent everything he had with him to her. She said there weren't any notes or anything pertaining to work. Just personal items."

"Is that his sister in Gainesville?"

"Yes. The college professor. Do you know her?"

"Sam mentioned her, yes. Would you happen to have her phone number," Jodie asked.

28

Mike signaled her from the other side of the newsroom, pointing impatiently to the clock, eager to leave. She held up one finger, needing another minute to make one more call. As she dialed the number Arthur Maxwell gave her, she saw Marvin Acker poke his head out of his office and say something to Mike. Then Marvin peered at Jodie. She had to make this quick.

On the phone, she heard the recorded message of an answering machine. Kate Rogoff wasn't home. She left a message, not saying what she was calling about, just saying that it was Jodie Simms with Channel 10 in Jacksonville and could Ms. Rogoff please call as soon as possible. Then she hurried out with Mike to shoot the Orange Park story.

When she got back shortly after lunch, the assignment editor stopped her on the way to the editing bay. She had a message that Sara Cassidy had phoned. Kate Rogoff hadn't called yet. Jodie left Mike to time-code the video and went to her cubicle to call Sara.

"Did you find out anything?"

"Yes and no," Sara said. "I called the World Health Organization in New York."

"So did I. How did you know about Rogoff?"

"Who's Rogoff? I called them about Dr. Stirling."

"Rogoff is a WHO epidemiologist I met in Mexico. Why would you call them about Dr. Stirling?" Jodie asked.

"Remember when I first told you about his clinic? I mentioned that he was involved in a program they called the Hale Project. I'm sure I told you. When I told you about his background. Remember?"

Jodie vaguely remembered Sara telling her something like that, but she had completely forgotten, dismissing it as having no bearing on what Stirling was doing now, on the cure for Alzheimer's he had developed. Suddenly it seemed important, something else connecting him to Rogoff.

"Yes, you told me," Jodie said. "What about it?"

"Well, I called them to try to find out a little more about Stirling for you, to see if they knew anything about the Alzheimer's treatment he offered."

"Did they?"

"They didn't know anything about the Alzheimer's treatment, no. But they did give me the name of a neurologist who worked with him at the National Institutes of Health. I called him and he told me some interesting things about Stirling."

"What did he tell you?"

"Well, first of all, he told me why Stirling left the NIH. Too much red tape, he said. He said Stirling complained that it took too long for him to get his projects into clinical trials. There's a whole long drawn out procedure they have to go through, first doing *in vitro* tests, then animal tests, all the way down the line before finally testing it on sick patients. Stirling objected to going through all that. He complained about it constantly. At least that's what this other neurologist said. But that could just be sour grapes," Sara said.

"What do you mean?"

"Well, the way it works in this kind of research environment is that each researcher is more or less in competition with all the others. And since Stirling was the top guy in the field, everyone else saw him as their main competition. He was more or less a target. That's what this doctor told me, for what it's worth. But he also said something else, something about when Stirling was down in Central America."

"What did he say?"

"Do you remember I told you about the Hale Project that Stirling was involved in? He joined the World Health Organization and went down to Central America to help bring specialized medicine to the people down there."

"I remember. That was a long time ago, right?"

"Right."

"What about it?"

"Well, do you know why his involvement ended?"

"I assumed the project was completed."

"It did end a few years ago, but Stirling didn't last to the end. The WHO discharged him early on. And do you know why?"

"Why?"

"This comes from the neurologist at the NIH, not from the World Health Organization. When I asked them about it, they wouldn't tell me much. They said it's their policy not to discuss the tenure of the doctors involved in various projects."

"What did the NIH doctor tell you?"

"Keep in mind that I don't know how accurate this is. Remember, I told you there's competition between—"

"Sara, for God's sake, just tell me what he said."

Sara took a breath and said, "Okay. He said Stirling was cut loose because of an incident in Guatemala."

"What incident? What happened?"

"No one knows exactly. At least no one who's willing to talk about it. But apparently there were some serious questions about what he was doing."

"I don't understand. What was he doing?"

"That part's a little vague, but it's something involving irregularities at a clinic for poor people down there. I don't know much at all about it . . . but, um . . ."

Sara hesitated.

"But what?"

"Jodie," Sara said, lowering her voice and sounding troubled. "It involves people dying."

Sara's words made Jodie shudder.

"What do you mean?" Jodie asked.

"I wish I could tell you more, but that's all I've been able to find out so far. Just that some people died and Stirling was blamed."

"Were they patients of his?"

"I don't know. But the WHO pulled him out of there right away. They were afraid that the local people might do something to him."

"This isn't making any sense, Sara."

"I know, but that's what the NIH doctor told me. He said it was a real tense situation for a while down there."

"Did Stirling do something that caused the people to die?"

"I guess that's what the people down there thought."

"Did the NIH doctor mention The Cure?"

"No, this happened long before Stirling developed that, I think. I'm still trying to find out more for you, but right now that's all I have. Give me some more time, okay?"

"As soon as you know anything, let me know."

"Absolutely. And Jodie . . . I, um . . . I wanted to tell you, I, um . . . I'm sorry. I should have found out about this before I came to you with it. I was so impressed by Libby Harden . . . and then when the book people in New York became interested . . ." Sara's voice trailed off, sounding as though it was squelched out by the weight of her guilt.

"I guess I got swept up in it . . ." she said. "I should have dug deeper."

"It happens . . ." Jodie said quietly, but she never would have thought it would happen to Sara Cassidy. And she never would have thought it would happen to herself, either. How easily smart people could be blinded, she thought, by the promise of a book deal.

Or a cure for a dying father.

≋ 29

Jodie found it difficult to edit the Orange Park story, distracted by what Sara had told her. She sat in the cramped editing bay, running the video of the high school principal explaining what had happened, but her thoughts kept returning to Stirling, to the mystery that had taken place in Guatemala, to the shots her father was taking.

It took all afternoon for her to put the package

together. She barely recorded the voice-over track in time. The five o'clock news had already started by the time she handed the tape to the engineer. Marvin Acker was standing outside his office, watching anxiously.

"Made it," she said timidly as she walked past him.

He just glared at her, not at all pleased with her performance.

Instead of watching the broadcast with the other reporters, Jodie returned to her cubicle and called Sam Rogoff's sister in Gainesville again, desperate now to talk to her. A woman answered the phone.

"Kate Rogoff?" she asked.

"No. Kate's in class. Who's this?"

"My name is Jodie Simms."

"From Channel 10? I know who you are! I watch that news a lot. I got your message on the machine earlier. I'm Tiffany. I live here with Kate."

She had a soft, young voice, youthful exuberance in her words. Probably a student. Jodie wondered how old Rogoff's sister was.

"Yeah," Tiffany said, "Kate'll be in class till six. She has office hours for her students after that so she won't be back until after eight tonight. When she gets in I'll tell her to call you. Oh, but you probably won't be at work then, huh?"

"No. Is there any way I can reach her now?"

"You can try her office. She's in and out. You can reach her there for sure tonight."

Tiffany gave Jodie the number. When Jodie called, a woman answered. It wasn't Kate Rogoff, either.

"I'm Terry, her teaching assistant. Kate's in class right now."

"Would it be possible to make an appointment to see her this evening?" Jodie asked.

"Sure. She has open between six-thirty and seven-fifteen. Does that work for you?"

Gainesville was about an hour away. It was a little after five now. Jodie said, "How about six-thirty?"

"You've got it. Your name?"

"Simms."

"You're down for six-thirty."

Kate Rogoff's office was on the third floor of Anderson Hall, the last door on the left. A teenage girl trudged out as Jodie approached. She was obviously a freshman, with braces on her teeth and red, fleshy cheeks. Tonight, she looked like a hapless defendant leaving court. She sighed and shook her head bleakly, distressed by what had happened in there but relieved she had more or less survived. As she walked past Jodie she whispered, "She's all yours."

The door was open, but Jodie knocked anyway. Kate Rogoff sat behind a massive oak desk. Neat stacks of term papers rose high in one corner, a Tiffany-style lamp was on the other side, and between them a peculiar collection of pen holders. Like medieval pikes, the long black styluses stood in defense of the woman in the worn leather chair.

Kate Rogoff peered over the top of her half-glasses. Her skin was darkly tanned and had a rough, pocked texture. Scars from severe acne, Jodie thought. The *surface* scars. Just looking at this woman's demeanor, Jodie was sure that scars much more severe lay beneath the skin.

She guessed Kate Rogoff was a few years older than herself, probably early forties. Her hair was bleached white and cropped close to her scalp. Had she cut it as a rebellious act? Jodie wondered. Or was it just a concession to convenience? Whatever the reason, it gave her the look of a tough opponent. The one word that came to mind to describe her was *hard*.

The lamp picked up the white outline of peach fuzz on her jaw. Her eyes were the color of granite and they fixed on Jodie with intimidating intensity. It occurred to Jodie as she stood in the doorway that it might have been a mistake coming here.

"And you are? . . ." Kate Rogoff said.

Jodie walked in cautiously. "My name is Jodie Simms."

"Simms. Yes, I saw the name on my appointment book. I didn't think I had a student by that name. Obviously I was right."

"I knew your brother Sam. We met in Mexico. I was hoping I could talk to you about him."

Kate took off her reading glasses and studied Jodie for a moment. "You don't look like his type," she said.

Jodie forced a laugh, feeling uncomfortable already.

Kate stood up, shook Jodie's hand, then gestured for her to take the wooden chair at the desk. Kate's body, covered in a plain beige blouse and brown slacks, was remarkably fit, considering the woman's age. Her arms had the definition of someone who worked out with weights, conspicuous veins evidence that she carried very little body fat.

"I can't possibly imagine why you would come see me about Sam," Kate said. "I presume you know that he died."

"Yes, I know. I'm sorry. It must be a—"

"It's not," she said, cutting Jodie off. "We weren't close." And she left it at that. "Now, what can I do for you, Ms. Simms?"

Jodie realized this woman saw no value in pleasantries. She liked things direct.

"Your brother was looking into something in Mexico," Jodie said. "Just before he died. I'm trying to find out what he learned."

"You'd be better served to call the World Health Organization."

"I did. They said they didn't have his notes from Mexico or a journal or papers or anything like that. They said all of his personal things were sent to you."

"They also should have told you that they called looking for his notes but that none was delivered to me. All I had was his laptop computer, which apparently belonged to the World Health Organization. I sent it to them immediately."

"They said there was nothing on it."

"I just sent the computer. I don't know what was or was not on it."

Jodie tried not to let Kate Rogoff's apathy discourage her. She needed information. Too much depended on it.

"I thought there might be something among his things that you might have missed," she said. "Something that might provide me with what I need to know."

"And what is it you need to know?"

"To tell you the truth, I'm not exactly sure."

Kate rolled her eyes and let out a breath, as though to say, *Why are you wasting my time?*

"I think what he was investigating down there," Jodie said, "might somehow have something to do with my father and the treatment he's been getting for his illness."

A hint of compassion breached Kate's hard exterior. "What kind of treatment has he been getting?" she asked.

"My father has Alzheimer's."

Kate hesitated. When she spoke again, her voice was an octave lower, a whisper softer. "I'm sorry to hear that," she said.

Not wanting to lose what little sympathy she had just won, Jodie decided not to mention Carl's improvement. Instead she said, "It's very important to my father's health that I find out what your brother learned down there."

Kate stood up and walked to a closet in the corner. From it she took out a blue cardboard box, the type lawyers keep case records in, and brought it over to the desk. She placed it in front of Jodie.

"This is everything the *Seguridad Publica* in Cancun sent," she told Jodie, "except for the computer which I returned to the World Health Organization and Sam's suitcase which contained only clothes. I already donated them to the Salvation Army. I haven't figured out what to do with these items. Most have no value. I'll probably just throw them out. You're welcome to look through the box if you think it'll be of some assistance to you, to your father. But I must tell you, I don't think you'll find anything useful in there."

The phone rang. Kate took the top off the box and gestured for Jodie to have a look, then she sat back down and picked up the phone.

"Hello. Hi, Tiffany." Kate glanced over a Jodie. "Yes, she's here right now. Television, huh?"

Kate did not sound impressed. Jodie turned her attention to the contents of the box while Kate talked to her roommate on the phone.

"No, I won't be able to make it," Kate said. "You go alone tonight."

Inside the box Jodie found a leather wallet that smelled of years of sweat, a Seiko wristwatch, a pocket calculator and several brochures for attractions near Cancun, like the nature park of Xcaret, the Hard Rock Cafe in the hotel zone, the Nautibus underwater sightseeing boat, swimming with the dolphins on Isla Mujeres, a timeshare called Mayan Cove, and Adventure Diving, a scuba school operating out of the Fiesta Americana Hotel.

Kate, on the phone, giggled, a sound Jodie found odd coming from this person. Kate turned her chair so her back was to Jodie and whispered something into the phone.

Jodie focused on the contents of the box again and noticed some writing on the Mayan Cove brochure. She took it out of the box. Scrawled along the edge of the brochure beside the photo of the timeshare was the name *Connor Wrye*. She wondered if that was a salesman who tried to sell Rogoff the timeshare. It didn't sound like a Mexican name, though.

"I'll see you around at nine-fifteen," Kate said. She turned her chair around and hung up the phone.

"Do you know who Connor Wrye is?" Jodie asked. She showed Kate the name on the brochure.

"I never heard of him. I assume it is a him."

"I don't know."

Below the name was written the word *Connection*.

"Connection to what?" Jodie wondered aloud.

"I would have no way of knowing."

Jodie, reading the rest of the scribbling near the bottom, said, *"Clinica Centro."* She thought about it a moment then said, "That must be the clinic he told me about, the one he was looking into."

Kate shrugged, looking uninterested in all of this.

Jodie opened the brochure and saw several other notes along the edges. Rogoff had written: *Who the hell is Cassandros?*

Jodie herself had been asking that same question.

The next notation said: *Why so much epilepsy?*

Jodie remembered Rogoff saying the same thing to her a month ago, at the beach. There were too many cases of epilepsy. But Jodie still didn't understand how that might be connected to her father and The Cure. *Maybe it isn't.*

The next note stunned her. Rogoff had written: *BDNF₂?*

Harrington had told her The Cure contained some

kind of protein which he called BDNF. It couldn't be coincidence that Rogoff had written the same thing.

She looked up at Rogoff's sister. "Sam wrote BDNF with a 'two' after it and a question mark."

Kate Rogoff glanced at it. "Yes, he did."

"Do you know what that is?"

With a breath of irritation, Kate reached back to the bookshelf behind her and slid out a thick medical dictionary. She licked her finger as she flipped through the pages. "Well, here's BDNF," she said. "It stands for brain-derived neurotrophic factor. I don't know what the 'two' after it signifies."

"What is brain-derived neurotrophic factor?"

"It doesn't expand on it here, but it shouldn't be too difficult to figure out. Brain-derived obviously means just that—derived from the brain. Neuro probably means nerves or the nervous system. All we need now is trophic . . ."

She flipped through the pages until she found the entry and read what it said. "Concerned with nourishment. Applied particularly to a type of efferent nerves believed to control growth and nourishment of the parts they innervate." She closed the book and stared at Jodie.

Jodie didn't know what "efferent" meant, but she didn't dare ask. She said, "So it more or less means nourishment for the nervous system?"

"More or less."

"So BDNF-two is something that comes from the brain that nourishes the nervous system."

"It would appear so," Kate said, replacing the dictionary on the shelf.

"Why would your brother write that?" Jodie said, thinking out loud.

"Why would you think I would know the answer to that?" Kate replied, peering across the desk at Jodie. Whatever sympathy she had felt about Jodie's father had already been used up.

"I didn't mean to imply that I think you'd know, I was just . . . it's was just the medicine my father is taking . . . I thought maybe . . . never mind."

Jodie felt oddly intimidated by this woman. She felt almost as though she were back in college, and this woman was her professor about to fail her in an important course.

She looked away and, trying not to think about the sharp eyes fixed on her, scanned the brochure again. She found another note scribbled along the edge of the page. It not only confused her but also made her very uneasy. It said: *What is he hiding?* She thought, *What is who hiding?*

One last note, written at the very bottom where there was barely enough room for the letters, was only one word. When Jodie read it, she trembled. The spelling was wrong, but she was sure it was the same man.

Rogoff had written:

Sterling

30

Jodie called American Airlines as soon as she got back from Gainesville and booked a seat on the next day's nine A.M. flight to Cancun. Next she called the Hotel Salida Del Sol and reserved a cabaña. She asked to speak with

Neil but the reservationist said he was in Campeche on business and would be back tomorrow, though he didn't know what time. Jodie hoped he'd return to Cancun early, thinking how much she could use his help. She packed, slept only a few hours, then drove down to St. Augustine while it was still dark.

Carl was in his bathrobe when she let herself in. He was sipping coffee on the living room chair, watching a fishing program on ESPN. He looked surprised to see her. And annoyed.

"What the hell? . . ." he said. "You think I burned the place down last night or something? What are you doing here?"

"Good morning to you too, Dad."

"Yeah, yeah, good morning. What are you doing here?"

"Fine, thank you. And you?" she said.

He threw up his hands. "For God's sake, Jodie . . ."

"Relax, I didn't come here because I'm worried about you." She walked over and kissed him on the forehead. "Even though I *am* worried about you."

"Then why are you bothering me so early?"

She went into the kitchen to pour herself a cup of coffee. "A visit from your only daughter is a bother?" she said from the other room. She didn't want to face him, afraid he would see in her face that she was lying.

"Go home."

She laughed. "Don't worry, I can't stay."

"Damn right."

"Listen, Dad, I've been thinking about getting away

for a couple days," she said, getting cream from the refrigerator. She noticed the box containing the syringes of The Cure on the shelf next to her father's beer.

"A vacation's a good idea," he said from the living room. "Your job is too stressful, and your old man's a pain in the ass."

"Right on both counts."

He laughed. "You didn't have to agree so fast."

She closed the refrigerator door but stayed in the kitchen, out of sight. "So anyway," she said, "I thought I'd go away for the weekend. Go somewhere warm."

He chuckled. "This is Florida. *This* is somewhere warm."

"Somewhere warm-*er*."

He got up with a moan and shuffled into the kitchen, his feet sliding around in slippers too large for him. "Where are you going?" he asked.

"Well, I thought I'd fly down to Mexico," she said as though it were nothing, and tried to hide herself behind a sip of coffee.

But he saw right through her.

"Mexico, huh? You just happened to pick Mexico out of a hat?"

"No, I didn't pick it out of a hat. I liked it when we went down there and I thought it would be nice to go back, just to relax."

"Who are you trying to kid?"

She forced a laugh. "What are you talking about?"

"I know why you're going down there."

"Dad, I feel like getting away for a couple days, that's

all. The beaches are nice there. It's warm. It's cheap. Granted, you can't drink the water, but who goes on vacation for a drink of water, right?"

Carl wasn't buying it. "You're going down there to see him, aren't you?" he said.

"What are you talking about?"

He just stared at her. He knew.

"Dad," she said, giving up the charade. "Let me try to explain."

He held up his hand to silence her. He walked closer and put his hand on her shoulder. "I was young once myself," he said. "I never left the country to see a woman, but times are different today. People travel more. Did you know I once drove all the way to Boston to pick up your mother, and that was before we were married. In those days that was like . . . like flying to Mexico to see that long-haired boyfriend of yours."

Realizing that he misunderstood completely, she vented her relief in a quiet sigh. "You always could see right through me," she said.

"You go," he told her. "I think it'll do you good. Get away from your old man for a few days. You be careful, though."

"I will, Dad."

"He seems like a decent fella, even with the hair."

"You're going to be okay, right?"

"Don't worry about your old man. Just enjoy yourself."

"I will. Oh," she said, as though it had just dawned on her. "As long as I'm down there, I might as well talk to Dr. Stirling, make sure the last supply of The Cure is the right stuff. Make sure there wasn't a mix-up, anything like that."

"And you tell him I'm paying good money, I want the real McCoy."

"I will." She kissed him on the cheek and said, "Don't take the next shot until I come back, all right?"

"Yeah, yeah, all right."

She wrote down the phone number of the Salida Del Sol and stuck it on the refrigerator door with a magnet. Then she made him promise that he'd call her if he had any problems, any at all.

From St. Augustine she drove straight to the airport on the north side of Jacksonville, speeding up I-95 most of the way so she wouldn't miss her plane. She checked in and had five minutes before her flight boarded so she called the TV station from a pay phone near the gate. She was relieved Lisa Kerns, one of the weekend producers, was in.

"What's up?" Lisa said.

"I need you to do me a favor. Could you locate someone for me? I'd do it myself but I don't have time. I'm leaving for Mexico in a few minutes."

"Mexico? I wish I had your life."

"No, you really don't. The name is Connor Wrye," Jodie said. "It sounds like a man's name to me, but it could be a woman. I don't know where he or she lives. Maybe Mexico, I'll check that end. But I need you to check here, in the U.S."

"Who is this person?"

"That's what I'm hoping you're going to tell me. Find

out as much as you can. You can call my place, leave a message on the machine."

"I'll do my best."

"Thanks. I owe you one."

⪡ 31

When Jodie landed in Cancun, she stopped at the Hertz counter and rented a yellow VW Beetle. The transmission was rough, it had no A/C and the ride was like a buckboard, but she hadn't thought ahead to reserve a car yesterday. She had to take what she could get.

She drove the long, straight road to the hotel zone, thinking about all she had learned yesterday and still unable to make sense of much of it. At the Hotel Salida Del Sol, Tomas, the front desk clerk, smiled when he saw her. He told her he had recognized the name on the reservation and had arranged for twin beds to be put in her cabaña. When he saw she was traveling alone, his jaw dropped.

"Is Neil Lancaster back yet?" she asked.

"No, señorita. Señor Lancaster is still in Campeche."

Jodie realized she was on her own. She went to her cabaña and unpacked, then found a phone book in the bureau drawer and looked up Connor Wrye. There was no listing for anyone at all named Wrye in Cancun or anywhere in the state of Quintana Roo. It must be someone Rogoff knew from the U.S., she reasoned. Hopefully Lisa Kerns would turn up something.

Next she found the number of the *Seguridad Publica,*
which Kate Rogoff had said was the agency that had sent
Sam Rogoff's possessions to her. It took several minutes
and half a dozen policemen before a man came on the
line who spoke English fluently. Jodie explained she was
inquiring about Dr. Rogoff's death a month ago.

"And you are who?" the man asked.

"My name is Jodie Simms."

"You are a relation of Dr. Roker?"

"Rogoff. His name is Rogoff," she said. "Dr. Sam
Rogoff."

"Rogoff, okay, yes."

Ignoring the man's question about being a relative,
Jodie said, "We received the few items you sent, but I'm
wondering if you have any additional personal items of
his."

"I think we sent everything."

"Could you check for me please. This is very important."

He sighed, annoyed, and said, "I will look and
telephone you later."

While Jodie waited for his call, she checked the phone
book again. First she found the number for Clinica
Centro, the hospital she believed Rogoff had been
investigating. She called, but the line was busy. She
wrote down the number and the address, then looked in
the Yellow Pages again, under MEDICOS, for the doctor
Rogoff had mentioned—Cassandros. No one by that
name was listed but she did find a name similar, a Dr.
Fernando Antonio Gozantro. She wondered if Rogoff
could have gotten the name wrong. Gozantro and

Cassandros sounded alike. Was Gozantro the doctor he had been investigating?

She dialed his office and let it ring a dozen times. No one answered, so she hung up and wrote down his address and phone number beneath Clinica Centro's. She would try again later.

An hour passed and no one from the *Seguridad Publica* called. Jodie tried Clinica Centro several times, each time getting busy signals. When she phoned Gozantro's office, twice no one answered, the next two times she got busy signals, then no one answered again.

She decided rather than spend the rest of the day waiting here, trying to get people on the phone, she would begin checking into a few things herself, in person. She left word with Tomas at the front desk that she was expecting a call from the *Seguridad Publica* and could he please take a message for her.

Next she went into the hotel gift shop and bought a map of Cancun. The store clerk helped her find Clinica Centro and traced the best route for her to take.

"Is that a good section?" she asked the clerk.

"Not a tourist section, no," he said. "But is good. All Cancun is good."

He also pointed out on the map where Dr. Gozantro's office was—less than a mile from Clinica Centro. Dr. Stirling's office was on the opposite side of the city.

Jodie was most curious why Rogoff had written Dr. Stirling's name on the brochure. Could the Alzheimer's cure somehow be connected to whatever Rogoff was investigating? The abbreviation $BDNF_2$ resurfaced in her thoughts. Rogoff had written it, and Harrington had mentioned it in connection with The Cure. Rogoff had also written the word *Connection,* and now Jodie wondered if the connection he was questioning referred to The Cure?

She was sure there was a connection between Stirling and whatever Rogoff was investigating—but what was that connection? Was the connection The Cure, or was it Stirling himself? Perhaps it didn't have anything to do with The Cure. Perhaps Stirling was somehow connected to Dr. Gozantro. If so, in what way?

Was it possible, she wondered, as she had been wondering for a long time now, wondering and yet denying that it was even a possibility . . .

Was it at all possible that Stirling himself *was* Dr. Gozantro?

⇒ 32

According to the map, Jodie had to pass Dr. Gozantro's office to get to Clinica Centro, so she stopped there first.

The street was too narrow to park her car there. She drove around the block and parked in a patch of gravel between two buildings. Stores were jammed close together on Dr. Gozantro's block, retail space so small Jodie was surprised people could conduct business in it. A shoe store. A bakery. A dress shop. A hardware store. All poorly stocked. Nothing here for tourists.

Small, dark Mayans crowded the sidewalk and the doorways, speaking a strange blend of Spanish and Indian, none of which Jodie understood. As she walked by, people stared. She felt oddly out of place here, an intruder in a section of the city these people reserved for themselves.

She quickened her pace as she searched for Gozantro's office. Few of the buildings had numbers. But she did find 25, the number she had written on the scrap of paper. It was painted on the stucco above a small *farmacia*. Certain she had written the right number, she wondered if the phone book could have been wrong.

A elderly man on a bicycle rolled up to her. His skin was tough like leather and as dark as espresso. He had the features of an eagle. Jodie was surprised at how black his hair was for a man his age. The pedals were missing from his bike, so he propelled himself by pushing off against the sidewalk with his bare feet. He smiled at her, not shy in the least about the teeth missing on the right side of his mouth.

"Tan a saatal?" he asked, the words sounding more Indian than Spanish.

Jodie pointed to the number on the building and said, "Dr. Gozantro. *Dónde?*"

He nodded and motioned her to follow him. He wheeled his bike to a narrow alley between the pharmacy and a putrid smelling fish market. Painted on the wall was the word ESCALERA and an arrow pointing down the alley. The alley wasn't wide enough for the man to go down on his bike but if Jodie turned sideways, she could walk it. He pointed to a door halfway down.

"Ka anal," he said, pointing upstairs.

"Gracias."

He nodded, smiled again and rolled away.

The door only opened part of the way before hitting the wall of the fish market. Jodie peered in at a stairway that seemed like an afterthought, narrow, dark, unusually steep. As she headed up, she felt the treads sagging under her weight and she worried the steps might snap.

The creaking announced her arrival to three children sitting at the top, playing a game with pebbles and a twig. They smiled at her and giggled when she spoke in English, asking them if they knew if Dr. Gozantro was in.

At the end of the hall was a plain wood door with no markings. It was the only door up here so she assumed this had to be Dr. Gozantro's office. She hesitated outside the door for a moment, wondering what she would do if she found Dr. Stirling in there. What would she say to him? Probably keep her mouth shut, let him do the talking, let him try to explain. But then she would have to say something, do something. What, though? She hadn't figured that part out yet. She would just wait and see how she reacted.

She felt nervous now. Even a little afraid. Not for her safety. But for her father. She feared that what she might find in here would somehow end up hurting Carl, and she didn't know how she would be able to live with herself if that happened.

She tried the door knob and found it unlocked. In an attempt to calm herself, she took a deep breath, cleared her throat and slowly opened the door. The cramped waiting room was filled with more than a dozen patients. She saw only four chairs in the room, all used by mothers holding children. More women leaned against the wall, children sat at their feet. One man sat on the floor reading the newspaper *Alarma!* Another man paced nervously, peering at Jodie for a moment, then resuming his continuous plod from the door to the hallway on the other side of the waiting room and back again.

Most of the people in here looked Mayan. Their whisperings as Jodie came in were mixture of Mayan and Spanish. Of the three windows, two were closed and caked with grime, the third was smashed, covered with pieces of scrap wood. No air conditioner ventilated the waiting room. The stuffy air smelled of unwashed bodies. Somewhere in the back a baby screeched. The phone started ringing. There was no receptionist, no nurse to answer it.

As Jodie stepped farther in and closed the door behind her, she felt uneasy. She definitely did not belong here.

A woman stared at her. Jodie walked over and said, *"Habla Ingles?"*

The woman nodded.

"Is this Dr. Gozantro's office?"

"Dr. Gozantro, si, aqui."

"Who do I talk to about seeing him? Is there a nurse or a receptionist, someone like that?"

"Si, Gozantro," the woman said, smiling, not understanding a word Jodie had said.

"Gracias," Jodie said and stepped to the side of the room. She leaned against an open spot on the wall and waited fifteen minutes before a short, chubby man with heavy Mayan features came out of the back, escorting a

woman and her two children. He was wearing a white lab coat and was remarkably light on his feet for someone his size.

"*Quien sigue?*" he said, looking around the room.

A woman with a tiny baby stood up and said, "*Yo soy.*"

The man started to take her back when he noticed Jodie. Dressed the way she was, and with skin much lighter than anyone in here, she stood out from all the other patients. He just stared at her a moment, as though measuring who she might be, then finally he said, "*Hola.*"

"*Hola,*" Jodie said. Her accent must have been obvious because he switched right away to English.

"Did you need to see a doctor?"

"I'm looking for Dr. Gozantro."

"I am Dr. Gozantro."

"You are?" Obviously she had been wrong about Gozantro and Stirling being the same person. But she still needed to find out how the two men were connected.

"If you have a moment, I'd like to speak with you," she said.

"Are you sick?"

"No."

He glanced around the room. "I have many patients waiting who are sick."

"It's very important, Doctor, and it'll just take a minute."

Gozantro looked around at the patients crowded into the room, then turned to Jodie and said, "Come along."

Jodie followed Gozantro as he led the woman and her child into the examination room at the end of the hall. A kitchen table was set up in the middle of the room with a stool for the doctor and little else in the way of equipment. There were no windows, no ventilation. The smell was so bad back here Jodie felt her stomach churn with each thin breath she drew.

The Mexican woman put her child on the table. Gozantro tickled him, coaxing a bright smile from the boy.

"Tiene algun dolor?" he asked the Mayan woman.

"Si. En la panza."

Gozantro gently palpated the boy's stomach and ribs, then he put his stethoscope to the child's chest and listened for a moment. He glanced over at Jodie.

"What do you want to ask?"

"Are you associated in any way with a doctor named Stirling?"

"I don't know him, no."

"Do you practice at the Clinica Centro?" Jodie asked.

"No. I have privilege at Medico Cancun and Clinica San Vitorio, not Clinica Centro. Why do you ask this?"

"I'm trying to find a doctor who might be associated with the Clinica Centro and possibly associated with a doctor named Stirling."

"You don't know the name?"

"I'm not sure. His name sounds like yours."

"I am the only Dr. Gozantro in Cancun," he said.

"I know. I checked the phone book. Do you treat patients with epilepsy?" Jodie asked.

When he heard this, Gozantro began to laugh. Jodie didn't understand what was so funny about that. Gozantro patted the baby on the head, said something to him in Spanish, then turned to Jodie.

"Is not epilepsy that is funny," he said. "I laugh because the doctor you are looking for to find. Not Gozantro. You want Cassandros."

"Then there *is* a doctor named Cassandros?" Rogoff had written the right name all along. "I couldn't find that name in the phone book," she said.

"No, you cannot find Cassandros. Of course not."

"Why not?"

"Cassandros?" he said with a chuckle. He shook his head. "No, no, is not in the phone book Cassandros."

He picked up the baby and carried him to a scale hanging from the ceiling. The scale looked like the kind found in old produce markets. He put the boy in the basket, waited for the dial to settle on one number, then brought the baby back to the table.

"¡Ijole! Que grande es él," he said to the mother. Then he peered over his shoulder at Jodie and said, "Do you speak some Yucatec?"

"Is that the Mayan language?"

"One of them, yes."

"No, I don't speak it. Why?"

He shook his head, disappointed in her. Then he said, "There is a word in Yucatec." He reached into his shirt pocket and took out a pen. He felt around his pockets for a piece of paper, couldn't find one, so he wrote on his palm. Then showed her his hand. He had written *K-A-S*.

"The correct way to say is *ka-aas*," he said, pausing slightly after the *K*. "But most people say only *kas*. Is the same meaning both ways. You understand?"

No, she didn't understand. She didn't understand why he was giving her this lesson in Mayan language.

"The doctor you look for, I am not a friend," Gozantro said. "But I hear of him. He is a *gringo* like you. He has patients with epilepsy."

"Yes. That must be him. Dr. Cassandros. But you still haven't told me why he's not listed in the phone book."

"You look for Cassandros, is not there. What is there is only the name."

"But you said that is his name."

He laughed. "No, no. Not Cassandros. Kasssss . . ." he said, hissing out the word as though he were a snake. Then he paused and nodded to her, making sure she was listening. Finally he finished the word, saying, "Andros. Okay?" he said. "Two word. Kas. And Andros."

"His name is Kas Andros?" Jodie asked.

Gozantro shook his head. "His name is Andros." And he spelled it for her. "A-N-D-R-E-W-S."

"Oh, Andrews?"

"Yes. Andros. Kas," he said, "the people add to the front of the name to describe."

"What does *kas* mean?"

Gozantro poked an otoscope into each of the baby's ears, peering inside, then probed the child's mouth with a tongue depressor and shined a light at his throat.

"*Se ve bien,*" he said.

He looked over at Jodie again. "In Yucatec, *kas* means bad. Kas Andros means bad Andros."

"Why is he called bad Andrews?"

Gozantro gave a vague shrug. "Many patients don't like him."

"But why?"

"For that, you must ask Andros. Or his patients."

≈ 33

As she walked down the steps and back through the alley, Jodie wondered if "kas" Andrews was the name the hysterical woman at Dr. Stirling's office had screamed two months ago. Had she heard it wrong? Cassandros and Kas Andrews sounded similar, especially when spoken hurriedly. Had Rogoff made the same mistake? Rogoff had written Cassandros on the brochure, but was Dr. Andrews the man he actually had been investigating?

Jodie stopped inside the pharmacy beneath Dr. Gozantro's office and asked the woman behind the cash register if she had a phone book. When Jodie looked under MEDICOS again, she found a listing for a Dr. William T. Andrews. Gozantro was right. *Maybe this is the doctor Rogoff was looking for?*

Jodie started to write the address of Dr. Andrews, but she noticed it was the same as the address of Clinica Centro. *This must be him.*

One thought echoed through her head: *Andrews is an American. Stirling is American.* The more she learned, the more she believed her father's doctor was the same doctor Rogoff had been investigating.

The woman at the pharmacy told Jodie how to get to the hospital from here. It wasn't far—two turns, then a straight shot, about ten blocks away.

The clerk in the hotel gift shop had been right: Clinica Centro wasn't in a tourist section. Few shops operated on this block. Several storefronts were empty. A clothing store had only a handful of items in it. Outside what looked like a deli, a dozen chickens roasted on a homemade grill, flames charring the birds an unappetizing black.

Over one doorway hung a sign: SPORTA. Inside it was empty except for a weight-lifting bench, a barbell with several iron plates on it, and a punching bag hanging in one corner. A barefoot boy, no older than five or six, lay on the bench, eating a pear. A large man, more flabby than muscular, drenched in sweat, pounded the bag with slow, powerful jabs.

Jodie parked near the gym. As she walked up the street, dodging potholes and piles of sand, she looked down one of the side roads. The road wasn't paved, but it had concrete sidewalks, she noticed. The street she was walking on *was* paved, but it had no sidewalks at all.

The houses down the side road were little more than glorified shacks. Some of them didn't stand a chance of keeping out the elements, let alone insects and rodents and whatever else might be scurrying around. Jodie realized she could never live in a shack like that, not with rodents coming and going at will.

Laundered clothes hung on barren trees, as though a heavy wind had sent shirts and pants and dresses tumbling through the air. Two boys played on a pile of gravel in an empty lot. A dog slurped black water from a puddle.

The hospital Jodie had come to see was at the corner, a small, two-story building with few windows and gray stone walls that looked unnaturally shoddy for such a solid material. The building resembled a factory or warehouse, she thought, certainly not a hospital. But she remembered Stirling's office and how it didn't appear to be a medical office from the outside, either. She had come to realize exteriors were often deceiving in this part of the world.

Situated between the clinic and the adjacent unoccupied building was a crude parking lot. A sign at the entrance had an "E" with a slash through it, which Jodie understood to mean "no parking." Painted on the side door of the building was NO ENTRADA, so Jodie walked around to the main entrance.

The doors in front were propped open with stones. Jodie walked into a lobby the size of her bedroom back in Jacksonville. Half the floor was tiled, the other half exposed concrete. Two workers were mixing mortar and laying rust-colored terra-cotta tiles. Wooden benches lined the wall on either side. Several Mexicans—patients waiting to see a doctor—stared absently at the workers. A mother cradled her sick child in her arms. In the corner, a man leaned against the wall, asleep on his feet.

Like Dr. Gozantro's office, this place did not have air conditioning. A slight breeze wheezed through the open doors and through a single window on the side wall, propped open with a stick. The hot, stuffy air smelled of body odor. Two ceiling fans hung above, but only one was moving—barely. The other fan dangled from a broken wire. The overhead lights were off, so the only illumination came from the doorway and the streak of sunlight spraying through the open window. Looking at the beam of light, Jodie could see dust from the tile work heavy in the air.

While the building needed renovating, Jodie noticed the place had some nice touches. High ceilings with ornate crown moldings. Old-fashioned transoms above the doors. The intricately hand-carved millwork on the sashes wasn't something often seen anymore.

Directly across the lobby from the door was a large wooden desk that looked like it came from an old schoolhouse. A woman in a white uniform sat at the desk, staring at a sheet of notebook paper with several names scribbled on it. Behind her was a long hallway with more benches lining it, more lethargic patients sitting, waiting. A few nurses scurried about, but mostly Jodie saw patients. She heard *chink chink* beside her as the laborer tapped a tile in place with his trowel. Aside from that the place was oddly quiet.

Jodie walked across the lobby to the receptionist's desk.

"Hello. Do you speak English?"

"Little bit."

"Where would I find Dr. Andrews's office? I'd like to see him if I could."

"*Qué?*"

"Dr. Andrews."

"Si, Dr. Andros. *Quirurgico.*"

"*Quirurgico?*" Jodie didn't understand.

"Um . . . surgico," the receptionist said.

"You mean surgical?" Jodie asked.

"Si. Surgicol."

"Can you tell me where his office is?"

"*Qué?*"

Jodie didn't remember much from her high school

Spanish class, but she took a stab at it anyway. *"Dónde está la oficina de Dr. Andrews?"*

"Dr. Andros no está en la oficina hoy." She struggled to find the words in English. "No in office today. Surgicol."

"He's operating today? He's in surgery?"

"Surgico, si."

"How can I make an apointment to talk to him?" The woman didn't understand, so Jodie said, *"Yo quiero hablar . . ."*

"No, no. No today. *Lunes,"* the woman said. *"Vuelva el lunes."*

Jodie didn't know what she meant. "Um, *como se . . . ?"*

From behind Jodie a voice said, "Monday."

Jodie turned and saw a tall, thin woman. She was in her early twenties, had light skin and European features, not the heavy Indian look of the Mayans. But what Jodie noticed most was what she was wearing, a heavy black nun's habit.

"She is telling you to return Monday," the nun said with only the slightest Spanish accent. "Dr. Andrews will be in his office tomorrow." Her eyes swept over Jodie's clothing. Then she asked, "You're not Dr. Andrews's patient, are you?"

"No. I just needed to talk to him, to *see* him really." *To see if he really is Dr. Stirling.* "Do you know him?" Jodie asked.

The woman nodded. She turned to the Mayan woman behind her. A little girl stood obediently at the woman's side. The nun spoke briefly to the woman.

"Yan in hok'ol. Pa'ten waye' ts'ats'aak."

Jodie realized right away she wasn't speaking Spanish. Probably Yucatec, she assumed.

Then the nun knelt down in front of the girl who couldn't have been more than five or six years old. She whispered kindly to her.

"Ma' ch'a'ik sahkil."

The little girl, looking pale and sick, nodded. The nun kissed her on the forehead, then gestured for Jodie to follow her outside.

When they were on the sidewalk, the midday sun beating down on them, Jodie said, "You were speaking Yucatec in there."

"Yes. Do you understand Yucatec?"

"No."

"I told them I had to leave but for them to wait for the doctor. And I told Gabriella not to be afraid."

"I do know one word in Yucatec. *Kas.*"

The nun nodded. *"Kas* Andrews." She looked around to make sure no one was listening. "He is not a good doctor, Andrews. You should find a different doctor. These people can't. They have no money and he treats them for no charge. But you aren't poor. There are better doctors for tourists."

"I'm not sick."

"Why are you looking for him then?"

"I'm trying to find out about him, what kind of doctor he is. I think he might be . . . well, it's kind of hard to explain. You said you know him, right? You know what he looks like?"

"Yes."

"Can you describe him?"

"Why do you ask what he looks like?"

"Like I said, it's hard to explain. Please, could you tell me what he looks like? Is he tall?"

"Yes, he's very tall. And very thin."

"How old is he?"

The nun thought about it a moment then shrugged and said, "More than fifty."

"Is he American?"

"American, Canadian, maybe English."

"Black hair?"

"Yes. Very sloppy. Sloppy clothes, too."

"Is he really light skinned, like he doesn't get out in the sun much? And he looks like he's distracted all the time, he doesn't look directly at you when he talks? And glasses that make his eyes look too big?"

The nun nodded. "You know Andrews already."

"I think I do, yes."

"If you are not his patient, then you must be a friend of one of his patients."

Before Jodie could answer, the nun touched Jodie's hand sympathetically and said, "Your friend is not the first patient of Dr. Andrews to die . . ."

〜 34

Her name was Sister Veronica Ignacia. She had come from Spain three years ago to work with the Mayans, first in some of the isolated villages throughout the Yucatan, but now at a Catholic church and school on the northern edge of Cancun, near Puerto Juarez. The priest only came to the church on Sundays. The rest of the time Sister Veronica and an elderly woman she called a *rezadoras* looked after the parish.

She told Jodie she had walked most of the way to the clinic with the Mayan woman and her daughter. The last kilometer or so they rode in the back of a pickup truck. The trip had taken several hours. Jodie offered her a ride back, hoping to pick her brain for more information about Dr. Andrews.

Sister Veronica gave Jodie directions through a section of Cancun where all Jodie saw were flimsy shacks constructed of sticks and rocks. Definitely not what the tourist bureau wanted visitors to see.

"Sometimes," Sister Veronica said, "when the children become very ill it is difficult to convince the parents to take them to the clinic."

She pointed down a road, scarred with potholes, and said, "Go here. Now go straight."

She continued what she had been saying about the people of her parish. "Most of the Maya would rather see a *hmen* than a doctor," she said.

"What's a *hmen*?"

"*Hmen* is the Maya word. Spanish is *curandero*. In English you say maybe shaman. He is a man who heals with herbs and sometimes elaborate ceremonies. Some of his cures are as ancient as the Maya themselves. *Hmen* are the same men who, centuries ago, sacrificed people to the Maya gods. Most Maya still go to the *hmen* for herbs.

Some go only to the *hmen*, never to the doctors. They have a strong belief in the power of herbs to heal."

"Do these *hmen* really help people? Can they really make people better when they're sick?"

"The people would not believe in the *hmen* if they did not do some good. In Mexico, there is a saying. 'When a rich man is sick he goes to a medical doctor; when he is desperate he goes to a *hmen*. When a poor man is sick he goes to a *hmen*; when he is desperate he goes to a medical doctor.'"

"I heard from someone that a lot of the people don't trust Dr. Andrews," Jodie said. "They think he's bad."

"They see his patients have seizures. It is a very frightening thing to see a person in this condition. The people don't understand what is happening. They think it is connected to the underworld."

"You mean organized crime?" Jodie asked, surprised.

"No. To the Maya, there are three worlds. Earth, Heaven, and the underworld. Spirits, good and bad, come from the underworld. When they see the seizures in someone, they think it comes from the underworld. When the person goes to a doctor and then begins to have seizures, they believe the doctor to be part of the underworld. They don't always understand what the doctor does. For some, the concept of being sick is no deeper than the symptoms they can see. What I mean is, if they have a headache, they don't look for the cause, such as a tumor. Doctors like Dr. Andrews treat the tumor, not the headache. A *hmen* treats the headache, not the tumor. You understand the difference? It is very difficult to change the way people see the world."

"Tell me, Sister. Is Andrews a bad doctor?" Jodie asked directly.

The answer Sister Veronica gave was not as direct. She said, "Who can know if it is the illness that kills the patient or if it is the treatment the doctor gives that kills?"

The nun pointed to a dirt road bisecting a gathering of rickety shacks built from sticks and palm thatching. "Turn here," she said.

They drove half a mile over bumpy road. Sister Veronica pointed to the narrow path between two buildings. On the right was a small white stucco shed with roofing made of rusted corrugated metal. A strong wind could easily topple it. The doors were open so Jodie saw the austere interior. Wooden benches without backs. Concrete floor. A single wooden cross behind the altar, colorful Mayan cloth draped over it.

"Is this a church?" she asked.

"Yes."

"Catholic?"

"Yes."

"That doesn't look like a Catholic crucifix behind the altar."

"That is called a *santos*," Sister Veronica said. "That is how the Maya make the cross. There is still much influence from the ancient ways in the Maya Catholic church. The people do not forget the beliefs of their ancestors. Like the underworld. They bring much of this to their Catholicism. I don't think the Pope approves of this, but as long as they are Catholic, what can he do?— Rome is far away. The dressing on the cross is called *iipil. Iipil* is the native dress for Maya women."

Jodie noticed the heavy black dress Sister Veronica was wearing and wondered how she could stand to wear it in the Mexican heat. A lightweight, light colored *iipil* would probably be much more comfortable.

Jodie drove up the path barely wide enough for her car. Across from the church was a school building. *Building* wasn't really accurate. It consisted of four posts and a thatched roof, earthen floor and no walls. In place of individual seats and desks, the classroom had five rows of wooden benches resting on stone blocks.

Today was Saturday and school was not in session. But half a dozen children kicked a ball around a patch of dirt behind the school. None of them had shoes and only the girls wore shirts. They were so skinny their ribs showed but they laughed as they played together. They didn't pay much attention to Jodie and Sister Veronica in the car.

At the end of the path was another thatched-roof shack. Jodie assumed it was where the nun lived. She drove toward the shack slowly, reluctant to let Sister Veronica leave. She still did not know enough about Dr. Andrews—who she now believed was definitely Dr. Stirling.

"Thank you for the ride," Sister Veronica said as she started to get out.

"Um, Sister," Jodie said.

The nun stopped, waiting for Jodie to speak. Jodie stared across the small car, not sure what to say. She decided the best thing to do was be honest, tell this stranger—this nun who was practically still a girl—tell her what troubled her.

"I think he might be treating my father," Jodie said.

Sister Veronica's questioning look told Jodie the nun didn't understand who she was talking about.

"Dr. Andrews," Jodie said. "I think he might be treating my father."

"Your father is ill?" the nun asked quietly.

"He has Alzheimer's disease. Do you know what that is?"

"Yes, I do. But Andrews is not a doctor for that. He is a surgeon."

"Do you know of a doctor named Stirling?" Jodie asked.

"No. He treats the tourists?"

"I think most of his patients are tourists, yes. Or at least people who come from other countries to see him, like my father and I did. I think most of them are probably Americans. He treats people with neurological disorders, like my father's Alzheimer's."

"I thought you said Dr. Andrews is treating your father?"

"I think they're the same man."

"How can they be the same?"

"I don't know. I'm not sure. I'm trying to find out what Dr. Andrews is doing, if it has anything to do with my father's treatment."

She looked directly at Sister Veronica. "I'm worried about my father," she said. "I'm afraid something might happen to him."

Sister Veronica stared at her, a look of empathy in her eyes. Finally she said, "There is someone I know who can perhaps answer your questions."

"Who?"

"Maria Ticas de Garcia. Perhaps she will tell you of Hector Itzá Garcia."

"Who is she? And who's Hector Itzá Garcia?"

"Hector was a patient of Dr. Andrews. Maria is his widow."

⇒ 35

They had to go on foot; Sister Veronica said the road for cars didn't go there. They walked a short distance up the dirt road, then they turned down a path that wound between scrub brush and several shacks, then they followed a canal for a few minutes and turned down another path to a small gathering of huts.

Each hut had walls constructed of thin vertical sticks, most with roofs made of green and brown palm fronds but a few with rusted sheet metal. The shape of all of the huts was the same—rectangular with rounded ends. Jodie couldn't imagine any of them withstanding a heavy storm. Even a minor hurricane would wipe out the entire village.

The hut Sister Veronica stopped at had a metal roof, a low, stone wall surrounding it, a squat banana plant in front and a piglet tied to a large stone outside. Beside the hut was a stick platform, five feet above the ground, about the size of a kitchen table. On top were homemade wooden planters and clay pots, every inch of space overgrown with herbs and other small plants. Four chickens roamed freely around the hut, getting along surprisingly well with the piglet. One chicken came outside the fence and over to Jodie where it pecked at her heel. Sister Veronica shooed it away.

Jodie detected the faint smell of sewage as she followed Sister Veronica toward the front door.

"Hola!" Sister Veronica called out. *"Hola, Maria!"*

A tiny Mayan woman appeared in the doorway. She looked like she was in her sixties with only a few wrinkles and no gray streaks in her black hair. Jodie realized that she hadn't seen many gray-haired Mayans in Cancun—actually she couldn't remember seeing any at all. They seemed to keep their hair color into old age.

Sister Veronica spoke briefly with the woman in a mixture of Spanish and Yucatec, then the woman stared at Jodie. Jodie noticed the woman was studying the angel pin on Jodie's blouse. Jodie unpinned it and offered it to the woman.

"For you," Jodie said. *"Usted. Por favor."*

The woman hesitated at first, then finally reached out and took it. She tried to pin it to her dress but had trouble with the clasp so Jodie helped her. The woman looked at the pin now hanging on her dress and smiled. Then she smiled at Jodie and gestured for her to come inside.

The house had only one room. On the left side, a hammock hung from the hut's support posts, a traditional Mexican blanket folded inside, adding the only color to the browns and grays of the hut. A kitchen made up the right side of the tiny space, with a homemade wood table, two short logs cut down for stools, and stones and a metal grate for cooking. It looked like something Robinson Crusoe might have lived in.

In the corner was a wooden shelf with a small *santos* cross, a statue of Mary also draped in an *iipil*, a tattered Bible and a photographic depiction of Jesus, a dark-skinned Jesus with noticeably Mayan features, not the Caucasian Jesus Jodie was accustomed to seeing.

Maria Ticas de Garcia looked shy and uneasy around Jodie. She wore a bleached white *iipil* dress with brightly colored trim. The leather sandals on her thick feet were falling apart. She said something in Yucatec.

Sister Veronica translated. "She wants to know if you would like a cup of *sa?*"

"What is *sa?*"

"A drink made from corn flower, water and honey."

It didn't sound very appetizing. Jodie noticed the cupboard near the stove, three shelves, no door or covering of any type. All the woman had was half a small sack of something—rice or corn or beans—and three unmarked tin cans.

"Would it offend her if I declined the drink?" Jodie asked.

"No."

Maria gestured toward the table. Jodie and Sister Veronica sat on the log chairs. Maria brought over a wooden bucket, turned it upside down and sat close to Sister Veronica.

Sister Veronica spoke first, asking in the strange blend

of Yucatec and Spanish if Maria would tell Jodie about her husband. Maria looked at Jodie and with stoic but solemn regard said:

"*Hector kimi kan dos meses yaax.*"

"She said her husband, Hector, died two months ago." "Would you tell her I'm sorry to hear that," Jodie said.

Sister Veronica did. Maria nodded, holding her emotion inside, and said, "*Dyos bo'otik,*" which Sister Veronica told Jodie was Mayan for "God pays it"—meaning "Thank you."

"What did Hector die from?" Jodie asked.

Maria spoke for a moment, then Sister Veronica translated.

"She said her husband had much pain in his side. They went to Dr. Andrews who told them that Hector needed to have surgery. To remove his appendix. He was in the clinic for three days. When he came home, he was not the same."

"In what way wasn't he the same?"

"*K'as ba'al ti' pol,*" Maria said, pointing to her head.

"He was bad in the head, she said," Sister Veronica told Jodie. "He would cry for no reason. Laugh for no reason. Sometimes he was violent."

"Did he have seizures?" Jodie asked.

Sister Veronica asked Maria and she said, "*Si, ataques.*"

Jodie couldn't remember exactly what Sam Rogoff had said to her a month ago about people having epilepsy. She had done her best to ignore him. Now she wished she had listened more closely. She realized it might be important in understanding how Stirling was treating her father.

"There have been several others with this condition in this area," Sister Veronica said. "That is not normal."

Maria spoke again.

"She wants to show you something," Sister Veronica said.

Jodie looked at the old woman and nodded.

Maria walked over to a shelf near the hammock where she kept a small cardboard box. It was tattered and flimsy but she carried it as though it were made of gold. She took out a tiny scrap of paper and handed it to Jodie. On it was neat block lettering which Jodie doubted this woman had written.

Convulsiones a causa de trauma.

"Traumatic convulsions, seizures," Sister Veronica said, looking over Jodie's shoulder.

Maria Ticas de Garcia spoke again. Sister Veronica translated.

"She said Dr. Andrews gave Hector the seizures. She said he is a witch doctor and does evil medicine. The *hmen* tried to cure Hector with herbs but they came too late for the *hmen* to stop the seizures."

"Beora ku kimen," Maria said sadly.

"Now Hector is dead," Sister Veronica said quietly.

Maria spoke again, angry now. Sister Veronica translated.

"She said she thinks Dr. Andrews took out more than just the appendix."

"Why does she think that?"

Sister Veronica asked, then translated the answer.

"Because after the surgery, Hector had a problem. The doctor took x-rays of Hector's head and said the problem was not related to the surgery, but Maria doesn't believe him."

"What kind of problem?"

"His nose kept bleeding."

"From an operation on his appendix?" Jodie said, pointing to the side of her waist, where her appendix was.

Maria nodded. She said something else that surprised Jodie.

"A man came to visit her a few weeks ago," Sister Veronica said. "He was like you, a *gringo*, a foreigner. From a health agency. A doctor. He came with a taxi driver who spoke Yucatec. The foreigner's name was Roga."

"Rogoff?" Jodie asked. "Could it have been Sam Rogoff?"

"*Wal*," Maria said, nodding. "Sa Roga."

"She says maybe it is."

"What did this man tell her?" Jodie asked.

Sister Veronica asked Maria, then told Jodie what the old woman said.

"He didn't tell her much. He asked many questions. He said there were too many people like Hector. He gave her that paper," she said, pointing to the scrap that said *Convulsiones a causa de trauma*. "He wrote the words," Sister Veronica said. "He believed Dr. Andrews was the fault. He said there are other patients of Dr. Andrews who have the seizures, who have the problems with the head."

Maria went on.

Sister Veronica said, "The American man told her he

was going to do something about it. But she hasn't heard
from him anymore. She wants to know if you know the
other man, since you are both foreigners."

Jodie nodded. "I know him. Tell her I'm sorry, but she
won't hear from him anymore." She took a breath and
said, "Sam Rogoff is dead."

Sister Veronica told Maria Ticas de Garcia, who
lowered her head and made a sign of the cross in silence.

⇒ 36

When she heard the knock at the door, Jodie rushed to
open it and fell into Neil's arms.

"Are you all right?" he said, holding her. "My God,
you're trembling."

"I'm so glad you're here."

"You sounded terrible when you called me. I came as
quickly as I could. What's wrong?"

"I didn't know what to do."

"I'm here now," he said. "It's going to be all right."

He held her in the doorway for a long moment, giving
her a chance to steady herself, then he closed the door
and guided her over to the foot of the bed where they sat
together.

"You should have told me you were coming down
here," he said. "I would have met you at the airport."

"I called last night but they said you were in Campeche. And this morning when I arrived, you weren't back
yet."

"The trip took longer than I thought. But I mean you

should have called me a few days ago when you decided you were coming down here."

"I decided last night, at the last minute. I had to check something down here."

"And I thought you came down because you couldn't stand being away from me. I'm crushed," he said, his hand clutching his heart.

She was too upset to joke with him. "Neil," she said, swallowing hard, struggling not to lose it. "It's Dad . . ."

"Is he all right?" Neil asked.

"I'm concerned about the medicine Dr. Stirling is giving him."

"I thought you said your father was doing better."

"He is. But . . ." She didn't know where to begin. "I found out some things . . ."

"What kind of things?"

"The shots Dad's taking—they're not what Dr. Stirling said they are." She told him what Harrington had told her, about the absence of porcine cells and the presence of human brain tissue.

"Are you sure about that?" Neil asked.

"The tests were done at the Mayo Clinic. They're the best there is, Neil. They know about that kind of thing. I'm sure the results were accurate. And there's more, too," she said.

"More about the medicine?"

"No. Dr. Stirling isn't who he says he is. I think he goes by another name."

"You *think* he does?"

"I'm almost sure. I learned about a doctor named Andrews. I met one of his patients today—actually the wife of one of his patients. I think Andrews did something to him, I don't know what, but something, and now he's dead. I met a nun, too, and she knows Andrews, and the way she describes him, the way he looks, the way he acts, he sounds exactly like Dr. Stirling."

"Do you know how strange this sounds, Jodie?"

"Damn it, Neil, I'm telling you the truth!"

"I believe you. I'm not saying I don't, I'm just telling you that it sounds bizarre."

"I know it sounds bizarre. It *is* bizarre. But it's all true."

"Did you see him? Did you see this Dr. Andrews person?"

"No, but like I said, Sister Veronica described him and I know it's the same man. I know it's Dr. Stirling. It has to be him."

"Just because a nun you don't even know thinks some doctor looks like your father's doctor—"

"It's not just that. Don't you understand, Stirling lied about what's in The Cure. He had me sign an agreement not to have it tested because he was afraid I'd find out that he was lying about what it was. But I had it tested and they said that there's human tissue in it. *Human*, Neil!"

"I find that hard to believe, Jodie."

"But it's true!"

"Just because some lab in Jacksonville told you—"

"It's not just *some lab*," she said. "It was the *Mayo Clinic*. They're experts, Neil. I know they were right about it. And I know that Dr. Stirling is also Dr. Andrews, and I know he's doing something to these people that he shouldn't be doing. *And people are dying,*

Neil. Hector Garcia. And others, too. They call him 'Bad Andrews' because so many of his patients die. Why is he killing people?"

"Whoa. Hold on, Jodie. You don't know for a fact that this doctor of yours is doing that."

"Yes I do. The World Health Organization was looking into that very same thing, that his patients were dying when they shouldn't be, that he was doing something wrong to them. He's done it before apparently, in Guatemala. They threw him out of the country or something. And now he's doing it again—*here!* There was a doctor, an investigator, down here a month ago. I met the man when I was here last time. You remember him? He was on the beach that day you came over to talk to me that first time."

"That guy you called a creep?"

"I thought he was hitting on me. Obviously he knew that Stirling was doing something wrong and he was trying to get information from me since he saw me and Dad at his office. He told me all this. He was trying to find Dr. Andrews but he had the wrong name, he didn't know Andrews and Stirling were the same person. What Stirling is doing isn't right, Neil. I don't know exactly what it is, but people are dying and it isn't right. Somehow it has something to do with a protein called BDNF."

"I never heard of that," Neil said. "What is it?"

"It's a growth factor that's produced in the brain, in the cortex. And it's in The Cure. My father . . ." she started to say, but emotion flooded her and choked back the words. She turned away and struggled not to cry.

"What is it, Jodie?"

She spoke quietly now. "Dad's been injecting himself with . . . with I don't know what. I'm afraid, Neil."

Neil put both arms around her and drew her against him. She lost it now and started weeping into his shoulder. He held her and whispered it would be all right, he would do whatever he could to make sure it was all right.

After a few minutes she regained control of her fears and dried her eyes. Neil poured her a glass of scotch from the mini bar. She drank a little, feeling the steadying warmth of the scotch strengthen her.

"What if the two are connected?" she said.

"What if what's connected?"

"The Cure and the patients down here who are dying? What if they're connected? What if Dr. Stirling's giving them the same thing he's giving my father and what if that's why they're dying? What if it's hurting my father too?"

"Is there anything wrong with your father?"

"Not yet, not that I can tell, but he won't go see his doctor back home to be tested. I'm worried that something might happen. The people down here have been having seizures. What if that happens to my father?"

"You're getting way ahead of yourself. You have no reason to believe that anything like that will happen to your father."

"Don't you understand? Stirling isn't who he says he is. I don't know what he's doing to Dad. I'm scared, Neil. I'm scared."

"What did you say about the World Health Organization looking into all this?"

"They were investigating the seizures and the deaths, but the man who was looking into it died before he could turn in any kind of report, so right now the whole thing is probably in bureaucratic limbo. We have to do something. We have to go to the police."

"The police?"

"People are dying, Neil!"

"Just wait a minute, Jodie. You have to understand something. In Mexico, the laws are based on the Napoleonic Code, which means you're guilty until proven innocent. You don't get a jury trial here. Accused people don't have the same rights they do back home. This is not the place to accuse someone unless you know for a fact that they're guilty. When you go to the police and accuse someone of something serious, you have to be absolutely certain about what you're alleging. Are you? Are you sure this doctor is doing what you say he's doing?"

"That's just it, I don't know what he's doing."

"That's all the more reason not to run right to the police and accuse him of something. Jodie," he said, taking her hands. "I've dealt with the law down here. It would be wrong to put someone through that if there's even the slightest chance that you're mistaken. I could tell you horror stories about Mexican jails and judges." He let that sink in for a moment. "And something else, too. It's not always the person who's accused that ends up in trouble. If you can't absolutely prove what you're saying, you could end up in trouble with the law yourself, and trust me on this, you do *not* want to be in that position."

"Then what am I supposed to do?"

"Let's talk to this doctor of yours first, see what he has to say and then go from there."

Jodie sank down against Neil and let out a thin breath of resignation. Maybe he was right. Maybe that was the way to proceed.

Neil put his arms around her. "I'll be there with you," he said.

She nodded, relieved that she didn't have to do this alone.

"And don't worry," he told her. "We'll straighten this whole thing out. I promise you that."

≋ 37

Carl hated driving on I-95. Ever since the state raised the speed limit to 70 MPH, he found the pace much too fast. He didn't feel comfortable driving at that speed, but if he drove slower everyone sped past him, usually blowing their horns, which also made him nervous.

So he took US-1 most of the way to Jacksonville, then cut across to the beach. He had a little trouble finding the street Jodie lived on but finally he pulled to the curb in front of her house.

She was always doing so much for him, the least he could do was keep an eye on her house while she was away. He would check the place today, turn a few lights on, leave the TV playing so people would think she was home. Tomorrow morning he would drive up here again to make sure no one had broken in overnight.

He let himself in with the key Jodie had given him. The first thing he did was walk from room to room, checking the windows. All of them were locked. He tugged at the sliding glass door, making sure Jodie had engaged the latch, then he took a measuring cup from the kitchen, filled it from the tap and watered the plants in the living room.

He hoped Jodie was having a good time in Mexico. God knows she deserved a vacation, deserved to think of herself instead of worrying about her old man. The last several months must have been hard for her. Now he understood all she had done for him and he wished he could repay her somehow.

When he finished watering the plants, he put the measuring cup on the sink board to dry, turned on the TV and left lights on in the living room and the bedroom. Satisfied he had done everything he could, he headed for the door.

The phone rang.

He picked up the extension in the living room. "Hello?"

"Oh, hi." It was a woman's voice. She sounded surprised. "I didn't think anyone would be there," she said.

He wanted to ask why she called if she didn't think anyone would be home but instead he said, "I'm here. I'm watching the place." He didn't want anyone to know the house was empty.

"Jodie told me she was going away for the weekend. I

was going to leave a message on her machine. Is this her father?"

"Yes."

"She's told me so much about you. I feel like I practically know you."

"I feel like I have no idea who you are," Carl said.

She giggled. "I'm Lisa Kerns. I work with Jodie at Channel 10."

"Oh, I see. Well, Jodie's away so . . ."

"Since I got you instead of the machine, I wonder if you'd mind giving her a message for me."

"Sure."

"She asked me to check up on something for her and she said it was important."

"What was it?"

"She wanted me to locate someone for her. Someone named Connor Wrye." She spelled the last name.

"Who's that?" Carl asked.

"I don't know. I just know it was important to Jodie. Would you tell her I tried everything. I ran the name through a computerized directory of phone books from all over the country, but I couldn't get a hit. I also ran it through InfoTrak, but that didn't turn up anything either."

"What's InfoTrak?"

"It's a service we use sometimes to find out things about people we're doing investigative stories on. You give them the name or social security number and they come up with all kinds of information—credit histories, past address, debts, bank accounts, all kinds of things. I tried it with this person, but it didn't turn up anything.

Whoever Connor Wrye is, he's not easy to find. Or she. I don't know if it's a man or a woman."

"Do you know why Jodie wanted to find this person?"

"No, she didn't say, except that it was connected to Mexico, because she was supposed to check down there to see if she could find out anything on that end. I hope she has better luck than I did. Tell her if she can come up with a social security number, that would be a big help. Or if she can narrow down where to look."

"I'll give her the message," Carl said.

As he drove back to St. Augustine, Carl kept thinking about the phone conversation with Lisa Kerns. Who was this Connor Wrye person Jodie wanted to find? Lisa Kerns said it was connected to Mexico, but the name didn't sound familiar. And Lisa Kerns said Jodie intended to look for this person down there. Now Carl wondered if that could have had anything to do with her going? She had said she wanted to get away, to relax. She hadn't said anything about looking for anyone. Had she lied?

And not only about Connor Wrye. Was there more she hadn't told him about her trip? Carl remembered their conversation a couple days ago, her concern about the injections he was taking. Was that part of it, too?

Anything to do with Mexico involved him, he told himself. Jodie must have gone down there because of him. But why? According to Lisa Kerns, Jodie had claimed it was important she find this person—Connor Wrye. Carl wanted to know why it was so important and what it had to do with Mexico.

When he got home, instead of going into the house, he hurried across the street and knocked on Jack Costello's door. He could hear the TV but Jack didn't answer, so Carl pounded on it again.

"Jack!" he called out. "Open the goddamn door!"

A minute later Jack opened the door, struggling to fasten his belt buckle. "Where's the fire, for God's sake?"

Carl pushed past him and walked in. "Where the hell were you?" he said.

"In the crapper. What's got you all wound up?"

"I need you to do something for me. That son of yours still an inspector?"

"You kidding? Bobby practically runs the regional office up there. He's a big shot now, you know."

"I need him to check somebody out for me. Run the name in that government computer they got up there."

"Carl, you know he's not supposed to do that kind of thing unless it's an official Postal Service investigation. He can get into trouble."

"You know I wouldn't ask if it wasn't important. It involves Jodie. There's something going on, Jack, and I need to find out what it is."

Jack Costello was silent for a moment, thinking, studying Carl's expression. Finally he said, "Give me the name."

"Connor Wrye." Carl spelled the last name. "A-S-A-P, okay, Jack?" he said.

"I'll call him right now. But it's Saturday. He probably won't be in the office until Monday."

"No, it can't wait. He has to do it now."

"Carl, it's Saturday."

"It's Jodie," Carl said. "It's my daughter."

Jack groaned as he picked up the phone. "Let's see what we can do."

≋ 38

Jodie listened as Neil made the call to Dr. Stirling. All he said over the phone was that it pertained to what he, Stirling, was hiding. Neil didn't give him a chance to pretend he didn't know what Neil was talking about.

"We're coming over there right now," Neil said.

Stirling appealed to him to wait an hour and come over at six-fifteen, after his last appointment. Neil begrudgingly accepted.

"No, we should go there and confront him now," Jodie said when Neil hung up. "This can't wait."

"It's better this way. He's not going to admit anything if we bust in there and lock horns with him in front of other patients. If its just the three of us there, I think we can get him to talk. Trust me."

When they arrived at Stirling's office, the door was locked and Stirling was in the waiting room, pacing. He saw them through the window and hurried over to unlock the door, then he locked it again when they were inside, looking worried the whole time. Darlene Cummings had already left for the day. The three of them were alone.

Stirling led them back to his office. Once they were

sitting, Neil said, "I think you know what this is all about, so let's not play games."

Stirling stared at them across his desk and adjusted his glasses. He looked first at Neil, then turned his attention to Jodie. He seemed to be considering what to say, how to respond. Jodie saw clearly in the troubled look in his eyes, magnified by the thick lenses, that he understood why they were here, what they had discovered.

"I wanted to go to the police," she said. "But Neil thought we should give you a chance to explain first. I don't know how you can possibly explain . . ."

"What is it you think I've done?" he asked abruptly.

"Tell me if this name means anything to you," Jodie said. "Dr. Andrews."

"Andrews?" He shrugged, avoiding direct eye contact. "No. Why? Should it mean something?"

Neil made no attempt to hide his contempt. "Cut the crap. We said no games, remember?"

Stirling stared at the desk again in silence, worry casting a shadow over his face.

Jodie said, "The Clinica Centro?"

Stirling reacted the same way he had when she said Andrews, the same guilty look. He didn't try to bluff this time; instead he glanced up at her and looked away quickly.

"You *are* Dr. Andrews," Jodie said. "Aren't you?"

"What . . . what makes you think that?"

"I've been to Clinica Centro. I talked to one of your patients. Maria Ticas de Garcia. You operated on her husband, Hector Garcia, for appendicitis. Do you remember?"

Stirling didn't answer.

"He died from seizures caused by traumatic epilepsy," Jodie said.

She saw in Stirling's face that he did remember.

"And I know about The Cure," she said. "I know what's really in it. I know it's not made from brain tissue of pigs like you said it was. Before you try to deny it—I know what I'm talking about. I had it analyzed."

He glanced up for only an instant and let out an uneasy chuckle. "Why would you do that?" he said. "You signed a—"

"Look," Neil said, impatiently. "You lied to her."

"It's not . . . not as straightforward as you think," Stirling told Jodie.

"I don't think it's straightforward," Jodie said. "Not at all."

"What I mean is . . ." Stirling searched for words. Finally he said, "Your father is better. You can't deny that."

"That's not the point."

"No, this is *exactly* the point."

"No, the point is you're doing something to these patients of yours and people are dying. *That's* the point."

Stirling stood up and came around the desk. He looked briefly for a place to stand, but he seemed awkward being so close to her. She saw perspiration on his forehead and upper lip. He walked across the room to a table with a coffee maker and bottled water. He filled a coffee cup with water, his hands unsteady.

"What . . . what makes you think . . . that?" he asked, his back to her.

"That your patients are dying? Or that you're doing something that's causing them to die?"

He turned toward her now. "You're making medical assumptions," he said. "Are you a doctor?"

"I don't have to be. I talked to Sam Rogoff from the World Health Organization. That's right," she said, seeing a surprised look on Stirling's face. "And he was a doctor. And he knew that you caused several patients to have epilepsy. And some of them died. Like Hector Garcia. So I don't have to be a doctor to make these medical assumptions. The World Health Organization already made them for me. The only reason we're here is to give you a chance to tell your side of it. If you don't want to, that's fine. We'll just go straight to the police and let them take it from here. Is that what you'd prefer, *Dr. Andrews?*"

Anguish swept through Stirling, changing his demeanor instantly. His neck muscles tensed as his face turned a shade whiter. In a nervous tic, he pushed his glasses up higher on his nose, then wiped his sweaty hands on his pants. He glanced at Neil and looked back at Jodie again.

"Epilepsy?" he said, again trying to bluff but failing miserably.

"Yes," she said. "So you see, your little secret isn't such a secret anymore."

Stirling chuckled, a forced, unnatural utterance. With his throat so tight, it sounded more like a whimper than laughter. "Really," he said, trying to act casual, innocent. "You're making it sound like some kind of cloak and dagger—"

Suddenly Neil slapped the top of the desk, the loud noise startling Jodie. She saw Stirling jump with fear. He looked like a frightened child.

"That's it!" Neil stood up and grabbed Jodie's arm. "Let's get out of here," he said, practically yanking her out of the chair. "If he's going to act this way, we're wasting our time. Let's just go to the police like you wanted to do in the first place. He can explain to them instead of explaining to us."

"No, no, wait!" Stirling said, no longer even trying to conceal his nervousness.

"We've waited long enough," Neil said. "If you want to play games, we're not going to sit here and play them with you. Either you start being straight with us or we're out of here."

"Okay, okay. Just sit down. Let's discuss this calmly."

"I'm not kidding," Neil said. "You jerk us around any more and I swear—"

"I won't. I'll try to explain. Please, sit down and let's discuss this."

Neil lowered himself into the chair. As Stirling walked back around the desk, Neil winked at Jodie. She realized the outburst had all been an act.

Stirling hesitated a moment, composing what he would say next.

"The Cure doesn't come from pigs, does it?" Jodie prompted. "It comes from humans."

Stirling shook his head. "No."

"I told you I had it tested and they found human brain tissue in it."

"No, what they found," Stirling said, "is exactly what I told you was in it."

"It's human, not porcine."

"What the tests you had done in Florida actually detected were the human DNA sequences within these transgenic pigs. Of course that's what they're going to find. Their results were accurate. Unfortunately their conclusions weren't."

"What's that supposed to mean?"

"If you recall, I explained that the donor source was cortex tissue from specially raised pigs into which I had injected specific human genetic codes. Do you remember?"

Jodie did remember Stirling telling her about the pigs being special, about there being something human introduced.

"This is done so that the growth factor produced by these animals will be compatible with the human central nervous system," Stirling said. "I'm sure I explained all this to you. Didn't I?"

Jodie glanced over at Neil who was staring her, waiting for her answer. "Did he?" Neil asked.

She managed a shrug which brought a questioning look from Neil.

"The porcine cellular components," Stirling said, "have to be purified out before NPEF-alpha is given to patients or else they'll have a terrible immune response. The whole purpose of using a transgenic donor source is so that the cells will be biochemically human. I do believe I explained this to you and your father when you first came here."

Jodie didn't say anything. Could she have misunderstood what he had told her? Could she have caused Dr. Harrington and the people at the Mayo Clinic to misunderstand as well?

"Let me reassure you," Stirling said. "NPEF-alpha is exactly what I told you it is, and the genetically altered porcine growth factor is absolutely safe. That's the reason we use it. Safety, above all else, is our number one concern. Your father is not taking anything that could possibly harm him."

Even if she had misunderstood what he said two months ago, that didn't explain everything else she had learned over the last few days.

"Then why are other patients of yours getting epilepsy and dying?" she asked. "What about that? And what about your secret identity—*Dr. Andrews?*"

"Will you allow me to explain?" Stirling asked, a little calmer now, a little more confident.

"There's nothing to explain. Patients are dying because you're doing something to them."

"The patients you're referring to are not AD patients," Stirling said. "They have absolutely nothing to do with NPEF-alpha."

"How do I know you're telling the truth? And what about what happened in Guatemala? Do you want to try to explain that too? That's right, I know about that. I know that people died down there because of what you did. You're going to tell me you have a good explanation for that, too?"

"It sounds like you've already made up your mind, just like you did about the components of NPEF-alpha being human. But as you now realize, the erroneous results of the tests you had done—"

"If you have something to say, just say it," Jodie said, snapping at him. "Go ahead and explain, for Christ's sake."

"Yes, it is true that some of the patients at Clinica Centro where I volunteer have developed epileptic symptoms, and in a few cases this has led to fatal seizures."

"They're dying!" Jodie shouted, rising out of her chair. "Patients of yours in Guatemala died, too!" She leaned over the desk, glaring at Stirling. "That's why the World Health Organization booted you the hell out of there, so don't make it sound like—"

"Jodie," Neil said, taking her by the hand and coaxing her back into her chair. "Let's hear him out, okay?" he said quietly. "Let's let him finish."

"Why, if he's just going to lie to us?"

"We haven't even heard what he has to say about any of that yet. Let him talk. That's why we came here. Let's see what he has to say."

Jodie blew out a breath of resignation, flopped back in her chair and crossed her arms in front of her, silently agreeing to hear Stirling out.

Neil turned to Stirling and said, "Go ahead. Say what you have to say."

Stirling looked at Jodie for a moment in silence, then in a quiet, sincere voice, said, "Miss Simms, I'm afraid you're misinformed about my tenure with the World Health Organization's Hale Project in Guatemala."

"I don't think so," she said in a sharp retort. "I *know* for a fact they kicked you out."

"Well, yes, there is some validity to that, but you obviously don't know the circumstances surrounding my withdrawal."

"People died. You were responsible. I know that much."

"People did die, but I assure you I was not responsible. Patients always die. They die here in Mexico, they die in Guatemala, and they even die at the Mayo Clinic. Some patients cannot be cured—that is an unpleasant but unavoidable fact of medical science. I'm sure you can appreciate that. Doctors cannot cure everyone of every illness. And no one died because of anything *I* did."

"I'm not stupid, Doctor. The World Health Organization wouldn't fire you if that's all it was, if some people were too sick to be cured. Stop trying to cover up."

"No. The reason the World Health Organization requested that I discontinue my participation in the Hale Project was because of the stories."

"What stories?" She wished Stirling would say what he had to say and stop being so vague and misleading.

"They started many years ago. I don't know exactly how, but I do know that they have spread throughout this entire region. All of the local people down here believe these stories, though no one will really talk about it openly."

"Believe what? Talk about what? What are you talking about?"

Stirling leaned a little closer, adjusted his glasses on his nose, and said almost in a whisper, "They are convinced that Americans, in particular American physicians, are harvesting organs from the poor people who

live here so they can ship them off to America to give to
rich people who need transplants."

"*What?*"

Stirling nodded and said, "Absolutely the truth. People believe it. It's become folklore in this region, much
like Big Foot up in Canada, or the Loch Ness monster in
Scotland. The only difference is that the monster down
here is foreign medicine, foreign physicians and sur-
geons. This belief and distrust permeates everything
having to do with medicine. Of course it isn't true, it's
ridiculous even to think such a thing could happen. But
most of these people are uneducated. They've been
brought up with a myriad of superstitious beliefs. The
politicians help perpetuate the lie because it promotes
distrust of foreigners. That way the electorate will ignore
what foreigners say about politicians stealing from them
and exploiting them. The stories are an integral part of
the culture."

"That's ridiculous," Jodie said.

"Unless you have actually encountered it yourself,
which would not be the case unless you actually lived
down here awhile, it is very hard to comprehend how
prevalent this belief is. But it is prevalent. I've encountered it, here and in Guatemala. I know the impact it can
have."

Stirling turned to Neil. "You live here," he said. "You
must have heard the rumors."

Neil looked at Jodie and nodded. "The part about
people accusing *gringos* of stealing organs," he said
quietly. "That is true, Jodie. The people really believe
that."

"And that is what happened in Guatemala," Stirling told Jodie. "That is why I discontinued my participation in the Hale Project. Not because I did anything wrong, and not because the World Health Organization believed I did anything wrong. I left because once the rumors start, they cannot be stopped, and my continuing presence would only hurt the project as a whole. But I'm not the first doctor who has encountered this prejudice. Not by any means. The World Health Organization will tell you that themselves. Just ask them. Just ask any charitable organization that comes down here to provide medical care for these people. All of them will tell you the same thing. They all encounter the same difficulty. Someone will accuse a physician of stealing organs and the whole project suffers. The sad part is, it is the people down here, the people themselves, who are the ones suffering the most from this. They believe the rumors, they stop going to the clinics, and they get sick. Sometimes they even die. You're right about it being ridiculous. It is absolutely ridiculous. But it is also absolutely what happens. And it happened to me."

Jodie didn't know whether to believe him or not. She looked at Neil again, and he seemed to believe what Stirling was saying. But even if the part about Guatemala was true, what about the rest? What about Stirling having two names? What about his patients developing epilepsy and dying? What about all that?

"Why should I believe anything you say?" Jodie asked Stirling.

"I assure you, Miss Simms, I have no reason to lie to you."

"You have no reason to have an alias either, do you?"

Stirling took a deep breath and considered his answer for a moment. He glanced at Neil, then turned to Jodie and said, "I admit that I do use a different name when I'm volunteering at Clinica Centro."

"Why? What are you hiding?"

"Obviously I'm not hiding anything, otherwise I wouldn't be telling you all this."

"All what? You haven't told me anything."

"I'm trying to be as candid as possible."

Neil spoke. "Jodie, maybe if we let him finish . . ."

Jodie was fuming again, but she forced herself to remain silent, crossing her arms over her chest, waiting for Stirling to explain himself.

Stirling nodded to Neil, a gesture that looked like he was thanking him, then he turned to Jodie and said, "I was concerned that if the patients found out about Guatemala, they would not come to the clinic anymore. I didn't want my participation in this clinic to interfere with the health care needs of these people, so I chose to adopt a pseudonym."

"You really expect us to believe that?" Jodie said.

"It is the truth."

"Jodie," Neil said quietly. "I have to admit, if you knew the way the people down here thought, you'd understand that it does make sense for him to do that."

"You believe him?"

"I'm just saying everything he's telling us is logical. So I guess . . . yes, I do believe him. On that, anyway. But what about the patients dying of epilepsy?" he said. "What do you have to say about that?"

"That is tragic. Very tragic."

"It's more than just tragic," Jodie said. "For God's sake, it's horrible. *It's criminal!*"

"Yes, I agree," Stirling said, which stunned Jodie. That was the last thing she expected him to say, to admit that he was doing something criminal.

"Which is why," Stirling said, "I was working with the World Health Organization and with Dr. Rogoff personally to determine what was causing this . . . epidemic."

"You were working with them?" Neil asked.

"Yes. Dr. Rogoff came to me and asked me to help him. We decided it would be best if no one knew of my participation, out of fear that the patients would become suspicious. They don't trust large international organizations like the World Health Organization," Stirling told Jodie. "For reasons I've already explained. They don't trust most things foreign. Dr. Rogoff enlisted my help to try to find out what was causing the cases of epilepsy that have been developing in this area. We're fairly certain it is something environmental, but we haven't yet been able to determine exactly what it is."

"I don't believe you," Jodie said flatly.

Stirling shrugged. "I don't know what I could say to convince you otherwise."

"You weren't working with Sam Rogoff. He told me himself that you were part of the problem."

Stirling looked befuddled. "He told you *that?*"

"Yes."

"Are you certain?"

"He told me you were a bad doctor—he actually called

you a quack—and said your patients were the ones who were mysteriously dying from epileptic seizures."

"I think you might have misunderstood what he said."

"I know what he said. And I know what Hector Garcia's wife said. She told me he started having seizures after you operated on his appendix."

"In regards to what Dr. Rogoff might have told you— could he have said that many of the patients that came to see me were also the same patients developing the unexplained seizures?"

"That's what I just said."

"Yes, but he didn't imply a causal connection between my care of the patients and the seizures."

"What the hell are you babbling about?" Jodie said.

"The reason Dr. Rogoff came to me was because most of my patients at Clinica Centro are Mayans from a particular area, the same area in which the incidence of seizures was detected. Dr. Rogoff enlisted my help because he thought I could give him access to these particular patients, not because he thought I was responsible. Obviously an appendectomy could not possibly cause seizures. Seizures stem from abnormalities in the brain. The appendix is all the way down here," he said, gesturing toward the side of his pelvic area.

"I know where the appendix is," Jodie said. "And I also know what Rogoff told me."

Neil put his hand on her shoulder and asked, "What did he say . . . *exactly*?"

"I don't remember his *exact* words. It was several weeks ago that we talked about all this."

"Is it possible that you misunderstood?"

"No!"

"Are you sure?"

Jodie wanted to insist that she was sure, but the questioning look on Neil's face made her challenge her own memory of that brief conversation on the beach. She had been trying to ignore Rogoff that day. The entire conversation had only lasted a few minutes and the only distinct impression she had come away with was that he was a creep.

Now, weeks later, was she sure of her memory of what he had said? Did he actually *blame* Stirling—*Cassandros*—for the epilepsy? Or had he really been saying something else? Could Stirling's account be more accurate?

With all that had been happening over the last few days, all she had been trying to understand, she realized she was a little confused about some things. In truth, she wasn't clear on *exactly* what Rogoff had said regarding Stirling/Cassandros.

Except that he was a bad doctor. Which is what Hector Garcia's wife said he was. Which, apparently, is what many Mayans also thought of him.

"Then why do they call you bad Andrews?" Jodie said.

"I told you, the people down here are suspicious of foreign physicians. Especially the poor people. They have a saying. When a rich man is sick—"

"Yeah, I know, I heard it," Jodie said.

"Well, when they are desperate, they come to me and sometimes by then it's too late for me to help them. If

they had come to me first instead of to the *curandero* . . ."
He just stared at her and left the rest unsaid, though the
meaning was clear. The people themselves were at fault.

"Anyway," Stirling said, "the people who don't trust
physicians in the first place see that a patient of mine
develops seizures and they don't understand it, so they
blame it on modern medicine, which they also don't
understand. In practicing down here, I have learned to
accept this prejudice, but I never anticipated that someone who didn't fully understand the peculiarities of these
people would interpret the superstitions as evidence that
I was doing something untoward."

Stirling turned to Neil. "Mr. Lancaster," he said.
"You've lived down here for some time. You certainly
understand the way the people are. You must understand
that I can't be blamed for cultural prejudices that have
existed for a very long time. You do understand, don't
you?"

Neil turned to Jodie again and just looked at her in
silence for a moment. The look on his face told her that
he did understand. He was in agreement with Stirling.

"He's right, Jodie," Neil said quietly.

Jodie didn't know what to say. She was no longer sure
about anything.

Neil turned to Stirling. "We want to make sure that
Jodie's father isn't going to start having seizures like
these other people she's heard about."

"I can assure you that will not happen. There is no
connection between them and your father, Miss Simms.
As I said earlier, they are not in the AD program. Your
father's therapy has nothing to do with them."

Neil nodded, then looked at Jodie and said, "What do you think?"

She just looked at him, still confused, wanting to believe Stirling, wanting to leave here confident that her father would be all right.

"Miss Simms," Stirling said, his voice soft and more human than she had ever heard it before. "I'm only trying to help people. The poor people who can't otherwise afford medical care. And people like your father. If you go to the police, I will get into trouble for practicing under another name, that is certain. They will likely revoke my license. Then I won't be able to help anyone, not the local people, and not my patients suffering the terrible effects of Alzheimer's. Please don't do that to these people and their families. Please don't take away their only hope. And please, don't do that to your own father."

≋ 39

The darkness made Jodie uneasy. As they drove over the small bridge into the hotel zone, the air coming off the water reeked of dying sea life.

"I don't want to be alone," Jodie whispered.

The wind, blowing through the open Jeep, sounded like a desperate hiss tonight. Jodie shivered as she fumbled with the top button of her blouse, trying to shield herself from the strange chill. She looked across the Jeep at Neil.

"Don't leave me tonight," she said.

He reached over and grasped her trembling hand, steadying her. "I won't leave you," he said.

He didn't turn into the parking lot of the Hotel Salida Del Sol. Instead he drove a mile farther up Kukulcan Boulevard and turned into a drive on the lagoon side, concealed by a row of green hedges. Cut into the shrubbery was a small jade sign with gold lettering. It said ISLA DORADA.

Neil slowed as they approached the iron gate and guardhouse. The guard, a young Mexican man in uniform, recognized Neil's Jeep and waved them on. The gate opened electronically.

A narrow bridge took them to a small spit of land in the corner of the lagoon. The streetlights here were old-fashioned, turn-of-the-century lampposts, but they sprayed a bright halogen light that quickly erased Jodie's uneasiness about the night. The cobblestone road wound past a collection of oversized mansions, rivaling the best neighborhoods of Ponte Vedra, where most of Jacksonville's wealthy lived. The architecture was an odd mixture of every conceivable style, the only common feature being all of the houses were built of quarried limestone.

Neil's house was at the far end of the island, so close to the water the rear portion looked like it dipped into the lagoon. Floodlights, submerged in the lawn, illuminated the massive stone pillars in front, pillars supporting a portico that reminded Jodie of the entrance to the White House.

Neil parked under the portico. As Jodie stepped out of the Jeep, she heard the steady sibilance of two fountains flanking the recessed entryway. From several nooks in the walls peered Mayan statues, ceremonial masks, ceramic vases. A large head looking like a combination of a snake and a bird stood in the middle of the walk, as though to greet guests. Jodie thought it looked familiar but she couldn't remember where she had seen it before.

"That's Kukulcan," Neil said as he came around the Jeep. "That's who the main street here in Cancun is named after. And the pyramid in Chichén Itzá, remember that?"

Now Jodie recalled where she had seen this figure, carved into the stone of that ancient city.

"Just about everything thing else around here is named after Kukulcan," Neil said with a chuckle.

"Is Kukulcan a Mayan god?"

"Well, legend has it Kukulcan started out as a ruler hundreds of years ago and then he became a god. The Feathered Serpent. When the tribes were good, Kukulcan watched over them. When they weren't so good . . ." Neil gave a wry look and said, "Well, they knew not to anger Kukulcan."

Neil led Jodie down the marble walk to a mahogany door so large and ornate it belonged in the entryway of a luxury hotel, not in a private home. She was surprised to see him open it without a key.

"You don't worry about burglars?" she asked.

"Not here."

As she walked inside and saw the interior of the house, she said, "I can't believe people actually live like this."

The marble floor continued past several other Mayan sculptures and a small collection of modern abstract paintings. A huge crystal chandelier hung from the cathedral ceiling. Farther inside was another chandelier, more marble and art, and an entire wall of glass overlooking the lagoon. The living room was as large as a hotel lobby. It was furnished minimally, but each piece looked exquisite. She liked the lean effect and the distinctly masculine feel it created.

Her footsteps echoed off the marble and stone surfaces surrounding her as she wandered deeper inside, overwhelmed by it all.

"This place must have cost a fortune," she said.

"A lot less than you think," Neil said. "I picked this place up for a song because it wasn't finished and because the man who was building it needed money desperately. Labor's so cheap here I was able to finish it for practically nothing. You can hire good workers for less than ten dollars a day. Mexico really is a place where you can live beyond your means."

Jodie followed Neil into the kitchen, which could have sustained a small restaurant. Stainless steel appliances shined as though someone buffed them daily. Cookware hung from the ceiling. The large island work area had two sinks, a large cutting surface scarred by knife blades, and a bin of fresh vegetables.

"You must be hungry," he said.

All she had eaten today were peanuts on the plane, almost twelve hours ago. She had been so preoccupied with Stirling she had ignored her hunger. But now that she had the answers she had come here to find, now that she was safe with Neil, she felt the emptiness in her stomach.

"Do you want me to fix something?" she asked.

"You're my guest. I'll make you dinner."

"You can cook?"

"Are you kidding? I'm one of the best chefs in Cancun, maybe the best in all of the Yucatan."

"You don't strike me as the type of man who spends a lot of time in the kitchen."

"If I were you, I'd reserve judgment until you taste my cooking."

He went into a small room off the kitchen and brought out a bottle of imported Bordeaux.

"The Mexicans know how to make mescal," he said as he opened the bottle and filled a glass for her. "But their wine leaves much to be desired. Do you like *Château Giscours?*"

Jodie chuckled. She knew the wine was red but she had no idea what *Château Giscours* was. "I usually drink *Château Ernest and Julio Gallo,*" she said. "But I guess I can stomach this for one night."

Neil smiled as he took a sip of wine from her glass, then handed it to her. She sipped a little and was impressed by his taste in wine.

He excused himself for a moment to change. When he returned, he was wearing shorts and a faded silk shirt, sandals, a trace of cologne. His hair lay loose on his shoulders. He brought a stool over to the counter for Jodie and said:

"Sit, and watch an artist at work."

She watched him prepare *pabil,* a Mayan dish of baked pork, seasoned with *achiote* and rolled in banana leaves, surprised at how comfortable he was in the kitchen.

"Where did you learn to cook?" she asked as she

watched him roll the pork and arrange it on a bed of rice on the plates.

"Oh, I picked up things here and there."

"You're just full of hidden talents, aren't you?"

He laughed and refilled their glasses.

Instead of eating in the dining room, Neil took Jodie outside onto the patio where they ate by candlelight, overlooking the calm waters of the *Laguna Nichupté*. He made a toast to, "Whatever the future has in store."

When Jodie tasted the *pabil*, she was amazed by the flavor and tenderness of the pork. "You really can cook," she said. "This is terrific."

"You didn't believe me?"

"I admit, I had my doubts."

"You should learn to trust me," he said.

"I do trust you," she told him. The words came out more weighty than she had intended—but she did mean it. She did trust him. And she was thankful to have him with her, desperately needing someone to trust.

Neil reached across the table and tenderly touched her hand. No further words were necessary.

They ate in silence for a long while. Jodie's thoughts drifted back to all that had happened today and she struggled to make sense of it. When she looked up, she saw Neil watching her. As though he could read her thoughts he said:

"You are all right with what happened today, aren't you?"

She let out a long sigh before answering. "I don't see that I have much choice about it, do I?"

"For what it's worth," Neil said, "I don't know this guy

Stirling from Adam, but I consider myself a pretty good judge of people, and I have to tell you, I think he's on the level. Oh I'll admit he's a little . . . odd," Neil said with a chuckle. "With the big eyes and the way he avoids looking directly at you most of the time. But I still believe his intentions are good. And I believe he's a good doctor. I don't think he's hurting anyone, Jodie. I really don't. But we both know that he *is* helping a lot of people, including your father."

"I just don't know what to think anymore," Jodie said quietly.

Neil held her hand again. "I know you're worried about your father. You don't want to see him hurt. He'll be okay. We'll make sure of that."

She and Neil didn't say any more about Stirling. Instead, Neil talked about his life down here and asked her about her life in Jacksonville. The hours passed quickly, easily. They finished the bottle of wine even before their plates were empty. Neil opened another bottle and they drank and talked some more.

After they finished eating, they left the dishes on the patio and Neil took her by the hand down to the edge of the lagoon. The moon glistened silvery over the surface of the water. Tiny waves lapped up on the sand. Far out in the darkness a fishing boat puttered along. Jodie took off her shoes and let the cool water touch her toes.

She and Neil strolled along the shoreline, and she let her thoughts drift further from all that had happened today. She let herself believe everything Stirling had told her. Her father needed her to accept it. His health depended on it. She needed to do this for him.

She tried not to think about The Cure and Clinica Centro, surrendering her thoughts instead to sensations of the present. The cool breeze. The quiet whisper of the water caressing the shore. The pleasant scent of the night. The touch of Neil's hand on hers.

They said nothing as they walked, just enjoying each other's company. Finally they stopped at the edge of Neil's property. A palm tree had fallen years ago, too tall and heavy for its shallow roots, for the soft sand, but it had continued to grow horizontally out over the water. Jodie and Neil sat together on the tree.

Jodie let her feet dip into the cool water. Neil put his arm around her and drew her against him. He felt warm, and his warmth made her feel safe, feel that everything would be all right. The troubled thoughts about the therapy keeping her father alive receded from her mind, becoming distant and faint like the sound of the lone motorboat somewhere out there in the darkness of the lagoon.

"Thank you for helping me tonight," she whispered.

"You don't have to thank me."

"I do. I don't know what I would have done if you hadn't been around."

"Why wouldn't I be around for you?"

"I just mean—"

He shushed her. "I know what you mean," he whispered.

His hand brushed her chin. She met his gaze, one that let her know something extraordinary was about to happen. Slowly, deliberately, he brushed the few strands of hair away from her eyes and stroked her cheek gently, with the tenderness of a lover. She reached up and found his palm. His hands felt smooth, but strong. The rousing scent of his body filled her lungs.

"I've been thinking a lot about you," she whispered.

"You're the *only thing* I've thought about," he said. "Each time we spoke on the phone, each time I heard your voice, made it harder to be away from you. And now that I'm with you again, I realize how much it's going to hurt to let you leave tomorrow."

"I wish I could stay longer, but I have to get back. I have my work, my father . . ."

"I'm just glad you're here tonight," he said. "Here with me."

She brought his hand to her lips and slowly kissed his fingertips, tasting the salt and sweat on his skin. The warmth and humidity in the air coaxed droplets of perspiration from her pores. Her blouse felt sticky against her skin. She strained to breathe. Her heart started racing.

He gazed into her eyes. "Last time you were here," he said, his voice soft and steady, "at the airport, when I watched you walk away, you can't imagine how much I wanted to go after you."

"Not as badly as I wanted not to have to go."

"Tonight . . ." He paused, looking deep inside her. "I don't want to let you leave," he said.

Jodie couldn't speak. All kinds of emotions rushed through her, all kinds of questions and concerns. She wondered if this was going too fast and then she asked herself, Why shouldn't it? She was old enough to trust her feelings, to know when it was real.

She drew a deep breath of his rousing scent. The moment was moving so quickly she felt dazed, a jumble of confused emotions. Tomorrow she'd be back in Florida and whatever *this* was—would it be over? She felt something special between them, something she hadn't felt in a very long time, something she hadn't allowed herself to feel.

She shifted, an awkward move that brought her hips against his. Their faces were nearly touching. For a brief instant their eyes connected in an enchanted gaze that stirred Jodie's passion and yet left her weak. As Neil leaned in to kiss her, her lips reached out to meet his.

She pressed herself closer to him and his powerful arms surrounded her, holding her as though he would never let go. His strength made her feel secure and certain this was right.

Without speaking Neil got up and took her by the hand. Jodie stood at the edge of the water. The breeze coming off the lagoon caressed her face. She quivered. In his eyes she saw a hunger and she realized she wanted this to happen as much as he did.

He brushed her cheek again and let his hand slip down to her shoulder, then across her chest, exploring her body with patient curiosity. She started to unbutton her blouse but he stopped her.

"Let me," he whispered.

He knelt down on the grass in front of her. She felt his breath against her breasts as he slowly undid the buttons of her blouse and spread it open. He kissed her nipple and she trembled. Her legs nearly collapsed beneath her.

She grasped his shoulders and held on to keep from falling.

His lips moved along her breast and down her waist to her belt. He stopped there and just lingered, kissing the light fleece around her belly button. Her eyes closed on their own and her head dropped back as waves of pleasure washed up her body.

Now Neil unfastened her belt and opened the front of her slacks. In an odd slow-motion flutter her slacks fell to her feet. She stepped out of them and stood barefoot on the grass in only her panties.

Her body quaked as she felt his fingers slide between the waistband of her panties and the soft, white skin of her thighs.

"Neil . . ." she whispered, feeling only the slightest concern for propriety. "Out here? . . ."

He answered without words, with one fluid motion removing her panties and moving in with such ardor that Jodie gasped and let out a rapt cry. Her fingers pinched into the muscles of his shoulders as she fought to contain herself.

Neil wrapped his arms around her and pulled her firmly against him. He rolled backward until her weight was on him, her hands tangled in his long, blond hair. Then he scooped her legs up off the ground and, leaning forward again, lowered her onto her back.

He knelt over her now, his legs straddling her. His face above her was red and flushed with blood. His hair brushed her face. He started to pull his own shirt over his head, still buttoned, but this time it was her turn to stop him. She pried his hands away and began unbuttoning the shirt, slowly at first, reining her passion, but then, as she got a glimpse of his chest, her hands trembled in anticipation. She began to have difficulty, and at last she just ripped the shirt open, popping the two remaining buttons. She struggled to pull the shirt down his arms, arms whose powerful grasp she longed to feel around her again.

Hurriedly, she undid his shorts and freed him, then she pulled him down against her. His member brushed her thigh and she felt it harden. The sensation of him against her skin sent a shiver of excitement through her.

His body was as lean and muscular as she had imagined. She dug her fingers into the ripples in his back and pulled him to her as tightly as two bodies could be. As his lips moved over her body, waves of pleasure washed through her. She tingled everywhere, her brain flooding with so much sensation she feared she would lose consciousness at any moment.

She slid her hand down his torso and took hold, stroking away the last remnants of softness. She could feel blood coursing. Neil wrapped his arms around her and let his weight settle upon her. She gasped for air, a quiver of delight rushing through her. His mouth pressed against hers and for a moment she could not breathe, nor did she wish to.

She felt his hardness leave her hand and brush her thigh again as he shifted position. When he entered her, the last gasp of air rushed from her lungs in a sudden uncontrollable cry and when she tried to breathe again, his scent was all she could taste. She held on tightly, her fingers pinching into his back. They found a rhythm quickly. It was as though they had been together many times before. It was as though they were meant for each other.

Time had no measure now. Nothing beyond this patch of grass at the water's edge, nothing beyond their coupled bodies existed anymore. For a brief, magical instant, Jodie knew rapture.

≋ 40

The phone awakened Carl. He lay on the couch. The basketball game was still on TV but he had no idea who was winning or even who was playing. He found the remote control between the sofa cushions and muted the volume, then he picked up the phone.

"Yeah? Hello?"

"Mr. Simms?" a man said.

"Yeah. Who's this?"

"Bobby Costello. My old man said you asked him about a man named Connor Wrye this afternoon."

"You're Jack's son." Carl finally shook the grogginess out of his head. "How are you? I really appreciate you doing this."

"No problem. Sorry to call this late."

"That's okay. I was up."

"Look, this guy you asked my father about, is he someone you know?"

"Not really. Not me, no. My daughter is looking for him. He's involved somehow with a doctor I've been going to in Mexico. I'm not sure exactly what it's all about, though."

"Mr. Simms, I'm going to tell you something. You tell your daughter the same thing. Okay?"

"What is it?"

"My advice to you and to your daughter is to stay away from this man."

"What are you talking about?"

"Stay away from him and anyone who's associated with him."

"I don't understand. Who is he?"

"I ran the name you gave my old man. Connor Wrye isn't his real name. That's an alias he goes by. One of several aliases."

"An alias? Then what's his real name?"

"His name is Lohr. Augustus Lohr."

"Lohr? . . ." It didn't sound familiar.

"Mr. Simms, he's not someone you or your daughter want to have anything to do with. He's an ex-con. He was in prison in California."

"Why? What did he do?"

"They sent him away for manslaughter but he's done a lot worse than that. Thing is, most of it he's done out of the country. Mostly in Latin America. Some in Africa, but for the most part he stays south of the border."

"Mexico?" Carl asked.

"He could be in Mexico. He's a mercenary, Mr. Simms. People pay him to fight for them, to kill for them. He doesn't do it because he believes in a cause. He kills people because someone pays him to do it."

"He kills people?"

"Among other things. He's a really bad man, Mr. Simms. I don't know why you're asking about him, but I strongly suggest—"

"My daughter is."

"She should stay away from him. You both should stay away from him. And if he's connected with your doctor in Mexico then stay away from that doctor too. I'm telling you this because you're my father's close friend. Stay away from this man. Please."

"I have to tell Jodie. I think she's trying to find him."

"Tell her not to. If this man doesn't want to be found, she shouldn't be looking for him."

"I have to tell her. I have to call her in Mexico."

"You do that. Call her. Tell her."

"His name is what again? His real name?"

"Augustus Lohr. But he goes by other names as well. Connor Wrye, which you already know. Some of the other names he uses are Dave Poole, Marcus Lanier, Neil Lancaster, Troy—"

"Neil Lancaster!"

"Yes. Why? Do you know someone by that name?"

"Oh my God!"

"Mr. Simms. What is it?"

"She went there to see him."

"Who?"

"Jodie went to Mexico to see Neil Lancaster."

"Can you reach her?"

"Yes. I think I can."

"Do it. Call her. Tell her she has to get away from him. Warn her, Mr. Simms. Do it now. Her life could depend on it."

Carl hung up and rushed to the kitchen to get the paper Jodie had stuck to the refrigerator. The paper with the number of the hotel Jodie was staying at.

Please, God, he thought, picking up the phone to dial. *Please let her be there.*

⟍41

Jodie wished this night never had to end.

By the time they were finished, they were covered with sweat. Sand clung to their naked bodies. Their arms and legs remained tangled together, their skin sticky.

"Do you want to go inside?" Neil whispered into the dark silence.

"I'd rather you just held me."

She felt safe with his arms around her. She felt everything would be all right.

"Jodie Simms," he whispered, his voice soft and guileless. "I think I'm falling under your spell."

"My spell, huh? Is that what you call it?"

"What would you call it?"

"I call it the intoxicating night air, the sea breeze, the moon. Maybe the watchful eye of an ancient Mayan god."

"Maybe it's just that we're good together," he said. "I've waited a long time to meet someone like you. And tomorrow you'll be gone. I don't want tonight to end."

"Neither do I."

They made love again. Afterward they sat on the patio in the damp night air, unclothed, gazing out at the lagoon and the few lights glimmering on the far shore. Jodie had lost all sense of time. All she knew was it was long past midnight and she didn't want morning to come.

As thoughts of all that had happened yesterday seeped back into her head, she said, "I hope we're doing the right thing, about Dr. Stirling and all of that . . ."

"I know we are."

"I hope you're right."

He wrapped his arms around her and kissed her on the forehead. "Trust me," he whispered.

They sat in silence for a moment, Jodie's mind wandering. Another question came to her and she asked, "Didn't you say you used to work in Guatemala? Weren't you a consultant down there?"

"Yes, I did. Why?"

"That's where Stirling had his problems with the World Health Organization. Do you remember hearing anything about that while you were down there?"

Neil laughed. "Guatemala isn't exactly New York City, I realize that, but it's still a decent sized place. It's not like Mayberry. Everybody doesn't know everybody else. It's a big country. A lot of things went on down there that I didn't know about."

"I just thought maybe you read about it in the papers."

"Their press isn't like ours. They run the stories that the government wants them to run. If that whole thing with Stirling didn't make the government look good, or didn't make the opposition look bad, it wouldn't show up in the papers, at least not prominently. Anyway, I wouldn't give it much credence. There's a lot of superstitious beliefs down there. And it's also like he explained, everything is political in these countries. *Everything*. It could just be the government didn't like people getting medical care from someone who wasn't controlled by the government, and they started the rumors. You really never know what you're dealing with in some of these banana republics."

Jodie was silent for a moment, thinking about that, thinking about home, thinking about her father, thinking about Neil.

"Are you ever going back?" she asked, finally.

"To Guatemala?"

"No. To the U.S."

"That depends."

"On what?"

He gazed into her eyes and asked, "Are you ever coming back down here?"

"I'm serious," Jodie said.

"So am I. If you don't come back, then I'm going to have to do something about that. Aren't I?"

"Are you?"

He took her hand and kissed it. Then he asked, "Will you be back?"

Jodie stared at the water, considering his question. Would she return? Would she take her father back to Dr. Stirling when his supply of The Cure ran out? She didn't see how she could deny him.

"My dad is so much better," she said.

"I guess the medicine Stirling is giving him works."

"But I'm concerned about the people having the seizures. I don't want that to happen to my father."

"That's not going to happen to him. I believe Stirling when he says that's not connected to your father's treatment. Personally, I think it's all environmental, some company is dumping chemicals or something like that, something they shouldn't be dumping, and it's getting into the water supply or the food supply. That's common down here, unfortunately. Too common. They don't have the kind of EPA regulations we have back home. And the laws they do have aren't really enforced. It's tragic, but it's true. And that what's causing those seizures, not any kind of medicine or anything like that. I'd bet my hotel on that. Your father's not going to have any problems like that, Jodie. I'm sure of it."

He did sound sure of it, and his assurances that everything would be all right helped to ease, at least to some extent, her concern.

"I have to admit," she said, "without The Cure Dad would be so much worse.

"That's why it would be wrong to take it away from him."

⇒ 42

Jodie wasn't there, at the hotel. At least, she wasn't answering her phone.

The fluorescent light above Carl in the kitchen hummed, as though warning him to do something, to hurry. He saw his own reflection in the sliding glass doors, a desperate, powerless old man bent over the phone. Outside, Sunny Palms was buried in an unsettling darkness. He felt a helplessness he had never experienced before in his life. Fear shuddered through him, all the way down to his soul. But mostly, he was overcome with guilt. Jodie was in Mexico because of him. If anything happened to her, it would be because of him.

The same hotel operator answered, the same man Carl had spoken to every thirty minutes since Jack Costello's son had called five hours ago. The man's voice was heavy with annoyance, but Carl didn't give a damn. He had to reach Jodie. He had to warn her.

"Ring the room again," Carl said.

The Mexican man didn't bother arguing this time. The last two times he had told Carl that he was sitting in the lobby and would have seen Jodie if she had come in—which she hadn't. But Carl had told him to ring the room anyway, thinking she might have been sleeping earlier, perhaps had too much to drink and didn't hear the phone. Or she could have been on the beach for a late night stroll, in which case the man in the lobby wouldn't see her return to the cabaña. There could be lots of explanations. He had to keep trying to get through.

After ten rings the operator came back on the line. "Sorry. No answer."

"Can you send someone to the room?" Carl asked. "Can someone go in and see if she's all right?"

"Señor, do you know what time it is here?"

"Yes, I know what time it is. That's why I'm so worried. My daughter should be there. She should be in her room. She should be answering the phone."

"This is Cancun, señor. It is a very romantic city. It is often that a young woman and a young man—"

"I'm afraid something's happened to her. She could need help," Carl said. "Just send someone to her room. Check on her. Please!"

"I don't have the authority to go in the room, señor."

"I'm giving you the authority. I'm her father. That's all the authority you need."

"No, I need for the manager to say it is okay and he is not here until morning."

"I can't wait that long. Please. She's my daughter. I think she's hurt. She could need help right away. If you don't do this, she could die. Please. I'm begging you."

The man let out an exasperated sigh. "Call back in five minutes."

Carl paced the kitchen floor, constantly checking the clock on the stove. Time felt like it was barely moving. The minutes seemed to stretch out for hours. He could only bear to wait four minutes before he grabbed the phone and dialed the number again.

The same man answered, out of breath.

"Your daughter is not in the room," he told Carl.

"You went inside?"

"Yes. I have the key. I open the door and turn on the light. The cabaña is empty."

"You're sure?"

"Señor," the man said with a tired sigh. "It is early in the morning here . . ."

"Was there anything suspicious in there, any sign that something could be wrong?"

"No, señor. Everything is normal."

"You're sure?"

"Yes, señor."

After Carl hung up, he paced the kitchen again, unable to stop thinking about what Jack's son had told him. It was four in the morning. Jodie should be asleep in her hotel room at this hour. Something was definitely wrong.

Realizing what he had to do, he hurried over to the drawer under the phone and riffled through it until he found Helen's MasterCard. He dialed 4-1-1 and asked for American Airlines. He tried to write the phone number down but he got confused halfway through. He was relieved when the recording offered to dial it for him.

The first flight with an available seat left at nine A.M. He reserved a seat to Cancun, then hurried into the bedroom to pack.

He hoped to God he wasn't too late.

≋ 43

When Jodie awakened, she was alone in Neil's bed, staring at the ceiling fan, whirling leisurely overhead. Sunlight shone through the wall of glass that faced the lagoon. She barely made out the two jet-skis speeding along the golden water in the distance.

The room was furnished sparingly, with an unusual dresser constructed of coral, a granite table at the foot of the bed, large clay Mexican tiles on the floor. The walls, done in rough stucco and painted the color of sand, were bare. A single sculpture stood near the door to the patio, a small limestone replica of a statue she had seen at Chichén Itzá. One of Neil's silk shirts was draped over part of it.

Jodie looked for a clock but couldn't find one. Her watch was wherever she had left her clothes last night, though she wasn't exactly sure where that was. She thought her things might still be outside near the lagoon. She couldn't remember bringing them in.

And she couldn't remember Neil leaving the bed either. He must have gotten up while she was sleeping. Feeling oddly out of place and vulnerable in his room by herself, she slid out of bed. The tile floor was cold under her bare feet. She padded over to the statue and put on Neil's silk shirt, buttoning just a few buttons. It smelled of his cologne, a scent saturated with memories of last night.

As she walked to the bathroom to see if he was in there, the smooth fabric of the shirt rubbed against her thighs, reminding her of the way Neil's hands had caressed her. She couldn't believe how wonderful it had been, couldn't believe a day that had begun as badly as yesterday had, had ended with such pleasure.

The bathroom was empty so she went out onto the patio to see if he was outside and to look for her clothes. It was a muggy morning. Not even the slightest breeze blew off the lagoon. The sun beat down harshly, letting her know it would be a good day to lay out on the beach, but not good for much else.

Her things, along with Neil's, were still scattered on

the grass and sand near the lagoon where they had abandoned them last night. She gathered everything up and returned to the patio. The wineglasses and a half-empty bottle of *Château Giscours* were near the chaise lounges. She brought them in through the kitchen door.

"Neil," she called out, her voice echoing through the empty house.

The dishes from last night were in the sink. An empty wine bottle was on the counter. The room still smelled of the spices Neil had used when he cooked. She rinsed the dishes and straightened out the kitchen a bit, then went into the living room, leaving her clothes on a chair.

"Neil," she called again. "Come out, come out, wherever you are."

There was no answer, only her own voice echoing off the tile and stucco and stonework everywhere. She walked down a hall toward two guest rooms, calling Neil's name. The rooms were empty and had the musty smell of places seldom used. On the other side of the house was another hall that led to a single room. The door was closed most of the way. She knocked, waited, but there was no response, so she eased open the door and peeked in.

It was a small room with an oak desk dark with age. An office or study, she decided. On top of the desk was a modern black halogen lamp that looked oddly out of place. Beside it was a half-empty bottle of tequila. The walls were decorated with military regalia, some of which appeared to date back hundreds of years, including a medieval suit of armor and several primitive tribal war masks.

Drawn by her curiosity about the man she had slept with last night, she stepped slowly into the room. She knew Neil wasn't here, but she wanted to have a look around, thinking it would help her get to know him better. They had been close *physically* last night, but she didn't know much about the man, about his thoughts when he was alone, about his passions beyond running a hotel and cooking exotic meals. If their lives were going to be intertwined—which, she had to admit, they already were—she needed to know who this man really was, what made him tick. And what better way to learn about a man than to explore the private realm of his study. In other words, to snoop.

She glanced back to make sure he hadn't come down the hall and wasn't watching her right now, then she walked deeper into the room, beginning her exploration at the bookshelf behind his desk.

She scanned the books, thinking it was a strange collection. Leather-bound volumes of *Moby Dick, War and Peace, A Farewell To Arms*, Sun Tzu's *The Art Of War*. She didn't know what books she expected to find, but not these. And yet the more she thought about it, the more they seemed to fit him. Nothing trendy. That wasn't Neil. No, he would have classic, serious, brawny sorts of books. Like the style of the house, like the military decor of this room. She wondered now if he had ever served in the army. Except for the hair, he did have a straight-laced, military quality about him. She decided he had been an officer.

She moved over to the desk now and lowered herself into his chair, the bare skin of her bottom sticking to the cool, worn leather. The leather smelled of Neil, the scent that had intoxicated her last night. For a moment she closed her eyes and breathed deeply, remembering the sensations of a few short hours ago.

She looked at the desktop now and focused on the small white pad beside the phone. The top sheet was clean of writing, but she noticed the imprint in the paper, the ghost of the note that had been written on the sheet above it some time ago, now torn off and missing. She recalled seeing in a TV show once—was it *Columbo?*—where the detective rubbed a pencil over the indentations, bringing the words up on the paper, revealing what had been written on the page above and solving the crime.

The idea of doing the same thing now intrigued her, not because she thought she was solving a crime, but because she wanted to see if it actually worked. And it might tell her a little more about Neil.

She glanced up at the door, feeling knavish just considering this. Neil wasn't in the doorway. She was alone. No one here to see her. Who would know? What harm would it do?

Why not? she finally decided, found a pencil in the top drawer of the desk and started to rub the side of the lead over the imprint in the paper.

She was surprised and delighted to see that the trick worked: the letters began to come into view. First an "S" then an "R" followed by a space. Jody wondered if "SR" was the abbreviation for Señor. Neil had probably written someone's name, probably someone with whom he did business.

She continued rubbing the pencil across the paper, bringing out the next letters. "V" then "E" then "R" then—

Before she could finish the next letter, she heard the front door open and close, then the sound of footsteps on the tile floor as someone came into the house. Neil, she reasoned. If he found her snooping in his office, what would he think of her?

She didn't want him finding her in here, didn't want him to think she was violating his privacy—which, she admitted to herself, she was doing, and which she also admitted was probably wrong. She tore off the top page so he wouldn't realize what she had been doing, stuffed it into the shirt pocket, put the pencil back into the drawer and scampered across the room to the door. She peeked into the hall to make sure he couldn't see her, then she darted out, closed the door behind her, and padded up the hall, her bare feet silent on the cold tile floor.

When she reached the living room, she saw Neil heading toward the bedroom, dressed in jeans and an olive tank top, damp with sweat. He stopped suddenly when he saw her, his eyes widening with surprise. He glanced down the hall where she had been, then looked again at her, surprise turning to concern.

"What are you doing, Jodie?" he said.

"Looking for you. You left?" she asked.

"Yeah." He glanced down the hall again.

"Why? Where did you go?"

"I had to run down to the hotel. Didn't you hear the phone ring early this morning?"

"No."

"I guess you were really exhausted. Anyway, there was a problem with the company that supplies the restaurant at the hotel. Trying to do business down here is like . . . well, it's nothing like doing business back home, that's for sure."

"Is everything all right?"

"Unless someone at the hotel wants eggs for breakfast," he said with a chuckle, the concern in his eyes now gone. "Everything's more or less under control."

"Good."

He came over and wrapped his arms around her, kissing her hard on the lips. He smelled of sweat. His muscular arms were damp around her. He was breathing heavily, as though he had just come from working out.

"What did you have to do at the hotel?" Jodie asked jokingly. "Wrestle with the guy who supplies the restaurant?"

Neil laughed. "It's hot out there this morning. Anyway, what about you?" he said, guiding her back toward the bedroom. "You okay? Sleep well?"

"Like a baby. You should have told me you were leaving. When I woke up and you weren't there, I didn't know what to think."

"I didn't want to disturb you. After yesterday, I figured you needed the rest. I'm just sorry I didn't get back sooner. I didn't want you to wake up alone."

"You could have left a note," Jodie said.

"I thought I'd be back before you woke up." He chuckled and asked, "Did you think I ran out on you?"

"It's your house. I knew you'd be back sooner or later."

"You would have waited?" he asked.

"Fat chance."

"No, you would have waited," he said, and this time it wasn't a question.

"Pretty sure of yourself, aren't you?"

"Yup. Tell you what, let me grab a quick shower then I'll make you some breakfast. Have you showered yet?"

"No, I just got up a few minutes ago."

"Care to join me?" Neil smirked. "The Mexican government encourages us to conserve water, you know."

Jodie unbuttoned the silk shirt and let it fall to the floor, then took Neil by the hand and led him through the bedroom to the shower.

≋ 44

Jodie's blouse was damp with dew and gritty with sand, so she put Neil's silk shirt back on and told him she was going to keep it as a memento of last night.

"Do I have any say in that?" he asked. "After all, it is my shirt."

"Nope. No say at all."

"Well, it looks better on you than it did on me, anyway."

After breakfast, he drove her back to the hotel. As they walked through the lobby, Tomas, the front desk clerk, hurried over.

"Señorita Simms. Your father call on the phone for you last night."

"Is he okay? Is something wrong?"

"He is worry for you, he say."

Neil said, "Fathers will be fathers."

"I meant to call him yesterday but with everything that happened I forgot. I better call him now and let him know I'm all right. By the way, did I tell you he said he liked you?"

"Your father has good taste."

"So does his daughter."

"I wish we could spend the day together," Neil said, "but unfortunately I have some work I have to do this morning. I'd like to see you later. Okay?"

"That's not something you have to ask."

"I'll call you."

"Stop by, why don't you," she said. "I think if you slip the manager ten *pesos*, he'll tell you what cabaña I'm in."

"I may just do that."

They kissed, then Neil went to his office and Jodie walked outside, feeling more alive than she had in a very long time. Romance had a way of rejuvenating her like nothing else could. She could not believe how good she felt, even after all that had happened.

The sun was warm this morning, the breeze off the water crisp and clean. She decided to spend a few hours on the beach, playing tourist. Hopefully Neil would come along before she had to leave for the airport. She wanted desperately to be close to him again.

When she got back to her cabaña, the first thing she did even before changing into her bikini was call St. Augustine. She let the phone ring at Carl's house eight rings before hanging up. She assumed he and Jack Costello had gone golfing. She would try again later.

She put on her bathing suit and was about to head to

the beach when the phone rang. She assumed it was Carl.

"Buenas dias, Dad."

"Mrs. Simms?" The man on the other end of the line had a Mexican accent.

"Uh, yes, I'm Jodie Simms. Who is this?"

"I am Luis Guzman with the *Seguridad Publica*. You inquired yesterday about the possessions of Dr. Samuel Rogoff, who died a month ago at his hotel here in Cancun."

"Yes."

"I have looked into the case and I can tell you that everything we found in his hotel room was sent back to Florida with the body."

Yesterday, she had gotten the answers she had been looking for. This dead-end, Rogoff's notes, didn't seem particularly important anymore.

"Well, thank you anyway," she said and was about to hang up when the man spoke again.

"However, there were some things we found in his car that are still here."

"Really?" The reporter in her was curious. "Were there any notebooks or pads?" she asked. "Anything he would have used for writing, maybe computer disks, something like that?"

"Computer disks, no. But yes, a writing book is here."

This intrigued Jodie. Even though she already knew what Stirling was doing, she was still interested in what Rogoff had discovered. Fourteen years as a reporter was impossible to override. Maybe she just needed to confirm what she had learned yesterday. Maybe that might make it easier for her to accept what Stirling had said. She also remembered one question remained—who Connor Wrye was and how he or she was connected to all this. She thought Rogoff's notes might tell her.

"Would you mind if I came down there and took a look at what you have?" she asked.

"You are family, you said, so it is okay, yes. We would like for you to take everything back to Florida when you leave."

Jodie agreed, wrote down the address, then changed out of her bikini and into slacks and a blouse, eager to find out what was in Rogoff's notes and sew up all the loose ends once and for all.

⇶ 45

All the people rushing through the airport confused Carl. The noise of the public address announcements was disorienting. He wasn't sure where to go. He saw people funnel through a metal detector so he followed them. A woman checked his ticket and told him which gate to go to.

It was all so confusing. His head felt funny today. He wondered if it had anything to do with not having had his shots this week. He had a vague recollection of feeling this way before, but it was a strange memory, almost as though he were remembering someone else's past.

He saw a pay phone and hurried over. He fished some coins from his pocket and dumped them on the metal shelf under the phone. One by one, he slid them into the coin slot, then he dialed the number Jodie had written.

"Salida Del Sol."

It was a different voice, a woman, not the man who had answered the phone all last night.

"Ring Jodie Simms's room," Carl said. "This is her father. It's very important. Please hurry."

Jodie locked the door behind her and started up the path toward the lobby. She had only taken a few steps when the telephone in her cabaña started ringing. Thinking it was either the police again or perhaps her father calling, she hurried back to the door, only to realize she had left her key on the bureau.

"Damn it."

Thinking she might be able to take the call at the front desk, she raced up the path toward the lobby.

Two rings. Three. Four.

Carl listened impatiently, the ringing in his ear causing his head to throb. The terminal around him was crowded this morning. Tourists—he could tell by the way they were dressed. Parents wearing *Lion King* shirts. Children with Mickey Mouse caps. Everyone was laughing, happy. Everyone but Carl. He was so worried he could barely think straight.

The phone rang five times. Six.

"Come on, Jodie, answer," he said to himself.

Over the public address, the airline agent announced the last call for his flight to Miami. Carl wasn't sure he'd have a chance to call Jodie from Miami when he changed planes to go to Cancun. He only had a minute or two right now. He needed to try to reach her, to warn her. If she was there, he would not have to board at all. He could tell her about Neil, tell her to stay away, tell her to come home right now. But if she didn't answer, then he would go, he would know she needed him.

Seven rings. Eight.

His forehead was damp with sweat. His hand trembled as he reached up and wiped his face.

"Where are you, Jodie?" he whispered. "Please answer."

Nine. Ten.

He glanced over at the gate and watched the last passenger, a college student, hand his ticket to the female agent at the jetway. After the young man walked through, the agent started to close the door.

Eleven rings.

"Come on, Jodie . . ."

Jodie ran into the lobby and over to the front desk.

"There's someone calling me," she said. "Cabaña twelve. Can I take it here? I locked myself out."

Tomas walked to a door at the side and poked his head in. A woman was sitting behind a switchboard. He spoke to her in rapid-fire Spanish.

"Please hurry," Jodie said.

Tomas came back over and shook his head. "He has hanged up already," the man said.

"Do you know who it was?"

"The operator said it is your father."

"Hold on!" Carl shouted. "One more passenger! Wait!"

He struggled with his bag as he doddered over to the gate. The agent smiled and tore off his ticket.

"Thought we were fixing to leave without you?" she said.

"I have to get to Mexico," Carl said.

"Well, you've come to the right place."

"I hope I'm not too late."

"No sir, they haven't closed the doors yet. We'll get you on. We'll get you to Mexico. You'll be there in less than three hours."

Three hours. It seemed like an eternity.

Carl lugged his bag down the jetway toward the plane, hoping three hours would be soon enough.

Tomas gave Jodie the phone and she called Carl's house in St. Augustine. There was no answer. She wondered where he could have called from. She tried her own house, thinking he might be there. When she got the answering machine, she pressed the code to retrieve her messages, hoping Lisa Kerns had called with the information about Connor Wrye. She hadn't. Jodie assumed it was up to her, here, to try to discover who Connor Wrye was and how he fit into all of this.

Tomas gave her directions to the office of Public Security in downtown Cancun. She left, hoping to resolve the last questions concerning Rogoff, Stirling, Connor Wrye, and whatever was going on down here.

⌇ 46

Neil found that if he ignored them, they would stare at him. But if he glared back at them when they peeked up, they would quickly turn away and not look at him again until he walked past them, and then only steal a momentary glance in his direction. The people down here were easily intimidated.

He grabbed the doorknob and cursed under his breath when he found it unlocked. Stirling was such an absent-minded asshole. He had to be told every few days to lock the damn doors. Neil locked it behind himself, walked past the desk and tried the door to the lab. It, too, was unlocked.

"Goddamn . . ."

He shoved the door open so abruptly that it startled Stirling, who was bent over a microscope, staring at a slide under the lens. He nearly fell off his stool when Neil threw the door open.

"Do you have to do that?" Stirling said, righting himself on the stool and adjusting his glasses which had slid down his nose. "Can't you just walk in like a normal human being?"

"No. Can't you remember to lock the damn door like I told you a hundred times? I walked right in here like it's some kind of fucking open house."

"I do lock it when I leave. But when I'm working in here, I don't see the necessity to—"

"*All* the time. I told you that. Lock the doors *all* the damn time. Do you know what all the time means?"

Stirling blew out a breath of irritation and looked away, not bothering to answer Neil.

"No wonder we've got so many leaks," Neil said. "The way things are going, they're going to rename this place the Clinica Titanica."

"Is that supposed to be funny?"

"Do I look like I'm laughing?"

Stirling resumed whatever he was doing at the microscope, fidgeting with the knobs, but then suddenly his expression changed to one of dire concern, and fear. He looked at Neil and said, "Did you take care of the—?"

"Done," Neil said. He took the syringe and the empty bottle out of his pocket and slapped them down on the counter. "That's one bird who won't be chirping anymore."

"Did you have any problems?"

"Nope."

"How long did it take?"

"Couple minutes. Same as Rogoff."

"The dose was right."

Stirling looked pleased with himself. But Neil knew that the egghead had no reason whatsoever to be proud of himself.

"For someone whose profession is supposed to be curing people," Neil said, "you're rather good at killing, aren't you?"

Stirling's expression changed instantly. He looked

offended. Tough shit, Neil thought. He meant to offend. If it weren't for Stirling's mistakes, they wouldn't have had all these damn problems that needed taking care of.

"Let's try to make this the last," Neil said.

Appearing concerned again, Stirling said, "Did Miss Simms suspect—?"

"You forget who you're talking to?"

"I just want to be certain that—"

"I can handle her. You just worry about doing your own damn part in this. One more screw up and it's not going to be so easy to smooth things out."

"How did *I* screw up?" Stirling asked.

"For one thing, you're not locking the damn door."

"Oh for goodness sake, will you—"

"And for another," Neil said, ignoring him, "what's taking so damn long to get this synthesis done? You said you'd have it ready months ago."

"I'm close. I'm very close."

"That's what you said months ago."

"You must try to comprehend all that is involved in this. We're breaking new ground, you understand. It isn't as easy as you'd like it to be. I can't just clone the actual growth factor. If I could, it would have been so much easier. I have to identify the processing enzymes because the difference is in the post-translational processing, not in the—"

Neil waved his hand in front of his face and said, "Save the jargon for someone who understands it. Just tell me when you're going to have this damn thing synthesized or cloned or whatever the hell you call it."

Stirling contemplated it a moment then said, "Soon."

Neil threw up his hands.

"I'm going as fast as I can," Stirling said.

"We can't keep this up forever, you know. You told me when we started that it was more or less safe. You said these people would have no problem compensating for the small amounts you were going to take out. You said that's why you were getting it from them, from these Itzás. That's why it had to be these particular Mayans. They could compensate, you said. They had the enzyme or protein or whatever the hell you called it. They had it inside them. Just them—no one else."

"That's true. I don't know why, but they are the only people whose nervous system produces this modified form of BDNF."

"Whatever. The point is, you said that since they have this mutant thing, they could compensate for the damage your procedure was going to cause. That's what you told me from the get-go."

"Well, actually, I did say there might be side effects," Stirling said. "If you recall, I mentioned that they might experience loss of spontaneity in behavior, reduced ambition, perhaps reduced inhibitions, and even the possibility of occasional violent outbursts."

"You said they wouldn't be able to smell things like they did before," Neil said. "That's what you told me was the main thing that would happen. Their sense of smell would be out of whack, which they probably wouldn't even notice and even if they did notice, no one would put two and two together anyway. That's what you told me."

"But I did say that when the cortex is affected like this, the chance of epileptic-like seizures is always a remote poss—"

"Cut the bullshit, Russell. You never said all these people would be dying. If it was a few—hey, it's the cost of business, I can accept that. But all these—no way, this isn't what I bargained for."

Stirling looked away again, embarrassment on his face. But it was not because he gave a damn about the people dying. Neil knew he didn't care one way or the other about them. Cost of doing business. Both of them accepted that.

Stirling's embarrassment, Neil realized, was because he had been wrong about how the patients would be affected by what he was doing, about how many would die from his procedure. His judgment was in question, and to Stirling that was the worst possible thing that could befall him. The genius might be found out to be a dunce.

"It's just a matter of quantity," Stirling said, defensive now.

"That's what I'm telling you. Too many people are dying."

"I'm referring to quantity of tissue. I have been forced to harvest more than I originally intended."

"And whose fault is that?"

"Well," Stirling said, avoiding looking at Neil now. "You have been insisting we accept more AD patients."

"Hey, keeping you stocked with all these high-tech toys of yours," Neil said, gesturing to the collection of medical equipment surrounding them. "That isn't cheap, you know. If you want to play, you've got to pay."

"I realize there is a cost associated with my research and that funding considerations are a part of all this. I'm not arguing that point. I'm merely explaining to you why the anomalies have occurred."

"Anomalies? Is that what the medical profession calls it these days?"

Stirling ignored the comment and said, "It's because I've been forced to increase the harvesting. In a perfect world, I wouldn't have to, but the world isn't perfect. I'm just doing what I must. If you'd rather we abandoned the whole project—"

"I'd rather you hurry up and clone the damn thing," Neil said, exasperated. "Then you won't have to worry about harvesting too much."

"That is precisely what I've been trying to do."

"Don't just try. *Do!*"

"Well, if we hadn't lost the lab in Guatemala—"

"I don't want hear any more about Guatemala. The only reason you're not an anomaly yourself is because I got your ass the hell out of Guatemala before Mendez did some harvesting on you."

"I'm only explaining—"

"I don't want to hear any more explanations. I want to hear you say it's done, you've cloned the damn thing. Until then, I'd rather you didn't explain anything else."

Sulking like a child who had just been scolded by his father, Stirling murmured, "Haven't you something else to attend to?" He turned away from Neil now and peered into the microscope again. "Shouldn't you be making sure Miss Simms doesn't give us any more problems?"

"I'll take care of her. You just take care of your end. We can't afford any more mistakes right now. It's bad enough the World Health Organization is on our ass. We sure as hell don't want the damn law down here looking into what we're doing. So for God's sake, no more *anomalies*, as you call them. You think you can manage that?"

Stirling looked up to say something, but Neil's glare squelched out whatever comment the doctor had considered making. Stirling was still sulking when Neil turned and headed out. The only thing the doctor had been right about was that there was one other thing Neil needed to attend to. And that was Jodie.

"And keep the damn doors locked this time!" he barked and stormed out, slamming the door behind him.

⇒ 47

An old man, no taller than a 10-year old boy, with skin the color of cocoa, stood at the curb waving a rag to direct Jodie into a parking spot a block from the *Seguridad Publica* building. The man's clothes were old and threadbare, two buttons missing on his shirt, leather sandals that were falling apart. He stood patiently beside her fender, smiling at her like a grandfather. She felt sorry for him and tipped him all the change she had, about twenty five *pesos*, then hurried up the sidewalk.

Luis Guzman's office was a tiny, featureless square room on the second floor. Two windows looked out over a square, crowded with vendors trying to sell tourists hats, leather belts, obsidian figurines. The odor of burnt tobacco hung in the air in Guzman's office. The ceiling panels were stained charcoal gray.

Guzman, a thin, light-skinned Mexican in a dark brown uniform, brought in a paper bag.

"These are everything," he told Jodie, handing her the bag.

She sat on the bench beneath the windows and opened it. "Why weren't these things sent back with the rest of Sam's possessions?" she asked.

"We didn't find them until ten days ago. Dr. Rogoff's rental car was not at the hotel so we didn't find it immediately."

"Where was it?"

"Here. In the commercial zone. On the street."

The paper bag contained maps of Cancun and Quintana Roo, a Pemex gasoline receipt for ninety-five pesos, an unopened pack of Wrigley's gum, three Imodium-AD caplets, and a small notepad.

Jodie took out the notepad. "Did the car break down?" she asked, curious why Rogoff had left it so far from the hotel.

Guzman shrugged. "It drives now."

"I don't understand why it wasn't at the hotel with him. Do you think someone stole it?"

"I don't think so, no. It was on the street for three weeks after, not locked, and no one did anything to it.

Cancun is not the same as the United States, you know. I lived in Texas for a year. We don't have the same crime you have there."

"If no one stole the car, then why wasn't it at the hotel where Dr. Rogoff's body was found? That doesn't make any sense at all. He wouldn't just leave it somewhere. I mean, how would he get back to the hotel without it?"

Guzman shrugged again. He didn't seem especially interested in knowing.

"Where was it?" Jodie asked as she opened the notepad and started to skim through it. It was filled with sloppily written notes, most of them impossible for her to decipher. "Where exactly was the car?" she asked without looking up.

"On the street. Not a tourist neighborhood."

Guzman walked over to a map on the wall and pointed. Jodie got up to see where the car had been found. She was surprised to see Guzman pointing to the street that ran in front of Clinica Centro.

"Are you sure that's where it was?" she asked.

He glared at her, as though offended by the question. He didn't bother to answer.

Jodie stared at the map. This didn't make sense. Why would Rogoff leave his car at Clinica Centro? And since he did leave it there, how did he get back to the hotel? Why did he even go to the clinic—*on the very same day he died?* That part—*the day he died*—kept churning up suspicion in her thoughts.

"Did you investigate Dr. Rogoff's death?" she asked Guzman.

"It was a *coronaria*," he said. "An attack of the heart. We have nothing to investigate."

"Who determined that it was a heart attack?"

"*El medico forense.*" Guzman struggled for the right translation. "In English you say the pathological doctor."

Jodie understood he meant the medical examiner. "Would it be possible for me to talk to this doctor?"

Guzman looked at her, his expression saying, *What's the point?*, but finally he relented, gave her directions and called to let the doctor know she was coming.

⇒ 48

Jodie rode the brake all the way down the dirt road, her car shuddering violently with each bump in the rough surface. The buildings here were industrial—two warehouses, a battery manufacturer, an auto body painting garage. Between them were large patches of sand, barren except for palmetto bushes.

Jodie steered around a washout in the road and continued on, looking from side to the side for the building Guzman had described. At last she saw it, a drab limestone box surrounded by scrub palms and set off on a lot by itself. The structure looked new, and remarkably solid, but it had about as much character as a highway toll both. A Volkswagen Beetle, much like her own rental car only older with badly faded paint, was parked on the strip of gravel near the door.

Jodie pulled in and carefully weaved her car around

more potholes. A large pile of sand had been deposited to one side of the building. Protruding from the nearby brush was a miniature front-end loader, a piece of equipment the size of a riding mower. Rust had rotted away much of the steel frame. The wheels were sunken into the sand. Jodie doubted it had moved in months.

On the other side was a narrow dirt path running between the building and the encroaching palm fronds, stopping at what looked like a loading dock near the rear of the morgue. Jodie assumed that was the entrance used for the dead bodies. She kept her distance from that doorway.

She parked alongside the VW. As she got out of her car, she heard a strange humming noise. It took her a moment to locate its source. It came from overhead, where a grid of power lines crisscrossed the sky. A nest of huge transformers hung off a flimsy pole thirty feet up, buzzing and droning like giant beehives. Jodie felt uneasy walking under it.

The door of the building was a heavy steel fire door. She tried to open it but it was locked. A button hung loose from the stone wall beside the jamb, held up by a wire snaking into the building. She pressed it and heard a buzzer sound inside. A few moments later a short, chunky woman with fair skin, stylish pink glasses and a light blue smock opened the door.

"You are Señorita Simms?" she asked Jodie.

"Yes."

"I am Dr. Rosita Ortega, the pathologist. Luis Guzman told me you are coming."

When they shook hands, Jodie felt ice cold fingers in her palm and the sensation made her squirm inside. She followed Dr. Ortega into a narrow poorly-lit corridor that ran the length of the building and watched her lock the door behind them.

Jodie noticed first how quiet it was in here. She wondered if Dr. Ortega worked alone. She also noticed the air was much chillier than in any other building she had been in, anywhere in Cancun. The thought of why it was kept this way gave her the creeps.

Dr. Ortega's leather soles clattered off the tile floor as she led Jodie through a cramped reception room with four plastic chairs and into an unusually neat office.

"Luis said you want to know of Dr. Samuel Rogoff," Dr. Ortega said, walking around her desk, a modern, metal work surface organized with half a dozen plastic bins, everything neatly in its place.

"Yes, I was hoping you could tell me more about how he died," Jodie said. "Mr. Guzman said it was a heart attack."

"That is correct."

Dr. Ortega already had Rogoff's file out and folded open on her desk. She skimmed through it and read from the report, following along on the page with her finger.

"*Ataque cardiaco funesto*," she said. "Yes, a very bad heart attack. It was fatal. He was dead when the hotel people find him."

"You're certain it was a heart attack?" Jodie asked.

"Certain, yes."

"Did he have a history of heart trouble?" Jodie asked.

"This I don't know. You are his family. You will know better than I know. Do you know of him having heart trouble before this?"

"No, I don't."

Dr. Ortega gave a vague shrug. "There must always be a first trouble. For him, the first is also the last."

The next question had entered Jodie's mind the moment she had learned where Rogoff's car had been found. Thoughts of Clinica Centro, of Hector Garcia's surgery, of Rogoff's investigation into "bad" Andrews, a.k.a. Dr. Stirling, of all the inconsistencies—inconsistencies she assumed had been settled yesterday—now churned in her brain again.

"Tell me something, Doctor," she said. "Is there any way a person can *cause* someone to have a heart attack?"

"I don't understand the question."

An image popped into Jodie's head—Dr. Stirling and his syringes. She said, "If a doctor wanted someone to have a heart attack, if he wanted to make it *look like* someone had a heart attack, is there a way to do that?"

"To do it intentionally?"

"Yes. And make it look like it happened naturally. Is that possible?"

Dr. Ortega considered it a moment then said, "Is possible, perhaps. Why do you ask this?"

"Could that have happened to Dr. Rogoff?"

Dr. Ortega stared at her, again considering this question carefully. Before she could answer, the buzzer at the back door sounded.

"Excuse me, please. One moment."

Dr. Ortega ambled out of the office and down the hall

toward the back of the building, where the repository and autopsy room were.

While Jodie waited, she took Rogoff's notepad from her pocketbook. She had left the police station right away and hadn't had a chance to look through it. Now she flipped to the last pages. She was interested mostly in the final notes Rogoff had written before he died, reasoning that those entries would explain why he had gone to the clinic that day. The last twenty or so pages were blank. She flipped forward through the pad until she came to a page with three brief lines of writing on it.

> *How does he do it?*
> *It must be trans-sphenoidal?*
> *Need films*

Jodie read the three lines over a few times, not sure what they meant. How does *who* do *what?* she wondered. And what did trans-sphenoidal mean? *Films?* What kind of film did Rogoff need? Was he talking about taking pictures of something? Or by films was he referring to x-rays, CAT scans, that type of thing?

Looking for an explanation, she flipped to the page immediately before the one with the three notations. On it were more hastily scribbled notes that were difficult to read. On top of that, Rogoff used strange abbreviations that Jodie didn't understand. She managed to decipher some of it.

> *Remark low incid degen brain disord. No Park. No*
> *AD. Stroke recovery phenom. Exception—epilep.*

Another entry farther down the page said:

Not gen pop. Isolat. Mayan only. Link? Must be. But what? 1st case—Oct (5 mths ago). Tot cases—9.

Jodie didn't take the time to try to decipher what else Rogoff had scribbled on this page; she figured she could do that later. Right now she wanted to skim through more of the pad, see what else she could find. She flipped back one more page.

Rogoff had written a list of nine names.

1. *Manuel Lamas Petán*
2. *Jose Maria Itzá*
3. *Franco Itzá Santamaria*
4. *Carmela Zapata de la O*
5. *Elena Fuentes de Itzá*
6. *Gabriella Epoc de Vasquez*
7. *Paulo Casillas Tikal*
8. *Teresa Rosado de Tuc*

The last name glared at Jodie as though the letters were eyes. It said:

9. *Hector Itzá Garcia*

For a moment she just stared, trying to make sense of what she saw. Rogoff had written no explanation for the list. Just the names. She checked the page immediately before it to see if there was some kind of explanation but there wasn't. Going back to the page after it, she saw the entry "Tot—9" and reasoned that it must be connected to the list of nine names. But she still wasn't sure who the nine people were.

She did know who Hector Garcia was, and she knew that Hector was dead. Were the others dead, too? More epilepsy deaths? *Link?* Rogoff had written. Link to what? She turned back to the last page on which Rogoff had written notes, to one of the last entries he had made.

How does he do it?

A possible explanation of what this meant came to Jodie's mind and made her shudder.

Could the *he*, she wondered, be Stirling, "Bad" Andrews?

And the *it* that he—Stirling—is doing, could that possibly mean the deaths of the nine people on the list?

Dr. Ortega came back up the hall now, carrying a clipboard and wearing latex gloves.

"I apologize for leaving you," she said. "They bring someone for to remain here until the family comes."

Word of the new arrival momentarily tore Jodie's thoughts away from the pad. Realizing that a dead body was here with her left Jodie feeling even more uneasy about this place than she already had been.

She watched Dr. Ortega set the clipboard on the desk, then peel off her latex gloves and toss them into the trash can. The same unsettling thoughts that made her shiver, thoughts about the dead body down the hall, also left her with morbid curiosity. She leaned closer to the desk and peeked at the clipboard.

It looked like a death certificate, most of it already filled out, hand-written in Spanish. Jodie's glare skimmed across the paper until she found the handwritten entry near the top, at the right corner, beside the caption *nombre*. The name Maria was written there. Jodie didn't make the connection until her gaze drifted farther left along the line to the caption *apellido*. The letters seemed to reach off the page and grab hold of her.

The full name of the deceased woman who had just been brought here was Maria Ticas de Garcia.

⟶ 49

Dr. Ortega told Jodie the name Garcia was common in Mexico, as was Maria. Ticas was also prevalent among the Mayans. The only way for Jodie to be certain was to see the woman who had just been brought in.

Dr. Ortega led Jodie down the corridor to a steel door near the back. When she opened it, a breath of icy air rushed out, making Jodie shiver. Dr. Ortega hit the wall switch and the overhead fluorescent lights flickered twice, then came on, humming steadily. This room, long and narrow, with ten bed-like steel tables arranged in neat order along one wall, resembled a dormitory for the dead.

Jodie followed Dr. Ortega into the repository. She saw a cloud of vapor rise over Dr. Ortega's head with each breath, looking as though the coroner were smoking. Jodie wondered why she couldn't see her own breath in the cold air, then she realized it was because she wasn't breathing at all. When she finally allowed her lungs to work, all they could take were quick, shallow gasps.

Even after fourteen years of working as a reporter, dealing with people's deaths, interviewing medical examiners, she had never grown accustomed to being around cadavers, never lost her feeling of uneasiness about death.

Only three of the ten "beds" were occupied today. Each of the three guests was sealed in a gray body bag. Dr. Ortega walked to the last body and stepped up alongside the table. Jodie stood near the opposite wall, watching intently but keeping her distance from the cadaver.

Dr. Ortega tucked the clipboard under her arm to free her hands, then with the same casual manner of someone opening a suitcase, unzipped the top half of the bag, exposing the face and shoulders of the corpse inside.

From where Jodie stood, all she saw was grizzled skin and mussed black hair. She could not make out the facial features from here. She realized she had to get closer.

As Jodie reluctantly stepped toward the body, Dr. Ortega moved sideways, allowing Jodie to see better. Jodie recognized the dead face instantly, the heavy Mayan features framed by the gray plastic body bag. It was the same woman she had met yesterday. Hector Garcia's widow.

Jodie closed her eyes and turned her head.

"How did she die?" she asked.

Dr. Ortega looked at the certificate on the clipboard. *"Ataque cardiaco,"* she said.

The words rang in Jodie's ears. Suddenly it was so clear to her. "A heart attack?" she said, staring at the coroner, waiting for a look of recognition on Dr. Ortega's face. But it didn't come. "The same as Sam Rogoff," Jodie said.

Dr. Ortega still didn't understand the connection. She gave a look as though nothing about this struck her as unusual, and said, "Yes, the same."

"I saw her yesterday and she was fine."

"You cannot tell with a coronary condition, not from looking."

"When are you going to do the autopsy?" Jodie asked.

"I don't do the autopsy."

"Who does?"

"No one. There is no autopsy for this person."

"Why not?"

"Her doctor already determine the cause of her death." She held up the clipboard to show Jodie. *"Ataque cardiaco,"* she said, looking satisfied with that. "We don't have the money to do autopsies on every person. If the doctor knows the cause, there is no need to do the autopsy."

"Is the doctor's name on there somewhere?" Jodie asked, thinking she should talk to him.

"Yes. Here."

Dr. Ortega pointed to the signature scrawled at the bottom of the certificate. Jodie had to strain to read it but she finally made it out what it said.

William T. Andrews.

Shocked, she murmured, "But . . . he told us . . . he wasn't . . ."

"I don't understand what you're saying," Dr. Ortega said.

"He lied," Jodie said, not even aware she was thinking out loud. "How could I be so stupid?"

Dr. Ortega, still not understanding what Jodie was saying, shrugged and started to zip up the bag. Jodie grabbed her arm and stopped her.

"Wait. You have to do an autopsy," she said. "You have to."

"No. I told you—"

"You don't understand. Remember what I asked you a little while ago? If you can cause someone to have a heart attack. You said yes, it was possible."

"Yes it is, but a doctor has signed—"

"Don't you see? *It was him!*"

"Who him? What do you mean?"

"Dr. Andrews! He caused it. He's the one."

"What are you saying? This is not making sense."

"Andrews did it," Jodie said. "I know he did. You have to believe me. You have to do an autopsy. You have to."

≋ 50

When Carl arrived in Miami to change planes, the hundreds of passengers rushing through the gate area overwhelmed him. He looked down the concourse and saw a solid wave of scrambling bodies. Over the PA a loud voice announced something in Spanish. The words confused him. A baby started crying right behind him, the noise ringing in his ear, making it more difficult for him to concentrate. He started walking away from the gate when a young woman cut in front of him, then stopped suddenly when her boyfriend rushed over and hugged her. Carl almost bumped into them. As he stepped around them, a man in a business suit hurried by, nearly knocking him over.

"Oh, sorry. You okay? Sorry." The man hurried away before Carl could even answer.

All Carl knew was that he was supposed to board another plane, a plane that would take him to Mexico, take him to where Jodie was, where Jodie needed him. He had to fly down there and warn her—if it wasn't too late already. He kept worrying he was going to be too late.

But where was he supposed to find that other plane, the one that would take him to Mexico? He looked around, lost in this strange, crowded, bustling place. Passengers hurried past him, walking in both directions. He couldn't tell from them which way he was supposed to go. But he knew he couldn't just stand here. He had to find the other plane.

So, carrying his single piece of luggage, a small valise that used to be Helen's, he headed up the concourse, studying the flight information at each of the gates, searching for the word MEXICO.

He saw ATLANTA, MEMPHIS, MONTEGO BAY. One sign said LA GUARDIA, which looked Spanish to him. He wondered if this was the plane for Mexico. A line stretched away from the counter. He walked to the back and asked a man wearing a tank top and gold jewelry if this was the plane for Mexico.

"Not even close, guy. Try New Yawk."

Carl didn't understand his answer. "Try New Yawk?"

"It goes to New Yawk. Mexico's the other way."

"Which way?" Carl asked, gesturing up the concourse. "That way?"

The man made a face and said, "Hell am I supposed to know?"

Over the PA a man's voice announced the gate had been changed to D-7, but Carl didn't hear which flight it was. He didn't even know the number of the flight he was supposed to be on. He waited for the announcement to be repeated, but a Spanish voice came over the PA and spoke words that held no meaning for him.

People got in line behind him. He realized he was in the wrong place and stepped out of the way. He put down his bag and opened his ticket jacket, deciding he should find out his flight number. On the ticket, all the numbers and times and codes confused him. He hadn't flown alone in years. He didn't know what he was doing. He couldn't make sense of his own ticket.

He picked up his bag and started walking again. The rush of passengers past him continued to disorient him. A woman wheeling a suitcase clipped his leg. She continued on without a word, not even missing a step.

Carl quickly became short of breath and his arm started hurting from carrying the bag. He thought maybe he had packed too much. But he needed it all. Only it was so heavy now. He wanted to sit and catch his breath but he knew he didn't have time. He remembered the ticket agent in Jacksonville telling him he had fifty minutes between flights. The first plane had landed fifteen minutes late. He'd been wandering for ten or fifteen minutes already. He realized he had only twenty or twenty-five minutes left to find the gate.

He saw a bank of telephones and suddenly had an idea. If he could reach Jodie now, by phone, warn her about Neil Lancaster, he wouldn't have to fly to Mexico, he wouldn't have to worry about rushing to find his plane.

He limped over to the phones, his leg hurting where the woman had hit him with her suitcase. He set his bag on the ground, pinning it between his legs so no one could steal it, and took out his wallet. He found the piece of paper on which Jodie had written the phone number of the hotel in Mexico. Then he fished a handful of quarters from his pocket and dumped them on the metal shelf under the phone. As he picked up one quarter and looked at the phone, he noticed it did not have a slot for coins. He just stared at it a moment, confused. Finally he dialed the number without putting any money in, thinking maybe calls were free here.

A woman's recorded voice came on. "Please enter your calling card number now."

"What?" Carl said.

After a brief silence the woman's voice came on again. "Please enter your calling card number now."

"I don't have one," Carl said.

Another brief silence.

"Sorry, please try again. Thank you."

Then a dial tone.

Carl tried again, and again he got the same recording. He dialed the operator. A man with a Cuban accent told him he needed a calling card to make a long distance call from this phone.

"I have MasterCard."

He tried to give the operator the number, just as he had done when he bought the airline ticket early this morning, but this time he had trouble getting the number right. The first time the man said he was two numbers short. The second time he was five numbers too many. Finally he got the right amount of numbers—and the right numbers, he hoped—then the man asked for the expiration date and Carl had no idea what he meant by that.

When he finally hung up, realizing he couldn't reach Jodie by phone, another fifteen minutes had passed. He had less than ten minutes to find the gate and board the plane. He feared he would never make it in time.

"—to Cancun, Mexico," the voice over the PA was saying. "will now begin boarding at gate E-4. All passengers requiring special assistance may board at this time."

As the voice repeated the announcement in Spanish, Carl's eyes darted around, searching for numbers on the gates nearby. So many people rushed past him, surrounding him, blocking his view, he could not see the numbers, even at the closest gate, twenty feet away. His hand trembling, he grabbed his bag and hobbled toward the gate.

He saw the number "9" over the counter so he started up the concourse. A little farther up and on the opposite side he saw "10" and realized he was going in the wrong direction. He hurried back, past "9," past the phones, "8" on the right, "7" on the left, "6" on the right. The concourse seemed to stretch out forever.

Finally, out of breath, he saw gate 4. Passengers crowded this area, carry-on bags littering the floor everywhere. As Carl squeezed between the seats to get to the counter, he tripped over a baby carriage blocking the narrow path.

"Hey!" the mother said, snapping at him.

"Sorry. I didn't see. I'm looking for gate 4."

"You should be looking where you're going. You could have hurt her."

"I'm sorry."

Carl glanced down at the baby in the carriage to make sure she was all right—she was—then he hurried toward the counter. As he got in line, he heard the woman with the baby tell someone: "Old farts like that shouldn't be allowed to travel alone."

Carl anxiously waited as the minutes passed. Finally it was his turn. He labored up to the counter, dragging his suitcase, then started searching his pockets for his ticket. The woman behind the counter stared, looking annoyed. When he finally found the ticket, the woman took one quick look at it and handed it right back.

"Wrong gate," she said. "You have to go to E-4. This is D-4."

Carl was confused. He looked at the number on the board behind her. "But this is four," he said.

"Deeee-4," she said patronizingly. "You want *Eeeee-*4. Concourse Eeeee. That way," she said, pointing. "Take a right, then another right." She looked past him and said, "Next in line."

A young couple with a baby stepped up, the wife nudging Carl out of the way. The agent took their tickets and tore at them, speaking tersely about boarding. Carl couldn't understand what she was saying.

"Where do I go?" he asked again.

The gate agent let out her irritation in a long breath. "Concourse E. Down that way. Take a right. Go all the way to the end. Take another right. You'll see gate E-4."

"How far is it?"

"Far," she said. She handed the tickets back to the young couple then said, "Next in line."

"My flight is boarding now," Carl said.

"Then I suggest you start walking, sir. I have passengers to board here. Okay?"

"Hey," a man in the back said. "Give the guy a break."

The agent ignored the voice, let out another annoyed sigh and fixed her attention on a businessman handing her his ticket.

Carl hefted his bag off the floor again and headed away from the counter. Disoriented, not sure where to go, he stepped cautiously out into the crush of passengers racing to get through the concourse. He started to walk in the direction the gate agent had pointed, afraid again he wouldn't make the flight. Thoughts of Jodie pushed him to walk quickly.

Soon he was out of breath, holding his chest and gasping for air. He looked at his watch. He only had two minutes to make his flight. He realized it was too late.

He dropped his valise and stood there, confused, afraid, devastated.

"You lost, sir?" a man's voice said behind him.

Carl turned. When he saw the electric maintenance cart barely a foot from him he jumped back, startled.

"Guess I snuck up on you, huh?" the maintenance man said. "Sorry about that."

He was a husky man in a gray uniform and a goatee. His teeth were discolored from tobacco but he had a friendly face and a calming, bass voice.

"You look lost," he said. "Are you with someone?"

"I have to get to Mexico. I have to find my daughter."

"What gate are you looking for?"

"Concourse E."

"E?" The man chuckled. "Buddy, you're not even close."

"I know. My flight leaves in two minutes. I'll never make it now."

"You'll make it. Hop in," the man said, taking his tool belt off the seat next to him. "I'm going that way myself, more or less. I'll give you a lift."

The man grabbed Carl's bag. Carl, still dazed and confused, hobbled around the cart and got in. The man drove him down the concourse, holding down his horn that sounded like a quiet bell on a bicycle.

"Didn't the airline have someone waiting at the gate to assist you?" the man asked.

"They do that?"

"Sure they do. You just have to tell them when you make the reservation."

"I didn't know."

"Now you know for next time. Which gate is your flight?"

"E-4."

They reached the gate just as the agent was closing the door to the jetway.

"Hold up a sec," the maintenance man said to her. "One more VIP, special delivery."

He helped Carl out of the cart, handed him the valise and said, "Have a good trip. My best to your daughter."

≋ 51

"It will take time."

"We don't have a lot of time," Jodie said.

Dr. Ortega held up her hands. "I cannot do the autopsy faster than it takes."

"All right," Jodie said. "As soon as you know something, anything, call me at the Hotel Salida Del Sol." She wrote down the phone number and the number of her cabaña. "If I'm not there, leave a message with Neil Lancaster. He'll know what it's about. I have to make a stop first."

"Where are you going? You said you wanted to know the autopsy results."

"I do, but I can't wait here. I have to go to Clinica Centro and check something."

Jodie stuffed Sam Rogoff's notepad into her pocketbook. She had to confirm that the names Rogoff had written were patients of Dr. Andrews. She had a hunch they were, but she needed to be certain, she needed proof. And more importantly, she needed to find out if, like Hector Garcia, these other people Rogoff had listed had died of epilepsy, or heart attacks. She needed to know if Stirling was killing his patients.

She started to leave but then turned back to Dr. Ortega with another question.

"I asked you if a doctor could cause a heart attack," Jodie said. "Can he also cause epilepsy?"

Ortega looked confused. She shrugged and said, "I don't know. Perhaps. There are drugs that may do this . . ." She thought a moment then said, "A wrong surgery to the brain, perhaps . . ."

"Surgery to the brain?"

"Perhaps. A surgery that damages the cortex or the—"

"The *cortex?*" Jodie said. Harrington had mentioned the cortex, that BDNF was secreted there. So had Rogoff; he thought an abnormality in the cortex was involved in the epilepsy cases he had been investigating.

"Are you sure surgery to the cortex can cause epilepsy?" Jodie asked.

"A damage to the cortex—surgical or traumatic—is possible to cause this, yes."

But if Stirling were performing surgery on people's brains, surgery that would cause epilepsy, surely the patient would know Stirling was doing this. A doctor can't cut into someone's head without the person either knowing in advance or finding out about it afterward. Hector Garcia's wife would have mentioned an operation like that. Unless . . .

"Is it possible," Jodie asked Ortega, "for a doctor to operate on a person's brain, on their cortex, without the person knowing it?"

"You ask these un-normal questions—"

"*Please!* Just tell me. Is it possible?"

"To operate without the patient knowing?"

"Yes. I mean . . . that's not really possible, is it?"

"With anesthesia, yes. The doctor can sedate the patient and do the surgery."

"But when the patient wakes up, he'll know something was done? His scalp will have been shaved and there'd be a scar where the opening was made, right? So he would know, right?"

"You ask if it could be done without the patient knowing *after* the surgery, knowing *ever?*"

"Yes. That isn't possible, is it?"

"Well . . ." Ortega said, the look on her face telling Jodie that she didn't agree.

"You mean it is possible?" Jodie asked.

"There are procedures that do not require shaving the head and cutting the scalp."

"What do you mean? How could a doctor get to the brain to operate on it without opening the skull somehow? I don't understand."

"If it is a small surgery, he can go through the nasals. In these places, the bone of the skull is thin. It can be easy for to punch through. This is done with certain procedures. To aspirate cancerous tissue sometimes is one example. There are others. Yes, I think it is possible for to do it without the patient knowing. There is no scar you can see. Very little pain. Perhaps minor bleeding after, perhaps not. But why do you—?"

"Nosebleeds?" Jodie asked, remembering what Hector Garcia's wife had said about Hector having nosebleeds after his appendix operation. "Would there be nosebleeds after that kind of operation to the brain?"

"If the surgery is through the nasals, it is possible, yes."

"How could you tell if an operation like that was done? Is there any way to tell?"

"To examine the patient, of course. If you know where to look, if you know it is something to look in particular. The hole would be seen on the x-rays. It will be small, difficult to see, but it will be there. There must be a hole, even with the—how do you call it in English—the surgery trans . . . um . . . trans-fee-no . . ."

Jodie opened Rogoff's notepad and quickly flipped through it, searching for the page she had read earlier, the word she hadn't understood. Her fingers were unsteady, struggling with the paper. Finally she found it.

"Trans-sphenoidal?" she said, reading Rogoff's notes.

"Yes. That is the word for this kind of surgery."

Jodie stared down at the notepad, at that same word—*trans-sphenoidal*—written right after *How does he do it?* Now she understood that it referred to some kind of surgery, a surgery on the brain, a surgery Stirling could do without the patient realizing it.

That must be what he's doing. Operating on patients without them knowing, damaging the cortex of their brains, causing them to develop epilepsy, causing them to die.

But why?

The answer, she realized, was connected to what Dr. Harrington had told her. He said he had identified traces of human cortex tissue in The Cure.

"You said a surgeon can suction out tissue with that kind of surgery?" Jodie asked.

"Yes. Tumors. Damaged tissue. It is aspirated with a tube and suction pump."

"Oh my God . . ."

"What is wrong?" Ortega asked.

Jodie couldn't answer her. Her thoughts were racing. She needed proof. She needed to be certain. She needed to convince herself, even though in her heart she knew there was no question.

Maria Ticas de Garcia had told Jodie that Stirling had taken x-rays of Hector's head when they went back to the Clinica Centro after the seizures began. The x-rays might still be there. And Stirling might have x-rays of the other patients on Rogoff's list. And those x-rays would show what Stirling was doing. Those x-rays would be proof.

Yes, she definitely needed to go back to that clinic and get proof. She needed to confirm what she already knew. More importantly, she needed to get something she could bring to the police, to prove it all to them, to get them to act on this. She needed to stop Stirling from killing people.

"Call when you know the results of the autopsy," Jodie said, rushing toward the door.

"Hotel Salida Del Sol," Dr. Ortega called after. "I will call."

As Jodie ran outside to her car, she thought about Maria Ticas de Garcia. If the heart attack had been caused by some kind of pill or injection, that meant the old Mayan woman had been killed. *Silenced.* The way Sam Rogoff had been silenced.

Jodie trembled as this thought seeped through her

mind. It wasn't just Stirling's patients who were dying, she realized now. If she was right about Maria Ticas de Garcia and Sam Rogoff, about the cause of their heart attacks, then anyone who knew too much, anyone Stirling viewed as a threat, was in danger.

Is Stirling murdering them?

Suddenly Jodie remembered that Sister Veronica knew about Hector, too. The nun knew as much as Hector's wife had known. She knew enough to get Stirling into trouble.

Did Stirling know about her? Jodie wondered, growing more worried by the second. If he did, Sister Veronica could very possibly be in danger.

Jodie knew she had to warn the nun—immediately.

She backed out onto the street, her rear tire bouncing in and out of a pothole. She sped away, tires spinning in the dirt, the image of Maria Ticas de Garcia's corpse warning her to hurry.

Since she didn't know if Sister Veronica had a phone where she lived, didn't even know the name of the church so she could look it up, she had to go there in person. She hoped she could get there in time. She hoped she could remember the way.

As she drove north through Cancun, she told herself she would go to the police later, after she made sure Sister Veronica was okay. There wasn't time to stop and try to explain everything to them now. Not only was there a language barrier, but getting them to believe what she would tell them, without having proof to back it up, and getting them to act quickly enough to insure Sister

Veronica's safety, would be impossible. No, she would find Sister Veronica first, then contact the police.

As Jodie left the congested center of the city and sped toward the northern outskirts, she suddenly realized something she had been too preoccupied to comprehend before now.

The one person who knew the most about what Stirling was doing, the one person most in danger, was herself.

It took her 15 minutes to reach Puerto Jauréz. She drove down the dirt road too fast, her car rocking violently, scraping the ground several times. When she pulled into the dirt drive at the church, she saw that Mass was being celebrated. The tiny building was crowded with Mayan women in colorful *iipils* and men in clean white shirts.

She parked alongside the building and hurried to the entrance. The priest stood at the altar, sprinkling Holy Water and singing in Spanish. Jodie stood in the back, searching the two dozen people in the pews for Sister Veronica.

She noticed a man standing in the corner and went over to him.

"Do you speak English?" she whispered beneath the priest's voice.

"Little."

"Do you know where I can find Sister Veronica?"

"Nah," the man said, and pointed out the door.

Jodie thought he was saying no, telling her to leave.

"Please. This is important. I have to find her."

"*Nah,*" he said again, took her by the arm and walked her outside. He pointed up the drive to the hut in the back. "*Nah. La Casa.*"

"In the house?" Jodie said. "*La casa?*"

The man nodded and went back into the church. Jodie hurried past the empty school to the small hut, far from the church. Even with all the people inside the church, she felt an eerie sense of isolation.

Jodie knocked at the flimsy door. She knew just from the scanty size of the hut that it had only one room, like Maria Ticas de Garcia's home. If anyone was inside, they would have heard her knock. But she knocked again anyway and listened near the door. It was quiet inside, no radio, no voices, not even the sound of someone moving around.

Her thoughts again fixed on the image of Hector Garcia's wife, lying inside a shapeless body bag in the morgue, and she shivered. She could not free her thoughts of the fear she might be too late.

She gently pushed open the door. This hut was similar to Maria Ticas de Garcia's, with two hammocks on the right side and a primitive kitchen on the left. Jodie noticed a refrigerator against the wall, one that looked thirty years old. She heard it humming and realized this hut had electricity.

The stove, slightly newer than Maria Ticas de Garcia's, had a black iron hood rising to the ceiling and a chamber beneath for firewood. Religious icons, likenesses of saints, covered the walls. A Bible sat on the kitchen table. A *santos* cross hung from one of the posts holding up the hammocks.

Near a small opening in the side wall—a window without a glass pane—was a crudely made wood and straw chair. The nun was sitting there, her back to the door so all Jodie could see was her black habit.

"Sister Veronica?" Jodie said quietly.

The nun did not respond. Jodie wondered if she was sleeping.

"Sister Veronica?" she said a little louder.

Still no response.

Jodie walked deeper into the room. As she came closer to the nun sitting by the window, still only able to see the back of her head, she noticed how still the woman was.

How her body was oddly slumped.

"Sister?" she said.

She reached the chair now and carefully, hesitantly, stepped around it so she could see the nun's face.

The first thing that registered was the pasty gray skin. Then the way the head hung forward. The way the hands drooped off the lap. Hands gnarled and wrinkled. A lap much thicker than Jodie remembered. She bent over and looked at the nun's face more closely.

Suddenly the woman's eyes snapped open, startling Jodie, sending her back-pedaling against the wall. The nun, a woman in her seventies, looked confused at first by Jodie's presence, but then she started giggling, amused by the way she had startled Jodie.

She said something in Yucatec and Spanish, words Jodie didn't understand, something friendly, almost teasing. Jodie assumed she was talking about the way Jodie had jumped back, but she was worried about Sister Veronica and quickly turned her attention to finding her.

"*Dónde está*—" Jodie started to say but the old woman interrupted her.

"I speak English," the nun said, her accent heavy, but Jodie could understand her. She looked Mayan. Jodie noticed mostly her bright, vital eyes, unusual for someone her age.

"I'm looking for Sister Veronica," Jodie said. "Is she here?"

"No."

"Do you know where she is? It's important that I find her."

"She go to the clinica."

"Clinica Centro?"

"*Sí*. For to see the *muchacha* who go there yesterday."

Jodie remembered Sister Veronica had escorted a girl and her mother to the clinic yesterday. That little girl must be the *muchacha* this woman meant.

"Do you know the girl's name?" Jodie asked, so she would know which room to find Sister Veronica in. "The *muchacha*? Do you know her name?"

"*Sí*. Gabriella Ruiz."

"Thank you."

Jodie started to leave when the nun said, "You are the second to look for Sister Veronica today."

A blade of fear sliced at Jodie as the woman's words bled into her brain.

"Someone else was looking for her?" Jodie asked.

"*Sí*. A man."

"A *gringo*?"

"*Sí*."

"Was he tall?" Jodie asked.

"*Si.*"

Stirling!

"Did you tell him she went to the clinic?"

The nun shrugged. "*Si*, I told him."

⟅ 52

Neil returned to the hotel when it was finished.

He walked down the path to Jodie's cabaña, feeling aroused—as always—by what he had done today, and imagining how good it would be to take Jodie to bed right now, with the thoughts still fresh in his mind.

He knocked at the door. No one answered so he used his passkey to let himself in. The cabaña smelled of Jodie's perfume, reminding him of their hours together last night. Her clothes from yesterday were thrown on the bed along with his silk shirt and a white bikini.

He picked up the bikini. She would look fine in this, he thought, her skin slippery with suntan lotion. Then he imagined himself ripping it off her, and the two of them going at it in the humid afternoon. He felt himself growing hard as he thought about Jodie, and he hoped to God she would hurry back so he could satisfy his craving before she returned to Florida.

He assumed she wasn't on the beach, since her bikini was here. She must have gone out somewhere, probably shopping. Though he would rather be naked and pressed against her right now, he decided this was a good opportunity to poke around a bit, make sure the explanation Stirling had concocted yesterday had satisfied her,

make sure she hadn't learned more, make sure she wasn't
bringing anything incriminating back to Jacksonville.

He didn't want her to become a problem because he
didn't want to be forced to deal with her, the way he had
dealt with the others who had threatened them. There
had been too many of Stirling's anomalies already. But by
the same token, he couldn't let her threaten what they
were doing, no matter how deep his lust for her.

Never mind about the fortune he and Stirling were on
the verge of making, he thought. As soon as Stirling
figured out how to synthesize The Cure, to manufacture
it in a laboratory without having to operate on the Itzá
Mayans to get the source, they could go legit and start
marketing the stuff all over the world, making a thousand times what they were bringing in now—which
wasn't peanuts either.

Right now, Stirling had over a hundred patients, each
paying close to seventy grand a year. Ten percent of
that—three quarters of a million bucks a year—was
Neil's cut. Nothing to sneeze at. Still, in a few years, he
would be making Donald Trump money.

But never mind that, he thought. Never mind the
money. More importantly, he had to know what Jodie
was doing. They never should have taken a patient whose
daughter was a reporter. Another one of Stirling's
mistakes. Too late to do anything about that now. All
they could do was keep an eye on her, see how far she
would go, determine whether or not she believed them or
would continue looking into the deaths.

The deaths were the problem. Many things you
could get away with in Mexico. Most of the everyday

legal bullshit could be circumvented if you knew the right way, knew the right people. But murder—that was not as easily swept under the rug. And Neil had spent enough time in this part of the world to know he did not, under any circumstances, want to face the judicial system down here for something as serious as that.

He walked over to Jodie's suitcase which lay open on the stand by the bureau. Most of her clothes were still in it. He assumed she hadn't bothered unpacking since she was only staying one night. He pushed her clothes aside and looked for any documentation regarding Hector Garcia or her talk with his wife or that nun, anything that might prove what she had accused Stirling of doing. He found nothing.

Next he opened the drawers of the bureau and checked them, then he looked in the closet to see if she had any bags in there, which she didn't.

Just then the phone rang. After debating for a moment whether to answer it, he decided to pick it up, see who was calling Jodie. If Jodie questioned him later, he could always say he had come here to see her, taking her suggestion from earlier today, and when he heard the phone ring, he thought it might be her calling for him so he answered it.

When he picked up the phone, the woman on the other end said, "I wish for to talk to Miss Jodie Simms."

"Who's calling?"

"Rosita Ortega."

The name meant nothing to him. "Miss Simms isn't here right now," he said.

As he spoke, he glanced down at his silk shirt on the bed and noticed the corner of a sheet of paper sticking out of the pocket. He picked up the shirt to see what he had left in there, thinking it might be something important. He pulled out the small sheet of paper that was folded once in half. He recognized it as a page from the pad on his desk at home.

"Why don't you try back in a couple hours," he said and started to hang up when the woman said, "I wish to leave a message with Mister Neil Lancaster."

"Yeah, I'm Neil Lancaster," he said as he unfolded the paper. "What's the message?"

Then he noticed the pencil shading on the paper and the first few letters of the nun's name coming through in white. The pencil shading was only in one corner of the paper so the rest of the nun's name didn't show through, neither did her address, but Neil realized instantly what this was, where it came from.

Jodie must have gotten it from his office. She must have been in there searching for evidence. She must suspect—

". . . blood test for Maria Ticas de Garcia," the woman on the phone was saying into his ear, the name she mentioned snapping his attention away from the paper.

"Hm? What? What was that?"

"I said, please tell Miss Simms," the woman on the phone said, "I make the test of the blood of Maria Ticas de Garcia."

Neil stuffed the note paper into his pocket and threw the shirt down on the bed. His full attention was on this strange woman on the other end of the line.

"Who is this?" he asked.

"Rosita Ortega. I am from the office of the *Medico Forense*."

Neil didn't understand why the Medical Examiner was calling Jodie, why she was telling Jodie about Maria Ticas de Garcia. But it definitely made him uneasy. In light of the note he had just found in the pocket of his shirt, he wondered how much Jodie knew.

Obviously she must have found out about the Ticas de Garcia woman. Neil had been certain she would never find out. After all, she was supposed to leave the country in a few hours. He decided it wasn't a coincidence that she had learned of the death. She must have been pursuing this thing. Last night's charade that he and Stirling had concocted hadn't fooled her a bit. Neither had the hours of intimacy at his house. Now Neil felt like the fool, like she had suckered him.

"Why are you calling Miss Simms?" he asked the coroner.

"She come to my office today."

"She did? Why? Was it about Maria Ticas de Garcia?"

"Not first, no. She had questions about another death."

"What other death?"

"She said you would know about it. An American doctor called Samuel Rogoff."

"She came there asking about Rogoff?"

"Yes. And later also about Maria Ticas de Garcia. It is about Maria Ticas de Garcia that I am calling. Please tell Miss Simms I make the test of the blood and I find the presence of *cloruro de potasio*."

Neil didn't say anything when he heard this, but he knew exactly what the woman meant. She had detected the potassium chloride Stirling had said would never be detected. Stirling had assured him no one would even look for it. Now the coroner's office had not only looked, but had found it.

But did they understand the significance? Neil hoped this second-rate stiff-dissector wasn't smart enough to make the connection. He had to find out.

"Potassium chloride?" Neil said. "What does that mean?"

"This much *cloruro*—um, potassium chloride—this much should not be in the blood," Ortega said. "Miss Simms asked if something in the blood can cause a heart attack. Tell her this can. Tell her she is right, I think is possible the death of Maria Ticas de Garcia was not from natural reasons."

≋ 53

Jodie parked on the street half a block from Clínica Centro. According to Luis Guzman, Sam Rogoff had parked a short distance from the clinic the last time he came here. He probably hadn't wanted to be noticed. He must have come searching for evidence.

And now Rogoff is dead.

Jodie shivered as she climbed out of her rental car. She felt a troubled chill, even in the midday heat. If this is where Rogoff had died, then coming here might be dangerous. But she had to go inside the clinic. Sister Veronica was there, and Jodie had to warn her.

She also had to see if her hunch was correct, if the names in Rogoff's pad were Andrews's patients who had died. She touched the notepad in her pocketbook to make sure she had it, then she headed up the street on foot.

She took some comfort in the sun glaring down on her face. Coming here in daylight was certainly safer than coming at night. Stirling couldn't do anything to her in broad daylight, with the entire staff of the hospital watching. She wondered if Rogoff had made the mistake of coming after dark.

With that thought running through her head, she trembled again as she headed up the street. Because of her job, she was accustomed to going into hazardous places, like the crack house in Jacksonville months ago. But she always had Mike Bono or another cameraman with her, taping everything, ready to help her if something happened. Today, going here, she was alone. If something went wrong, she was on her own. And that made this feel so much more dangerous than anything she had done at work. She could not get it out of her mind that her life might be in danger.

But so was Sister Veronica's, and that's why she had to do this.

She quickened her pace, feeling urgency. She had to locate Sister Veronica and make sure she was safe, warn her about Stirling.

She reached the clinic in less than a minute, out of

breath and damp with sweat from hurrying in the Mexican heat. When she walked through the open doors of the clinic, her heart was racing. The tile job still wasn't finished but the two men weren't working today, Sunday. No patients waited in the lobby, either. All the benches were empty. Only the receptionist, a young Mexican girl of seventeen or eighteen, sat behind the old desk.

Jodie approached her, struggling to catch her breath. She felt a tightness in her chest that made it even more difficult to breathe. Calm down, she told herself. She needed to be calm in order to think straight, to act prudently. She wiped the perspiration from her forehead and took a few slow breaths.

The young girl in a white uniform peered up from the sheet of paper on the desk. *"Buenas tardes, señorita."*

"Buenas tardes," Jodie said. She knew the Spanish word for room so she said, *"El cuarto de Gabriella Ruiz? Dónde?"*

"Doce."

Jodie didn't understand.

The girl must have seen confusion in Jodie's face because she held up ten fingers then two fingers and said, *"El cuarto número doce."*

"Oh. Twelve?" Jodie said. "Room twelve?"

"Sí. Twelve. *Y la tercera cama."* She held up three fingers.

Jodie wasn't sure what that meant, but she would find room twelve and go from there.

"Gracias," she said and started to leave but the woman stopped her.

"Firme aquí," she said, pointing to a grammar-school

type composition pad on the desk. *"Su nombre. Y cuarto número doce."*

As Jodie wrote her name and room number twelve, she scanned the list to see if Sister Veronica was here. She saw the number "12" written several lines up the page. The name scribbled beside it in a large scrawl was *Sor Veronica Ignacia.*

Jodie pointed to the name on the page and asked the receptionist, "Is she still here?"

"Qúe?" The woman didn't understand.

"Um . . . *aqui ahora?"* Jodie said, pointing to the name. It meant "here now?" but the girl seemed to understand what Jodie was asking.

"Sí, la hermana religiosa está aquí. No se ha ido todavia."

All Jodie understood was *"Sí"*—yes, Sister Veronica was still here. That was all that mattered.

The receptionist pointed the way to the room and Jodie hurried down a long hallway to the other side of the building. She saw only one nurse the entire time, a dark woman in her fifties wheeling a cart with medicine from one room to the next. A few patients had visitors, but not many, half a dozen people in all. The hospital was unusually quiet.

With so few people around, the place had a forsaken feel to it, as though the building were on the verge of being closed, as though the patients here didn't matter to anyone. Jodie would have felt better, felt safer, with more people around, more eyes watching, but she told herself again at least there were some people, and it was the middle of the afternoon, it was not dark.

She found the room marked 12. The entrance was

wide open, no door. She took a step inside and looked around. The room was oddly shaped, like a bowling lane—fifty feet long, but barely wide enough to accommodate the beds, beds set up parallel to the side wall. She wondered if it had been a hallway at one time. That was the impression she got as she stared down it.

All six beds were against the left wall, allowing just enough space on the right side for a person to walk by. Faded green curtains hung between the beds. The overhead lights were off and there was only one tiny window at the far end, leaving the room in depressing shadows.

The air smelled stale, ripe with the spoor of sweat and urine. The pregnant woman in the first bed rolled over, moaning as she did. Someone deeper in the room had a tinny portable radio playing strange Mexican rap music. Jodie heard coughing from another bed and the quiet sound of two women whispering in Spanish from the back of the room.

She walked deeper into the room. The smell became awful the farther she went. She found it difficult to breathe. She understood now why Sister Veronica had such difficulty convincing people to come here.

An elderly woman lay sleeping on the second bed, snoring softly. Jodie walked past her and over to the third bed. As she peered around the privacy curtain, she saw Gabriella Ruiz lying in bed. A short, heavy Mayan woman Jodie's age sat on the wooden footstool beside her, holding Gabriella's hand. In the woman's other hand were rosary beads. Jodie recognized the little girl

and her mother from yesterday, when they came in with
Sister Veronica.

"Hello," Jodie said.

"Buenas tardes," the mother said cautiously, not recognizing Jodie.

"Do you speak English?" Jodie asked.

The mother looked at the little girl in the bed who
said, "I do."

Jodie came closer and smiled at the young girl. "How
are you feeling, sweetheart?"

Gabriella shrugged.

"I'm a friend of Sister Veronica's," Jodie said.

Now Gabriella smiled, as though she were looking at a
friend of her own. "Sister Veronica is to come to see me
today," she said. "You know when she is to come?"

"Hasn't she been here yet?"

"No."

"She signed the book in the lobby," Jodie said.

"She don't come to see me," Gabriella said, looking
sad now. She sniffled, as though she might cry, then she
wiped her nose and turned away.

"I'm sure she will," Jodie said. "She probably stopped
to see someone else, that's all. I'm sure she'll be here in a
little while."

"I hope," Gabriella said, and as the words came out,
Jodie saw a thin rivulet of blood seep out of Gabriella's
left nostril.

She realized instantly what that meant, and the horror
of it left her staring in shock, speechless.

"Ay! Virgensita de Guadalupe!" the mother said, quickly

springing up and wiping the blood off Gabriella's lip with a tissue. Then she held the tissue against her daughter's nose and said, *"Ka'teen. Ba'axten ni' segertik k'i'ik'?"*

Gabriella spoke to her mother in Yucatec, calming her down. Finally the mother let Gabriella hold the tissue and she sat on the edge of the footstool again, holding her daughter's hand.

"My nose is again to bleed," Gabriella told Jodie. "Mama is afraid."

"Did you . . . ?" Jodie had difficulty getting the words out. "Did you have any kind of surgery today or yesterday?" Jodie asked. "Any operations? Did Dr. Stir—I mean Dr. Andrews operate on you? Did he do anything to you?"

"No operate, no. Dr. Andros give me medicine. The pills. At night."

"But he didn't operate on you? Are you sure?"

"I sure. I sleep right away after the pills. I sleep through the night."

Sleeping pills? To put her out right away? Dear God, no!

"Did your mother stay with you?" Jodie asked. "Was your mother here with you all night?"

"No, Dr. Andros say she must to go home. Is the rule of the hospital."

"You were alone all night?"

"No. The other patients are here," Gabriella said, gesturing to the other beds in the room. "And Dr. Andros is here, too."

"Oh my God . . ." Jodie whispered.

The girl's mother saw the frightened look on Jodie's

face and anxiously questioned Gabriella, wanting to know what was wrong. Gabriella asked Jodie.

"No, nothing. I was just . . . I'm going to go look for Sister Veronica," she said. "I'll be back later." Then she hurried out.

In the hall, Jodie fell against the wall and struggled to catch her breath. Stirling had operated on that little girl. Stirling had punched a hole into Gabriella's skull, by way of her nose, and had done something to her brain. Aspirated some of her cortex. That has to be what he's been doing. And he did it again last night.

Oh dear God! That poor little girl. If the same thing happened to her that had happened to the others . . . *Oh God!*

Besides being frightened for Gabriella, Jodie was also worried about Sister Veronica. The nun should have been here already. Could something have happened to her? One thought rushed through Jodie's mind. Had Stirling silenced her, too . . .

Jodie raced back down the long corridor to the other side of the hospital, to the empty lobby. For a minute, she tried frantically to question the receptionist about Sister Veronica, but the teenage girl did not understand what Jodie was asking. Fortunately a man walked in as Jodie and the receptionist were trying to communicate and he offered to help. He spoke fluent English. Jodie had him ask the receptionist what time Sister Veronica arrived.

When the man told Jodie the answer, she knew for certain something was very wrong.

"She arrived two hours ago," he said. He pointed to the receptionist and told Jodie, "The señorita said the sister you are looking for has not left the clinic yet."

≈ 54

Rosita Ortega completed the preliminary autopsy on Maria Ticas de Garcia, confirming what Jodie Simms had told her. The Mayan woman's death had likely been caused by the excessive amount of potassium chloride in her system. Dr. Ortega didn't understand exactly how it got there, but she knew it did not belong. Further inquiry was warranted. She would refer it to Luis Guzman.

She peeled off the latex gloves and threw them into the trash bin, then headed up the hall to her office to type the report. She wasn't sure what to write down under "determination of death." Jodie Simms had said Dr. Andrews—who had already signed the death certificate—was involved. But how? What he had done? Dr. Ortega did not know, and Jodie Simms hadn't stayed long enough to explain it all.

Dr. Ortega was eager to complete this and turn it over to Guzman, let him take over. If anything criminal was going on, he was the one to investigate.

As she loaded the form into the typewriter the buzzer rang. Someone was at the front door. Wondering if it was Miss Simms, Dr. Ortega walked through the waiting room and opened the front door.

The man standing outside had a large square jaw and

long, blond hair tied in a ponytail, obviously an American. But he spoke Spanish without an accent.

"Are you Rosita Ortega?" he asked.

"Yes."

He extended his hand. "I believe I spoke with you on the phone a short time ago," he said. "I'm a friend of Miss Simms. Jodie Simms. I was at the hotel when you called."

"Oh, yes, I recall. Mister Lancaster?"

"Yes. Miss Simms asked me to come here."

Dr. Ortega stepped aside to allow him to enter. She noticed he had a brown paper bag in the pocket of his silk shirt, rolled to the size of a fat Cuban cigar. It looked strange since he was otherwise dressed sharply.

"I am completing my report now," she said.

"Report on what?"

"The autopsy of Maria Ticas de Garcia."

"You haven't turned it in to anyone yet?"

"No, not yet. Did you give Miss Simms my message from before, about the blood test?"

"Yes. She thanks you. She asked me to stop by and take a look at everything you have. I'm a little more familiar with this type of thing than she is and she wanted my opinion."

"I don't have much," Dr. Ortega said as she led him into her office. "Just the preliminary findings from the autopsy. And the file on the American man who died of the heart attack a few weeks ago, Dr. Rogoff. I checked his record. There was some blood work done on him, by mistake. The potassium chloride level was very high also.

Miss Simms thinks his death might not have been a simple heart attack, you know."

"Yes, I know."

"I think I agree."

"I'll need to look at Rogoff's file, too. At everything."

Dr. Ortega gathered everything together and brought them into her office. She found the American man sitting behind her desk, in her chair. His audacity irritated her, but she knew *gringos* were like that, always taking over as though everything were theirs.

Thank God this wouldn't take long, she told herself. He'll be gone in a few minutes. She said nothing about him sitting in her chair. She just dropped all the files on her desk curtly and stared at him.

"This is everything?" he asked.

"Yes. Except the autopsy report. That's still in the typewriter. I haven't finished it yet."

The man turned to the side and scanned the form in the typewriter. He turned back to Dr. Ortega.

"You haven't spoken to anyone else yet?" he asked her.

"No, not yet. I'm getting ready to call Luis Guzman, the investigator who handled Mister Rogoff's death."

"But you haven't talked to him yet?"

"No."

"Or anybody else?"

"Just Miss Simms and you," Dr. Ortega said.

She stared down at him now, rankled by all the questions, and still upset about him sitting in her chair. The only reason she was telling him anything at all was as a courtesy, because she thought he and Jodie Simms had some connection to Dr. Rogoff. But her patience was wearing thin.

"Why are you asking all this?" she said finally.

He reached over to the typewriter, pulled out the unfinished autopsy report and put it on the desk in front of him along with the rest of the documents pertaining to the deaths.

"Why did you do that?" she said. "I told you I didn't finish that yet."

"I just want to make sure this doesn't go any further than this office," he said.

"What do you mean?"

He reached into his shirt pocket and took out the small paper bag. Dr. Ortega watched curiously as he unrolled the bag, reached in and took out a vial of sterile water and an ampule of crystals. She didn't understand what he was doing, and he still hadn't answered her question. Confused and irked by him, she stared as he reached back into the bag and took out a hypodermic syringe.

"What are you doing?" she asked.

"Just one second and I'll show you."

He mixed the crystals from the ampule into the sterile water, then took the plastic protective sheath off the needle and drew the milky liquid out of the vial and into the syringe.

Now he stood up. "Okay," he said. "Come here."

"Why?"

"I'm going to show you."

Dr. Ortega stood on the other side of the desk, not coming any closer.

"What is that?" she asked.

"Let me see—what did he call it?" He picked up the ampule again and read the label. "Tubocurarine chloride."

"Tubocurarine chloride? But that's—"

"Yes, I know. Did you know that primitive tribes of South American Indians use the plant form of this on the poison darts they hunt with? It's very effective."

He stepped around the desk. She took one step back, maintaining the same distance between them.

"We felt it would be a good idea to get away from potassium chloride," he said. "Too many heart attacks might raise suspicions."

He took another step toward her and suddenly she realized what he was doing.

"*Oh dear God,*" she said in a gasp of terror.

She wheeled around and rushed into the waiting room, trying to get to the front door, but he easily caught up and shoved her forward, knocking her off balance and sending her tumbling to the floor.

She screeched as she landed hard and skidded into one of the chairs. She started to roll over so she could stand up, when he pounced down on her, his weight pressing her to the floor.

"You should have accepted the good doctor's death certificate without question," he said.

He pulled up the sleeve of her blouse, exposing her arm and shoulder. Then he jabbed the needle into the fleshy part of her arm. She let out a strange *eek* that he thought sounded funny. She was too shocked to scream out. She just stared at the needle stuck in her arm. She was unable to free her hands from underneath her so she couldn't pull it out. She couldn't do anything. He was in complete control.

"If you had just accepted the death certificate as is," he said, "you might not have driven yourself into respiratory failure."

"No, no, don't!"

She squirmed and rolled and managed to free one arm. In desperation, she reached back for the needle. He grabbed her wrist, pressed it to the floor, then depressed the plunger, emptying the solution into her arm.

"You are a bit overweight," he said. "You should know it's not healthy for a person like you to get too excited about something like this. You never know what could happen."

Again she squirmed beneath him, but he had her pinned too well. She couldn't get away. Finally, as though it suddenly clicked what he was doing, she started screaming for help.

He made no effort to stop her. "No one can hear you," he said.

Her pleas for help continued, gradually becoming weaker until finally they petered out into hopeless sobs. The sobs were less noisy than the screams, which Neil appreciated.

"Thank you," he said.

He pulled the needle out of her arm. He continued to sit on top of her, holding her down, waiting for the poison to work.

It only took a few minutes.

≋ 55

Away from the in-patient wing, the halls were nearly deserted. Jodie passed one orderly wheeling an empty gurney and saw an exhausted nurse carrying an IV bag up the hall. The RADIOLOGIA E IMAGEN room was closed. The LABORITORIO farther down the hall was also dark and empty. She followed signs that said URGENCIA to the emergency room, where two dozen patients huddled in a cramped waiting room and in the hallway. Three nurses and one doctor rushed around, trying to care for these people. Jodie smelled vomit in the hot air. The din of Spanish voices and moans and sobs made it difficult for her to communicate with anyone, but she finally got one of the nurses to tell her Sister Veronica had not been this way today.

Jodie went back to the in-patient wing and peeked into each of the rooms, looking for Sister Veronica. The nun wasn't anywhere. She went back to Gabriella Ruiz's room and asked if Sister Veronica had been in to see her in the last fifteen minutes, thinking she might have missed her.

"No," Gabriella said, even sadder than before. "She say she will see me today."

"I'm sure she will," Jodie said. "She probably had an emergency. You wait and see, she'll be here later."

Jodie did not believe her own words as she left the room and headed up the corridor again. Thoughts of Maria Ticas de Garcia and Sam Rogoff stirred in her head, leaving her fearing the same fate had come to Sister Veronica. Jodie didn't want to accept it, didn't want to believe harm had befallen this woman who had helped her, but the longer she looked without finding Sister Veronica, the more difficulty she had thinking anything different.

Jodie didn't know where to search next, but she knew she couldn't give up. She decided to try the emergency room again. As she followed a different hallway to that side of the building, she saw a sign that said QUIRÚRGICO and an arrow pointing down another hallway. She remembered from yesterday that the word meant surgical. The receptionist had told her that's where Dr. Andrews's office was. She stopped and stared down the hall at the double doors at the end, the word QUIRÚRGICO stenciled on them.

His office might contain files on his patients, medical records, maybe even x-rays. *Evidence.* She thought about the list of names in Rogoff's notepad. She needed verification that Stirling had killed them, proof that he was operating on them to get what he needed to make The Cure. She realized this might be her only chance to get it.

She looked around. No one was here to stop her, so she walked up the hall, trying to place her steps quietly, unable to mute the echo off the walls. Nervous, she kept glancing back, hoping no one would see her. Finally she reached the doors and eased them open. The surgical wing was dark and empty. No one was working here at this hour. She glanced back one last time, then slipped through the doors.

Moving cautiously, she headed up the hallway, looking for Stirling's office—or rather—Andrews's office. She stepped around the nurse's station and walked past the two recovery rooms. Next she came to double doors marked NO ENTRADA. The operating room. She stopped only briefly to see if anyone was in there, if Stirling was operating on someone right now. The room was too dark to see inside, but she was sure it was empty.

She continued up the hall to the last door. It was marked JEFE DEL DEPARTAMENTO DE CIRUGÍA. She wasn't sure what that meant, but this was the only other room on the hall; it had to be Andrews's office.

She pressed her ear to the door and listened, hearing nothing on the other side. So she tried the knob. It was locked. Not sure what to do now, but still convinced she had to get into this room and gather the evidence about Stirling, she studied the door, considering her options.

Her gaze found the transom above the door. She stared up at the small pane of glass. It was open a few inches to ventilate the office but she could tell by the way it was hinged that it could open much more. Perhaps enough for her to crawl through.

She looked around for something to use as a ladder to get her up high enough to reach the transom. At the nurse's station were two straight back wooden chairs. She hurried over, grabbed one and dragged it back to Stirling's door.

She climbed up onto the chair and peered through the glass pane. The lights were off inside the office but some illumination came in through the transom—not much, but enough for her to see the room was empty. She saw another door behind the desk. No light bled out from underneath it. A closet, perhaps? She didn't see any file cabinets or even a computer and wondered if this was the secretary's room and that other door led to another office rather than a closet. Could the evidence she needed be behind that door?

She turned her head and checked the hall behind her again. Still no one coming, so she pulled gently on the glass above the door. The transom creaked open. She looked up the hall one more time, then grabbed the sill and hoisted herself up through the tiny opening over the door.

She was glad she was small and fit, because it took a lot of strength to pull herself up and there wasn't much room to squeeze through. Getting down on the other side was even more difficult. Since she went through head first, she had to swing her legs beneath her while contorting her body sideways and holding on tightly to the sill. Finally she got her feet below her and she dropped to the floor.

She left the light off and went straight to the door behind the desk. She tried to open it but it was locked. She peered up but saw that this door didn't have a transom for her to climb through. Hoping to find a key, she went to the desk and began searching the drawers in the dark, feeling around among the pens and pads and paper clips. She would have preferred to be doing this with the light on, but she didn't feel comfortable turning it on. If someone came down the hall they would see light through the transom and know she was here.

She pushed aside scissors, rubber bands, pricked her

finger on a staple remover, felt some items she couldn't identify. Then her thumb brushed over the jagged edge of a key. She snatched it from the drawer, hurried back to the door and tried to unlock it, but the key wouldn't fit in the lock.

"Damn it!" she whispered.

She was going to go back to the desk to look some more but then she tried turning the key over and this time it slid easily into the lock. She twisted the knob and the door opened.

She peered in. This room was completely dark, no light at all. She got a sense that it was larger than the office she was in, and cooler, much cooler. And it had a very different smell. A *medical* smell. But a different medical smell from the rest of the clinic. The air in this room somehow reminded her of the morgue.

She slowly stepped inside, closed the door behind her, and felt along the wall for the light switch, confident no one in the hallway would see the lights in here. Her hand swiped over the switch and fluorescent lights flickered on, one after the other, illuminating a long, narrow laboratory.

The equipment in this lab looked more modern and sophisticated than what she had seen in the rest of the clinic, even though she had no idea what most of this equipment was used for. All of the new, high-tech gadgetry reminded her of Stirling's other office, where he treated Americans. She was certain this was his lab.

She felt uneasy being in here as thoughts of Sam Rogoff and Hector Garcia's wife went through her head.

She thought, too, about Sister Veronica being missing and about Gabriella's nosebleeds. Stirling was dangerous. And right now she was alone and vulnerable inside his lab.

Yes, she felt very uneasy being here. It had only been minutes and already she wanted to get the hell out of here. But first she needed proof, she needed to stop him. She would stay only long enough to get that proof and then she would be gone.

She noticed a bank of wooden file cabinets along the wall. As she headed toward them she spotted more than a dozen wire cages stacked on a shelf, each cage containing a tiny black mouse. The mice were eerily silent and they all seemed to stare right at her.

A shudder ran up her spine as her childhood fear of rodents filled her head with thoughts of the little creatures somehow getting loose and attacking her. For an instant, she was back in her grandmother's cellar as a little girl, afraid for her life. But she told herself she wasn't a little girl anymore, and these mice weren't going to get loose. She had nothing to fear from them.

She turned her attention back to the file cabinets, believing that they were where the evidence she sought would be.

She found the drawer marked G–J unlocked, so she pulled it open and started searching through the folders for Hector Garcia's medical records.

All the patients whose names began with G, H, I and J were together, but beyond that they weren't in any particular order. It took her a few minutes to find Hector

Garcia's folder. When she pulled it out and opened it, she saw at the top right corner of the chart MÉDICO: ANDREWS, WILLIAM T.

Information about his age, height, weight, medical history, that type of thing, was typed in the preprinted spaces near the top. In a red stamp was the word MUERTO, which she knew meant dead, followed by a date handwritten in black ink—28 noviembre 98.

Jodie turned her attention to the notations typed on the bottom half of the page.

POSITIVE FOR BDNF$_2$ PRECURSOR.

Dr. Harrington had told her that something resembling BDNF was in the sample of The Cure he analyzed in Jacksonville. If she understood this notation correctly, Stirling had tested Hector Garcia for the same growth factor and found it present in him. Had he done something to Hector to get the growth factor?

BDNF came from the cortex, Dr. Harrington had said. Trauma to the cortex could cause epilepsy, Dr. Ortega had said. Jodie, putting two and two together, could not deny the obvious. Could Stirling really have removed part of Hector Garcia's brain in order to make The Cure? It seemed too incredible to believe. But that's what everything indicated.

The next notation on Hector's chart said: FAMILY AVAILABLE: IMM—son, sister, brother. EXT—grandson (1), cousins (11), nephews (6), nieces (4). And he listed all their names.

Jodie wasn't sure what that meant. Hector had family

available. But available for what? To be operated on, too? Stirling couldn't possibly mean that. He couldn't possibly be listing people for prospective surgery. *Could he?*

The next notation said: PROSPECT—9+. Another entry she didn't understand. But she did understand the last notation. And as she read the words written by Stirling's hand, a chill rushed up her spine.

Watch for this lineage.

Obviously Stirling *did* list Hector's relatives in hopes of getting the chance to operate on them next, to remove pieces of their brains as he did to Hector. PROSPECT— 9+. Did that mean on a scale from 1 to 10, the prospect that they also contained $BDNF_2$ was a 9+?.

"Oh my God, I'm right," she said out loud, realizing that everything she had thought about Stirling was true. He was operating on these people, taking chunks of their brain to make The Cure, and they were dying because of it.

But her father was better because of it.

That doesn't matter!

As badly as she wanted to believe that it really didn't matter to her, she could not erase that thought from her head. Her father was definitely better because of what Stirling was doing. So was Libby Harden in Daytona. So were hundreds of people suffering from the horrendous affliction of Alzheimer's. Better because of what Stirling was doing. Better because these people were—

No, it doesn't matter! Stirling is killing people down here. Nothing can justify that. Nothing!

Jodie realized that, no matter what the consequences were, Stirling had to be stopped.

Needing the last bit of proof, she quickly flipped through the loose pages in Hector Garcia's file, searching for his x-ray, the film that would show the scar from Stirling's secret trans-sphenoidal operation. She was sure Stirling had ordered an x-ray on Hector. Maria Ticas de Garcia had told her so. But it was not in the file.

Jodie glanced at the closed door to the outer office, listening to the silence, afraid someone might come. She was nervous about being here. She felt she had to hurry.

Hector's x-ray was gone. The notations about BDNF would have to suffice. But maybe there were other x-rays of other patients. She had to look. And she still needed to confirm that the names Rogoff had written were other patients Stirling had killed because of his surgery.

She took Rogoff's notepad from her pocketbook and turned to the page with the list of names. The first name was *Manuel Lamas Petán*. She tucked Hector Garcia's medical chart under her arm, closed the G–J drawer and opened the drawer in the next cabinet, marked O–R.

She kept watching the door as she searched for Manuel's chart. When she found it, she opened the folder and saw Andrews's name on the top along with the red MUERTO stamp and the date: 11 *enero* 99. In the box marked *edad* was typed 10 *años*. The boy was only ten, Jodie realized.

Stirling is killing children too? she thought in disbelief. *This can't be happening.*

Struggling to keep her emotions in check so she could do what she had come in here to do and then get out, Jodie scribbled "yes" in Rogoff's notepad beside Manuel

Petán's name to indicate that he was a patient of Andrews and was deceased.

Now, scanning the bottom of the chart, she noticed the typewritten notations. POSITIVE FOR BDNF$_2$ PRECURSOR. A long list of relatives was typed on the page followed by: PROSPECT—7. Not as good as Hector's relatives, she realized, but probably still a family Stirling wanted to get his hands on.

Jodie turned her attention back to the cluttered folder and looked for the boy's x-ray or CAT scan. As with Hector Garcia's records, this folder did not contain either. She went back to the file cabinet, thinking there might be another folder for him, certain the boy would have had an x-ray of some type. But there was no other folder. There was no film on him or Hector. Stirling must have taken them out, trying to cover what he had done.

She stared at Manuel's chart and wondered if by itself, or even with Hector's chart, it was enough to prove what Stirling was doing. Without the x-rays showing the scar from the secret surgery, would the authorities believe her?

She wasn't sure, but if that's all she had, she would have to go to them with it. She wanted more, though. She wanted proof that Stirling would be unable to refute. At the very least, she would present the police with records from all nine names on the list. And hopefully Dr. Ortega would come up with something as well.

She tucked the dead boy's chart under her arm along with Hector Garcia's and continued checking the medical records of the rest of the names on Rogoff's list.

≋ 56

As the jetliner began its descent, Carl stared out the window at the turquoise Caribbean below. It held no beauty today. All he wanted to see was land, Cancun. He could not stop thinking about Jodie. He needed to get to her soon, but this flight was taking forever.

Finally he saw the beach below, waves rolling onto white sand. Then a long wasteland of scrub brush and swamp as they neared the airport. He unbuckled his seat belt and stood to get his bag from the overhead compartment. As he struggled to tug it out, the flight attendant hurried over.

"Sir, you have to remain in your seat while the 'fasten seat belt' sign is on."

"I'm getting my bag."

"You have to leave that stowed away until we land."

"But I need it."

"You have to wait until we land. Please sit down."

She coaxed Carl back into his seat and stayed to make sure he buckled his seat belt. He watched her return to the rear of the plane, not sure why she was making things difficult for him.

The plane shuddered now as the landing gear hit the runway. Carl popped up right away and tried again to get his bag.

"Sir!" the flight attendant called out, rushing over again. "You must wait until the plane comes to a complete stop at the gate," she said, irritation in her voice.

"You don't understand!" he said.

"Sir, *you* don't understand. All passengers must remain seated until the plane comes to a full and complete stop. Now I'm going to have to insist that you sit," she said, practically putting him back into his seat.

Carl felt that every second mattered. He could barely keep himself seated as the plane taxied toward the terminal. When they finally stopped at the gate, all the other passengers jumped up, clogging the center aisle. He tried to stand up but too many people crowded him and he couldn't get out of his seat until people started filing off the plane. He struggled to pull the bag from the overhead compartment, but people kept squeezing by him, bumping him, and the bag was wedged in by another suitcase. He couldn't get it out. A tall woman Jodie's age finally helped him pull the bag down. He rushed up the aisle, his legs sore from the flight, the suitcase heavy in his hand.

The terminal wasn't nearly as crowded as Miami airport had been, but there were still a lot of people, which made him uneasy. He didn't know where to go at first, but he noticed that everyone was moving in the same direction so he followed the rest of the passengers down an escalator to a large room where immigration officers checked passports.

The line at the far right was the shortest so he tottered over and waited fifteen minutes for his turn. The Mexican man in uniform took forever to flip through his passport and stamp it. When the man handed it back, Carl hurried past the baggage claim. He only had the small valise he had carried on the plane. He headed straight toward Customs.

Three young girls handed out coupons for free drinks at various restaurants. They kept pushing papers in front of his face, confusing and scaring him. He staggered past them to the Customs checkpoint.

"Press the button, please, señor," the woman in uniform told him.

Carl did. A red light blinked: ALTO.

"Come over here, señor," she said, directing him to a table off to the side. She pointed to the valise. "Is this your only baggage?"

"Please, I'm in a hurry," Carl said.

The woman tilted her head to the side and suddenly looked at him suspiciously.

"Is this your only baggage?" she asked again.

"Yes."

"Open it, please."

"I don't have time for this. Don't you understand? My daughter . . ." he said.

"Open the baggage," she repeated. A man in uniform came up behind Carl now. Carl noticed the pistol strapped to the man's hip.

"And open your pockets too," the woman said.

≋ 57

It took Jodie twenty-five minutes to find and check all nine names on Rogoff's list. Each of the medical charts said the same thing: each patient had tested positive for $BDNF_2$, each patient had as physician Dr. William T. Andrews.

And each patient had died.

But not one of the patients' charts contained a CAT scan or x-ray of any type, nothing that would show the opening Stirling had made in their skulls, nothing that proved he was secretly operating on them, suctioning out pieces of their brains.

She looked at the stack of files in her hand, the charts of the patients on Rogoff's list. Perhaps the police could make a case against Stirling from the charts alone—no, not alone, the charts plus her and Neil's testimony. She just hoped that would be enough.

She glanced at the door again, still worried someone would come in and find her. She'd been here too long already. She had to get out and contact the police.

Sister Veronica returned to her thoughts now. *Where is she?* Jodie remembered that the old nun at the church had sent Stirling here to find Sister Veronica. She hoped to God he hadn't already gotten to her. But Sister Veronica was nowhere to be found. Jodie had searched the entire building. It was becoming increasingly difficult for her to believe the nun was all right.

Jodie decided she could not delay any longer. She had to go now. She started to turn to leave but lost her grip on the patient charts. They slid out of her hand and fluttered to the floor, scattering all over. She hurriedly knelt down and started picking them up, wanting to get out quickly, worried someone would come, when she spotted the unmistakable gray film of an x-ray under the table in the middle of the lab.

She reached under and pulled the film out. Printed on the edge was GARCIA, HECTOR ITZÁ. With nervous excitement prodding her to move quickly, she rushed over to the x-ray viewer, turned it on and held the film up so she could examine it.

It took her a few moments to find it but suddenly she saw the tiny light colored circle in the front portion of the skull. Is that the hole Dr. Ortega told her would be there? Jodie wondered. Is that the hole Dr. Ortega said would be left by the surgery she described?

It must be.

A shiver of excitement rushed through her as she stared at it, realizing she had found the evidence she needed, irrefutable proof she could show the authorities to convince them of what Stirling was doing.

Finally satisfied that she had what she came here for, she slid the x-ray into her pocketbook, stuffed the other patients' files in beside it, then hurried to the door to leave. As she turned off the light and opened the door to the outer office, the door across the room leading to the hallway opened and through it came Dr. Stirling.

His eyes met Jodie's for only an instant, but in that instant Jodie saw quite clearly he would not allow her to leave this place alive.

She ducked back inside the dark lab and for a moment just stood there, staring at the door, not sure what to do, where to go. Then she heard footsteps hurrying across the office, the sound of Stirling running to the door. She turned the latch. But then a horrifying thought came to mind. She remembered she had left the key in the door.

Frantic now, she turned the lights back on, saw the chair across the room and rushed over to get it. She brought it back to the door and jammed it under the knob just as Stirling turned the key and shoved the door. The chair ground against the tile floor, holding the door shut.

Jodie saw a phone on the counter and raced over. When she grabbed it and put it to her ear, she heard the sickening sound of silence. No dial tone. She didn't know what number to dial—9-1-1 didn't work here, and she didn't know what the emergency number was in Mexico.

Stirling thrust his weight against the door. The chair inched back, allowing the door to open several inches. The chair would not hold for long.

Jodie saw Stirling's eye peer in at her and she froze, the phone in her hand. He stopped pushing the door, stopped moving altogether. The room fell into deathly silence.

"Before you do something stupid," he whispered, his voice a chilling hiss. "We should talk."

Jodie managed to move her hand enough to press numbers on the phone, not even knowing what she was pressing, just dialing in desperation. But the line remained dead.

"The switchboard operator is not working today," Stirling said.

Jodie didn't want to believe him. She continued trying the phone, pressing "9" several times, hoping to get an outside line, then jabbing desperately at "0."

Stirling thrust his weight against the door again. The chair skidded back several more inches, the opening almost wide enough for him to get through. He pushed again, opening the door a little more. The scraping sound of the chair's legs on the floor frightened Jodie. She dropped the phone and jumped back. Stirling reached in through the opening, grabbed the chair and began trying to pull it loose.

Jodie, desperate for a way out, looked across the room and saw the door near the back. She ran over, hoping to God it wasn't locked. She tugged at it and it opened. Relieved it wasn't a closet, wasn't a dead end, she stared down a short, dark hallway with stairs at the end.

A crash blasted through the room as Stirling threw the chair aside and shoved open the door. Jodie whipped her head around and saw him rush in. He took a moment to close the door behind him and turn the latch, then he grabbed the chair and lodged it under the knob again. Only when the door was wedged closed did he turn toward her.

For the first time, she noticed he had a syringe in his hand.

As he stepped toward her slowly, she spun away and rushed through the doorway, into the hall, tugging the door shut behind her. She was in total darkness now. She reached out and found the wall. Feeling along the cold surface, she made her way hurriedly down the hallway. Suddenly the floor gave way to the stairs and she almost lost her footing. Her hand hit the railing as she started to fall. She grabbed hold of the rail and caught herself. Then she scrambled down the stairs.

Behind her the door opened. A streak of light washed away the darkness and she saw another door at the bottom of the steps. Hoping it was an exit, she rushed toward it.

A shadow blocked the light behind her now and she knew without turning around and looking—*Stirling was coming!* His shoes stomped the floor as he rushed after her.

She bounded down the last few steps. As she finally reached the bottom, she heard Stirling closing quickly behind her. She shoved open the door and ran through.

≡ 58

The Customs agent stared at the collection of shells spread on the table. She picked up the can of WD-40 and shook it. Then she tried to unscrew the bottom, looking for a hidden compartment for drugs. Finally she shrugged, said something in Spanish to the man with the pistol, then told Carl he could go.

Carl quickly gathered his shells together and stuffed them back into the suitcase. He put the WD-40 on top. When he tried to close the suitcase, the zipper got caught. He struggled with it for a minute, first trying to force it shut, then trying to open it again. Finally he gave up on it, grabbed the half-open bag and headed for the exit, spilling shells as he went.

Men lined the corridor, calling out names of hotels and tour companies. A girl was handing out Cancun information booklets. People stopped to talk, others gathered at a booth in the middle of the corridor, changing currency. A group of Spanish children were laughing. One man was sweeping the floor, whistling. The noise and commotion disoriented Carl. For a minute, he wasn't sure which way to go.

"Taxi, señor?"

Carl looked to the side and saw a man dressed in white, grinning at him.

"You like a taxi, señor? Air condition!"

"A taxi, yes," Carl said. "Yes, I need a taxi."

"Very good." The man took the suitcase from him. "Come, señor. I take you."

He led Carl through the terminal and outside to his cab, parked at the curb.

"You go to the hotel zone, señor?"

"Hotel, yes."

The man held open the door for Carl, then hurried around and got in behind the wheel. He started the engine and turned the air up high.

"Nice, yes, señor?"

"Please, I'm in a hurry. I have to get to my daughter."

"No problem, señor. What hotel?"

Carl reached into his pocket and pulled out the paper Jodie had stuck on the refrigerator. All she had written was the phone number. Not the name of the hotel. Carl tried to think of the name but he couldn't remember.

"The hotel, señor?"

"I . . . I don't know . . ."

"The Fiesta Amaricana?"

"No. No."

"The Malia Turquesa?"

"No, it didn't sound like that."

"Ah," the driver said, sure he knew it now. "The Ritz Carlton, señor. It must be the Ritz Carlton. Very nice hotel."

"No, it was something different." He showed the

driver the paper. "This is the phone number. That's all I have. I don't know the name."

The man looked at the paper for a moment, looking as confused as Carl was, then he turned to Carl and grinned. "No problem, señor," he said. "I will call and ask."

"Yes, yes. Call and ask. But hurry, please. Hurry."

"One minutes, señor," the cabby said.

He left the engine running and walked back into the terminal. Carl kept checking his watch, not exactly sure what the hands meant, how much time was passing, then peering up at the terminal door, anxious for the cabdriver to come back. His palms were soaked with sweat, as were his pant legs where he kept rubbing his hands.

He could not stop thinking he was going to be too late.

≋ 59

Instead of finding the blistering heat of a Mexican afternoon when she threw open the door, Jodie found herself staring into a morbid black hole of a basement. The stench of mildew and fecal matter hit her like a blow to the face. For an instant she faltered, fearing what lay ahead. The thought of running blindly into this unknown hole unnerved her.

But then she heard Stirling rush down the stairs behind her. She thought she felt the heat from his body. She lurched forward into the darkness, swatting the door closed as she ran.

It slammed with a harsh metallic sound, like a trap springing shut. And as that sound reverberated through the basement and through her head, the first thought to afflict her was that there might not be another way out of here.

But she knew if she stayed put, if she did not keep running, Stirling would catch her and she had already seen in the cold grizzled face of Maria Ticas de Garcia what would happen if he did.

She ran forward through the blackness, her hands outstretched like someone bracing herself for a fall, trying to feel ahead for obstructions. The basement had no light whatsoever, not even windows to offer the scantiest wattage of illumination. She heard a motor sputtering somewhere in here, a pump or a fan or a piece of equipment of some kind. And she thought she heard water dripping nearby as well.

Then she heard Stirling fall against the door behind her and turn the knob, and from then on, only those sounds echoed in her head.

She rushed forward, pushing herself to go faster. The stink of sewage was much stronger now. Each strained breath she drew felt like it was corroding the lining of her lungs. She ran through a puddle of cold water. Her shoes were open in front and her toes soaked up the chilled water instantly, numbing her feet and her legs, making it harder for her to run. The sheet of water made the concrete floor slippery. She had to slow down.

The door behind her opened with a sibilant *whoosh*, the kind of sound a body makes when it's dragged quickly along pavement. A broth of light poured into the basement—dim, cloudy light that gave a murky cast to the objects surrounding her. But at least she could see now, and what she saw were massive tanks, cast iron pipes, a rumbling boiler, and aluminum ducts reaching out in all directions like arms of a huge metal squid. Straight across the floor, perhaps fifty feet away, was another doorway.

She stalled only for an instant, just long enough to glance over her shoulder at the doorway behind her. A rectangle of light was cut out of the blackness. And in the rectangle stood Stirling's dark silhouette, his right hand held out at his side, the syringe protruding from it.

A bullet of fear struck Jodie, weakening her legs and taking her breath away. She grabbed for something to hold onto and her hands found the steel boiler. A blast of searing heat shot through her fingers. She shoved herself off immediately and started running again. Now she stepped on dry concrete and sprinted toward the door on the other side of the basement—a door she desperately hoped was an exit.

Stirling let the door behind him close slowly. Jodie watched the wedge of light begin to shrink, the basement gradually capitulate to the darkness. The last few inches went with a sudden snap and Jodie found herself surrounded by pure black again.

She could no longer see the door ahead of her. With the image still in her mind, she continued running forward, through another puddle. She didn't stop to listen for Stirling, to see if he was coming. She just ran, her arms outstretched before her.

Her hands hit suddenly, before she could brace herself.

Her elbows collapsed and she ran smack into the steel door, banging her face so hard that for a second she lost all sense of direction. As her head cleared, she heard footsteps on the floor behind her, the *clack-clack-clack* of leather shoes running on concrete. Then she heard a splash as Stirling rushed through the puddle of sewage.

Jodie brailled along the door until she felt the handle. She yanked at it with wet, trembling hands, but the door would not budge. *It was locked.* She began feeling along the surface for the latch but heard Stirling continue toward her and realized if she stood here a second longer he would surely catch her.

She darted away from the door and edged her way to the side, hoping the darkness would hide her. She moved as quickly as possible, feeling blindly for what she had seen a moment earlier. Her hands finally found a steel tank, this one cold. Keeping her palms pressed against it to maintain a sense of where it was, she worked her way behind the tank, into the crevice between the steel tank and the stone wall.

She heard Stirling collide with the door, a loud *clack* that made her heart jump. Then she heard him pull at the handle, heard the door struggle against the latch. Then silence.

Even the fan motor she had heard earlier was no longer humming. It had stopped some time after the frightening sight of Stirling coming down here, but Jodie hadn't noticed its absence until now. Now, the quiet in here was so deep she could hear blood pump past her temples, hear her own strained breath as she struggled to inhale the dank air.

Stirling's shoes scratched the floor now as he turned around, turned away from the door, turned to face the bowels of this black basement.

She pressed herself flat against the wall and squeezed her eyes shut, feeling like a child afraid of a make-believe monster, hoping if she didn't look, it would go away and leave her alone. But she was not a child and this monster was not make-believe.

"Jodie . . ." he said, his voice hissing like a rattlesnake about to strike.

Jodie opened her eyes to the blackness.

The sound of his voice speaking her name quivered down her back, weakening her spine so that she could barely stand. Like a rock climber clinging to the face of a mountain, she held as tightly as she could to the coarse concrete wall. Her legs shuddered beneath her.

"I know you're still here, Jodie," he said. He spoke quietly, but his voice echoed off the harsh surfaces all around, making it sound like he was everywhere.

"Jodie," he said again. "We need to talk."

He was trying to get her to speak, she realized, trying to get her to give away her position so he could find her. But she wasn't going to let him do that. She wasn't going to let him trick her.

She started to inch along the wall, creeping farther behind the line of tanks when suddenly she heard a snapping sound and realized what it was an instant before the overhead lights blinked on.

Her eyes were accustomed to the darkness, and now the sudden flash of light stung. She squinted, afraid to peek out between the tanks to see where he was, fearing he would see her first.

She tilted her head back slightly and saw the naked bulb hanging from the ceiling above her. A few other bulbs were spaced across the length of the basement, but the one glaring on her, the one most threatening to her, was directly overhead.

She wondered if Stirling had turned on the lights himself or if someone else had come in—someone who could help her?

Or is it someone who will help Stirling?

She remained silent and still, listening to see if someone else was here. No one called out. No sound of footsteps from the other side of the basement scratched the silence. No one else was here. Just her. *And Stirling.*

"You can't hide forever, Jodie," Stirling said. "You know I'll find you."

The scrape of his shoes on the concrete floor as he moved out across the basement made her tremble. He would eventually find her back here. She had to move. But go where? There was no place else to hide. She was trapped. Like those mice in the cages upstairs, she was trapped and at the mercy of this demented doctor.

Then Stirling spoke again, and this time his words seized Jodie's attention like a hand clutching her throat. "Jodie," he said. "You don't want to see your father die horribly, do you?"

Is he threatening Dad? Can he really do anything to Dad? No, it's talk. He's just trying to frighten me. In his desperation, he's trying again to trick me.

Desperation? she thought. *His* desperation? He wasn't

the one who was desperate—*she was*. She was the one trapped down here. She was the one right now fighting for her very life.

"He will die," Stirling said, his voice a little louder, a little closer. "What you're doing . . . your father will die. Is that what you want?"

I want you to stop killing people. I want you punished for the people you've already killed. That's what I want. This has nothing to do with my father. She wanted to yell this in his face, but she knew that was exactly what he wanted her to do. He wanted her to give her position away, to reveal to him where she was hiding.

She bit her lip and remained silent as she tried again to think of a way to escape.

"Because that's what will happen," Stirling said. "Your father will die."

Leave my father out of this! This isn't about him. But in her heart, she knew that it was.

"Think of your father, Jodie," Stirling said. "I'm sure we can come to an understanding."

Stirling remained silent now, letting his words fester in her head. She tried not to think in terms of what all this had to do with her father, but it was difficult not to consider him. Indirectly the deaths she had discovered were keeping her father healthy and ultimately alive. If she exposed what Stirling was doing—

No! People can't trade lives. It isn't up to me to decide that one person will die so another can live. No one has that right. Not me. And certainly not Stirling.

Stirling was silent now for a long moment. Jodie didn't even hear him moving. She began to wonder if she had lost track of him, if he was moving so stealthily that she couldn't hear him anymore. He could be right behind her!

She snapped her head quickly, sure she felt his presence next to her, sure she felt his breath on her neck. But he was not there. She was too nervous to breathe. She kept moving her head from side to side, repositioning her ears in a desperate attempt to try to hear him, his movement, his breath, anything.

Then he broke the silence.

"Can't we just talk?" he said to her.

Jodie heard him move across the concrete, heard him draw closer. From the sound, she realized he was coming toward the tanks.

She turned her head and saw the narrow passage between the row of tanks and the wall. It was a tight squeeze but she could slip through. Once at the end, she could dash to the door. Stirling would surely see her when she ran out from behind the tanks, but she might be able to make it to the door, up the stairs, through the lab and office and out into the corridor before he could catch her. And once she was up there she would be safe. It was her only chance.

"Jodie . . ." he said again. "Come out and talk to me, please. For your father's sake."

Stop talking about my father!

She tried not to listen to him, but his voice seemed to be part of the musty air she breathed, part of the room trapping her, echoing off the walls, off the steel tanks, off the concrete floor and wooden ceiling, off the inside of her skull. What he was telling her was as undeniable as the light glaring in her eyes. Her actions would hurt her father. She didn't want to listen, didn't want to believe, but she knew it was the truth.

Still, Stirling was killing people, and under any circumstances, that could not be justified. He had to be stopped.

Even if it means Dad's Alzheimer's will return? Even if it means he will suffer and die when he doesn't have to?

The answer was painful, but she knew it had to be "yes." Stirling had to be stopped, no matter what.

Keeping herself pressed flat against the wall, she began sliding her way to the side, taking tiny steps, careful not to let her shoes scrape the gritty floor. She made up her mind to make a break for the door right now.

She had only taken a few steps toward the opening between the tanks when she heard it. At first it sounded like the kind of squeaking a shopping cart makes when it has a bad wheel. But this sound did not come in regular intervals. This had no order, no pattern. Just random, high-pitched sounds. Then a faint scratching sound. Then more high-pitched *eeking* sounds.

Not understanding what the noise was, Jodie hesitated, wondering if Stirling could be doing something, something she should know about before it was too late, like opening a valve, flooding the basement with water or a deadly gas.

She leaned toward the gap between two of the tanks and started to peer out, hoping to catch a glimpse of where he was, what he was doing—that's when she felt something brush against her toe.

Her gaze dropped instantly to the ground, and when she saw it she could not control the wave of fear that washed from her foot to her brain, leaving a wake of horror in every nerve of her body.

Barely an inch from her foot and moving toward her was a swollen, grizzled rat, brown teeth visible through its open mouth.

Jodie shrieked and bolted through the gap between the tanks. She did not see Stirling and Stirling did not see her until she rammed into him. He was turned the other way, not expecting the hit. She ran full force into his ribs, knocking him off balance and sending him stumbling into a grill of pipes lining the opposite wall. His glasses flew off. The syringe came loose from his hand and clattered to the floor. He dropped to his knees to grab it.

The collision knocked Jodie backward against the tank. But she managed to keep her balance and remain standing. When she saw him reach for the syringe, she rushed at him and shoved him from behind, knocking him forward again. This time his head clanged against one of the pipes and he collapsed flat on his stomach.

Jodie didn't wait to see if he was going to get up. She turned and ran across the basement toward the doorway leading to the main floor. She had only gotten a few yards when she saw the plywood table she had missed before, when it was dark.

It was set up against the wall, partly concealed in shadows. And even though Jodie was running past it, even though she barely glanced in that direction, she saw clearly the body lying atop it.

Sister Veronica's eyes were frozen open. Her jaw hung down as though her face were locked in the throes of a painful gasp for life. For an instant Jodie heard the nun screaming, but then she realized she herself was the one screaming.

Horror seized Jodie. At first she couldn't move, she just stared and screamed at this young woman who had tried to help her, this young woman who was now dead.

Then she heard Stirling move, a sound that broke the paralysis in her limbs. She sprinted toward the door, gasping, letting out involuntary whimpers of fear.

Her hands were trembling and clammy with sweat. She grabbed the handle but her fingers slipped off. As she grabbed a second time, holding as tightly as she could, she listened for the sound of Stirling running after her but heard only her own strained breathing. She did not dare take the time to look back. She tugged open the door and clambered up the stairs, two at a time.

She raced up the hallway to the lab. The chair was propped against the door where Stirling had left it. She knocked it out of the way, yanked open the door and dashed through the outer office to the next door, pulling that open and rushing out so quickly she didn't see him until it was too late.

His body was solid, barely reacting when she ran into him. She started to flop backward, but he quickly grabbed her and held her up. She almost screamed, then she saw his face and collapsed into his arms.

"Thank God it's you!" she said.

"What's wrong, Jodie?"

"He's trying to kill me! Stirling is down in the basement! He tried to kill me! He killed Sister Veronica! She's down there! We have to do something!"

Neil hushed her and held her tightly. "I'm here now," he said. "I'm going to take care of everything."

60

"Salida Del Sol," the cabby said as he climbed back in behind the wheel.

"Yes, yes, that's it!" Carl said. "That's the place! I have to get there right away. Hurry, please!"

"No problem, señor."

The driver backed out slowly and drove around the circular drive in front of the terminal. He slowed for the speed bump at the exit, then headed up the road at about forty miles per hour.

Carl leaned forward. "Please. I'm in a hurry. I have to get to Jodie's hotel. Can't you go faster?"

"The road is dangerous, señor."

"My daughter may be in trouble. I have to get there right away. Please!"

"Si, señor."

The driver sped up, taking the car to about sixty miles per hour. That still didn't seem fast enough for Carl. The road was narrow, but it was straight and empty and surely they could be going faster.

"I'll pay you extra," Carl said. "Anything you want. Just go faster."

"I am go faster, señor."

"More faster!"

The driver grimaced as he pressed the accelerator and added another ten miles per hour to his speed. The palm trees alongside the road were a blur now. The cab vibrated as the tires struggled over the rough asphalt, much bumpier than roads back home.

They came up on another car going much slower.

"Go around him," Carl said before the cabby could slow down. "The lane's clear. Go around him."

The cabby did as Carl told him, slowing only slightly as he changed lanes. Carl sat forward, close to the driver, watching out the windshield, making sure nothing delayed them.

As they approached the junction to the road going south to Playa Del Carmen and north to Cancun Centro, the cabby slowed.

"What are you doing?" Carl said.

"I have to stop." He pointed to a line of cars stopped in the lane ahead.

"Why aren't they moving?"

"Maybe a crash, señor. I told you, this road is dangerous if you drive much fast."

"Go around it. Can you go around it?"

"I can take the turn to Cancun Centro, go round and come down from the other side to the hotel zone."

"Is that faster?"

"I don't know how long we wait here."

The cabby slowed the car to little more than a roll now. Carl glared at the line of cabs and rental cars near the junction. He could just barely see flashing lights of a police car far ahead.

"Go around!" he said, hoping it was the right choice.

"Sí, señor."

The cabby maneuvered around the line of cars to the junction, then sped up Highway 307 toward downtown Cancun.

61

"Where is he?" Neil asked.

"He's down there. Down the stairs. In the basement. I pushed him and I think he hit his head."

"I'm going to go down there and check."

"No, wait . . ."

"Jodie, I have to check, see if he's hurt. I'll be right back."

"He killed Sister Veronica. He's dangerous."

"I'll be all right. You stay here."

"He has a syringe," she warned him. "That must be what he used to kill the others, to make it look like heart attacks."

"I'll be careful." Neil squeezed her hand, gave her a reassuring look, then left.

From where Jodie stood at the doorway she watched him walk across the outer office and disappear into the lab. She heard his footsteps on the floor as he walked to the back of the room, then the quiet click of the door closing behind him as he went downstairs. Silence followed, a heavy, unsettling quiet.

Jodie tried not to fixate on the quiet. She glanced up the corridor behind her, looking for someone to draw her attention, to ease her fear. No one else was around. Just her. And she noticed now how silent the entire building had become. She felt a strange surreal sense of desolation. She looked back into Stirling's office, fear slowly seizing her again. She wished someone else would come—a nurse, another doctor, a janitor, anyone. Waiting here by herself, she did not feel safe.

Growing more troubled by Neil's absence, she stepped inside the lab, still staring at the door in the back. It bothered her that she couldn't hear what was happening in the basement. Just silence. Cold, unnatural silence.

Something is wrong. Very wrong.

Realizing she could not leave Neil down there, but still not sure what to do, she moved past the file cabinets and around the table in the middle of the room. On the table was a large metal stapler. She quickly snatched it up, thinking she could use it as a weapon, something heavy to swing. The coldness of it settled quickly into the bones of her fingers, leaving her hand numb.

As she approached the back door, she slowed, placing each step carefully, ready to jump back at the slightest sound. She started to reach for the handle. Her hand was trembling. The last thing she wanted to do was to open this door and go back down into that dank pit, but Neil was down there, he was helping her, and now he might need her help. She had to do it.

Her hand touched the cold metal doorknob, sending a shiver through her body. She stopped breathing now. Her gaze fixed on the door. She started to turn the knob when suddenly the door flew open. She shrieked and lurched back. Someone—it happened so fast she couldn't see who it was—rushed through the darkness toward her, his hands grabbing for her, and she realized instantly that Stirling had killed Neil.

With the little strength she had left, she raised her right arm to swing the stapler but he caught her wrist before she could strike. He held her so tightly she could not break free. She was about to scream when he whispered:

"Shhhhh. It's okay. It's only me."

The moment she recognized Neil's voice her body went limp in his arms.

"I thought you were him," she said. "I thought you were dead."

"It's okay." He hugged her until she stopped shuddering, then he grasped both her shoulders so she could see his face and he said, "Jodie . . . he's dead."

The words didn't register right away. But then all of a sudden their meaning clicked in her head and she realized what Neil was saying. The shock of what she had done left her unable to speak. *She had killed a man.*

"You said he hit his head when you pushed him?" Neil said.

She nodded weakly, drew a thin breath and whispered, "He . . . he hit the pipes." She shook her head, trying to rid her brain of the image of him falling. She looked up at Neil and wanted desperately to explain what had happened, to defend what she had done. "He was . . . I was just trying to get away," she said.

"I know. It'll be okay."

She forced down another breath, trying to calm herself. Neil's presence helped. His understanding eased her fear.

"You'll stay with me when we call the police?" she said.

"I'm not going to leave your side."

She hugged him, and he told her again everything would be all right.

"I found proof," she told him, still holding him tightly.

"Patients' records, Hector Garcia's x-ray. Enough for the police."

"You have it now?" he asked.

"Yes. Yes, right here." She showed him the charts and the x-ray stuffed in her pocketbook.

"Hang on to those," he said.

"Will you call the police for me?"

"Of course."

"I just don't know if I can do it."

"Don't worry about that. I'll take care of it. But we shouldn't do it here."

"What do you mean?"

"It's not safe. We don't know who was in on it with Stirling."

"Do you think someone else is here?"

"I don't see how Stirling could have done all this alone. Someone must be working with him. They could be here in this building right now."

"*Oh God . . .*" She peered across the dark room at the hallway beyond. "I just want this to end."

Neil took her by the hand. "It'll all be over in a little while. I promise."

≋ 62

Jodie left her rental car on the street near Clinica Centro and rode with Neil in his Jeep. She shivered in the wind, clutching her pocketbook with one hand and Neil's hand with the other. Neither of them spoke until Neil drove past the turn for the *Seguridad Publica* building.

"Is there another police station?" Jodie asked.

"We're going back to the hotel."

"We are? Why?"

He peered at her, a strange look in his eyes that made her uneasy.

"Jodie, you killed him," he said.

"It was self-defense."

"I know, but remember I told you about the judicial system down here? We have to be careful how we handle this. I know a man who's connected with the federal police. I'm going to call him before we call the local cops. My friend can help us handle this the right way."

"You think that's what we should do, call him first?"

"Trust me on this."

"Will he be working on Sunday?"

"I'll call him at home."

When they got back to the hotel, Neil parked around the side of the building and took Jodie in through the service entrance. She didn't understand why he was going this way but she was too nervous about what had happened at the clinic and about facing the police to question him. Which door they used seemed unimportant compared to everything else that was going on.

They hurried through the laundry room where three dryers were twirling sheets. The machines, noisy, rusted monstrosities, appeared to be vented right into the room, blowing hot air across Jodie's face as she followed Neil toward a door in the back.

Neil held her hand and took her down a path that circumvented the pool area, a back trail through the palm bushes used by hotel workers. They came out behind the cabañas. Jodie remembered she had locked her key in the room earlier today, but fortunately Neil had a passkey. He unlocked the door and took her inside the cabaña.

The constricting bands of anxiety that had been tightening around her all day began to loosen now. But she was still anxious, still afraid, especially about the police. Her hands were trembling as Neil took her to the bed and sat her down.

"You need a drink," he told her. He left her for a moment and went to the mini bar. "Scotch, okay?" he asked.

"I really don't need a drink."

"You're a wreck, Jodie. You need something to calm your nerves."

He took the miniature bottle into the bathroom and returned a moment later with a glass half filled with scotch.

"Just have a little," he said. "It'll help settle you. Trust me."

Jodie took a sip. The warmth of the scotch felt soothing going down her throat.

"Thanks," she said. "Maybe I did need this." She took another sip and said, "What do we do now?"

"Now I call my friend."

Neil picked up the phone. Jodie took another sip of scotch. She was already feeling the tension leaving her body, feeling her nerves settle. Neil was right about her needing the drink. It was a big help. She watched him dial the number. While he waited for someone to answer, he looked over at her and smiled.

"Don't worry," he said. "We're going to make everything right."

She nodded and took another sip. She was glad he was

with her. She didn't know if she would have been able to handle this alone.

Neil turned away and spoke to someone on the phone in Spanish, quietly, rapidly. Jodie's mind was jumbled with all she had been through; she wasn't able to pick out any of the words he was saying. She really didn't even try. He knew what he was doing. She was just relieved to leave everything in his capable hands.

He hung up and came over to the bed.

"What did he say?" she asked.

"That was his wife. He's not home right now, but she knows where he is. She's going to call him and have him call us here."

"Will it take long?"

"No. Just a few minutes." He put his arms around her and drew her close. "Everything's going to be all right," he told her.

"I know," she said, and looking into his eyes she truly believed it would be.

She noticed now how sleepy she was beginning to feel. All that had happened must be catching up with her. She took a deep breath to steady herself, then had another sip of scotch.

"Are you okay?" Neil asked.

Jodie felt her eyes getting heavy. A dizziness came over her now, a feeling of unsteadiness she had never experienced before. The room began to sway.

"My God . . ." she whispered.

"Jodie?"

She started to get up from the bed to go into the bathroom and splash water on her face, clear her head, but her legs buckled beneath her and she grabbed for the bureau. The glass fell from her hand and shattered on the floor. Neil rushed over and held her.

"I don't know what's wrong," she said. "I'm . . . I can't stand up."

"Let me help you."

He guided her back to the bed and practically placed her on her back. Her head felt too heavy to support. It sank into the pillow.

"I don't understand what's wrong with me," she said.

"It's just exhaustion."

"No . . ."

"It's going to be okay," Neil said.

He looked fuzzy to her now. She reached up to hold his hand but he was much farther away from her than she thought. She realized he was backing off from the bed.

"Neil? . . ."

Still facing her, he stepped over to the door and opened it. Jodie hadn't heard a knock and wondered if he was leaving the cabaña. But he didn't walk out. Instead he stepped to the side.

Another man appeared in the doorway carrying a small black satchel. The bag looked like the kind physicians used. Sunlight glared behind this man, making it difficult for Jodie to see him clearly. He and Neil exchanged looks and whispered words Jodie could not hear, then the man walked into the cabaña.

Could he be Neil's friend from the federal police? she wondered. That could be an evidence bag he was carrying. How long had it been since Neil hung up the phone? A minute? An hour? She didn't know anymore. But didn't Neil say the man was supposed to *call*?

Her vision grew increasingly blurred. She blinked and rubbed her eyes but it didn't help, her vision didn't clear. She still could not see all the way to the door.

The man Neil had let in stepped around the foot of the bed and came closer to her, and she finally saw his face. Suddenly she couldn't breathe. Shock swept through her. Then a sick feeling of disbelief. Then a bone-chilling fear.

"How are you feeling, Jodie?" Dr. Stirling asked. Blood seeped from the small cut on his forehead. His glasses were cocked, the frames bent.

"But you're . . . you're dead . . ." She turned, searching for Neil. "Neil . . . ?"

He came up behind Stirling and peered down at her.

"Wha . . . what's . . . going . . . ?" She tried to say the rest but the words would not come out.

When she attempted to sit up, her body would not respond. It was as though she had lost all control of her muscles. All she could do was lie still and face what was about to happen.

Neil stepped around Stirling and came close to her. "You didn't leave us any other choice," he said.

As his words echoed through her head and his face came in and out of focus, she suddenly realized what he had done.

The scotch. He had put something in the scotch. He had drugged her. And he had brought Stirling here to her. *But why?*

"You should have left well enough alone," Stirling said to her, reaching down and touching her wrist, checking her pulse. She tried to pull away but he easily held her arm still. She had no strength.

"I had hoped you would have understood that sacrifices have to be made when one is on the verge of an important scientific breakthrough," he said.

Jodie watched helplessly as Stirling felt her forehead, then took the stethoscope from his black bag and listened to her heart. When he was done, he said, "I admit that the outcome on a few of the procedures turned out . . . unfortunate. But one must weigh that against the fact that NPEF-alpha, The Cure as you call it, is helping so many people. There is always a downside, always a price to pay. But I think it's been worth it. I had hoped that after you saw the change in your father you would have felt the same way. Too many people count on what I'm doing here. I can't let you jeopardize that."

"Money . . ." she said, barely getting the word out. "All . . . just . . . money."

"No," Stirling said. "Not to me," he added, glancing over his shoulder at Neil.

"Keep telling yourself that," Neil said bitterly. He stepped around Stirling and came a little closer.

Jodie could barely keep her eyes open now.

"I'm sorry," Neil whispered to her. "You should have been satisfied just having your father better."

"No," she murmured, not even sure the word came out. "Don't . . ."

He reached into her pocketbook and took out the folders and the x-ray she had jammed in there. Stirling grabbed them quickly from Neil and stuffed them into his black bag.

"This is the only proof she has, right?" Stirling asked.

"That's it."

"The woman at the morgue?"

"Taken care of."

"Do you think either of them told anyone else?"

"They didn't have a chance."

Neil turned back to Jodie and said, "You're going for a little ride." Then he looked over his shoulder at Stirling. "Did you bring her car?"

He nodded. "I parked it alongside the building, like you said."

"Good." Neil turned to Jodie. "Some of the roads down here are awful," he told her. "Unfortunately, tourists have accidents all the time."

"Neil . . ." she said, barely able to speak the name of the man who had made love to her just last night, the man who was now betraying her.

"I'm sorry, Jodie. I really am. But you left us no other choice."

He slid his arms under her and lifted her from the bed. In desperation, she held the sheets as tightly as she could, pulling them off the mattress as Neil carried her away from the bed.

"Don't be difficult, Jodie," Neil said.

Stirling pried the sheets from her hand and threw them back on the bed in a ball.

"Get the door," Neil said.

"If we take her outside like this someone will see us."

"No one will see. We'll go through the laundry room. Just open the door. Hurry up."

Through her blurry vision Jodie saw Stirling scamper over to the door. He turned the knob and eased the door open only an inch so he could peek out and make sure it was clear before he opened it all the way. When he stuck his face close to the opening, the door suddenly jolted open, smacking him in the forehead. His glasses flew off, and he tumbled backward and fell to the floor, clutching his face and squealing like a wounded animal.

"What the—?" Neil started to say.

The door flew open the rest of the way, revealing Carl standing outside, holding a paisley valise, glaring at Jodie and Neil, first shock on his face, then anger.

For a brief instant, Carl and Neil just stared at each other, neither speaking, neither moving. Then as Neil started to say, "What are you doing here, old man?" Carl let out a furious howl and charged into the room.

Neil turned and flung Jodie onto the bed, then he recoiled just as Carl came near, striking him backhanded across the jaw and knocking him into the bureau. Carl let out a gasp of pain and crumbled to the floor. The suitcase he was carrying smashed against the wall, spilling shells across the room. The can of WD-40 clattered to the floor.

Carl struggled to stand, rising onto one knee before Neil rushed over and pounded him on the back of the head with interlocked hands, knocking him down again onto his stomach. Then Neil rushed over to the door and quickly closed and locked it. Stirling was still on his back, holding his head, squirming in pain. Fresh blood streamed down his face from a second gash in his forehead.

"Get up," Neil barked at him.

Jodie, seeing her father in pain on the floor, gathered all the strength she could and rolled herself to the side of the bed. She dropped her legs to the floor in a weak attempt to stand.

Neil stepped over Stirling and came to the bed. He put

his hand on Jodie's forehead and shoved her back down. She flopped backward onto the mattress, unable to resist. Carl struggled to stand again, rolling over onto the scattered shells.

Neil turned and glared at Stirling. "Will you for God's sake get up!" he said, gritting his teeth, struggling not to shout. "Get something out of that goddamn bag of yours. Make it look like natural causes, like the others. And do it fast."

Stirling managed to push himself to his knees and put his bent glasses back on. Neil grabbed the black bag from the floor and threw it to him.

"Hurry!"

On the bed, Jodie pulled herself up again and tried to stand.

"Stay down!" Neil hissed. He rushed over and shoved her to the mattress again.

"Bastard!" Carl said in a weak, rabid voice. He lifted his hobbled body onto one knee again.

"Hurry with that shot," Neil told Stirling as he stomped toward Carl, his fist ready to strike again.

"Dad . . ." Jodie cried out.

Neil turned his head for an instant when he heard her, then he turned back to Carl to strike him. As he cocked his arm back, Carl raised his hand. Clutched in his crooked fingers was the can of WD-40. Before Neil could react, Carl sprayed the oil, coating Neil's eyes and mouth and nose.

Neil threw up his hands and screamed as the oil burned into his eyes. He couldn't see, couldn't defend himself. Carl thrust himself to his feet and swung the can at Neil, hitting him in the side of the head. Neil fell sideways into the bureau. Blood poured from a gash in his temple. Carl thrust the WD-40 can with all his strength into the bridge of Neil's nose. Neil's legs buckled and he fell to his knees. Carl swung again, this time nailing him in the forehead. Neil's head snapped back and hit the bureau. He flopped forward onto the floor and lay motionless. Carl hobbled closer and started spraying WD-40 into Neil's face.

"You bastard," he yelled at Neil, who was unconscious and bleeding badly. *"You son of a bitch!"*

Suddenly Stirling rushed at Carl and shoved him into the other bed. He jabbed Carl in the kidney with his left fist, then came at him with his right hand—holding a syringe.

Carl managed to grab Stirling's arm before Stirling could inject him. They began to wrestle, Stirling on top, blood streaking down his face. Stirling drove his knee into Carl's stomach. Jodie watched in horror as Carl's arms collapsed and the needle jolted close to his chest. But Carl, struggling, managed to hold onto Stirling's wrist and keep the needle away.

Jodie squirmed to the edge of the mattress again. Her body was slow to respond, as though the messages were delayed going from her brain to her muscles. She dropped her feet to the floor and pushed hard against the mattress to sit upright.

Stirling pulled his left arm free of Carl's grip and punched him in the face. The blow didn't have the power of Neil's punches earlier, but Carl didn't have much strength left either and his head snapped to the side. He tried to grab Stirling's arm again but could not find it in the air above him. Stirling hit him in the throat, sending Carl into a fit of coughs.

Jodie saw Carl's hand slip off Stirling's right wrist. Now, nothing held off the syringe. Stirling pulled it back slightly, the way one draws his fist back before a punch. As he started to thrust it forward, Jodie threw herself off the bed. Her legs would not support her weight so she just tumbled forward, toward the other bed, toward Stirling and Carl.

She collided with Stirling an instant before he could jab the needle into Carl's chest. She and Stirling crashed to the floor, tangled together. They rolled across the shells. She heard him let out a hideous scream, then he flung her off. She hit the wall, and for a moment lost her senses.

As her vision slowly returned, she saw Stirling rise to his knees. Protruding from his chest was the syringe. The plunger was depressed all the way. He glared down at the hypodermic needle, fear and utter disbelief on his face. He stared up at Jodie. He started to reach out for her but then his face contorted, his eyes widened and his mouth dropped open. He clutched his chest. A gurgling sound emitted from his throat. His eyes rolled back and he toppled forward, smacking the floor directly in front of Jodie.

His face was only inches from hers. Saliva dripped from his mouth. He made one attempt to raise his head, lifting it only slightly off the floor, then it dropped back down. The gurgling sound stopped and Stirling lay perfectly still. Jodie didn't have to check his pulse. She knew he was dead.

As she struggled to get up, Carl crawled across the floor to her and wrapped his arms around her. He was crying. He was holding her, protecting her, and crying. She sank against him and started to cry, too.

➤ EPILOGUE

Carl walked slowly along the beach, scanning the tide line for shells. He spotted one in the sand a few feet away, let go of Jodie's arm, and rushed over to snatch it up before a wave could wash it away. He stared at it for a moment, unsure whether to keep it or not. Finally he sprayed it with WD-40 and stuffed it into his bag. As they walked on, he took Jodie's arm again, and held on as though he was afraid of falling. But Jodie wondered if he did it just to feel safe.

She noticed how much thinner and weaker he had gotten in just the last couple of weeks. His gait was unsteady. Everything he did, he did with uncertainty. The decline was coming more rapidly than she had expected. More rapidly than he was prepared for, too. She saw bewilderment on his face all the time.

The breeze off the ocean picked up, bringing a chill to the evening. The sun settled below the tops of the apartment buildings bordering the beach, leaving a long, uneven shadow across the sand. Jodie glanced at the filled Publix bag in Carl's hand.

"I think we'd better start heading home, don't you?" she said.

He tested the weight of his bag and gave a satisfied nod.

As they lumbered up the beach, Carl started breathing

heavily, wheezing like a smoker. They had to stop at a bench on the edge of the sand so he could catch his breath. These days he tired easily. A half-hour walk was as much as he could stand.

As they sat down, Jodie smelled a mixture of sweat and the ocean on him. His pants were rolled up halfway over his calves. His sneakers were wet and covered with sand. He turned to her and studied her face for a moment.

"What?" she said.

He shook his head, then turned and peered at the waves.

"It was a nice day, wasn't it?" she said, trying to make conversation.

He didn't answer. She wasn't even sure he heard her. He looked at his watch. For a moment he just stared at it, his eyes showing confusion. He was trying so hard to make sense of what he saw, but finally he shook his head in disgust and stared across the beach.

"It's almost six, Dad."

He nodded, then he turned and stared at the water again. "Little thing like that . . ." he murmured.

"It's okay," Jodie said.

He shrugged and continued gazing at the surf.

She wondered if he was thinking about Mexico.

She often did.

So much of what had happened down there was still unresolved. But one part was very clear, Neil Lancaster's fate. He had told Jodie about Mexico's legal system and how much it differed from U.S. courts. But he hadn't mentioned how swift Mexican justice was. At least in this case. The government had needed only one month to convict him of murdering Sister Veronica, Maria Ticas de Garcia, and Dr. Rosita Ortega. Now he was in a prison, where he'd spend the rest of his life.

Jodie tried not to think about him, about the night the two of them had been together, about the feelings she had had for him. But she often lay awake in bed at night, memories of him playing with her emotions. Hurt, anger, hatred. He had done such terrible things; he deserved to be punished. She sometimes even wished Mexico had the death penalty, because that was what he deserved. This man whom she thought she could have loved . . .

She looked at her father now and saw that he was staring at her again.

"What?" she asked.

He was silent for a moment longer, then he said, "Have you heard anything?"

She hesitated. He asked the question often and it was always the same answer. She wished it could be different, but she knew it never would be. Finally she said, "No."

"Nothing?"

She shook her head.

He looked oddly resigned now. He gazed at the ocean again, as though some answer, some solution lay out there.

The Mexican authorities had been stingy with the details. The World Health Organization hadn't been able, or willing, to tell her much. She had spoken with several officials from the State Department, but they had been more interested in asking questions than in answering them. The newspapers knew less than Jodie did. Sara

Cassidy had gotten some information, but even she was having trouble getting past the roadblocks the Mexicans had put up.

But from what Jodie had been able to piece together, approximately a hundred patients had been receiving The Cure from Dr. Stirling. That meant one hundred lives Jodie had altered drastically, not to mention the lives of the people who loved these patients. If only there had been some way for her not to have hurt so many, so deeply . . .

Her father turned and looked at her now.

"Maybe it's still too early to tell anything," he asked. "You think so?"

"I'm not sure, Dad."

"I mean . . ." He stalled, at a loss for the right words. "Did they say . . . ?" He looked confused and desperate. "Can't they . . . somehow . . . get *any?*"

Jodie shook her head.

He stared at her for a moment, looking like he wanted to say something, but finally he turned and stared at the water again.

Jodie gazed at his profile silhouetted by the setting sun. His proud, sad face. She had already told him what she had learned. With Stirling dead, the Mexican government had cleaned out his lab and office, confiscated all his records and all remaining supplies of The Cure. Rumors circulated that a German pharmaceutical company wanted to buy The Cure from the Mexicans and make it available in a synthetic form, but nothing had come of it. Even if that did happen, that would take years of research. From what little information Jodie had gleaned from U.S. and Mexican health officials, she held out little hope The Cure would be available in any form, anytime soon. Certainly not in her father's lifetime.

She had told him all this before.

But he would not surrender hope.

Tonight, staring at the surf, he murmured, "There has to be . . . some way."

She just looked at him, thinking how difficult it must be for him. He had to understand that he was getting worse. He had to know that soon he would need to be taken care of again. And that was something he must be deathly afraid of. In a very short time, he would lose his identity, become that other person, that lost, helpless child. It must be tearing him apart.

And what must be worse for him, she realized, was knowing that it was because of his own daughter.

Emotion swelled in her throat. She bit her lip and had to look away.

How could I have done that to him? How? . . .

He turned to her again. "You know, maybe," he said. "Maybe if we talk to them, if we explain . . ."

She took a breath. "I've talked to them, Dad."

"But there must be someone else we can talk to."

"I've talked to everyone."

"Well," he said, desperately grasping at straws. "We can talk to them again. Can't we?" he asked, staring at her. "Can't we try again?"

He continued staring at her, a sad, pleading look on his face. She had to look away. She just stared at the sand, struggling to hold in her emotions. She knew he was staring at her, but she couldn't look at him. She knew if she did, she'd lose it altogether.

"Jodie?" he whispered.

She took a deep breath and slowly turned to face him again. The anguish in his face was gut-wrenching. Biting down on her lip again, she reached over and touched his hand, stalling until she could speak.

"Daddy," she said, so softly she could barely hear herself.

She hesitated again, looking for strength somewhere.

"The shots . . ." she whispered. "There won't be any more."

He stared at her as the words registered. She saw the loose skin on his throat tighten as he swallowed hard. He cleared his throat and took a breath.

"You mean," he asked, "not ever? . . ."

She nodded. "I'm sorry, Daddy."

He slowly turned toward the water again, looking like he had just been told of a relative's death. Only this was closer than a relative. This was himself.

"Well . . ." he said quietly. He thought for a moment, then finally sighed and nodded silently.

He looked at his watch again, but could not figure out the time.

"Maybe we'd better get going," Jodie said.

He nodded, then shrugged, then said, "We could stay a few more minutes."

"Sure. If you want."

"A few more minutes . . ."

They sat in silence for a moment, then he looked at her.

"People died?" he asked.

It took a moment for Jodie to realize he was talking about Mexico. "Yes," she said.

He sat in silent thought for a moment. Then he looked like he was going to say something, but instead he just shook his head and remained silent.

The breeze from the water made Jodie shiver. Carl noticed and put his arm around her to keep her warm. The instinctive way he reached to protect her, to comfort her, to *father* her, overwhelmed Jodie. She fell against him and wept.

"It's okay," he whispered. "It's going to be okay. Don't cry."

He hushed her and rubbed her shoulder, trying to console her.

When she looked up, she saw the face of her father, of the strong man who had always been there for her, always protected her as a child. And she was still that child, *his* child. And he was still her father. But she knew their roles would too soon be reversed.

This moment, she realized, may be the last time he held her this way, the last time ever.

She wrapped her arms around him and hugged his thin body.

"Daddy, I love you," she said.

He smiled at her and said, "I love you, too, Jodie."

In this embrace, she realized she was saying good-bye to her father.